ETERNITY LEAVE

SIMON KETTLEWELL

ISBN: 979-8-7004858-7-6

In memory of Shelagh Nicholls
who loved maps and uncommonly
used words. You are missed x

Two roads diverged in a wood, and I—
I took the one less travelled by,
And that has made all the difference.

Robert Frost

My bruddas don't dab, we Vossi bop.

Stormzy

1

BEFORE

Fact: Number of nappies changed, 23,698

Dear Chloe, Emma, Ruby, and Ollie,

I am applying for the position you haven't advertised, has no specific job description and no hope of fiscal reward. I am applying because I have this misguided belief that it will look like it does on the cover photo of 'The Complete Guide to Childcare' where everyone appears relaxed and bright-eyed, not knackered, irascible or covered in snot. The hours, I believe, are those required to undertake all tasks, which will keep coming interminably and never actually be completed. While the exhaustion will be akin to an extreme bout of glandular fever. I see there is no provision for sickness or holidays; any 'breaks' I might desperately need, you will be accompanying me, at my expense. I am told by other jaded and cynical workers in this line of work that it will also be necessary for me to provide all facilities, entertainment, emotional support whilst looking like I know what I'm doing when I don't have any sodding idea. I also notice there is no provision for training and the learning is exponential to the task in hand, though even the grizzliest jobs look clean and easy in 'The Complete Guide to Childcare'. I understand there is no system for making complaints. If I do submit a grievance, I can expect a response in about twenty years along the lines of 'you chose to have children so suck it up'. While this might be true, it is a long time to wait for such a crappy, patronising answer, which I could have come up with myself.

I am only heartened by the belief that most of the time you will be asleep, or at least that's what it alludes to in 'The Complete Guide to Childcare' because the pages are packed with blissfully sleeping babies. However, the authors have since produced a sequel, 'The Second Complete Guide to Childcare', which begs the question *What did they miss out of the first 'complete' guide?*

My credentials for your disinterest are as follows:

1. I am a man. Despite the often-promoted myth that there are men falling over themselves to look after their offspring and change a pile of nappies as high as Kilimanjaro, the statistics prove there are still only a handful of those who do. There are even less who take on such a task full-time as it is easier to get a 'proper job' with a 'proper' reward and a 'proper' title to give people something to talk about at social functions (this has been unanimously verified by 'the lads' down the 'The Final Furlong'). I can't do the 'Mrs Doubtfire' thing. I am six foot three with size eleven feet, and I have enough problems remembering who I am without impersonating somebody else.

2. I have no experience with this type of work. I have never held a baby. I have, if I am being entirely honest, thought of this sort of work as rather repugnant and demeaning. I have only recently stumbled into it by getting together with your mother, Brigit, who, since we met, has become quite an expert at conceiving and giving birth even if she did insist during the birthing process that it was all my fault – a bit rich given her

complicity and a bit vulgar in the midst of what I recall as such a beautiful and collective moment.

3. My exposure to this type of employment has been limited because, where I come from (a working-class town in the Midlands), the only men who looked after their children were unemployed. I am currently in the position (through a couple of hasty ill-thought-through decisions on my part) of being unemployed. I therefore suppose I am suitably qualified in this sense. I like to call myself a novelist and a yet-to-be completely self-sufficient, organic smallholder, as it is something tangible for people to talk about when they tire of talking to your mother about the NHS. When they find out I haven't yet had a book published or am not a proper farmer, they move quickly away to look at someone's holiday snaps from the Forest of Dean. However, I should point out that, when I complete the final draft of my 'work in progress' it sells for a six-figure sum and is optioned for a film, my resignation will take place with immediate effect. Please take the crayons out of your mouths and make a note of this. Pin it on the fridge between the jammy handprints and that line of slime no one actually wants to touch as it looks like some sort of disease.

Points in support of my application:

1. I have a car. It is an old Ford Sierra, which your mother says is a 'death-trap'. I place it at your disposal to spread whatever fluid – yoghurt or otherwise – on the upholstery, as its resale value is about seventy-five quid with a full tank.

2. I don't know any nursery rhymes; most of them are medieval and sensationally politically incorrect. I only sing in the shower, but brilliantly.

3. I have never changed a nappy, or done anything with powdered milk or talcum powder, though they do look very similar to each other and, in the right light, a bit like cocaine, and I apologise if there is on occasion a crossover. Not with the cocaine of course. I shall be keeping that for myself.

4. I don't do rashes or purulent skin eruptions. Apart from highly paid dermatologists, who does?

5. Pureed food makes me want to vomit. Along with vomit itself. And diarrhoea. Even the word makes me want to vomit.

6. I don't like Winnie the Pooh. I think he is a self-centred, honey-troughing layabout who sponges on people's emotional vulnerability. Tigger, in my view, has a personality disorder and should be in some sort of secure facility. As for Eeyore – a shed-load of anti-depressants should do the trick. Piglet would make maybe a couple of neurotic pounds of greenback bacon and go well with a blob of maple syrup. I do like Stephen King and will be happy to read some of his work out loud.

7. I can't tolerate whinging and whining or protracted bouts of noise, or crying as I am quite emotionally cut off. Your mother classifies this trait as 'being slightly sociopathic'. I don't like 'small-talk'. Can you be slightly sociopathic?

8. I think children should be seen and not heard, and preferably not seen as well if at all possible.

9. I am resourceful, a natural leader, a good organiser, but have limited experience with play dough as it wasn't invented when I was a child. I am available as I live

quite nearby, but you mustn't let this influence your decision as I'm sure there are better, more qualified people than me, billions of them in fact, and yes, mainly women.

10. I am reliable, but being present doesn't necessarily mean I will be useful.

11. I love the Ramones, the Sex Pistols, the Clash, and compressed cheese and onion sandwiches. Oh, and your mother, which is why I am in this desperate situation in the first place.

I'm sure I'm not suitable for the job, but should you not receive any other applications, I am literally, your man.

Yours sincerely,
Dad.

****

Dear Chloe (born), Emma (born), Ruby (born) and Ollie (not yet born),

Thank you for not writing to let me know I have the job. The crushing gravity that I am solely responsible for three girls under the age of two wasn't truly apparent until your mother's maternity leave ended and she left for work this morning. So far, she hasn't come back, and it is now ten o'clock and you are all screaming. In my head I am screaming too. I want to lie down in a dark room and sob. I am covering my ears and closing my eyes as I am in such a state of helpless desperation, sensory denial is the only reason I haven't run down the road. I do know though that when you are all asleep for most of the day, (which I'm sure I read in 'The Complete Guide to Childcare'), I will be writing that great novel and getting the hell out of town. So far this sleeping thing hasn't happened and that familiar feeling of hopelessness is hovering over me like an alien spacecraft waiting to beam me up. Take me now!

Yours for the time being (hopefully very, very, very briefly)
Dad.

2

BEFORE

Fact: Number of children's outfits changed, 17,112

On a plane returning from seeing a friend in Toronto, I watched a film. It was 'Father of the Bride 2'. There is a scene near the end when the father (Steve Martin) is standing in the corridor of a maternity unit, holding a newborn baby in each arm. This was his line: **'It was at that moment, with my daughter in one arm and my grandson in the other, that I realised life isn't going to get much better than this.'** I was in my mid-thirties and living a life I knew would suit someone else far better than it suited me. This was the line running through my head: **'It was at that moment, with nothing in my arms, and an inedible in-flight meal that I realised, unless I was reckless and bold, my life would never be better than this.'**

I left my job and the life I was living then. I threw it all to the wind; the one which blows over the Carpathians. Instead of going 'west, young man', I headed east where it was bleak and people trudged around wearing furry hats looking grim and slugging straight vodka because they were so miserable and cold. I discovered that being 'reckless and bold' often appeared from the outside as nothing more than belligerent and stupid. I returned home, short of money, without a job and exhausted. Still in the clutches of being reckless and bold, I met and fell in love with a woman called Brigit Wheeler who enjoyed and was far better working with the vagaries of healthcare than I was.

We were in a pub in Moreton-in-Marsh. There is nothing 'reckless and bold' about Moreton-in-Marsh. Despite abandoning my other skills, I was becoming adept at whining.

'Maybe, I should go back to offices and board rooms and the "internal market".'

Brigit regarded me with an undisguised look of disgust.

'Why would you do that?'

'Because it's familiar. It's safe. It pays well.'

Brigit stood up and put ten pounds on the table. She held out her hand for me to shake. 'That's it then.' She shook my hand, picked up her coat and started walking towards the door.

I went after her. 'Why are you going?'

Brigit looked at me as if I were stupid. 'Because we're done here.'

'Done?'

'That's right. Done, over, caput.'

'Why?'

'You're a fraud. All this talk about living a different life. It's bullshit. Anyone can talk. I thought I was spending time with someone who had put his money where his mouth is. I admired you, despite everyone else thinking you're a nutter. Now I know you're a nutter with unpredictable flashes of inspiration that fizzle out like a damp firework.'

'Jesus! I left my job. I went away. I did some good things for people. You didn't do that. I was in The Cats Protection League for three years. I saved cats!'

'You can't legislate for other people. If the reason you ran away was to try and diminish everyone who doesn't, then it was a waste of time. People don't care how flamboyant your gestures are if they're empty. I love what I do. I think I can make a difference where you clearly think you can't. I'm there because I believe in it. You'd be there because you want to feel safe. That, in my book, coming from someone who makes nothing more than a bit of theatrical drama, is pathetic.'

'I didn't run away.'

'If you didn't, then why are you running back so quickly? Seems like a whole lot of running to me.'

'So what am I supposed to do?'

'You tell me. You were the one who spent his time telling everyone how dull their lives were because they weren't 'doing it differently'. So I suggest you go and do it 'differently'.'

'I'm not sure I know how. I just ended up on my own in Transylvania. It's not the top place to be on your own.'

Brigit looked me directly in the eyes. It was unsettling. I find the 'eye to eye' thing very unsettling.

'Work it out.'

Brigit left me standing in the pub with her ten pounds and a group of elderly people playing bridge, staring at me and probably thinking I got what I deserved. We had come in Brigit's car. She left me in Moreton-in-Marsh to contemplate my increasingly apparent stupidity. Such a sad come down after my visions of a 'different life'. Moreton-in-Marsh certainly wasn't one of the places on my bucket list, that was for sure.

I didn't hear from Brigit after that. She was done with me. Two weeks later I went to her flat to find she had moved away, to a new job in the southwest. It took me a week to track her down.

Brigit answered the door. 'You,' she said, eyeing the rucksack on my back.

'Yes, me.'

Sensing Brigit's reluctance to let me in straight away, I arrived quickly at the obvious conclusion. 'Have you met someone?'

'Yes, I have.'

I felt a genuine spear-like jab in my belly. 'Right, I'm pleased for you.' This was going to be done and dusted quicker than I thought.

'Wait,' she said, 'there's a problem though.'

To be honest, I didn't give a flying fig about any problem Brigit might be having with some new bureaucratic boyfriend with a flash car and a shiny suit.

'I don't know if he's what he really seems? That's the problem.'

'How would I know?' I felt pretty pissed off, having come all this way, to find Brigit wanted me to resolve a problem with her love life on the doorstep.

'Because you would know,' she said.

Confronted by what felt like Brigit's curtness, I'd forgotten the pretence I was going to use to justify my unannounced arrival at her front door. I handed her the ten-pound note she'd left in the pub.

'I actually came to give you this. I didn't need it. I sold my suits to one of those 'pre-loved' shops. I won't be needing those either.'

She did that 'eye to eye' thing again. There is too much of the 'eye to eye' thing.

'Then the problem is solved.'

'It is?'

'Absolutely. You can come in.'

I followed Brigit into her little front room with the fire burning in the grate. The next day I started to write the novel that I believed would change the landscape of literature as we know it and our lives at the same time. It was crap. It changed nothing. I even sent it out to a few people in the book business so they could reassure me it was as crap as I suspected. I had visions of one day becoming a literary giant when the blistering truth was that I would amount to little more then a tall man holding a book. I rapidly slumped into an abyss of abject panic and self-doubt.

It has lasted so far for nineteen years.

3

NOW

(19 'CHILD-CARING YEARS' LATER)

Fact: Number of school pick-ups, 9,289

Yesterday I was standing on the Ghats in Varanasi, India, with our eldest daughter, Chloe. She is nineteen and about to go to university and have a ball, party, love, kiss a load of frogs, live and all that boring sort of stuff. I pretend to feel no envy. I live a lie. Youth is not wasted on the young, as some of those who are no longer young will have us believe. How can it be wasted on anyone else?

On these Ghats where life is laid bare, they were burning bodies as they do before slinging the ashes into the Ganges where they float, coagulate and reform once again, hopefully in the right molecular order for the deceased to re-emerge into the next life where it won't be so blisteringly hot. Maybe Moreton-in-Marsh.

'You need to keep drinking,' I kept telling Chloe. 'I mean all the time. You need to make your pee crystal clear. It's forty degrees.'

'It's still their summer,' she pointed out. 'No one comes to India in the summer except for idiots like us. This was your idea.'

It was. I crashed her gap year. I needed to get away from the madness that is the place where I live.

My heart was beating like Delia Smith whipping the mixture for a jolly light sponge.

'I don't feel so good,' I said to Chloe. 'My heart's going crazy.'

'You'll be fine.' That's what the family says to me. *You'll be fine.* Words no doubt they'll use when I'm three breaths from taking my last. Dying will be my final defiance and I won't be there to say 'I told you so!'

Chloe closed her eyes. 'It's really spiritual,' she said, as the ashes of human bodies settled on our clothes and the sun blistered my skin like the crackling on a hog roast. In a building only metres away from the burning pyres were people who, instead of going into a nursing home near Frinton-on-Sea, had come to the banks of the Ganges to die. If they had wanted to accelerate their demise, all they needed to do was take a dip in that sludge-coloured snake of a river and swallow a mouthful.

I sat down on the steps. 'I feel really, really unwell. I mean really unwell.'

A man wearing a long robe came up the steps towards us. Ah, help, I thought. He crouched down in front of me and unravelled the material belt around his waist. I was in no mood to be propositioned. He revealed some little foil wraps.

'You like something?' He was totally oblivious to my obvious failing health. I wouldn't have been surprised if he'd said 'you'll be fine' in Hindi. My head was swimming. My heart was thumping so fast and hard it would have given Mike Tyson a fair old slug in the chops. 'Opium?' The man unrolled one of his little foil balls. 'Or maybe a little heroin?'

'Do you have any water?' I asked in this weak and pathetic voice. I was feeling quite desperate.

The man shoved his hooky wares back into his belt, stood and spat on the ground, a gesture that told me this was the only moisture I was going to get. Little did he know,

I would have given him more rupees for a bottle of water than he wanted for several grams of the gear he had stashed uncomfortably close to his testicles.

I walked to the top of the Ghat. My legs gave way and I sat helplessly down on the road. A crowd gathered around me. Chloe was backing off. I was an embarrassment in India instead of being one at home. Anyone under the age of thirty was sniggering at this red-faced Englishman with his heart trying to slam its way out of his chest. An elderly woman, not much shy of ninety with skin like a turtle, started fanning me with a brush. A couple of Japanese tourists went past, pretending this wasn't happening right in front of them.

'Could you buy me a bottle of water?' I called after them in a fading voice.

They slowed and regarded me warily. We were talking thirty rupees. They looked at one another with expressions of panic.

'I am very dehydrated. I need water.'

They weren't keen. They had clearly been programmed not to trust Englishmen sitting on the ground asking for water while ninety-year-old Indian women fanned them with reeds.

Chloe persuaded them. Like her mother, Chloe has this way with reluctant people and very big eyes into which young men are beginning to helplessly fall to their emotional deaths. The Japanese couple yielded. I was grateful to them and promised to visit Tokyo very soon. I could see, even in my desiccated state that they were quite alarmed by the prospect of me turning up on their doorstep.

I spent the rest of the day rehydrating and feeling like a right twat. Chloe had the whole thing on Instagram before I could get my first mouthful of special minerals and salts bought from the chemist. By lunchtime the episode had received three hundred and fifty-seven likes and eighty-two comments with that laughing, tearful emoji thing.

'You'll be fine,' she said. I was seven thousand miles from being fine or home.

Now it is Friday afternoon. Less than twelve hours after touch down at Heathrow, I am here in England like a transported crewmember from Star Trek, sitting in the car waiting for the school bus to arrive. In India it is bedtime. I am fully hydrated. Chloe was right this time – I was fine. My head is still in the developing world while my body is here where the pavements are clean and there are no beggars with sedated babies pleading for twenty rupees.

It isn't refreshing to be back, it's simply different.

We are at the end of a heat wave. Dark clouds are congregating, joining together as a prelude to some seriously horrible weather. Only a couple of weeks ago 'they' – whoever 'they' are – were talking about 'stand pipes'. Only the very young children were excited about this prospect because they crave a type of managed adversity absent from their gilt-edged lives. People with security cameras and electric gates do not expect to stand around a single tap for a bucket of water. They might as well live in India. It is a very thin line. Our family doesn't have security cameras; we don't have anything valuable enough to steal. Nor do we have electric gates for the same reason. We've given our cash to the kids.

I am waiting for our son Ollie and his seventeen-year-old twin sisters, Ruby and Emma. Ollie is in year eight, about to become a teenager. Ruby and Emma are in the sixth form. The only thing identical about them is that they are girls. Where they saunter in what appears to be an 'I don't give a flying fuck about pretty much anything' sort of way, Ollie runs at pace to the car to bag the front seat and tell me about the new downloads on PlayStation.

'Shotgun front seat!' he yells.

'And Ollie takes gold once again!' He is the last of the line and still at the lovely side of puberty where the grunting has not yet begun. One day this malarkey will stop and I won't see it before it does. It will come out of nowhere, an emotional sniper's bullet, and end something so special and fleeting I will always mourn its loss.

Ollie throws his bag into the foot-well and slams the door.

'Good day?'

The answer is always the same. 'Boring!'

'A good day then.'

'We did sex education. We know it already.'

'You do?'

'Course.'

'Really? All of it?'

'It's obvious.'

'It wasn't obvious to me when I was your age. Make sure you have the facts.'

He takes a crumpled leaflet from his bag and drops it in my lap. 'The facts. With diagrams. If you think you need it.'

I open the leaflet. It is graphic and clear. Nothing is left to the imagination. This would have been classed as pornography in my day. 'Right, the facts. Good.' I look at my precious twelve-year-old boy, searching his face for any sign of perplexity. I want to take this knowledge away from him and protect his wonder at the world a little longer. I'll soon be losing him to that existence of relentless masturbation and the agony of unattainable girls. I'm losing so many things. I can't do with losing my son at the same time.

'I'm getting a new skin,' Ollie says as if it is the most normal thing.

'A new skin? What's wrong with the old one? What do you think you are; a snake?'

'Duh!' He means his PlayStation controller. When I try and limit the hours he plays I am told it is a 'human rights issue'. I thought those were simple things like food, shelter and safety, not games designed to undermine most of them.

An old lady with a walking frame shuffles along the pavement. Ollie and I do this thing…

'Bet you a pound she's going to get into that car,' I say.

15

'Nah.'

The old lady edges around the back of the battered Ford Fiesta parked in front of us, opens the boot and shoves in the walking frame. Putting the lid down, she edges to the driver's side, pulls the door open and hangs onto it, shimmying as if she is on a ledge with a thousand feet of air below. When she finally gets into the seat, you can tell it's taken everything out of her.

Ollie claps. 'She did it!'

'You owe me a pound.'

He just shrugs. The thought of paying me is as absurd to Ollie as tidying his bedroom. We watch the old lady lurch out into the traffic, oblivious to the mummies in their 'active wear' honking from their four by fours while learning Spanish from a Michel Thomas CD in readiness for their holidays on the Costa Perfect.

Emma and Ruby saunter along with two boys I've seen before but don't know. They used to wave at me. Now they eye me with suspicion. 'What's he doing here?' I can see them thinking. Well, I've come to give my children a lift home as I have done for the last fourteen years.

'Skirt Gate', as we call it in our house, has clearly had little effect on Emma. She keeps pulling hers down as it rides up to a point even she thinks is beyond acceptable. This is a matter of principle as far she is concerned. We had a call from the school last week.

'I'm afraid it's a significant problem,' the deputy head, Mrs Chambers told me.

'A significant problem?'

'She's upsetting the middle year boys. It is a boys' school. The girls are only here for the sixth form and they should comply.'

I tried to talk to Emma that evening.

'Comply! Comply! It's a school not an army camp!' (These kids are good with their rights; human and otherwise.) 'It's their problem. They should look the other way if they can't deal with it. They can go to the toilets. It's not difficult.'

'Go to the toilet?'

'Yes, you know.'

Unfortunately I did know. I couldn't help but recall my own teenage years and remember only secret anguish and silent despair, the dull ache in my loins like impacted wisdom teeth. I just didn't want to know that Emma knew. My little princess who'd never be seen without a tiara, enraptured by 'The Little Mermaid' for hours on end. This adult before me must have kidnapped that little girl and swallowed her whole.

The next day Emma marched into the Bursar's office demanding the policy on skirt length for sixth formers. 'We don't actually have one,' the little man said, probably quaking in his little shoes. 'Good,' Emma said, leaving him wondering how things went so horribly wrong.

'Sorted,' Emma informed us later. 'As a concession I'm going to get a longer skirt.' The new skirt was no more than a centimetre longer, but longer.

'I have complied,' Emma announced proudly. 'Don't make it an issue of scale.'

'I got a behaviour mark,' Ollie tells me now.

I like to think he's bright enough. We all like to think our children are bright enough. Then again, we live in a place where you can barely stick a pin between the geniuses, in the 'Gifted and Talented Academy'. It must be stuffed to the gunnels.

'A behaviour mark's good then?'

'For talking.'

'Oh. Not so good then.'

'I actually got three.'

'Three!'

'I gasped when I got the first one, and he gave me another and then I said 'what?' and I got another. They're so tight. Billy farted and he got a behaviour mark too. He said 'even the Queen farts' and then he got a detention for being rude about the Queen. He's right. She does.' Ollie blows a raspberry.

'The Queen doesn't fart,' I say. 'She's far too posh.'

Ollie looks very serious. He is twelve, and farting is a serious business when you're twelve.

'Course she does. Everybody farts. Even Ed Sheeran farts. On stage!'

I can't put into words the love I feel for my boy. It is so expansive, so wide and tall, deep and all consuming, it hurts. Right now, we are mates. I know though, that one day this banter, this free-flowing thing, will stop. And so will those moments when we go to the football and Ollie slips his hand so instinctively into mine when we are weaving through the crowds. I imagine there will be a last time when he lets go and probably won't take it again until I am infirm and in need of him for support and probably can't remember who he is. The experts say it's all 'positive progression'. There's always a shiny-headed, four-eyed expert from some pumped-up university in London on the 'News at Ten' reducing feelings to some sort of anthropological formula. To me it is nothing but another lance piercing my already ragged heart.

The girls get into the car, showering Ollie and me with their disapproval. We are soaked within seconds.

Emma shoves Ollie in the back because little brothers need to know their place. Ollie doesn't give a fig.

'It's disgusting. You encourage him, Dad. You're supposed to be the grown up. Remember? The Queen's an old lady who deserves some respect.' This is rich coming from Emma who thinks anyone in authority is an idiot.

Ollie pipes up. 'Dad says she and her family are benefit scroungers.'

'Jesus, Dad. One day he's going to say something to someone and they aren't going to find it funny.'

'He's hardly likely to be chatting to the Queen.'

18

Ollie has already committed the sin of repetition and I've paid the price of silence and icy stares from the people three doors away. I'm told they will never speak to me again.

Emma leans forward. 'What was it he said, Dad? That little pearl of wisdom in the Post Office?'

'Leave it, Em. We don't need to go over old ground.'

'We do if you don't learn.' This is what happens to teenage girls who are encouraged to speak their mind. I should have dressed them in Boden, made them ride ponies and keep their opinions to themselves and use only mine instead. 'Oh yes, I remember. Ollie said, *My dad says you think we don't like you very much. My dad says it's not true.*'

Ollie fills in the gap. 'I said, *My dad says it's not true. My dad says we don't like you at all.*' This creases Ollie until he's dribbling like a baby.

Ruby stops texting whoever she saw ten minutes ago because so much has happened since. 'Can we go home please, Dad? We're just sitting in the car having a pointless argument and I've got stuff to do.'

We leave the mothers in their vast shiny clean vehicles and their perfect children exchanging the highlights of their day, achievements and educational aspirations for the evening. We are squabbling behind filthy glass windows and probably look to the perfect people like one of those documentaries I watch on late-night TV when I've had too much to drink and don't want to lie down in a spinning house.

'Roddy Quail's dad's got a Ferrari,' Ollie announces.

I immediately take this as a criticism and another tick against the long list of things at which I have failed as a parent. We do not have a Ferrari. Ollie of course is impressed, which only adds to my pain. Sometimes we fail as parents. It hurts me like a wasp sting hurts because it feels like such a personal stab at what has been the main facet of my life for the last nineteen years; my *raison d'etre*. They are, to quite a large extent, the product of my work and their problems, according to them, caused by me. Unlike sitting at the peak of a glittering career, it's more like squatting precariously on top of a restless volcano.

Diane and Richard Quail, to the visible eye, are perfect with their taut, angular bodies and sharp jawlines. Richard Quail's jaw is so sharp it could slice the atom. He makes Gaston out of Beauty and the Beast look like a chinless wonder. Confidence drips from the Quails like the water rolling down the panels of Richard's executive-car-clean-services waxed Ferrari.

The Quails are beautiful to look at. They have special skin that people brought up in industrial towns don't possess. Their children, Jemima and Roddy, are even more beautiful with names selected effortlessly so they will slot into their perfect lives like a perfect key into a perfect lock. How can you go wrong with names like Jemima and Roddy unless you live in an industrial town and have skin like the hide of a rhinoceros's arse because the air is thick with dirt? The Quails do things I've never even thought about, including buying a Ferrari and owning a house on a Greek island with a name I thought was a part of the large intestine. I wouldn't even know where to buy a Ferrari. Is there a Ferrari shop? Diane Quail is one of the country's leading cosmetic dentists. The Quails have teeth so white and perfect they don't need to put their headlights on in the Dartford tunnel, should they ever need for some unfortunate reason to visit Dartford. They are the sort of people who, simply without doing anything, could cause an outbreak of self-loathing on a global scale.

For a moment or two I torture myself with these images, all the things the Quails are, all the things I am not. I need Ollie to be impressed by me, not someone else's dad on film-star wages. Tricky when all I get is the odd cheque from the electricity board for having one of their poles in the garden.

'I've got a cheque for having an electricity pole in the garden,' I once informed the gathered family. 'I mean, how many people get cheques every six months for having electricity poles in their garden?'

'They took the wires off and buried them two years ago. You should call them and return the money,' Brigit said while we were eating a Saturday breakfast where everyone lists their punishing schedules for the week and subsequently the locations where I am required to be.

I waved the cheque. 'It's thirty-four pounds, eighty-seven pence. Every penny counts.'

Brigit scrolled the calculator up on her phone where she was illegally perusing Twitter under the table. 'Times two. That's—'

'You have your phone at the table!'

Everyone grinned at me sympathetically and pulled out their phones from under the table. In one minute, nineteen years of work walked out the front door to be replaced by technology-infused zombies.

'Sixty-nine pounds, seventy-four pence,' Emma confirmed. 'Plus interest of twenty-four percent APR. That's…'

'I don't want to know.' I ripped up the cheque into little pieces and let it flutter over the table. 'Give me your phones.'

People actually handed them over. Brigit made hers disappear.

'And yours.'

'The hospital is full. I have to keep in touch. We're on red alert.'

'So close the doors. Give me the phone! You're the parent. You have to set an example.'

'God, we're such a dysfunctional family,' Ruby added. 'I mean, most people don't eat at the table. They eat in their rooms or watching the TV.'

Brigit handed me her phone. 'Yes, and that is why the social infrastructure is crumbling.'

People looked at the ceiling as if there was something more interesting up there. I had the sense to sit down and eat my breakfast in silence.

Right now, in the car, Ollie is still banging on about Ferraris. 'A Ferrari is so sick. So sick.'

I've tried hard not to let these things grate, but it is difficult to rise above a wave that even the most ardent surfers couldn't ride, despite their manly claims. My sense of self has been eroded over the years, for reasons which will become clear. Doubts have gnawed away at it like the rat that nibbled through the main electric cable to the house, fried itself to a crisp and cost us a very large amount of money. The children of course felt sorry for the rat. I was glad the bastard was dead despite the huge amount of money spent to bring about rat genocide within fifty metres of the house. Though judging by the scratching and banging in the roof, I assume one of its distant relatives is back, the size of a domestic cat and plotting revenge.

Still on the subject of the Quails, because it is a big subject, Richard Quail is a neurosurgeon. The Quails are wealthy and empirically successful by anybody's standards. If they are ten on the scale, I used to think I was probably one, unless of course you fractionalize the measure, then I would be several zeros after the decimal point. They live in a large sprawling place where local people 'do the garden' and clean the house. These local people are grateful for the work, as all the farms have been rented out to people from London weekenders who stuff their faces with clotted cream and say 'ooh arr' to amuse themselves as they tuck into their local venison, imagining there is a 'Wurzel' lurking around every corner. These are the disciples of the columnist, Toby Walters who extols the virtues of this little part of the country where only rock stars and Tories can afford to eat out and Toby came as a child and doesn't want to give it over to the 'pikeys and the people with the tattoos and the bloated bellies' as he so delicately referred to them in his little column.

Jemima and Roddy Quail are privately educated and will run the country in one form or another after their gap year 'travelling' to see the 'poor people' in their corrugated shacks, and forgotten by the time these golden progeny arrive at Bondi Beach. I could lie and rubbish the Quails, but Diane has been a friend to me over the years when things have been quite difficult. Besides it is hard to find anything bad to say about them. Not that they do anything endearing – apart from cure people, that is – and give dour-looking 'horsey' women a smile like Julia Roberts, and a good chance at Ascot. But how can you ever feel equal to a man who has at some time had his fingers inside your head where every memory and ounce of consciousness resides and where, with a slip of the blade, he can take away everything you ever were or ever could be? You wouldn't want to fall out with Richard Quail. Me? Anyone can change a nappy.

I steel myself from rubbishing a Ferrari, which isn't easy when you're sitting in a Skoda, trying to convince the people in this car that they are what the smart people are driving. All I can do is grip the synthetically covered steering wheel and take slow deep breaths and think about the fuel economy and my two free years of roadside assistance both in the UK and Europe plus floor mats.

We drive home with Ollie extolling the virtues of Ferraris. He is animated and he is certain he will be buying one when he is seventeen. He looks at me in anticipation.

'Don't look at me. I like Skodas. You wouldn't catch me dead in a Ferrari.' This is true, but it's a fiscal thing rather than a choice.

'You can't drive if you're dead.'

I like to pretend we are in a plane when I'm driving. I've done so much of it over the years, I have to transcend the reality of being behind the wheel. My inner child is alive and well. I wonder if Richard Quail imagines his Ferrari as a plane. I mean why would you need to imagine a car like that to be anything else?

'Welcome ladies and gentlemen and little irritating sprogs to Coconut Airlines. I am your captain for this flight and your co-pilot is Ollie. We will be flying at an altitude of approximately twelve inches in this smart-thinking person's aircraft.' Ollie gets out the chewing gum and starts to pass it around. 'There will be a selection of inflight meals mainly restricted to chewing gum. Our cabin crew will now do the safety drill.'

Emma ignores this. 'God, Dad, you're so childish.'

Ruby, now off her phone, takes the lead. 'There are emergency exits to the front and rear of this idiot's thinking car, and all seat belts should be worn during the flight because there is a maniac at the wheel. If we are going to crash, which could be at any time, please put your head between your knees and kiss your ass goodbye.'

'It's arse, not 'ass'. Ass is a type of mule-thing,' I point out, ever the stickler for correct English usage.

I hand over the controls to Ollie while I get my inflight meal out of its packet. He holds on to the wheel like a consummate professional and changes the gears when I depress the clutch and say 'now'.

Emma hits me on the shoulder. 'Jesus, Dad, a twelve-year-old is driving the car!'

I ignore this. Ollie knows the drill.

'The weather at the house of the many unfinished jobs is much the same as it is here and the kitchen still looks like it did this morning because I have been writing down our life story, which is not a pretty thing now it's on paper, and you will all never ever speak to me again. This could be a good thing.'

Ruby shouts from the back seat where she usually balls out her advice on how to drive since passing her test. 'What do you mean you're writing a book about us? I thought you wrote novels.'

'His novels don't sell,' Ollie points out. 'He's a failed author.'

'You got a behaviour mark.'

24

'That's an achievement.'

'I thought I'd write what I know - a life of unforgiving hospitality.'

'Is that why you keep jotting things in that little notebook?'

'Yup.'

'Jesus, Dad. You can't do that. We're dysfunctional. We don't want everyone to know.'

'Rube, they already know. You keep telling them.' I feel quite heartened by this slightly panicked reaction.

'It'll be so boring. Who wants to read about some guy who looked after his kids?'

'What about the Kardashians and the Osbornes. They made a fortune.'

'They're famous. You're not.'

'They must've started somewhere. Kim married Kanye West. I live with Brigit Wheeler. Everyone knows who she is.'

'Only in the hospital.'

'Everyone goes to hospital. It's a world stage.'

'Well, she won't speak to you either.'

The idea is becoming more tempting by the minute. 'Just do the safety drill, woman, and let the men fly the plane.'

They're hot on equality, so rest assured that the comment emerging from Ruby's lips would appear on a documentary about dysfunctional families as a series of bleeps.

4

NOW

Fact: Number of times I said 'and what's the magic word?', 32,120

Brigit's car is in the drive when we get home. After all these years, the house is still unfinished. I feel it imploring me to go to B&Q and conceal its embarrassment from the other consummate dwellings with their smooth lines and exterior gloss, all culled from natural earth ingredients by poor people in the east. Both the internal and external walls look like the patchwork on Elmer The Elephant because no one can settle on a single colour. The hallway is decorated from seventy match pots from Wickes and the window frames are almost fifty shades of grey. I find, along with the term 'positive parenting', family democracy to be a complete pain in the arse. Bring back the Victorian father sitting at the end of the table, expounding his views on the world while the rest of the family sit transfixed in stony silence at the sheer majesty of his intellect. Four children are also very expensive, but I am reminded by those unsympathetic children: 'you chose to have them, so suck it up'. Oh, how I will relish the day when the boot is on the other foot and they have children. If I am still turning out to 'be fine'.

It is unusual for Brigit to be home early. She leaves at 7.30 in the morning and rarely gets back for at least twelve hours. She is the Chief Executive of the local major hospital and is either loved or loathed depending on who is not getting their own way. Where I am very proud of Brigit, and imagined the children would be too, they feel only embarrassment. Parents are meant to be hidden unless they are, according to Ollie, Ronaldo or some rapper from the Bronx. In some ways Brigit and I have very similar jobs; we both deal with squabbles between people who act like children, except Brigit has a badge on a lanyard around her neck and gets paid, and I deal with disquiet between people who are still largely children, have what sometimes feels like a noose around my neck and a shed-load of abuse for being 'tight' as Ollie so succinctly puts it.

Brigit comes straight out of the living room to greet us.

'Darlings!'

I don't know why she uses this term. It is a guarantee to rile teenage girls and prompt a twelve-year-old to walk straight past.

'Lovely day?'

Ruby gives Brigit a hug. I can see the tears forming in Brigit's eyes. All it takes is a hug from one of the girls for everything to come rushing out. It has not been easy for Brigit to leave a large portion of the care of our children to me for reasons I could list extensively. Brigit harbours guilt and, I know, considerable regret at leaving four vulnerable little people in the hands of an incompetent maniac as he learnt, very slowly, the tricks of the trade.

Ollie and the girls have dropped their bags in the middle of the multi-coloured hallway. I fall over them and swear. It is 4.45pm and, as anyone who has looked after a truck-load of kids for a very long time will know, it is a very sweary, God-I-need-a-big-drink-but-I-probably-have-to-drive-to-football time of day. Everything sags.

'Dad!' Ruby says. 'That's so unnecessary. You're supposed to set an example we can follow.'

Brigit and Ruby glare at me in an anti-swear unison. The hypocrisy bounces off the walls like a Ping-Pong ball.

'Then you can start with the breakfast dishes that are still on the table.'

Ruby gives me such a pained look; I might as well have asked her to be nice to Ollie. 'I'm hugging Mum.'

Brigit sticks her tongue out. 'So, what have you been up to today?' she asks.

I'm about to list the tasks when I fall over another bag. 'You could move the bags!' I call after them. I can't help myself for acting this out for Brigit's benefit so she can sense my Groundhog Day-style suffering now she is home. As if on autopilot, I pick up the bags and the words of protest dissolve like the cash in my wallet.

Emma and Ruby zip into the kitchen like soldiers under enemy fire, grabbing food from the cupboards and the fridge as if running for their lives. They hole up in their rooms to talk to the people they have just left in case there's been some world catastrophe since they last spoke minutes before. I recall the days of the telephone with the wire and the cheap calls after six and my mother hovering in the hallway to make sure I didn't stay on longer than three minutes. It is not possible to sound cool and pour out your heart to a girl when you have to speak at the speed of someone reciting the 'terms and conditions' on a radio advert for mobile phones.

'You could put the bread and the cartons and the butter away,' I shout after them.

But they are gone. I might as well talk to the dog. At least he's stupid enough to look as if he's listening.

'One hour,' I tell Ollie as he retreats to his room with a peanut butter sandwich and a glass of something pink. This is for the PlayStation where he re-joins his friends to shoot the shit out of one another.

'God, Dad, you're so tight. Eddie stays on all night.'

'I don't care about Eddie. His parents are irresponsible.'

'You can't say that.'

'Just did.'

'Eddie's dad's loaded.'

'Good for Eddie's dad.'

With these gun games I have battled against the counter arguments of discrimination, isolation from friends, improved dexterity and social integration and lost. He closes his door and it is only seconds before he is yelling.

'This internet is so laggy!' he shouts at a friend who I presume is Eddie who is at his own home; probably a mansion with gold taps and one of those crummy Ferraris in the drive with more data than he knows what to do with, shouting back. If Eddie's dad's so 'loaded', perhaps he could give some of Eddie's data to us. I don't know if 'laggy' is actually a real word.

Ollie comes out of his room, waving his controller like an old person waving a stick in rage.

'This internet is so bad. Why can't we have better internet?'

'Look, Ollie, I've told you before, we live in the country where there is only a single strand of copper wire. People in the country don't play computer games. They go out and forage in the hedgerows, spot birds and suck insects into those little vacuum cleaners we used to have when you were lovely and little and we used to count their legs.'

Ollie gives me the sort of look you would give someone who has lost everything with no hope of getting it back. 'That's so sad.'

'So you wouldn't need internet. We could make a set of wooden dominoes.'

'You could phone someone.'

'Who do you suggest?'

'Someone. I hate living in the country. Eddie's got 'superfast broadband'.'

'I'll call the Queen,' I suggest. 'She'll sort it out when she's stopped farting.'

'You're not funny.' He returns to his room and slams the door. If I were in an elimination game for quality parenting, I would be going home.

Brigit has gone from the hallway to sit on the sofa with her laptop. She is on the phone talking to someone about ambulances and how they are 'stacking up'. I didn't know you could stack an ambulance. Brigit's job has the potential to seep into every corner of her life. It is a battle to keep time for the family sacrosanct, but she manages this and I have to confess that sometimes it grates. Sometimes I need her to be inadequate for no other reason than to vindicate me for my incessant moaning.

Brigit holds up her hand to me when I go into the lounge. I have been stopped in my tracks until she is finished. I am riled. I have been halted, stemmed by someone impersonating a traffic policeman.

'Sorry. I had to make that call.'

I don't ask her about the call. We don't talk about her work. People think we do. People think I'm privy to every little detail. I know nothing. It isn't a rule. I've had to listen to people drone on about the NHS whenever they meet Brigit for years. I'm surprised they don't bore themselves to death. I'm amazed politicians don't fall asleep simply talking about it. Conversations about 'bed capacity' and 'never events' should become an Olympic sport available in tablet form for insomniacs.

'Hi!' she says in this cheery tone generally adopted by children's TV presenters. There is silence from the rooms where the younger people are now holed up. I often wonder if the cost of Brigit's absence from the children over the years has been worth it, and often chastise myself for moaning on days when we both imagine how great it might have been to change places. I could have swapped a used nappy for a financial standing instruction, both of which appear much the same.

I hand Brigit a glass of wine. I can see from her face she has clearly not had a good day. There are people in the hospital right now with their clipboards and questionnaires, going through the place like a Barium meal. Brigit looks tired. I'm tired. It is not a good basis to start a conversation.

We can't help ourselves. We hurtle towards it like the Starship Enterprise getting sucked into a black hole.

'Why don't we have a few minutes?' Brigit gestures for me to sit down like an interviewee.

'I've got to make tea.' I am trying to avoid a 'tiredness conversation', which will send us over the waterfall and into the pool before we have the sense to stop.

Brigit gives me an earnest look. 'How's your day been?'

Yep, this is the first line of a 'tiredness conversation'.

'I took Chloe to Ikea to get stuff for university.'

'That's nice.'

'That's nice' could be taken in several different ways. I choose to take it as you're-lucky-to-go-shopping-with-our-eldest-daughter-while-I'm-trying-to-fit-three-patients-into-each-bed. (I call it cosy.)

'Ikea? You mean going to Ikea is nice?'

'Yes. Time with Chloe.' Brigit does the darty eyes. Beware the 'darty' eyes! 'Did you have the Swedish breakfast?'

'We did.'

'And the bottomless coffee?'

'It's really weak.'

'But bottomless.' Brigit does the 'darty' eyes again.

'We went shopping. I don't see shopping as a pleasure. I could draw you a detailed map of Tesco if you want. Such familiarity isn't fun.'

I know Brigit's had a bad day and, to make the point, she's spinning something magnificent and memorable out of a trip to a 'flat-pack' furniture store where they only show you the stuff when it's built and not the impossibly heavy boxes you have to lug from the warehouse to the car, take home and start a war with the whole family because the Scandinavian families are better at 'Lego' than we are.

'Did you buy anything for yourself?'

'It's Ikea! There is nothing I want from Ikea! They don't sell Harley Davidsons at Ikea. I already have a rubber whisk and a rubber egg box, which is bloody useless because we don't have bouncy eggs like they obviously do in Stockholm!'

'I want to tell you something,' Brigit says.

'This sounds ominous. You're leaving me.'

'Don't get your hopes up.'

Sometimes I wonder what it might be like living in an anonymous bedsit in Truro. I could pretend to be Poldark. Perhaps not. He didn't, as far as I know, look after the kids. No one gets the reputation of being a swashbuckling hero from looking after the kids. 'You want to tell me something?'

'I went to a carers' seminar today.'

Brigit likes 'a catch up'. I am a full-time parent and sometimes 'a catch up' can feel like reliving a nightmare. Retelling the arguments over FIFA points and how a spoon got stuck down the drain system in the dishwasher simply achieves nothing but distress. I think I have a cumulative form of Post Traumatic Stress Disorder. I don't go to meetings where there are agendas and processes for resolving things. Some days I feel like the empty-handed negotiator dealing with a bunch of teenage terrorists who can pull the pin whenever they want. Some days I could do it myself.

'It was very interesting.'

'So who ran the hospital while the audience were stuffing their faces with mini pasties and Scotch eggs?'

We should really stop this conversation because we both know it's going to get scratchy. We simply can't help ourselves.

Brigit clasps her hands together. 'I want to tell you something really important.' Ollie screams. He runs out into the hallway. 'Oh my God, why is this internet so

bad?'

Emma shouts from upstairs. 'Can you kill him please? I'm trying to concentrate.' Emma needs to concentrate so she can catch up with the first year of sixth form, which has passed her by like a high-speed train.

'I told Ollie I'd phone the Queen,' I call to Emma.

'That's so childish. I'm trying to work.'

'That's only because you didn't do any in year twelve,' I call back.

Emma slams her door.

Brigit folds her arms. 'That's hardly helpful, is it?'

It mentioned this facilitative, non-confrontational approach of Brigit's in 'The Complete Guide to Childcare' (that glossy slab of distortion and untruth which is now languishing in some landfill site in Cornwall propping up affordable housing). Brigit leaves to tell Ollie to tone it down in a 'facilitative' way.

Ollie changes the tone, but not the volume and squeals like an injured rabbit. There are no flies on Ollie. He doesn't sit still long enough.

Brigit returns and recomposes herself, takes a glug of wine and re-focuses her mind. This is beginning to feel like 'bedtime stories'.

'There was a man giving a talk.'

I am glazing over because I am so much more tired than she is. Brigit senses this drift because she is big on engagement when it comes to conversations.

'I want to tell you this. I think it's important. I can see what's happening.'

'What's happening?'

'To you.'

'To me?'

'Yes, to you.'

I laugh.

Brigit doesn't.

We sound like the Chuckle Brothers. I like the Chuckle Brothers. They've been important to me over the last twenty years.

Brigit waits for me to stop grinning. 'If you can't take this seriously...'

'I can. We sound like the Chuckle Brothers.'

33

Brigit ignores this. 'I listened to this talk by a man called David Shaw. He chatted to me afterwards. He gave up his job to look after his mother when his father died. She was very disabled, and David had no other family.'

People tell Brigit their intimate stories in the most public places. Sometimes they stop her in the hospital pasty shop where all the cardiac surgeons buy their lunch before returning to their offices to wipe the short-crust pastry crumbs from their shirts and tell the public to cut down on stodgy food. Ruby and Emma now tower over her; Ollie is racing to meet her head on, and only Chloe, our eldest daughter, matches Brigit's height. This does not reduce Brigit though, nor the alpha males who are constantly surprised that she is the CEO of a huge hospital. 'I wasn't expecting a woman,' they sometimes say. 'And you weren't expecting a kick in the balls,' she often thinks.

'David's mother died.'

'I'm sorry.' I smirk. I'm tired. I've been to Ikea. It's hard to take anything seriously when you've been to Ikea and bought twenty slabs of compressed wood chippings, which you have to build into a state of the art piece of furniture.

'You didn't know her.'

'I didn't know David Bowie, but I cried when he died.'

Brigit starts to get up but falls back into the seat. It is really low because I took the casters off after Ollie and I broke it practising goalie dives.

'I wanted to tell you this because it's important and I haven't said hello to the kids properly yet. David's mother died. Now he has nothing. His reason has gone. It was really moving. He told us how he spent every day looking after her, cooking meals, taking her out, being with her because she needed round the clock care.'

'Well, I do that, just with perfectly able-bodied people who could do it for themselves.'

'He was a carer.'

'And I'm a slave.'

'Now she's gone.'

Ollie is shouting about the Internet again.

'And my charges are alive and well.'

'When his mother died, David's world simply stopped, his job stopped, just like that. He didn't know who he was anymore. He was a someone who 'did' for someone else for years. He said after his mother died, he didn't know where to start.'

I am expecting at any moment for Brigit to produce a collection box for this man to buy him, perhaps, something from Ikea. I want to laugh, but I can see Brigit is welling up. She is a woman in touch with every neuron and molecule of her emotional self. It must be bloody exhausting.

I take Brigit's wine glass and empty it on her behalf. It is well into the sweary God-I-need-a-big-drink time.

'When David was talking, I thought of you. I thought of how the kids are on the verge of leaving the nest. I know Ollie's only twelve, but he'll be almost an adult soon and it will change. You know it will.'

'My mother's still alive and I will not be moving in with her!'

She is ninety-two and I'm beginning to believe she'll be cheerfully reading the eulogy at my funeral, telling everyone what a disappointing son I've been and how for the last twenty years I could have saved her the embarrassment of explaining to the WI why I don't have a 'proper job'.

'David's going to volunteer with the League of Friends.'

It takes events such as the election of Donald Trump, Brexit or the death of Joe Strummer to stun me into silence, but this does. I am flabbergasted. I make a sound from which I feel disassociated.

'How old is this man?'

'Seventy-five.'

'Seventy-five?'

'So you think after all this…' I make a sweeping motion with my arm to indicate nothing in particular, 'that I should join the fucking League of Friends?'

'Do you have to use that sort of language?'

'Do you have to tell me depressing stories about lonely people joining the League of Friends?'

'I'm saying that after twenty years of looking after the family, you need to think about what comes next. I was using it as an illustration. You really don't need to swear.' Brigit gets up from the sofa and falls back onto it. 'This sofa drives me mad! Can't you do something about it?'

'I'll talk to the Queen. I can do it when I'm talking to her about the Internet if she isn't farting herself to death.'

Brigit grips my arm and looks me in the eye. No one understands how disturbing I find the 'eye to eye' thing.

'I'm trying to help.'

'I don't need any help, Brig. You stick to running hospitals and I'll do what I know best.'

I leave the room to go and empty the dishwasher and think about 'what I know best'. Like a bully, I give the dishwasher a kick because it can't fight back. It sustains a smooth dent from my foot. It can be knocked out with a kick from the other side. I know this because it is not an unfamiliar routine. Those with gym membership, and time to go to them, sweat it out with punch bags to vent their hatred. I have the dishwasher. I have so many reasons to hate it. That white almost cubic thing has taken days of my life. What do I have to show for it? Glasses with opaque blooms, that's what.

Emma comes into the kitchen where over the years I believe I have forged a little furrow in the dirt of the stone slabs. I tell them it'll be the place they find me when I die, curled up and crispy. They laugh it off. 'You'll be fine,' they say.

'I need to talk about the car.' Emma is the dog with the bone. She is the sort of dog who will lose its life before giving up the bone.

I am holding the Ikea whisk. It is a little worn and I suppose I could have bought another one, a little gift for myself. 'What about the car?' I am whisking eggs while we have this conversation and listening to Steve Lemacq interviewing Peter Hook from New Order about an up-coming box set I don't think will be available in Ikea.

(If someone tells you only women can multi-task, they are lying. It's the only way to survive three children under the age of two without anyone incurring serious injury from every known and unknown hazard in the house. I am also an unqualified child health and safety expert.)

'We need another one. She,' Emma jabs a finger in the direction of her sister's room, 'doesn't stick to the schedule. I need to learn, and I need the car.'

'Okay. I'll talk to her.'

'Talking's no good, Dad. We are beyond talking. This requires action.'

'What's beyond talking? Me buying another car, or you assassinating your sister?' I can see she's considering the assassination thing. 'Assassination would be cheaper. I could sell the car while you're doing time.'

'Ha ha, funny man. We need another car.'

'We can't afford it. The insurance is too expensive. It would be cheaper to insure a moon rocket where you can't hit anything other than space debris. I didn't have a car when I was your age.'

'They didn't have cars when you were my age.'

'I cycled everywhere.'

'Ha!' Emma goes off to confront Ruby. There will be nothing facilitative about this. An assassination could be imminent.

Brigit comes into the kitchen. She is changed and ready to become super-mum as well as the head of a large teaching hospital. She starts by chopping and then frying onions and beef for the Bolognaise. I am riled. I make a perfectly good Bolognaise. I need to make this Bolognaise. It is my job which is being eroded every day because the girls need me less and less until the point when they won't need me at all and I will stand in the corner like an old broom without the bristles until someone chucks me out.

'I was doing that.' I try to snatch the wok.

37

'I'm trying to help.'

'But this is my job. You come in and you start doing my job. I don't turn up at the hospital and tell you how to get some sort of formula for the admission and discharge rates for people over the age of seventy-five with specific complex needs.'

Brigit glares at me. She glares at me because she knows I've got views on this sort of thing and I could, if I felt bloody-minded enough, work out a formula, which might in theory just cut it. I know she is thinking about Twitter and my rant one evening when I was drunk, about the incompetent management of the NHS, seen by hundreds of her staff. It took me hours to delete. What happened to free inebriated speech?

'I just want to help.'

We do a bit of wok grabbing, which is very dangerous given that it contains hot oil and singed onions. I should really tell the children not to try this sort of thing at home, but realise there is little danger of this happening because it involves the cooker and cooking utensils and the making of a proper meal.

'I'm fine. I know it's a job anybody can do, as it isn't hard, but it's my job. I'm not ready for the League of Friends. I cook, I serve, we eat and the people I raised from miniature versions of themselves go back into their rooms to do whatever it is they do!'

Brigit looks at the ceiling because it's better than looking at me and encouraging me to go on. She touches my arm very gently. 'Are you okay?'

'Yes, I'm okay.'

'You seem a bit agitated.'

'I'm fine. Honestly.'

'Okay. I know you're not. I was only trying to be helpful.'

'Did you bring me a form to fill in?'

'A form?'

'For the League of Friends?'

I get a beer from the fridge and return to the lounge. Brigit follows me. She takes my hand like I'm a confused old person who needs reminding of the date and that the Luftwaffe aren't about to drop their payload on my head.

'It's okay, lovely,' she says.

'Don't call me "lovely". You're not Cornish.'

'I'm trying to be helpful. You've done a fantastic job, but things are changing and we need to plan. We have to help you think about the next few years.'

I'm so ground down by Brigit's good intentions, she could sprinkle me on the drive. 'I know you're right. I know things are changing and it's hard.'

Brigit looks relieved.

'I'm a man who's done a job without a job description for nineteen years. I'm isolated because I'm not a woman and emasculated because I'm not like other men.'

Brigit puts her arms around me. 'Is that it? After all these years you still can't reconcile that what you've done isn't legitimate?'

'That's about the size of it.'

'That feels a bit self-indulgent.'

'Maybe it is. I have time to think about it. You go to work and one day when you leave, someone will make a speech and tell you what a wonderful person you've been and there will be a litany of achievements. Maybe a dame. There's a case in point. A man becomes a 'Sir' and the wife becomes a 'Lady'. Not so the other way round.'

'And someone who will come in and change everything because they will feel they need to. It's a passing thing.'

'It's a marker. It's a measure of what you've done.'

'God, can't you see it? You're in danger of missing the point. Take a look at the kids. What a great job you did.'

Emma screams. We hear her stomping down the stairs. Ollie's bedroom door opens and he screams. They are both shouting. Ruby is running now because she is a rescuer and rescues people when they need rescuing and in fact sometimes when they don't, leaving them occasionally quite

39

scarred as a result of not needing to be rescued. There is three-way shouting.

'Sounds like the 'great job' I've done.'

Emma stomps back up the stairs and slams her door. Calm returns. Ruby puts her head around the lounge door.

'It's okay, she didn't kill him.'

Brigit hugs me.

Ruby does the two fingers to the back of the throat thing. 'That is so wrong. I mean, so wrong. You're old people!' She leaves us to our wrongdoing.

'I don't even know where to start,' I say to Brigit who's still hugging me well beyond the point of necessity. I don't know whether she is feeding or draining me.

'You start at the beginning.'

'That's bloody profound. And where's that supposed to be?'

'Well, it's now.' She reads a lot of those very expensive books on 'smart thinking' which aren't reduced to buy one get-the-cheap-as-chips one half price', where people write about obvious simple things no one has the time or the energy to think about anymore.

'What, here? In the lounge?'

'Yes, you change the way you see things.'

She follows me back into the kitchen but, no matter how I stare at it, the place still has the feel of some catastrophic disaster from which the previous incumbents have fled and those remaining will have to clean up.

'There's a massacre in the town square where the bodies were strewn everywhere and the people don't know what to do…' I raise my hand to stop this moral flood pouring from Brigit.

'I've heard it," I remind her. 'They start moving the bodies so the flies don't eat them, the water turns poisonous and they don't get cholera.'

'So, the moral is?'

'So, the moral is, don't leave bodies lying around. No? Ok, the moral is, do something.'

'Exactly.' Brigit looks satisfied that I have the message.

I survey the kitchen. 'I'll start clearing the dishes then.'

As I start to clear the dishes, the analogy doesn't feel quite as profound as dragging dead bodies out of the sun.

5

BEFORE

Fact: Number of bottles of formula milk made and given, 17,520

We spotted the house on a walk. I had enough money for a deposit. The house was small. There was a long garden, completely overgrown. I was feeling reckless and bold. I saw myself in that garden, in that house, renovating, tilling the earth, building a composting toilet and a shed where I could brew my own beer and shit through a hole in a plank. I saw myself morphing into a cooler version of Hugh Fearnley-Whittingstall. I realise, looking back, that the person I saw doing all of those things was probably not me, but I was panicking too much to do anything rational. We put in an offer and commissioned a survey.

'The place wants gutting,' the surveyor said when I went to meet him in his office to challenge the four hundred and thirty-two structural issues he had identified which were wrong with the house. I wanted this house. It had my name on it and no one else's because they weren't stupid enough to buy it.

'We can deal with those. I'm handy.'

'You'll need to be a miracle worker. There's wet rot and dry rot, the floorboards will have to come up. There's a risk of flooding and there's a bulge in one of the outside walls.

The window frames are rotten and there is no damp proofing whatsoever. Need I go on?'

'You don't want to buy it then?'

'I suggest you don't either.'

'What if I reduce my offer?'

'By at least a third.'

'Then it's a good deal?'

He didn't comment.

'I'll take that as a yes then.'

'Be very clear – I didn't say that.'

I left him with his ginger nuts and his Newton's Cradle and a photograph of his ugly children. I imagined his wife had left him for someone with hope in their heart.

I went to visit the vendor because they lived in a large farmhouse not far from the cottage. They agreed to a reduced price because they were 'asset rich and cash poor'. This is not something we are ever likely to be. They knew it was a 'pig in a poke', and the pig was still in residence. The building society agreed with a series of provisos. We bought the house. This was it!

Not only was the house itself a 'structural issue', it was also a fleapit; a run-down pile of bricks down an overgrown lane. It was called Riverside Cottage because it was close to a flooding river. The house had its own well with its own brand of bacteria and a colony of fleas only the council could eradicate. A man in a white suit and a badass attitude got out of his unmarked van and waddled towards me. I informed him of my plan to live 'off the grid'.

'Oh, I expect to be self-sufficient by the end of the year.' I was talking to a man in a suit that made him look like 'Big Hero 6'.

'Good for you. You're lucky there's a Tesco a quarter of a mile away when your engine seizes up with the chip fat.'

I hate that kind of cynicism. It only leads to despondency.

The man in the suit entered the house and came straight out again, brushing at his body frantically. He was covered in little jumpy black things.

'You shouldn't let a house get in this sort of state. It's cats! Cat pee. I like to be blunt with people. You can't mince your words with pest control. It's a critical thing. Clarity.' He held up a fat finger between us. How do people get fat fingers? Fingers do lots of exercise. I felt like biting it. I thought about his wife and all the other women who have to live with jumped up, pedantic arseholes like that. I imagined him running a white-gloved finger over potentially dusty surfaces for 'clarity'. Those women have my sympathy and permission to leave.

I delivered the fatal blow. 'We don't have a cat.'

'Somebody does.'

'Well, that's true, but we don't, and we've never lived in the house. We've just bought it, only got the keys yesterday.'

'Ah, the people with two houses.'

'No, just the one. We rent a house.'

This took the wind out of his suit. He re-entered the house like someone tackling radioactive fallout and started to spray. I saw him in the upstairs window; a spaceman with his nozzle, killing whole populations of fleas with children and other relatives. A mercenary.

Finally he emerged from the only door and took off his helmet. He looked like a beetroot. Without a word he packed up his spray and thrust a clipboard at me. 'You need to sign this.'

'So I'm taking responsibility for the genocide?'

'Just the fumigation. Leave it for twenty-four hours. You might want to wear a mask for a couple of weeks.'

'We're moving in on Friday.'

'Well, I'd still wear a mask.'

I could imagine him and his wife sitting at the dinner table wearing masks. I couldn't imagine Brigit. I watched him go in his little white van, chuntering, and off to bollock someone else for letting cats piss in their house.

There was a trail of official people beating a path to our peeling front door through the head-high nettles. A man from the water board came and shook his head like someone with severe St Vitas Dance. He made a sucking sound with his teeth. It would have been nice to have met someone positive.

The water board man, whose name I learnt was Dave, pointed at the little motor and the hole leading to the well very disparagingly. 'Can't use that.'

'Why not? It's been tested. We're using it now.'

'Not tested by us. That's some private company. You can risk it if you want, but I hope you've got a good septic tank. You'll be shitting through a slot machine.' With a long fingernail, he tapped the piece of paper I was holding.

'So, we die of thirst?'

I got a second opinion. They told me it was okay. It was the answer I needed. We didn't die.

I hit the garden like Alan Titchmarsh on speed. I was hoeing. No one told me what a life-sucking job hoeing actually is. Brigit walked up the garden. I remember it was a Sunday. She was holding a long white plastic stick with a blue line in the little circle.

'I'm pregnant.'

I dropped the hoe. My hoeing days were numbered.

The impending arrival of Chloe filled our lives with joy. I plastered a wall, papered it and painted it white. It looked like the Alps. I hired a man to smooth it over.

'Jesus! Some idiot's made a pig's ear of this,' he said rather insensitively.

'Yes, it was like this when we bought it.'

He pulled back a piece of wallpaper. The glue and the plaster were still wet. I avoided eye contact.

I had not considered the ramifications of chucking a child into the mix of our lives. I watched Brigit's belly getting closer to the steering wheel as she headed off to implement whatever fantastic scheme the government was introducing to get 'more for less' in the NHS. I toiled on the land and worked around the skilled tradesmen putting my DIY ineptitude right. Brigit was good at it what she did. She had a great career ahead of her. Mine was receding in the rear view mirror. I was convinced I was good enough to sustain us in other more imaginative ways. I could also, I was sure, cope with one single, little child. We discussed the idea. We had nine months for Chloe and the idea to gestate. The decision for me to stay at home felt pragmatic at the time. Looking back, if I had known what I know now. Well, what if I'd known what I know now?

We went to a dinner party with some of Brigit's colleagues. I didn't have any colleagues. People aspiring to self-sufficiency, I discovered, don't tend to have colleagues. I think that is what the 'self' generally means in the term 'self-sufficiency'.

'I think it's wonderful you'll be looking after baby,' a woman called Cynthia Wellbank said after at least one bottle of red. 'Refreshing.'

'Refreshing' wasn't a word I became familiar with over the years.

There were other people equally sanguine about our up and coming arrangement, and when people are effusive it engenders well-being. All of this was theoretical though. Where Brigit was in both body and mind preparing for the real situation soon to occur, the whole idea and image of the birth and what was to follow was simply in my imagination. It was a fantasy.

I bought a book called 'The Complete Guide to Childcare'. It was big and heavy, glossy and full of tips and scenarios. It was one of those books which end up in bargain bookstores because, appearing attractive, they are the books anyone with any ounce of sense or knowledge of the realities of childcare would never want to buy. The authors made it look as easy as Madhur Jaffrey makes knocking together a Gajar Matar Aloo from the rawest authentic ingredients as she beams out beautiful and elegant from the cover of her equally glossy books. I have never completed a Madhur Jaffrey recipe without succumbing to a jar of Lloyd Grossman's Tikka Masala.

'I've bought a book.' I put the weighty tome on the table in front of Brigit. The table wobbled. 'It's all in here. I'm reading it from cover to cover.'

'We haven't talked about it properly,' Brigit said when nut pralines were occupying ninety percent of her waking thoughts and Waitrose were struggling to keep up with demand.

'It'll be fine.' I didn't know then how significant and meaningless in times of emergency this phrase would eventually become.

I was as keen as a puppy to take care of our impending child. The book made it appear easy; broken down chapter by chapter into simple tasks even an idiot could follow.

'Right,' I said to Brigit. 'We're in this situation. You've got a good job, I'm making a go of the self-sufficiency thing and I can do other stuff too. I've got a great idea about sex trafficking.' Brigit was mildly alarmed. 'My novel. It's about sex trafficking from my time in Romania.' (I did actually finish the thing and get it published fourteen years later. I averaged about twenty-eight pages a year.)

'I don't know,' she said.

'I can do it.' I knew nothing about children except they irritated me in public places. It was a low baseline to begin with, but Neil Armstrong had never walked on the moon before taking the 'first giant step for mankind'.

The months crept by. I saw the event on the horizon far enough away not to concern myself too greatly. This was a mistake. Where Brigit was preparing by cleaning, changing curtains and painting a Noah's Ark mural in Chloe's room, I was still using the hoe and beginning to loathe the thing with a similar intensity to the way I loathe cauliflower.

In the days leading up to the birth, things were good. I grew a never-to-be-repeated crop of vegetables on a plot of ground made up of weeds and chicken shit. I know now it had nothing to do with my extensive hoeing. The substrate

47

was as fantastic as substrate gets, the perfect storm of rotting organic material. I was living like I imagined Hugh Fearnley-Whittingstall lived. I regarded the earth with wonder, panning it through my fingers as if I were looking for gold. I even started to grow my hair and found a green jacket with ripped pockets in a charity shop.

I started the novel about sex trafficking, but realised I knew very little about the subject. That aside, everything felt so, well, poetic. I hung a copy of the poem 'The Road Not Taken' by Robert Frost in the kitchen to remind myself I was on that road in the yellow wood and all that. I was going to become a father and take care of our child and it would be glorious every single day. I looked at our refuse with new eyes. I was thinning the Tesco shop down to the bare minimum. I was baking, making 'hearty' vegetable stews and interesting things with fennel and other vegetables I had never encountered before. I was gobbling up 'The Complete Guide to Childcare', and Hugh Fearnley-Whittingstall was guiding me into the labyrinth of a thrifty and industrious life. I was his acolyte. One day I knew we would meet and he would shake my hand and we would be like brothers, an unspoken understanding between us; an unbreakable bond.

I was gathering useful things I found on my walks.

'You're becoming a bloody Womble,' Brigit said.

'There's a use for everything.'

'A bicycle wheel without a bicycle?' She started calling me 'Uncle Bulgaria'.

'I'm going to make a spinning wheel.'

'You need help.' She was right; I never did make the spinning wheel.

One day a man calling himself William with long grey hair tied back in a ponytail and wearing a smock leant over the fence where I was still religiously hoeing the vegetable patch.

'Good to see,' he said. 'You talk to them?'

I stopped hoeing. 'No, I thought it was just Prince Charles who had that sort of time on his hands.'

'It really works.' He took an old wooden recorder from his battered man bag and started to play. He came through the side gate with the one hinge like the Pied Piper without the rats. He started with the courgettes and then moved on to the carrots and so on. He played with such earnestness; I couldn't help but believe this worked. I was vulnerable. Maybe Brigit was right; maybe I needed help. When he stopped, I made him coffee and we sat under the blossom of a cherry tree which would never yield cherries because the bees had pissed off somewhere else.

William told me an ancient unverifiable story about a man who discovered his true wealth after searching all over the world, only to discover it was buried under a tree in his own garden. He left me thinking about digging up an old apple tree at the top of the garden just in case. I felt this spiritual wave consuming me. I lit joss sticks and candles. I bought a CD of Native American chants and joined a Buddhist centre. The head man called himself 'Dhalaray' and was in fact a plumber called Pete who came to fit a new cistern in the toilet and demonstrated none of his cosmic karma when he cracked the toilet bowl and had to replace it. I gave up the Buddhist thing because the meditative position absolutely buggered my knees and on three occasions in the midst of a mindful silence, the stabbing pain caused me to shout out the sort of words Pete used when he broke our toilet bowl. I realise now how dangerously close I had come to putting basalt crystals under my pillow to enhance well-being and welcome the spirits into our home.

'You'll set the house on fire,' Brigit said when she came home to find me asleep on the floor with the house stinking of cinnamon.

In the early hours of Chloe's due date, the lingering smell of cinnamon still in the air, I woke up to the sudden sound of rushing water. Assuming it was the pipes creaking under the weight of Dave's prophesised bacteria coming up from the well, I leapt out of bed. I was wrong. Brigit was in the bathroom bending over and hanging onto the edge of the sink.

'My waters have broken.' Her voice was unsurprisingly strained. 'She's coming today.'

'Today?' Despite knowing this, I was not ready. I needed this child to come when I was ready. Now was far too soon. I wasn't ready for this day. Days, I have discovered in life, have this habit of turning up when you aren't ready for them.

'Yes, today! I need a towel and I need you to fill the bath.'

I was on point. I grabbed a towel and handed it to Brigit. I ran the bath. We hadn't discussed the bath. We had discussed the plastic sheet, the changes of clothes, the baby stuff, the changing table and the storage of enough equipment to set up a franchise of Mothercare. After all this, I didn't think Brigit would need a bath. It seemed an odd time to take a bath, and a bad time to question her aggressive logic. I ran into the bedroom to collect my clipboard. I had one job; to record the contractions, severity and the interval. Brigit had made a chart. I can't do charts. Brigit is a chart person with the 'chart gene'. I am not.

Brigit climbed into the bath with, according to the man from the water board, a kazillion bacteria for company. Proving Archimedes was onto a good thing, Brigit displaced the equivalent body volume in water over the side of the bath and onto the floor. I was about to complain when Brigit winced in pain, making a jungle animal sort of noise of such magnitude that if I'd known she was capable of this, we wouldn't have been together. I would probably now be living in Moreton-in-Marsh.

'Was that a contraction?' I enquired, wanting to be sure. I had never heard the response to a real-life contraction before. If that were it, I wouldn't miss it again.

'Well, it wasn't wind!' came the rather unnecessarily acidic reply.

I ticked the box and set the stopwatch. I was on this.

I sat on the toilet seat looking at Brigit's vast belly, inside which Chloe punched and kicked like a puppy in a Tesco bag. I felt like someone waiting for a precious parcel, which would be my responsibility in a few months time for most of the day. I can't lie, I was nervous. I had this thought, and I am almost too ashamed to admit it. I had this thought because I am a man and Brigit is a woman, and men can't have babies and women can. I thought, 'I'm so glad it isn't me who at some point in the next few hours is going to pass a whole human person, probably the size of a large and genetically modified cantaloupe melon, through a space that currently only a small tangerine should rightly fit'.

Brigit was eyeing me suspiciously.

'I know what you're thinking,' she said.

'I bet you don't.'

'You're thinking…' A contraction with the strength of a sternum separator took Brigit in its grasp. I must ask her one day if she knew what I was thinking.

I didn't bother writing this one on the chart. 'I'll call the midwife.'

Brigit didn't argue. Chloe was to be born at home. We had a number. The midwife answered. Half an hour later, the midwife was knocking on the door. I was standing behind it, willing her to arrive and practising looking calm.

A small woman fizzing with energy stood on the doorstep. 'I'm Sylvia Banks,' she announced with the commanding tone of someone who had come to take over. 'What can you tell me?'

'Well, Brigit's upstairs and she's in labour.'

Sylvia Banks put her hands on her hips. She wanted more.

'I've been recording the contractions. Well, the first one anyway.' I wanted to sound like a man in control and bloody useful. I waved my clipboard. Sylvia Banks ignored it. 'It's all here, recorded.'

'One isn't that helpful really, is it? You need two to know the interval. You can't measure a distance with one post, can

51

you? A few would have been better than just one. Surely she's had more. Please don't tell me you've called me after one contraction. I'm sorry to be so abrupt, but I've got three mothers in labour right now and two midwifes off sick.'

'I didn't know. I was calling you when it happened.'

'What's the dilation?' She might as well have asked me the inside leg measurement of Prince Charles.

'I don't know.'

'Well, you should.'

'How would I know?' It wasn't in 'The Complete Guide to Childcare'. Sylvia Banks did not look impressed. I was searching desperately to do or say something, which might impress these women. I concluded that giving birth would probably be the only thing.

'You look, you feel.'

I looked at my chart with its one tick. 'You look, you feel,' I said to myself. I could see immediately this woman was capable, making other, less capable people feel useless.

'Right,' Sylvia Banks said when she'd finished assessing the situation. She took the clipboard from me. 'You won't be needing that. Put the kettle on, make it strong. Two sugars and warm water for my colleague.' Behind Sylvia stood a short, young woman in a black coat and woolly tights. This young and probably very warm woman also wore a perm last seen on the head of Michael Jackson singing 'Rockin' Robin' in 1972. It was the middle of July and on the previous day it had been thirty-four degrees. It wasn't the climate for looking like Paddington Bear.

'This is Christine Wallace. She's a student. They have to learn,' Sylvia said as if it were a truth simply to be borne. 'You okay with that?'

Who was I to argue? 'Oh yeah, of course. The more the merrier,' I said to Christine who didn't smile. Who would wear a thick coat and woolly tights in over thirty-four degrees if they had a sense of humour? The only thing I would have objected to right then was going through what Brigit was going through. The thought that imminently an unnaturally large object was about to be expelled from my body and rip me open from my pubis to my epiglottis, leaving a ravine the size of the San Andreas Fault, made every molecule in my being wince. Underneath her layers Christine finally smiled weakly at me and followed Sylvia up the stairs where Brigit was lying on the bed. I went to boil the kettle in the half-finished kitchen. It was such a small and unimportant task in comparison to what everyone else was doing above me. Anyone can make a cup of tea. I wanted to do something no one else could do.

I bobbed in and out of the bedroom, checking for no useful reason. I cooed at Brigit, but it did nothing to smooth her demeanour. I felt like an interloper in the world of women. A feeling I've experienced many times since. I went back into the kitchen to make more tea for the sake of making tea. I was slushing and quite woozy with tea.

'Right, now, push Brigit,' I heard Sylvia Banks say quite firmly. I ran up the stairs like a shot with the purpose of someone determined to be useful. I watched as Brigit gave birth, humbled by her strength and determination to do this without drugs. A pharmacy-full wouldn't have been enough for me, and in that moment I felt my male weakness laid bare. Chloe was born pretty much on time at exactly three fifteen in the afternoon, a characteristic she has failed to employ since. Sylvia Banks was in full charge, and Christine still wearing her black coat and woolly tights, watching and learning.

I looked down at Chloe all slimy and perfect. 'It's a baby,' I said. I sounded like a sleepwalker who's uttered something utterly sublime in the most ridiculous place.

Sylvia shook her head. Why wouldn't she? She eyed me with an expression worn by someone entirely familiar with hopeless new fathers. 'What did you expect; a puppy?'

(I discovered in the long run that a puppy would've been a great deal easier because, apart from Scooby Doo, they can't talk.)

'You can cut the cord,' Sylvia suggested.

53

I had a job. I was going to cut the cord! I was going to surgically separate this child from its mother and release it into the wild! In truth, it was more along the lines of a mother offering a child the chance to stir the cake mix when the job is already done. Sylvia clamped the cord and handed me the scissors. I was reminded when the blades faltered on the flesh of cutting an old plug off a lamp. The image rather reduced the moment. I separated Chloe from Brigit and handed her over like someone given a small line to say and then pulled off the stage. This was women 'doing their thing', and behold, they are so good at it. Yet in six months I'd be the one this tiny person would rely on during the day. How could this be? Where would I fit in? It is a question I have asked myself many times since and, now, nineteen years later, I guess I am asking it again.

6

NOW

Fact: Number of times dishwasher filled, 14,367

My mother has agreed to give up her car. At ninety-two she has done well not to instil fear into the hearts of other innocent pedestrians and road users whenever they see her coming. They do see her coming because I insisted that this car was bright yellow and visible from the space station on a foggy day.

Emma has taken her test once and failed. She feels bitter and, if I'm brutally honest, I was slightly relieved because of the imminent cost of insuring another sweet, innocent teenager who, when they hit the road twenty minutes after passing, morph into Lewis Hamilton, but not as good.

Emma is ready to go, jangling the keys at me.

Ruby runs into the hallway.

'You've got an hour. The car is mine. It's on the chart.'

'Ooh, you've got an hour,' Emma says in this whiny voice.

'I mean it. I want you back.'

We reverse out at a horrifying speed, presumably because we only have an hour. We almost collide with the person standing in the road.

'Christ!' Emma shouts with the window wound down.

Despite almost being crushed against the bank, Harriet Rickard is smiling. She waves. 'I wanted to catch you,' Harriet says. Emma revs the engine to demonstrate her impatience. 'I wanted to ask how the girls were after their disappointing exam results. I know it's hard. Spence did so well. We're so proud of him, and of course, Archie and Becca. We'll have plenty of lawyers when things go wrong. You know, when those less fortunate, less educated get into trouble.'

'They're all doing just fine,' I assure her.

Harriet looks agitated.

'Are you okay, Harriet?'

'Oh yes, yes, absolutely fine. Couldn't be better. Life is as good as it gets.' Harriet notices the L-plates and makes this strange hooting noise I couldn't emulate. 'Ours passed first time. Naturals. Can't all be, I suppose. Some people simply have it.'

'Of course.'

'How's Brigit? Must be hard, what with everything against her. I often think about what Caroline Waters said about her never being able to sleep at night.

Emma revs the car very hard. Caroline Waters has said a lot of things over the years.

'I think she sleeps just fine. Is there anything else, Harriet? I need to get Emma on the road.'

'Yes, I've got an exhibition of new paintings coming out next week.' Harriet digs out a piece of paper from her pocket and unfolds it. She hands it to me. There is a picture of David Hockney. He has a new collection at the Tate.

'This is about David Hockney, Harriet. Are you working with him?'

She giggles.

'Oh turn it over, silly man.'

There is an advert for vitamin supplements on the back.

'I'm not sure I understand. This is an advert for vitamin supplements.'

'That's the one,' she says.

'Right, I look forward to it.'

Harriet snatches the paper from me. 'Yes.' Harriet stands away from the car.

I try to imagine an exhibition of vitamin supplements. I suppose with Tracey Emin's 'unmade bed', the Turner Prize might be a possibility.

'Good luck,' she says madly, cheerily. 'They do apprenticeships for the less academic, you know.'

Emma pulls away. 'The woman's nuts,' she says loudly with the window still wound down.

I can see Harriet running after us. Even though the ground is wet, I notice she is wearing slippers. Harriet puts her head in Emma's window and shouts at me. 'I forgot to mention that last year I saw some people putting all these Christmas lights on their house and the house was falling apart. I told them they should spend the money on the house instead.'

'What did they say?'

'They were very rude. They told me to, you know, 'F off'. Then again you would expect that kind of language from those sorts of people. Will you be having a lot of decorations this year?'

'I expect so. We like the bling. Brigit's from Liverpool.'

'Yes, well, I'm not implying anything by saying this, but lights are very expensive. You could buy a pot of paint.' Harriet steps away from the car. She starts directing with her arms. I wave at her.

'Just drive, Em.'

'I got ten A stars by the way,' Emma shouts. 'I'm going to be an astronaut.'

Martin the postman hears this and puts his thumbs up. Maybe it was his second choice of career if he didn't cut it as a postman. I bet astronauts don't get a box of Cadbury's Roses every year for leaving parcels behind the gate rather than just one of those 'sorry we missed you' cards when they're not bloody sorry at all.

We pull away at speed, leaving Harriet gripping the postman's arm and standing in the middle of the road.

Emma is off the grid and pushing the rev' counter into the red.

'Steady on!'

'I know what I'm doing!' Emma is shouting even though I'm just a foot away from her. 'I only got two majors in my test! You make it out like I can't drive!'

'Yes, but they're the ones where you are a risk to life and limb. It isn't anything to brag about. You don't get sympathy points the next time you take the test.' This is not a good time to provoke a teenage learner when they are behind the wheel and giving the clutch a serious seeing to. I have no dual controls. It is like challenging a gunman with a peashooter.

We hurtle towards the junction. I close my eyes. We turn left and my stomach lurches the opposite way with my breakfast close behind.

'The mirror is that thing in the centre of the windscreen, which is not just for checking your chops.'

Em ignores this.

We drive into town. I see Geoff Tiller, one of our neighbours parked up down a side street. Em decides to turn into this street and keep the manoeuvre a secret to herself. I go one way and my internal organs go the other.

'Jesus, woman! No indication, no slowing down. This isn't 'Starsky and Hutch' you know. You need to share with other people what you intend to do.'

'Ooh, do we now. Who's Starsky and Hutch? Mates of yours?'

'I don't have any mates. They all ran away when I became a boring full-time babysitter. The Dukes of Hazzard, then.'

'Nope. Never heard of them either. People you went to school with?'

'Grand Theft Auto then, which your brother shouldn't be playing because he's only twelve and conned your mother

58

when she was vulnerable with bogus reviews on Mumsnet written by morons or twelve-year olds.'

"There's a Dadsnet.'

"I know. I checked it out. The whole of Aberdeen has got forty members."

Geoff Tiller is in the midst of a heated argument with an attractive young woman who I recognise as Phoebe Cannon, the barmaid at the Final Furlong. Phoebe is crying. I assume this might be because she is stuck in a car with Geoff Tiller. It is something likely to make any woman cry. Geoff Tiller looks like Homer Simpson, but he does have a lot of spare cash from his mysterious work with 'banks'. I see all this in detail because Emma has now stalled right next to them.

'You made me stall!'

'I can't make you stall, Em. Only you can make you stall. Just get the bloody thing going.'

Brigit would be horrified at the lack of facilitative interaction here. 'So, how do you feel about stalling?', she would probably say.

Geoff's wife Gaynor is a housewife. She and Geoff have one son, Brian, who, according to Harriet Rickard, 'has that look about him' which, when you examine Brian, you can sort of see in a very un-PC sort of way. When he was fifteen Brian broke the jaw of a young man standing at a bus stop minding his own business. There appeared to be no motive and Brian was given community service. During this time, he hit someone again, at a bus stop. Realising Brian Tiller had a grudge against people standing at bus stops, he was placed in a juvenile detention centre. Brian now works abroad, but nobody knows where or doing what. There was a rumour he was working for MI6, but there was also a rumour that Elvis was living on the moon, and some hope that Brian Tiller might become his neighbour.

We are alongside Geoff and his young emotional passenger who is married to Dan Cannon, a plumber with a temper. Dan would snap Geoff in half if he knew he was upsetting Phoebe on a Saturday morning in his car.

We stall again.

'You might want to put the handbrake on,' I suggest, to stop us rolling back into the terrified man in the polished-within-an-inch-of-its-life Audi just behind us.

'Stop shouting at me!' Emma shouts.

'I'm not shouting.' I bloody well should be. I have Geoff yelling at Phoebe on my left and Emma on the right. The man in the Audi throws his hands up in horror because he has now forgotten when he took his test and everything he ever learnt about road etiquette. He gives us the finger. I take this on the chin. We deserve this. We deserve a whole lot more. We deserve a kick to the bodywork. The Audi man doesn't know how lucky he is that Emma hasn't got out of the car and punched his windscreen. I live a precarious life. I am sitting next to a psychotic teenager in a yellow dot of a car with my neighbour on my left having a row with another man's wife. The man in the Audi is quite clearly saying that 'learners should not be allowed on the f…ing road' or words to that effect. Right now I am inclined to agree. Geoff Tiller has seen us and slides down in his seat. He is quite tall. Even for a small person it is quite a task to get right down into the foot-well. Geoff turns to look at us with his Homer Simpson face. Phoebe turns too. I wave meekly at Geoff. He does not appear smug. Instead he looks mortified. I imagine Geoff with one of Dan Cannon's U-bends embedded in his forehead, looking like a rhinoceros.

Emma is quite systematic in her approach to the world. She applies logic where others slot in emotion. She is convinced, through the process of probability, that she is able to predict, with some certainty, the test route she is likely to get. She has a chart of all the sixth formers who have taken their driving tests over the last couple of months, the routes they took, the instructor, and whether they passed or not. From this data she has calculated that the route she is almost certain to get is the one we are doing right now. If she gets the female examiner called Geraldine, she is doomed, but Kevin, apparently compliant depending on the shortness of the skirt, is the man to get.

'This is definitely going to be the route I'll get,' Emma assures me.

'If you say so.' Even I know this is not a good time to argue.

Through my extra mirror where I can see oncoming danger, but can do bugger all about it as Emma knows best, I see an ambulance with its blue flashing lights weaving its way through the traffic. Just when you think things can't get worse…

Emma responds and, quite rightly, swerves in front of the poor bugger in his Audi, missing him by a balding person's perished hair and almost giving reason for the ambulance to stop and pick people from the wreckage.

'Well done!' I say, because that's what you're supposed to say when the intention is right even though the potential cost both in human and financial terms is incalculable. We are round the test route with a couple of parallel parks, a reverse around a corner and five islands in record time.

'If you speed on the test, you'll fail. It's not a race.' This was one of the two reasons why Emma failed in the first place. The other was turning left at thirty-five in a thirty limit without slowing down.

'I won't speed.'

'You're speeding now.'

'I won't then. That's then and this is now.'

'That's great to know then. I feel reassured.'

We leave the town for a country lane where I brace myself as surreptitiously as I can against the dashboard.

'You're going a bit fast.'

'The speed limit is 60,' is what I get back.

'But it's a single lane.'

'Still 60.'

'Still bloody dangerous! You don't have to do 60. Just because the limit is 60, it doesn't mean you have to stick to that.'

'Stop shouting!'

'I'm frightened. That's why I'm bloody shouting.'

This prompts Emma to stick her foot to the boards. Fear is not a currency here. 'You don't need to swear.'

'Yes, I fucking-well do! You need to slow down.'

'You need to stop shouting.'

'I'm shouting because I can't hear myself above the noise of the bloody engine!'

We swerve towards the pavement where a woman with a pushchair, realising we may shortly be on the pavement ourselves, is clearly thinking about throwing herself into the road where it could quite possibly be safer.

'You need to stop!' Yes, I am shouting.

Emma pulls into a garage, slams on the brakes, the car stalls, and she gets out. She storms off across the forecourt mumbling expletives to herself. She stands about a hundred metres away with her hand on one hip and her phone in the other. I am being reported to the highest authority.

I get out. 'Why are you calling Mum?'

She ignores me.

I storm over and try to snatch the phone.

Mr Fratton, one of my mother's neighbours, comes out of the garage and looks at us. My mother will hear about this within the hour and I will no doubt get a phone call to tell me 'this never happened in my day'. I wave at Mr Fratton. He is on his mobile phone and staring me out. He is eighty-seven. I think about snatching his phone and pushing him over.

'I'm phoning Mum to come and fetch me.' Now I know that Brigit, with her guilt complex about not sharing enough time with the kids, will be in her car as fast as Batman and Robin get out of the bat cave and will be down here to pick poor old Emma up with her bruised sensibilities.

'Don't be so bloody stupid. You nearly killed that woman and her child.'

'She shouldn't have been there.'

'She was on the frigging pavement!'

'It's not a proper pavement.'

'Jesus!' I am brimming with anger. I can feel my blood pressure up there with the gods, and if it stays there I will shortly be joining them. 'Emma, get back in the car.' I snatch the phone and start running away across the forecourt. People filling their tanks are watching. This has newspaper potential. I shout into the phone breathlessly, 'You don't need to come.'

'Sounds like you've upset Emma.'

'She nearly killed us and a woman and a child on the pavement. I'm not sure that warrants a sack-load of sympathy right now.'

'You sound out of breath. What's the matter with you?'

'I'm running from our daughter.'

Emma is laughing.

'I'm coming to get her.'

'Don't be so bloody stupid.'

Brigit slams the phone down and doesn't pick up again. I wait for a text. It doesn't come. I hit the phone because I am enraged and it is a good enough excuse. I get into the yellow car where my knees come up to my chin. I start the engine and stall. Emma is still laughing. I drive away, leaving her on the forecourt with her hands on her hips and a pout which would give Posh Spice a bloody good run for her money.

Brigit passes me on my way home.

I wave.

She ignores me.

I arrive home.

Ruby is in the driveway looking at her phone where she's been timing us on the stopwatch.

'Eighty-five seconds late. Did you fill it up?'

I walk past her, the last of my energy draining through my feet. 'No. I forgot.'

'Mum's gone to get Em.'

'I know.'

'She says you shouted at her.'

'She nearly killed a woman and a child and us. She's a maniac!' I imagine repeating these hopeless facts until I go insane. Emma is the child and I am the parent. I should know better. I am only human. Right now it doesn't feel as if it is enough. What else am I supposed to be?

I close the door and sit down on the bottom step of the stairs with my Scottie, Claude. He smells of something horrible he's been eating, but he doesn't care, and right now neither do I.

'I love you, Claude.' I notice he has conjunctivitis in both eyes. Despite this, he looks genuinely pleased to see me through his crusty lids. Right now, I need someone on my side and a smelly dog will have to do.

7

BEFORE

Fact: The volume of Calpol administered, 4 litres

After Chloe was born, we had six months of joy. The weather was perfect and Chloe had wall-to-wall parents. At least that is my untainted memory. I was tending my crops and even writing a few pages of the utterly crap tome the first draft of my novel would eventually become. Our life was, as I flicked through the glossy pages of 'The Complete Guide to Childcare', everything the authors said it would be and more. This was my bible. I wanted to keep my copy as pristine as the people and the children on and between the covers. These experts knew what they were talking about, and we were walking along the same road in holy trinity. We were this little family with two full-time parents, a triangle; that tough little shape the spiritualists call 'the door to wisdom', a shape the Egyptians loved so much and Pythagoras too. There were sleepless nights, of course. I couldn't do what they call 'controlled crying'. What's controlled about crying? It is an unleashed emotion without containment, like training a jellyfish to do the quick step. Apart from the little things, this period felt to me like a piece of cake. I believed I really could be the main parent. This would be as smooth as the bottom of our first child.

Brigit had some concerns. She was the mother and I understand, now, that the bond between the mother and child is never really broken, but only stretched. I have never asked Brigit if she kept a 'paper trail' of our agreements and understandings for use when I started claiming I never agreed to anything. Her ability to dredge up conversations from the past however is very unsettling.

'You have to be sure you want to do this. You can't take this on and then change your mind a year down the line. This is not like having a hamster.'

'I've never had a hamster.'

'You've never looked after a child.'

'They're hardly the same. You can't equate a child with a hamster.'

'If you stay out of conventional work, you won't easily get back in, and Chloe needs consistency. This is very hard for me to do. I am sacrificing more than you could ever know for the sake of our family.'

I brushed this off. It would take me years to see how much this really cost Brigit. I didn't see then, because it didn't apply to Brigit, how easily and often gratefully and quickly men will return to work after the birth of their child. I didn't register that 'The Complete Guide to Childcare' only referred to the mother in the caring role. The book wasn't intended for me at all.

'I can do it. I want to do it. I want to live a different life, off the grid. I'm growing stuff; it'll be totally brilliant. Anyway, I'm going to write that novel. It's just a matter of time.' No-one, apart from someone who loved me and knew I wanted the best for our little family, would have given a milligram of credence to my logic.

About a month before Brigit went back to work, I began watching Chloe carefully. This was a real, breathing, dribbling and crying miniature person who thought the hands attached to the ends of her arms belonged to someone else. Chloe was turning from an image in a glossy hardback book into something undeniably and disconcertingly real.

I could see how natural Brigit was with Chloe, and how hard it would be for her to leave for whole days at a time. I saw this, but I didn't say anything. I wonder now whether it was pride or delusion or both. If I had spoken, shared my doubts, things could have turned in that moment, and it would be Brigit sharing her thoughts about child rearing and telling millions of other women what they already know. Instead it is me. I count the lucky stars I found along the way.

'I don't know if I can do this,' Brigit said on several occasions with increasing distress.

I was thinking this too, but one of us had to remain positive, and to be honest it was usually Brigit.

'It'll be fine. It's going to be one of us. Why can't it be me? You'll be home before you know it.'

The day that I'd imagined during our six months would never arrive, arrived. I remember it was icy and there was frost clinging to the trees, adhered by a biting northerly wind. I was not prepared. There is nothing to prepare a man with no physiological bond for suddenly being alone with a six-month-old child. What would we talk about? It took until the moment just before Brigit's departure for me to appreciate the magnitude of this unpreparedness. I'd deluded myself into thinking I wouldn't feel alone or anxious because I had Chloe and we'd share everything. But 'I', in the singular adult sense, was alone. I had no plans for the day. It was too cold to stay out for long, and I was lost for where to take her. I don't know why it hadn't occurred to me that Chloe was not going to be an equal partner in this thing. I'd be spending my days with someone to whom the world at large made no sense at all. Starting with a baby is like beginning with a dementia patient and working backwards until once again they become whole. 'Benjamin Button' in reverse.

I watched Brigit drink her coffee in the unfinished kitchen. Never had the drinking of a cup of coffee felt so brief.

'Would you like another?' I offered her another really hot coffee.

'I have to go.'

I could see Brigit's eyes were red. But didn't Brigit realise what this was like for me? I was being deserted. I was screaming inside, silently. 'Please don't go! Please don't leave me with this child. It's a mistake. It's all been a mistake. I have never looked after a child on my own before!' I had this image reeling through my mind where, as she walked out of the door, I was clinging to her leg as she dragged me to the car, begging her not to leave because I was about to start a job for which I had no legitimate qualifications. I felt like a fraud. I felt like someone claiming to play a musical instrument and then being asked to perform at Wembley Stadium in front of thousands of people.

Chloe sat in her high chair spreading goo over the tray and loving it.

Brigit finished her coffee.

'Another?'

I noticed the car was covered in ice. I was going to make a big thing of the ice.

'I'll scrape the ice off the car. Maybe the roads are too treacherous.' I walked out slowly into the freezing air with the scraper and cleaned the windows. Alan Burton, our neighbour, was pulling out, heading off to school where he was the headmaster. He waved. I waved back and watched him disappear to a structured day of timetables, bells and detentions, of yelling teenagers and bloody noses. I wanted to be a headmaster with a headmaster's badge and pupils queuing outside my office rigid with fear. For a fraction of a manic second I imagined grabbing his car door and jumping in beside him. He was going off to run a school. He had purpose and I… I was in charge of a six-month-old child for a whole day. And then another. And another.

Alan's day was already laid out like a list which must be completed before the bell when he could come home to his pipe and slippers and a doting wife called Marlene from Watford. Alan was educating the future generation. He had long holidays. What the hell was I doing? If anyone knew, it was the people in 'The Complete Guide to Childcare', but it certainly wasn't me.

When I went back into the house, Brigit was kissing the top of Chloe's head and crying at the same time.

'This is it then,' Brigit said.

My stomach was in a knot. Chloe started crying. Oh God, don't leave me with a crying child. I'd calmed her before, but Brigit was always there like one of those safety nets under a trapeze.

I could see Brigit was in pain. I was in pain, but for a different reason. Perhaps then, if we'd both declared our own individual pain and done a swap, the children might have turned out differently and Ruby wouldn't still be telling me what a 'dysfunctional family' we are. I couldn't feel Brigit's pain anymore than I could with the birth, but I did understand. She was leaving the child she had nurtured for nine months with the utmost care, and delivered her into the world utterly perfect, and then handed her over to me; a fraud, masquerading as someone who pretended to know what they were doing. I was living a lie. Not a comfortable place to dwell.

'You will look after her, won't you?'

'Of course I will. I promise.'

What else would I do?

I followed Brigit to the door. I was like a dog desperate for a walk.

'Don't come with me. I just need to go.'

Oh my God, she was going to do this. She was actually going to leave me with our child. Brigit Wheeler actually believed I could do this.

I stepped back inside the house. Brigit started the car. It stalled. The AA would take at least an hour to come. It was a legitimate excuse. The car started, pulled away and bounced along the pot-holed lane. Brigit was gone. Only the mist from the exhaust hung in the air as evidence she was ever there. In seconds the mist was gone too. I could hear the growl of the cars on the bypass, the noise of 'the commute', of people going somewhere to do things in a world I had so readily, unthinkingly departed, and now suddenly craved.

I went back to find Chloe crying in the kitchen. There was a lot to cry about in the kitchen. It was half-decorated. There were wires hanging out of the walls waiting for lights we couldn't afford. I took Chloe upstairs to change her. I lay her in the cot where she settled quickly with the expression of a drunken person on the brink of unconsciousness. I crept downstairs to my computer where I intended to spend the morning on my masterpiece. I had a sudden surge of well-being. Maybe this was going to be okay.

Chloe was asleep for twenty-five minutes. I hadn't written a word. I went from trying to structure a serious literary novel with no plot to watching Winnie the Pooh and Noddy and bloody Teletubbies – the thing of nightmares – in just over half an hour. We went on to build towers and knock them down. No; I went on to build towers and knock them down. Panic spread through me like a virus until I ached with it. I was a man looking after a child, imprisoned in a room with building blocks and gruesome cartoons and no prospect of reprieve.

Brigit rang at lunchtime.

'How's it going?'

I took a moment to look at the wreckage of the room and leapt to grab Chloe from sticking her saliva-covered fingers into the plug sockets. Chloe had just learnt to crawl.

'We need some of those plug covers. She nearly stuck her fingers in the socket.'

'Oh, my God! What the hell were you thinking?'

I was thinking, *I'm trying to write a novel, become Hugh Fearnley-Whittingstall and pretend I am not the sole carer for a six-month-old child requiring round the clock supervision in case she lights herself up like Oxford Street at Christmas.*

'It's fine,' I said. 'It's a learning process. I'm watching her.'

'I miss her so much.' Brigit started to cry. 'Will you put her on the phone?'

I held the phone to Chloe's ear. She pulled it away as Brigit talked into Chloe's toothless mouth.

'It's okay,' I said when Brigit had finished talking to Chloe's gums.

'Are you okay?'

'She won't sleep.'

'At all?'

'Twenty-five minutes.'

'She'll get into a routine.'

I think we've made a mistake teetered on the end of my tongue. Brigit had given up so much. I knew this. She'd given it up so I could have the time to write and live outside the system. It wasn't her fault that Chloe only slept for twenty-five minutes.

'I've booked us into a playgroup on Wednesday.'

'That's so great. I have to go.'

It struck me then, that Brigit could go, back to the world I had chosen not to re-join. Instead, I had made a leap into something I knew nothing about. I'd made rash decisions before, but nothing with such long lasting consequences as this. I couldn't be the only man in this part of the country to take on this job full-time, surely? I would begin my search for a kindred spirit to share and support.

I decided to take Chloe to Tesco. It would be fun. Looking back, I can now see how far I slipped and how quickly; within just a few days I was going to Tesco for fun. The next thing would probably be standing on the bridge, watching the traffic on the bypass for a right laugh.

I strapped Chloe into the little seat in the trolley. I became good at Tesco. I knew where the shitake mushrooms were. They were next to the broccoli and asparagus combinations; three for the price of four, including sweet and sour sauce or a chow mein. I could have worn a badge. On one afternoon when Chloe actually slept, I sketched out the Tesco layout on the back of an envelope. I compared it to the real thing. The only error was aisle 23, which they'd moved to 27 since our last visit following a flood from the fish freezer.

A woman appeared from behind the end of the toilet roll aisle. She pointed at me.

'You're Brigit Wheeler's husband.'

'We're not married.'

'Oh, partner thing then.'

'Yes, partner thing.'

The woman held out her hand. 'I'm Mandy Chaucer.'

'Any relation to the writer?'

'Oh yes, my husband is a distant cousin a couple of generations removed, I believe.'

Of course he was.

'Dick Chaucer. He's a renal surgeon at the hospital. Brigit will have talked about him.'

'Not sure she has.'

'Dick's got a lot of time for Brigit.' (She was then the Director of Operations.) 'No time for that idiot, John Taylor. Couldn't organise the proverbial in a brewery. Be glad when he's gone.'

'You work there too?' I asked.

'I suppose in a way I do. We're all on the same team, you know.'

I was trying not to smirk about a renal surgeon having the name Dick.

'Like a sort of job-share, you mean?'

'Exactly like that. We must have you round for supper now we know one another.'

I wasn't sure a brief 'hello' in the bog roll aisle at Tesco constituted an intimate relationship. Perhaps someone should have pointed that out to Bill Clinton.

'Your day off? The hired help away?'

'No, this is our daughter, Chloe.' Chloe blew a thick saliva bubble. 'I look after her.'

Mandy looked at Chloe and then at me, as if we were as incongruent as a gazelle and a lion.

'You? All the time?'

'Yes, me. I mean, I'm becoming self-sufficient as well and write novels.' I guess the self-sufficiency thing didn't look that good standing in the toilet roll aisle in Tesco when we should have been wiping our backsides on old passed-down copies of 'Farmers Weekly'. 'I don't just do this.' Admittedly, my portfolio career didn't possess the same kudos as Dick flushing out bladders.

'Oh, I must get one of your books. Recommendations?'

I was once again the musician claiming to play and now being asked to prove it.

'Not published yet, I'm afraid.'

'Oh, bad luck.'

Actually, it had nothing to do with luck. It was mainly getting to the keyboard that was the problem. The other was when I did get there, pages of crap flooded from the ends of my fingers.

'Well, it's not luck really. It's the time.'

Chloe started to cry. I'm only glad she couldn't talk and tell Mandy Chaucer what a fraudulent father I was and we were in Tesco for entertainment.

'I'll check the diary and get Dick's people to call your wife's people.'

Mandy was off and round the corner as fast as Hamilton takes a bend. They never invited us to dinner before they moved away. Dick had an affair with an anaesthetist called Jane which, Brigit told me, spawned a multitude of schoolboy jokes.

Chloe wouldn't go to sleep that night. She is still like this today and wanders around the house turning the lights on and flushing the toilets I assume to stop the septic tank from 'backing up'. I sang to her and kept winding up the Winnie the Pooh mobile where the four main characters dangled like the victims of a multiple public hanging. As her eyelids grew heavy, I started to tiptoe out of the room. After two steps she woke up because she was watching me with those wide beautiful eyes young men are still hurling themselves into. I sat on the floor and sang desperate songs, sinking lower, until I was on my belly and swimming across the varnished floorboards. I drank two large bottles of ice-cold beer very quickly and fell asleep in the chair.

Brigit woke me up.

'Jesus. You can't just go to sleep.' She saw the bottles on the floor. 'You've been drinking! God! I can't leave you for five minutes!'

I stared at her in disbelief. 'It's actually been eleven hours without a break.'

Brigit put her hands on her hips. 'Duh! I've been out for the same amount of time.'

'I think that's how time works.'

Brigit ignored me and went straight to Chloe. The next minute she was standing in the doorway cradling Chloe in her arms. She'd been back two minutes and my work had been unravelled like the seam of a dress.

'She was asleep. You've woken her up. It took me ages.'

'Wide awake now.'

Chloe actually grinned.

After Chloe finally went to sleep, Brigit and I sat down to eat some of my homegrown produce. I was knackered. I barely had the strength to lift a pan.

'I met a woman at work who runs this 'informal' parent support group,' Brigit said. 'She invited us, but I think you should go and I'll stay with Chloe.'

'What sort of group?'

Over the years I have been to many groups and, I would say to anyone with small children, be particularly wary of 'informal' groups.

'She's quite religious, but a lovely woman. Her husband looks after the children, they've got two. They're at school now, but they have this meeting of a few parents every couple of weeks where they talk about childcare issues and offer support for people with problems.'

'I don't have problems.'

'You might find it useful. There are other men.'

This made it all sound pretty desperate. I was joining an 'informal' group to meet 'other men'! I believe these days they call it 'Grindr'.

Despite overlooking the term 'informal' group, I should have registered the alarm bells at the words 'quite religious'. I believe you are either religious or you are not.

8

NOW

Fact: Number of bedtime books read (including repeats), 9,256

Young people appear late on Friday nights. They deposit themselves in various parts of our multi-coloured house. They make my teenage years look like an episode from 'Little House on the Prairie'. These young people emerge the next morning like the 'living dead' crawling from their graves.

Despite people and noise in the kitchen and some rapper belting out sixty words a minute about 'trailer trash, bitches, hoes and designer clothes', I get up to let the dogs out. Claude, my Scottie, has left a pile on the kitchen floor because no one, despite his pleas, has let him into the garden. For some reason he's got it into his head that he'll receive a biscuit for doing a poo wherever he is and not just outside. This morning he is looking pretty pleased with himself because he's done the shit and now he wants his prize.

In the kitchen there are two girls who I've never seen before and three boys. Emma and Ruby are here too. They have been to a party down the road.

'The dog's done a poo.' I point at the offence.

'Oh, I didn't see it,' Ruby says as if she actually believes this.

They all wanted dogs. I didn't even like dogs, but I caved in because I was water-boarded with syrupy pleas about how emotionally underdeveloped people without pets can be until I couldn't breathe.

'How can you possibly have not seen it? Someone out of …' I count them '…the seven of you would, simply through the process of probability, have stood in it. Instead you've walked around it.'

I sound like a fool. I sound like one of those parents who care about clean windows and bedding plants, painted guttering, and gleaming Sunday-waxed Vauxhall Astras. I sound like someone to whom anything remotely youthful, spontaneous and joyful has leaked out like a bad bout of incontinence. I am talking about dog shit on the kitchen floor first thing in the morning with the sublime idea I might still appear to them as a 'cool dad'. There is no such thing!

The people I don't know, who aren't my sons and daughters, are all staring into my fridge as if it is the gateway to some magical kingdom. One of the boys takes out my maple-cured bacon and sniffs it. He looks at me as if I'm somehow responsible.

'It's in date,' I assure him. I have never in my life gone into someone else's fridge and taken out their maple-cured bacon, put it in a frying pan and fried it in front of the owner's eyes. I struggle for a suitable word, but audacity will have to do.

Chloe appears wearing barely nothing but a few strategically placed straps. The other girls are dressed similarly. The boys seem unfazed. They have seen it all and my teenage self, buried under layers of what we refer to as wisdom and restraint, envies them completely.

'This is Amber and Katie,' Chloe says as if it could be anyone coveting my maple-cured bacon.

'Hey,' they both say together.

'Hey', I have grown to learn, means 'hello' in translation.

'Hay is for horses, Stanley.'

Ruby shakes her head in despair. It's a line from 'Flat Stanley' for anyone who has enjoyed a literature-filled childhood.

Ruby punches my arm. When did punching people's arms become a friendly gesture? 'Mum's the seventh most powerful person in the city.'

A boy with the sort of hair one gets from being permanently submerged in the sea and is now holding my maple-cured bacon speaks. 'Yeah, it's in the paper. Respect.' He does this thing with his fingers and his fist. He lightly touches his head. 'I'm Niall.'

I shake his hand. He has a vice-like grip. I try not to wince.

Ruby laughs. She saw me wince, slightly.

'So who's number one then?' I ask, imagining this to be a joke.

'That bloke with the Ferrari. Cool car.'

Oh my God, it's Richard Quail. Richard Quail is the most powerful person in the city! He's got a Ferrari and the respect of everyone who ever had anything wrong with their brain and an epidermis like something in a Clinique advert.

'It's the bloke who owns the tyre places,' Niall informs me.

I feel brighter. 'Ferraris are ten a penny round here. My friends, the Quails, down the road own one.'

Ruby and Emma shake their heads. This does, I cannot argue, sound desperately pathetic.

'It's out of fifty people,' the boy says. 'That's pretty cool to have forty-seven people behind you.'

'No, it's forty-three,' I feel the need to point out.

Niall does this twirly, pointy finger thing. 'Just testing yah.' Niall leaves, wearing only a pair of tight, nothing-left-to-the-imagination boxer shorts. He returns with a copy of yesterday's 'Chronicle'. He hands it to me.

I should really jab his eyes out, just like Jackie Chan would. Fuelled by the image of Niall taking me down in one simple manoeuvre, I resist the temptation and open the paper.

'Page twenty-three.' Niall takes the paper from me and finds the page. God, do I look like I can't open a paper? Obviously!

'Oh, so not near the front then.'

There is a list of names, a brief biography and a photograph compiled by someone no doubt in the back office of the 'Chronicle' with two pages to fill and no real news. There are a couple of business people, doctors, lawyers, and a novelist! A bloody novelist! An important novelist! A novelist with power! There are no child carers. There are academics and engineers, and Brigit, beaming out of the newspaper at number seven. I am thrilled for her. She has a well-paid vocation, empirical measures for progress and now power in the city. What is the saying? 'Whenever a friend succeeds, a little something in me dies'? By all rights, I should be dead!

'There are only fourteen women,' Niall says. 'Bit biased with thirty-five men.'

'Thirty-six,' I correct him.

'Right. Good job I'm not doing a maths degree.'

'It is. What are you planning on doing then?' Apart from coveting my maple-cured bacon. I imagine mechanic might be an option as long as he has someone to count the nuts and bolts.

'Medicine.'

'Right.' I only hope he doesn't have to treat me for anything requiring adding or subtracting.

'Brigit is the top woman on the list,' Niall adds. 'So cool.'

There are new people appearing at the house these days – people beyond the safety of the school gates where I have delivered the children for years and watched them go through in the knowledge that they are secure. Now there are people with histories and secrets, and other lives I know nothing about. This lack of intelligence unnerves me. The girls don't bother introducing the other two boys, but

79

Dylan, a boy I now recognise, shakes my hand, quite firmly and introduces the other boy, Bret. They all nod and turn their attention to spreading my organic ketchup on my pumpkinseed bread. They seem okay kids, though I'm not sure why I think this when they are rifling my fridge. To me, a stranger taking things out of my fridge without my permission is no more than a common thief.

I tip my coffee pot to find it empty and my coffee jar devoid of coffee. I could swear now, but I don't. I sit down at the table and Chloe comes and puts her arms around me. She is a perceptive young woman and, even at moments like this when my kitchen is being ransacked, I feel real pride and privilege to be with these young people. I guess this is my gong for doing the time and not a spot in the top fifty along with the other novelist who probably writes garbage. People will buy anything.

'Don't you wish we were still in India?' I say.

'Not really. It was time to come home.'

She is right of course. Chloe was fed up with being stared at, sized up and chatted up by boys with wives standing just behind them. These young, beautiful western women are constantly being visually touched up by men three times their age, and any man who doesn't believe this should take a walk down any high street with them on a sunny day.

On the kitchen table is an old Sunday supplement. It is open at a regular column where a man talks wryly about his family life and how the weekends are some sort of comic farce in which he plays only a walk on part. He tells us how exhausted 'the Mrs' looks on a Friday night in a house that appears like it's been subject to a Viking attack. I hate these smug men. I burn their columns quite ceremoniously in the wood burner and watch their faces crinkle to ash while I empty the dishwasher, cook a meal, answer the phone and moan bitterly about the cliché that men are unable to multi-task. It is not true and 'the Mrs' knows this but, more often than not, doesn't like to say (a rocking boat on this vast sea is the last thing she needs!). I do not possess such refined etiquette. I say – like the piles of washing I have done over the years on sunny days – 'let it all hang out!'.

I tear the magazine up. They make money from parodying something I have done seriously for nineteen years. It is not a farce. It takes the most inwardly reflective people to mine the joy from the angst, and the tears from the laughter.

'Footy!' Ollie shouts as he comes into the kitchen wearing his goalie kit and gloves before he's had breakfast. 'Pancakes?'

'Sure,' I say. He plays his best games on a couple of my pancakes.

I look across at the cooker and the work surfaces. Despite the autumn chill, the young Gods and Goddesses, still scantily clad, have gone into the garden to eat my bacon between slices of pumpkinseed bread with lashings of organic tomato sauce. I make the pancake mixture among the greasy frying pans and the crumbs, the butter and the ketchup. There is an open bottle of beer in the door of the fridge. I close it before the temptation breaks my resolve.

After spitting on them 'for grip', Ollie takes off his gloves to wolf down his pancakes. All the great goalkeepers turn up for breakfast wearing their gloves. I take Brigit a cup of tea. She is checking her e-mails in bed.

'You're the seventh most powerful person in the city.'

'I know.' Brigit has a streaming cold and the little drips on the end of her nose keep splashing onto her phone. It crosses my mind to take a photo and put it on social media. I have Facebook and eighteen friends who use it as often as I do to say thank you for the birthday wishes from the other seventeen if they are still alive.

'Niall thinks it's so cool. He did this little salute and said 'respect'.'

'He's such a lovely boy.'

'Can't add up though.'

'Emma says he's in the top five percent in the world at Chemistry.'

I forgot to mention that Niall is also handsome with the body of an Olympic athlete. I take little comfort in his lack of numeracy skills.

'You've got to admit these lists are a load of rubbish. Look at number one. Dave Meakins. He gives them money for advertising his tyres.'

'You sure you're not saying that because you're a teeny weeny bit jealous?'

'No. Of course not.'

'Good. There's no need to be. I'm just checking my media.'

We have become insanely defensive about our use of mobile phones in the house. Brigit's Scottie, Mop, lies on the bed languidly and growls at me.

Brigit looks up from the Twitter feed where the the Sylvanian families are commenting more coherently than the government on the state of the country. 'Have you thought any more about what I said yesterday?'

'No, I'm afraid I haven't. I'm struggling to look at the people raiding the fridge in a different way. No matter how hard I try, they are still frying up my maple-cured bacon.'

'Okay. Well, try. You need to put some things in place.'

'What sort of things?'

'Strategies for not reacting and wading in.'

'They're eating my bloody bacon! I was looking forward to my bacon.'

'We can always get some more. How about that for looking at it differently? These are young people.'

'Then they could bloody well walk to the shops and get their own.'

Brigit is scrolling through the NHS Twitter feed now, where interesting people write interesting things about Bowel Cancer Networks and Diabetes UK.

'Before you go, I think you need to take a look at this.' Brigit hands me an envelope. It is from the university. It is crinkly and cream. I read it. Twice. I frame my response.

'Oh my God! That's so amazing. I mean incredible, fantastic. Oh my God.' I have overdone it. My face is resisting my smile and making it ache.

Brigit eyes me suspiciously. 'So, you're pleased for me?'

'Oh yeah. I mean it's amazing, incredible. Respect.' I do the hand thing and look stupid.

'You can be such a tosser,' she says.

Brigit has been awarded an honorary PhD from the university. I kiss her on the top of her head, close my eyes and think about that novelist in the list of powerful people.

'I'm so proud of you. You so deserve all of this.' I can see Brigit is genuinely pleased. This is a real honour for her.

'How long have you had it?'

'A couple of weeks.'

'A couple of weeks!'

'I felt, you know, a bit of a show-off.'

'It's brilliant."

'You know what I mean.'

'That no one will give me an honorary PhD? I don't need one.'

'There's a big ceremony. I want everyone to be there.'

'I'll let you lead on that one. I've got to take Ollie to football. I am really so proud of you,' I say again, just to make sure Brigit knows and can't sense yet another part of me in its death throes.

'You said.'

Her bloody Scottie misses nothing and lies at Brigit's feet like a fanged henchman. That dog can smell the scent of death. She growls and bares teeth intended for a much larger dog.

'Fuck off, bitch,' I whisper under my breath.

Brigit looks up from her phone. 'What did you just say?'

'I said I've got an itch.'

'Liar.'

9

BEFORE

Fact: Number of meals cooked, 64,871

Chloe and I were three days into our new life. I thought I was doing okay. Brigit was phoning every hour to make sure I was doing everything right. The strain was palpable between us. The truth was, at that moment, we both wanted to be where the other person was, doing what they were doing. We could have invented the saying 'the grass is greener…'.

'Do you check the temperature of the milk?' Brigit made it sound like an inquisition.

'Look, I'm the one who's read 'The Complete Guide to Childcare'.'

'Do you change her when she's wet?'

I check Chloe. She is wet and saggy. 'Immediately?'

'Immediately. Good. And it's too cold and wet for her to be out.'

I didn't respond to this. In my hallowed book it said 'fresh air is vital for the growing child', and also for the parent who is beginning his climb over the skirting board and up the wall. Of course the parents in 'The Complete Guide to Childcare' looked so smug anyone would think they'd just won the Euro Millions rollover.

The weather was wet and cold, but eminently preferable to Noddy and his 'little red and yellow' heap of shit. We visited the little zoo where we wandered around the animal enclosures in the rain singing songs about the rain as if the wetness itself wasn't enough. I was as wet as Gene Kelly, but looked more like a Ned Kelly in my wellies and yellow poncho bought from a depressed-looking man at the ticket desk.

'Don't know why you'd want to come here in this weather.'

'I wouldn't go into marketing.'

'Don't intend to.'

'We're here because a person can only watch Noddy drive around Toy Town so many times in pursuit of two naughty goblins.'

'I like Eastenders.'

'Thought you might.'

I was very taken by a little cat. It stared at us intently with big eyes, making me feel quite responsible for it's incarceration. It seemed to me just like the cat living next door, which I now realise was the catalyst for the flea explosion in our house.

A man wearing an official hat sidled over to us. We were two of only a handful of people there. He was clearly keen to impart some information.

'Very rare, that cat,' he said, pointing at the domestic-looking cat.

'Is it?'

'Very. On the verge of extinction. It's a fishing cat.' He said this to Chloe who had ice cream all over her face, adeptly applied by the hands she still thought belonged to someone else.

'I thought all cats liked fish.'

'Fallacy. Imagine the worst of all worlds – your favourite grub in a medium you're terrified of.'

'Isn't that to protect the fish?'

The man shook his head at my obvious idiocy. 'The fishing cat has developed very long claws to hook the fish out. The perfect example of evolution.' With that definitive response he walked off.

I chatted to a young woman called Angela, pushing twins around. Unlike Chloe they were sleeping. She was thin and worn out, with rings under her eyes like black slings. I imagined I would soon take on this emaciated demeanour. Angela wore a coat that hung off her shoulders. She eyed Chloe's ice-cream smeared face. I was yet to become adept at the constant wiping required to avoid the telltale appearance of the Dickensian child.

'Here,' she said, offering me a wipe. 'You got the job then.'

'I did.'

'Wife not around?'

'She's at work. I look after Chloe.'

'Oh, that's so great.' She looked as if she was about to cry. 'A man who's prepared to get his sleeves rolled up. My Steve's useless. Comes home from work, can of beer, feet up. Thinks his job is done.' She gripped my arm. 'There should be more like you, but they won't do it. Too much like hard work.'

Another considerably older woman wearing a headscarf came over holding two cornets.

'This is my mum, Sheila,' the young woman said. 'She's helping me out just now.'

Sheila handed the cornets to the now awake twins who also seemed to think the hands on the ends of their arms weren't theirs and proceeded to smear the ice cream over their faces.

'Twins?'

'Thirteen months.' Angela looked at her mum who squeezed Angela's hand. 'Little angels. Blessings, both of them. Make the most of it while you can.' It sounded heartfelt. As we parted I realised I hadn't told her my name.

Several months later, I saw Sheila again at the zoo. Chloe and I were watching the fishing cat. It was still peering longingly into the fish-less pool.

'Hi,' I called. The twins were walking now like two little drunk men, holding onto the buggy. Sheila made her way over to me.

'Oh, hello. You're here again,' she said.

'We've got a year's membership. The animals are fed up with seeing us. Your daughter not with you?' As soon as I said this, I could hear Angela's words, telling me to value every day with Chloe; that she was a blessing.

'Angela passed away.' Sheila's voice cracked. 'Two months ago. Cancer. She was thirty-one.'

I looked at Chloe. One of the twin boys was holding her hand.

'He's full of love,' Sheila said. 'Just like his mum. Rory's more like his dad, I'm afraid.'

'I'm so sorry for your loss.' I realised then that Angela hadn't just been tired, she was gravely ill. I looked at the boys. They had curly hair and, despite their tragedy, they were happy there at the zoo. What I meant was, I was so sorry for the boys' loss. Their mother was gone and in a way Brigit was absent too, at work, though she would come home and shower Chloe with her love. Angela would never be able to do the same for her boys. I realised in the zoo with the fishing cat watching us, that Sheila and I had something in common; we were the guardians of these new people on the planet. We weren't the ones who had brought them into the world pure and whole. It was Brigit and Angela who had done that. Angela, wherever she was in the scheme of things, could rest assured, as well as Brigit, that Sheila and I would do our very best.

I never saw Sheila again, and often wonder what happened to little Rory and his brother, and the fishing cat of course, who is more than likely sitting on a cloud with his little fishing rod, if you believe that sort of thing. Having looked after children and lived in a fantasy world for so long, often preferable to the real one, I feel I am entitled to believe that sort of thing.

I watched Sheila trudge away with her two grandsons. I hoped then, with all my heart, that Steve might seize the opportunity to make a rich and life-long relationship with his boys. I returned to my car and I wept. My eyes are blurring now as I recall this so many years later. I think of Ruby and her description of us as a 'dysfunctional' family and how we laugh at the context in which she draws this conclusion. It is the laughter I will remember until they say 'you'll be fine' one last time and they let me go from what became a much more beautiful life with them in it.

Later that day when Brigit came home and took over, I went to the meeting with the 'quite religious' people.

'Doreen's my Personnel Manager, lovely woman. I know you'll like her,' Brigit assured me.

It is fair to say that Brigit has a greater propensity to like people until proven otherwise than I have. Where she sees potential, I see lost causes. It was the thought of a kindred male which propelled me out of the house in search of a soul mate.

Doreen Taylor lived on a modern estate on the other side of the city in a cul de sac. My Ford Sierra sounded like a Harley Davidson because the hole in the exhaust was now the size of a large hand. I found the house and left the car.

The only reason I walked past the six foot statue in Doreen Taylor's front garden was because no one would have expected it to be there. I knocked on the door and turned to look behind me. I saw the statue. It was the Virgin Mary of the scale you might see at Lourdes. It looked like it was made of marble so I tapped it. It was hollow; some sort of resin. At her feet was a small pool with trickling water, and beneath the water were little blue lights spelling out the word LOVE. If I'd seen this from the car I would have legged it.

Doreen was at the door before I could turn away. I could tell she was disappointed.

'You must be Brigit's husband.'

'We're not married.'

Doreen was wearing one of Demis Roussos's dresses. I waited for her to break into 'Forever and Ever', waxing lyrical about 'tea and lemonade'. Instead she gestured at 'our lady', or 'her lady', as I was having nothing to do with this sort of suburban madness.

'No Brigit?'

'I didn't think she was meant to come.'

'Well, I thought she might if you could get a babysitter.'

'Brigit is the babysitter.'

She laughed at this, though I could see she didn't think it was funny. Doreen had beautiful, even teeth, just like Demis Roussos. Perhaps they shared the same dentist. Perhaps it was Diane Quail.

Doreen gestured to the statue. 'Isn't she beautiful?'

I was trapped between a woman wearing a Greek bell-tent and a giant statue of the Madonna. What do you say? *No, it's the most hideous and weird thing I've ever seen in the front garden of a Wimpey Home.*

'It's incredible,' I said. Which was true. I was punch drunk with tiredness. I would have given Doreen my life savings of three hundred and twenty seven pounds minus the twenty I'd paid for 'The Complete Guide to Childcare' right then if she'd said I could go home.

'Come in,' Doreen said, beckoning me like the Grim Reaper to follow her.

Given the evidence, the decision to enter into that place where the inhabitants thought a six-foot shrine to the Virgin Mary would enhance the sale price was simply asking for trouble. I followed Doreen as meekly as a lamb, which was ironic given the edifice in the garden, and the Christian propensity for sacrifice of the said creature.

'We're rather bohemian,' Doreen pointed out as we made our way along a hallway draped with mandala-inked sheets like a Bedouin tent. I would have said 'insane'. It made the place look like a cave. A couple of coats of Dulux

Apple White would have given it the lift it badly needed. I was imagining the blurb on the estate agent's advert: *Requiring some sensitive upgrading, a bloody big skip and possibly an exorcism or two.* The sheets fluttered along with Doreen's loose-fitting attire like something from The Onedin Line.

The main room was no lighter. On the walls were vast canvases depicting scenes of men in boats under furious skies, women with babies hanging onto nipples and lambs dotted about in places you would never expect to see them.

'Welcome to our humble home,' Doreen said.

I could see nothing humble about a house with aspirations to be a satellite of the National Gallery and the Vatican rolled into one. 'Thanks.'

Doreen put on a couple of lights to reveal the extent of this madness. 'We were just having a quiet moment before you came.' The light cast its glow over five other people, sitting on a sofa and a couple of armchairs. There were two men and three women.

'This is Brigit Wheeler's husband,' Doreen said. They looked impressed. I told them my name. It didn't have the same reaction. I'm amazed Doreen didn't apologize on my behalf. 'He looks after little Chloe. His wife, Brigit is my boss. She's very important.' Doreen looked at me with an expression of what I could only interpret as disappointment.

'We're not married.' I could feel the six people take sharp intakes of breath, sucking the air out of the room like a vacuum packing machine.

'Oh,' Doreen clapped her hands together. 'That's fine then. We're open house, aren't we? All sorts?' At least I didn't have a six-foot Madonna in my front garden. 'We were rather hoping Brigit might have come along, added a bit of gravitas to the proceedings.'

Doreen pointed at a bald man sitting in the far corner next to the television. 'This is my husband, Dave.' Dave didn't move, or say anything. He had this glazed appearance as if life had got the better of him and rendered him stationary. 'Dave looks after Jeremiah and Job. They're at school now but, as you will know, it's a never-ending task. It's great to have another man on the team.'

God, she already had me signed up!

The other man stood up. This man made Peter Crouch look petite. He looked like a radio mast.

'This is Tony, and his wife, Topsy.'

Tony wore a pair of jeans which forgivably stopped four inches above his ankles and a shirt so frayed I could see his chest hairs. Tony had enough hair on his chest to provide Dave with a thick toupee. Topsy was short, and immediately I imagined them having sex; Topsy's face buried in the tufts of Tony's manly chest hair while his extensive legs dangled over either side of the bed. Where Tony's handshake was like holding a wet piece of halibut, Topsy tapped her feet together and gripped my hand like a vice, making the wrist joint click.

'Is Topsy short for anything?' I asked for the sake of a spot of light banter. I could only think of Topsham.

'Had you anything in mind?'

I didn't say Topsham. 'Not really.'

'Just Topsy.'

I liked Topsy. She had a glint in her eye and one of those smiles, which had another agenda one can only guess at. She winked at me. Perhaps she liked tall men. In that department, with Tony, she had won the top prize.

Doreen touched Topsy's arm and nodded at Tony.

'We have a daughter,' Topsy said quietly, 'Sian.'

'Oh, that's nice.'

'She's four.'

The two remaining women sat together. One was very young, early twenties at the most and she looked nervous, so I wasn't alone on that score.

'This is Stacey.'

Stacey was wearing jeans and a sweatshirt with It Started With a Kiss on it.

'She has Ethan who is one.'

The other woman stood up as Topsy sat down. 'I'm Debbie. I have Sam and Sarah. They're twins. They're four months.'

I shook her hand and she sat slowly down. I realised then that everyone, for one reason or another, mainly due to childcare, looked exhausted.

We had snacks in little bowls and tea made from things I didn't know it was possible to make tea from. After we had eaten, we watched a short video about calming and reinforcing good behaviour in difficult children. I was falling asleep. We talked about the video. I was so tired I felt as if I were in a parallel universe.

'Sian has cerebral palsy,' Topsy said.

I wondered why she had suddenly said this. I realised after a moment she was talking directly to me. I looked at Doreen who nodded sagely, stroking the crumbs off her Demis Roussos design. I didn't know what Topsy wanted me to say. It felt like a test I know Brigit would have passed with flying colours. I had already poured out my emotions in the car over Angela's tragic death and her now orphaned boys. Tony squeezed Topsy's hand. There was silence. I looked across at Dave who had only moved to slip in the video, the exertion clearly taking everything he had.

Doreen broke the silence. 'Thank you Topsy. That was for you,' Doreen said to me. 'We take the time to share with the group something at least one person may not know.'

Topsy interjected. 'I wanted, we wanted you to know that. It's important if you come again.'

Doreen clapped her hands. 'Okay, I'll go. I have a small lump on my left breast.'

Small gasps. I wondered what was coming next.

'I've had a biopsy and the surgeon feels confident that it will be benign.'

Dave suddenly came to life like a robot powered up. 'I'm a recovering alcoholic.' His voice was slurred and I realised then that this was a lie. Dave was not recovering at all. He was an alcoholic, and that was why he was at home all day

92

with pre-cooked meals in the fridge and a list of things he rarely completed because by ten o'clock in the morning whatever it was he chucked down his throat had hold of him as tightly as a boa constrictor.

Doreen did the lot. She had Brigit as a boss and Brigit always takes the time to see the whole person, their potential and not their faults. It didn't matter that Doreen dressed like a Greek pop star and had Jesus's mam in the garden. People have 'stuff', and I had a lot to learn.

Stacey started to speak in a tiny little voice. 'I'm not married either.' She was looking directly at me.

'I didn't know that,' Doreen said.

'I didn't like to say, but now someone else's said it, I thought it would be okay. My mother says I live in a dark place.'

'Of course, of course,' Doreen said. 'All sorts.' She looked across at Dave who clearly couldn't give a shit.

'Ethan's dad was killed in a hit and run before he knew I was pregnant.' Stacey stared down at her hands.

Doreen stood up and went over to her and kissed the top of Stacey's head. 'It's alright, love. It truly is.'

Debbie coughed. 'I want to say that I have two healthy twins. I'm dead lucky. I have a husband who loves me and them and I feel blessed.'

I could feel my anxiety rise. I wanted to run down the quilted hallway, out past the six-foot icon and blast my roaring Ford Sierra down the road. It was my turn next.

Doreen clapped her hands together. 'Wow,' she said. 'Haven't we done something amazing here tonight?' She turned her attention to me. 'Give us something we don't know about you.'

I looked at each one of them in turn. I looked at Dave and wondered what state his liver was in, at Tony still holding Topsy's hand and maybe wondering if it was his fault for being too tall or Topsy's for being to short which caused little Sian to have cerebral palsy. I looked at Stacey who was thinking of her partner and how he never saw little

Ethan, and what life might have been like if he had. Stacey was crying. I wanted to cry, because in the same way Sheila at the zoo and I had something in common, so did Debbie and I. We had a healthy family, and it was something to celebrate. I can't in all honesty say that I saw this with such clarity then, but something incredible happened in that house with the resin imitation of the Virgin Mary in the front garden and our host wearing a frameless yurt. I realised that having things go your own way all the time teaches you very little.

'Well?' Doreen said. 'Come on.'

I looked at them all, reflected briefly on the quirkiness, their different lives and their honesty, here in the crazy house in a cul de sac where I had always imagined people's lives to be so simple and ordinary.

I took a deep breath.

'I feel diminished by looking after a child. I don't feel like a proper man. I'm ashamed to say this, but it's true. I don't know how to make the feeling go away.'

There was silence. I waited. I thought they might be able to help me and give me an answer. I didn't know then that I was only seventy-two hours into the search for an answer that I would eventually find nineteen years later when we were putting up a Christmas tree.

I returned only once to Doreen's house. Things had changed. Doreen had stolen another dress from Demis Roussos, Stacey had met someone called Darren, a floor manager from Tesco who probably knew the layout less than I did. They left to live in Ipswich where apparently she was very happy and had turned her hand to writing greetings for Christmas cards; a market I had imagined was already pretty well covered. Debbie didn't really need us any more because she was so lucky and utterly replete with her lot. I hope her lucky run continued. Dave, the alcoholic, still hadn't reached the 'recovering' stage of his illness and seemed perpetually pissed. My guess is that he's probably sitting next to our little fishing cat by now, with Angela, the mother of the twins and a bottle of Jack Daniels between them, having a good old laugh at us all scrabbling about down below. Tony and Topsy got into Scientology and made little sense after that. They did have matching key rings though bearing a very fetching picture of Tom Cruise. Three new people joined, but we didn't bond. 'Bonding', I had learnt from Brigit, is all about finding common ground.

I was still searching.

10

NOW

Fact: Number of miles driven, 587,567

As soon as we are in the car and on our way to football, Ollie connects his phone to the sound system before I can press the button for '6 Music'. Someone is calling me a 'mother fucker', which I can really do without on the way to a football tournament at nine o'clock in the morning.

'Turn it off,' I tell him, jabbing the screen and missing the button thing because it isn't a real button. Instead it is a picture of a button.

'You're so tight!'

'I don't want someone swearing in my car.'

'Ruby and Emma do. Chloe as well.' This is all true. Ollie makes a cogent point. I am the parent, Emma keeps reminding me, and so I have to initiate the war of attrition. I hate the war of attrition. 'And they drink at parties and have sex, and smoke and do drugs.' Ollie is full of revelations, of which some are true and the rest he makes up from a variety of dodgy sources including Instagram and Facebook where his alleged age is twenty-three! I choose for myself the things I want to believe about my daughters and discard the rest to the trash can in the back of my head until evidence materialises and I pretend I'm on a separate plane of existence where I can still breathe.

'Yes, but you're twelve.'

'I know all the words and worse.'

I am tempted to find out what 'worse' means, but decide I don't want to know.

I make a suggestion. 'What about The Vossi Bop? That's okay apart from the 'body shots'. I don't agree with the gun thing.'

Ollie creases up with laughter. 'You're so not cool.'

'My job as a parent is to manage this.' God knows why I'm sharing this responsibility with Ollie. I can feel myself beginning to fade. *My job as a parent…* What is my job as a parent right now? I watch the mothers and I've seen a lot of them over the years. They seem so consummate at managing the young children. They offer them a variety of exotic fruit instead of a Mars Bar, or they sing a couple of lines from 'the Wheels on the Bus', and it makes me wonder if someone punched the heart out of solid parenting. I'm sure 'the mothers' kick the shit out of the waste bin when they're on their own. *No, they don't*, Brigit has informed me on more than a few occasions when a kitchen appliance has taken the brunt of my lonely rage. *People don't behave like that.* I firmly believe that those mothers, those Stepford wives, are all a front, and if I shook them for long enough, springs would start bouncing out of their ruby-lipped mouths. No one is that good that consistently if they live, breathe and possess a beating heart.

Ollie puts on the Crazy Frog song and in this moment I'd rather have some rapper telling me I'm 'a mother-fucking bitch' than a squeaking frog.

We pick up Brutus Collins on the way. Brutus and Ollie used to be friends, but now, apparently, Brutus is 'so not cool'. Brutus lives on a farm without fields. They live in a series of linked barns where cows used to live and now there are people who aren't allowed to put up television antennae because the cows didn't watch TV and the whole thing needs to be in keeping with buildings full of shitting bovines.

97

'Oh, thank God you're here,' Penny, Brutus's mother, says. 'Nancy's chucking up and Giles has got a court case in Nottingham.' (On a Saturday? I'm not aware the courts do Saturdays.) 'There's a lot to prepare.' (I imagine when there's a vomiting child at home and a nerve-shredded wife there's always a lot going on at the courts on a Saturday.)

Penny pushes Brutus at me. I imagine, if I asked, she would probably let me keep him. Brutus looks about as happy to get into the car as Ollie looks to have him in it.

'I like him to wear a vest.' Penny hands me a perfectly folded and pressed vest. Ollie sniggers. Even I know that a vest is 'so not cool'.

'He wears a vest!' Ollie whispers loud enough for Brutus and his mother to hear.

'Brutus is going home with the Carter's,' Penny informs me.

At least it's only one way.

I turn the music off because Brutus will not be used to being called a 'mother fucker'. He will be used to Mozart and Beethoven not rolling over. We sit in stony silence. I feel it is my duty to break it.

'How are you, Brutus?'

'Good.'

Ollie shakes his head and concentrates on his phone. I am usually asked not to speak to any of his friends. Brutus though is different; Brutus is 'so not cool'.

'Ollie's mum is the seventh most powerful person in the city,' I announce.

Ollie looks at me as if I am insane for saying this. 'No one cares, Dad.'

'I care.'

Brutus leans forward. 'My dad thinks Ollie's mum earns too much. He thinks she's a waste of public money and it should be a man.'

Even Ollie looks up from his phone.

'And what do you think about that Brutus?' I say.

'I think he's right.'

I turn the music on and a man from the ghetto saves me the trouble of telling Brutus he is a 'mother fucker'.

I drop Ollie and Brutus at the gate of the tournament, which looks like a big affair. Ollie leaves Brutus actually putting on his vest. He obviously wants to be the subject of ridicule. I leave him to it. Without looking back and not wanting to be associated with someone wearing a vest, Ollie runs across the field at speed to find his team.

The car park is on a small industrial estate. I can see, even before I get there, the lines of VW vans with their roof racks and bull bars, despite the woeful absence of bulls, and the stickers for Sex Wax, and Rip Curl, and Carving the White, which I thought was a drug thing. I squeeze my 'smart person's' Skoda between two silver vans and slide out of the door like a newborn calf dropping from its mother's womb.

'Ah, It's you!' When people shout at me like this, I feel immediately accused and my instinct is to run.

The woman now racing towards me is Jilly Green. Jilly runs a lot. She is adorned from head to foot in 'active wear'. The women pick up their kids in their 'active wear'. They limber a lot outside the school gates, chatting as they do. I have never felt comfortable with limbering in public. When did all this lunging, calf-stretching and rotational shoulder shrugging start? Is it no longer possible to talk to a mother without her tilting right and left like a bloody metronome?

Jilly Green is married to a Barrister, which is someone who Ollie thinks makes coffee in Starbucks. Gerald Green has never made a cup of coffee in his over-privileged life. 'That's women's work' he would no doubt say, and the same phrase used by his son, Charles Julian, when he saw me using a vacuum cleaner one Christmas when he'd been sent to us while Gerald and Jilly went for drinks and those little savoury things barely big enough to fill a tooth. This was at the Skinners who, at the time, were living a luxury lifestyle they couldn't actually afford. They ended up in a maisonette on Bowler Street where men in responsible jobs drive slowly in the early hours of the morning.

'Why has he got two names?' Ollie asked me when Charles Julian was perusing the bookshelves and Ollie was annihilating a mystery opponent on FIFA.

'So he can use it as an alias,' I said.

'What's an alias?'

'Something you use when you want to be somebody else.'

'That's so cool.'

'Just play with him until two thirty, then we'll do something normal.'

Charles Julian liked to play croquet, but all that was on offer at our place was a sledgehammer and a tennis ball.

I was running the hoover over the carpet.

'Why do you do women's work?' Charles Julian asked me.

'It's not women's work. It's just work, Charlie,' I said after my voice got over the shock and came back.

'My name is Charles Julian.'

'It's not women's work, Charles Julian. Really, anybody can do it. There's just an on/off switch and then you just push it around.' Just like they probably do at your pumped-up public school for being such a pompous little brat, I thought to myself.

Jilly gleans and then spreads confidential news like warm Nutella, denying later she ever knew anything about it. If she was Walter White from Breaking Bad, this is the thing at which Jilly is the 'absolute best'.

Jilly grabs my arm, with such a look of desperation I am immediately concerned.

'I'm so sorry,' she says in this voice, which oozes insincerity like an infected cut leaks pus.

'Why are you sorry?' I am walking. Jilly has short legs. She is jogging, always jogging. When she's not jogging she is limbering, lunging and in the 'downward facing dog'.

'About Brigit. I mean, it's so unfair.'

I stop. Jilly stops. We collide. Her head hits my chest. Jilly is still smiling though. Mind you, the woman does have a lot to smile about. She has no qualifications, has one child being thrashed at some boarding school in the Home Counties for his own blinking good and learning that it is only women who do all the menial jobs. Jilly lives in a house the size of Birmingham Arena, has five horses, which can't be easy as you can only ride one at a time, and the life of Riley, which is a name that will substitute for Gerald's first wife, Norma, who Jilly ousted with the consummate skill of someone who'd clearly done that sort of thing before.

I start walking again because Jilly is contorting her face in preparation for what she obviously thinks is news so powerful it will change everything. Jilly is back to jogging as if we are attached by an invisible wire.

'What's so unfair, Jilly?'

'All the breaches, the faults they've found at the hospital. That terrible report. She must be worried sick. There's all those wonderful people saving lives and yet the system is failing them. It must be heart-breaking.'

'I'm not aware she's worried sick. I'm sure it's all rubbish, trumped up by the press because they don't have any news.' I don't actually know what she is talking about. I only do healthcare as a patient.

Jilly grabs my arm. 'Oh no, this is on the QT. Gerald says the eagles are involved.' This is what she calls the lawyers as if they're likely to swoop down and steal their prey, when in fact all they do is empty your wallet and wear stupid wigs. 'Sam Waters spoke to him about it. They're all so worried. We're worried. We're all worried. We're birds of a feather.' No we're not. I'm from a Midlands industrial town and Brigit is from Halewood in Liverpool where they make a lot of cars. We're not even birds!

'It's not really my department, Jilly. I do the domestic stuff.' The stuff her son thinks should be done by the women.

'No, I suppose not.'

I text Brigit.

Got collared by Jilly Green. Says something about a terrible report and how worried everybody is about you.

Brigit pings straight back. She can do both thumbs.

Don't tell her anything. She's a nosey cow.

Nothing to tell.

Tell her to …..! Off!

Sometimes, Brigit is not quite as facilitative as she seems to the rest of the world.

The people in Ollie's football team are all new to us and so are the parents. Martin, the coach, comes and shakes my hand. 'Ollie's settling in well. It's great to have him on the team, and good to have another dad along.' What he means is that this is a whole day tournament, and many of the dads are out on their carbon fibre bicycles, kings of the road, Bradley Wiggins with their lycra-covered arses in the faces of motorists driving at fifteen miles an hour because the git in front thinks he's in the *Tour de France*.

Our team have a gazebo. A woman who looks like a bag lady because she is in possession of a lot of bags is sorting bottles and crisps onto a table for the boys. She sees me.

'Ah, my sister works at the hospital.'

I am sometimes viewed as an empty conduit to Brigit, a hollow tube. 'Right.' What else do I say? 'Good for her.'

'I'm Denise.'

I wait for her to give me more information, but she doesn't. Normally I get 'I'm Chris Rayner's wife', or the appendage of some other high achiever. Chris is an orthopaedic surgeon who breaks and mends bones and fucks his secretary at the Futures Inn next to the hospital where Brigit has seen them disappear on a Thursday between seven and nine when he's allegedly sucking the cash out of the purses of the suffering because they are in too much pain to wait for the NHS. Olivia Rayner is aware of this extra-curricular activity, but the consequences of actually slapping the thing on the table and looking it in the eye are simply too terrible to contemplate. Jilly Green is already well ahead of the game with this little juicy joint and has been through all the computations to ascertain the best type of vice Olivia should use for Chris Rayner's balls. When it comes to the 'silently suffering wife', Olivia is a professional, her upper lip as stiff as her husband when he's with his secretary in the Futures Inn.

'Nice to meet you, Denise,' I say to the woman laying out the snacks.

'My sister's a phlebotomist.'

Again, in any other context, you might wonder why she's suddenly talking about her sister and her blood-sucking job. This is a way of informing me, in the form of one of those games you get on a place mat in Pizza Hut where you have to link the knife and fork via lines of spaghetti to a pizza, that she knows that I know I live with the head of the local hospital.

I help Denise lay out the crisps and the drinks. It isn't hard, but she makes a meal of it, literally, by opening a packet of cheese and onion and apologising as if it is an addiction which, judging by the way she's ramming them into her mouth, it probably is. I am pleased that her sister is a phlebotomist, and so is she. She doesn't mention Brigit, but Brigit hangs in the air between us.

Ollie is playing well. It is hard being the parent of a goalkeeper, especially when a couple of goals slip past. I feel the need to apologise to the parents of the outfield players as if we have collectively let them down. There are seven matches and we are in the play-off for some sort of plate. The boys don't want a plate. They want the trophy, but it is clearly going to a team with players who are not in a month of blue moons under thirteen, when two of them have beards as thick as King George V.

'It's okay,' I say to Ollie as we drive home.

'The defence were crap,' he says indignantly. 'Brutus needs to be dropped from the team. He wears a vest.'

'You can't just drop someone from the team for wearing a vest.'

Ollie looks at me in disbelief. 'Duh.'

'You obviously can then.'

'Did you see that last goal? There was no one there! Brutus should've been

there.'

Well, there was you, Ollie.

But I don't say this. His confidence is precious. I must protect it as if it were a rare egg the unscrupulous want to steal.

11

BEFORE

Fact: Number of baby wipes, 134,000

In the first year I spent with Chloe I miraculously wrote a novel. It was terrible. One agent bothered to write: 'I receive 1500 manuscripts a year. Of these 1500 maybe five, possibly six, are good enough to pass muster (had to look up 'muster'). If you think you are among this tiny percentage then you should press on.' I tried to read between the lines, but there was nothing there but double spacing.

I wrote a collection of poems. They were utterly crap. I have never written any poems since – though I did enter a local limerick competition for which I won a box of Milk Tray at the parish hall. Chloe clapped. Her hands were so small, no one could hear her.

My vegetables stopped growing. Chloe absorbed my days like one of those sink holes that appear in the strangest of places when you least expect it. We went to many groups for babies and met lovely people, but in most cases I was the only man doing full-time childcare. I was panicking. I wasn't enough. This little girl was filling my heart with love and yet I was filling her days with consummate incompetence.

One evening Brigit made an announcement. We were sitting in the still unfinished kitchen with the concrete floor, the rest of the house largely uncarpeted and a porch that lay in the garden like a felled body.

'I'm pregnant.'

Chloe was a year old.

We went for a scan. Brigit lay on the bed and I sat next to her, watching the screen, bouncing Chloe on my knee. Brigit couldn't see the screen. The image appeared. I noticed the slightest change in the scanographer's expression.

'There's more than one.'

Brigit burst into tears. 'Oh my God!'

'Two.' 'The Complete Guide to Childcare' said nothing about 'two more'.

We discovered they were girls and non-identical. We called them Emma and Ruby. I bought a book called 'The Complete Guide to Twins'. Oh, yes I did.

'I feel like a whale, and I'm a bit scared,' Brigit said by the time she looked like she'd swallowed a couple of good-sized puppies scrabbling to get out. I could see the whale thing coming on nicely and I personally would have been bloody-well terrified at the thought of not one but two cantaloupe melons emerging from my body cavity.

'It's okay,' I reassured her with no confidence whatsoever.

Brigit sensed my anxiety. This sense spawned her misgivings. 'There'll be three little people. I don't think I can leave three little people.'

I didn't know what to say. Leaving them was one thing. Leaving them with me was absolutely another. Anything I said would have been squirrelled away and thrown back at me, very hard. I didn't recognise this at the time, but leaving Emma and Ruby as well as Chloe was infinitely hard for Brigit times three.

'The Complete Guide to Childcare' said nothing about looking after three children under the age of two. There were pictures of mothers with two children, but sensibly spaced in age by maybe three or four years. These were people into planning their lives, setting things out page by

106

page. The whole book was sensible. It was about sensible parenting; about sensible mothers doing sensible things with other sensible mothers who all lived sensible lives. They appeared to live with sensible partners wearing sensible and immaculate clothes doing sensible jobs. Nowhere could I find anyone like us; sensible only by the fact that we kept breathing in and out and putting our children first so that slowly we, like many parents, began to disappear. As far as I could see, the people populating the pages of this increasingly doubtful tome had two hands and not three. The men, looking relaxed and bloody-well pleased with themselves, had the propensity to wear slacks taken from an age where tailors thought nothing of sticking a tape measure up between the legs and asking 'if sir dresses to the left or the right'. Reading 'The Complete Guide to Twins' was like passing through a portal into a future apocalyptic nightmare where I could see, with terrifying clarity, a landscape of soiled nappies and a tidal wave of milk lapping at its shore.

I tortured myself with 'The Complete Guide to Twins'. Ignoring the thing about cats and curiosity, I couldn't resist looking at it, each time hoping the images and the text wouldn't be so stark about the need to manage what could be an overwhelming workload. There were double buggies, two high chairs, a chapter on 'sequential feeding', emphasising the importance of varying the order to avoid one twin feeling less important than the other. There were methods to help try and understand the communication, which sometimes develops between twins. All of this was very interesting to someone not on the cusp of being sucked into the vortex of this world, but only served to increase my panic. This was all well and good, I thought, when I finally reached the index, but what about the third child and the days with only twenty-four hours? I was a father, not a child psychologist. I was a man in a sea of mothers who made the whole thing look easy and only served to strengthen the case against me for being a fraudulent interloper who should be out in the world putting Wonderloaf on the table. Did all mothers know this stuff? Was it genetic or passed down through the matriarchy by some sort of osmosis? I searched the pages for the 'third child' with the desperation of a dodo looking for a mate long after being the last of the ferociously ugly breed left alive. Nothing! Nowhere in 'The Complete Guide to Twins' was there a 'third child' or a man engaged in the care of the first or second. I am sure that 'The Complete Guide to Twins' has brought great joy and salvation to countless parents of twins. Whatever misconceptions, doubts and fears they left within the pages, I swept up and took for myself.

By thirteen months Chloe still wouldn't walk.

'Please, beautiful. I need you to walk.'

'Am are bootiful,' she said, sounding uncannily like Bernard Matthews in his advert for turkey fillets.

'I know, but I could really do with you being able to walk. There are two sisters on their way. I am only human. I have only two arms. I am a bloke. I am the last dodo. Have mercy on me.' I could hear myself whine. I was begging our child to accelerate the evolutionary process and become bipedal.

'Am are bootiful.'

At fourteen months Chloe took three steps across the living room. Imagine my elation, followed by the intractable disappointment, when she sat down and refused to get up until a week before Emma and Ruby were born.

Brigit kept working during her pregnancy, saving as much of her maternity leave as she could. I whooped silently to myself when another day passed, which would add to the interval between the birth and the day when I was handed a weight almost too much to contemplate in daylight hours. 'The Compete Guide to Twins' sat on a shelf and taunted me until I moved it and put it under the bed.

I was dipping in and out of playgroups and gatherings for parents and toddlers like a socialite might appear at parties but never throw their own. I was trying desperately to socialise Chloe with a variety of scenarios, where women changed nappies with one hand while balancing a child on a knee and giving a bottle. I watched from the corner of my eye. I practised at home and nearly caused Chloe a head injury. I chatted with women whose names I couldn't remember. It was like one-sided speed dating where it became clear that it was only I in search of that elusive second date.

'We should organise a play date,' I heard women say.

Chloe was interacting with a little boy called Luke. I introduced myself to his mother.

'Abby Ball,' she said. 'They seem to be getting on well.'

'They do.'

'Perhaps we should organise a 'play date',' I suggested.

If there is a way to stop a conversation and change the molecular structure of the atmosphere around it, this was it. Abby Ball gave me such a look of disgust, one would imagine I'd suggested we made a threesome with her friend, Alysha, who was heading our way, and throw in a couple of studded whips and collars while we were at it.

'Maybe another time,' I said.

She glared at me. 'I'm not sure my husband would be comfortable. I'm sure you understand.'

I'm not sure I did. I wasn't actually inviting him for the three in a bed thing anyway. I didn't ever suggest another 'play date' again. I only accepted offers; warily.

Apart from the 'play date' faux pas, everyone with little children seemed nice. Little children prompted this phenomenon where 'niceness' flowed like the sap from a tapped tree. Yet I couldn't rid myself of the notion that there was something fundamentally flawed about a man looking after his child. Looking back, I imagine it must've been very wearing for these women, often married to successful men, holding a conversation with someone who saw his only salvation in becoming Hugh Fearnley-Whittingstall or Ernest Hemingway as compensation for everything else.

'There are loads of men looking after their children these days,' a well-spoken woman called Kitty wearing 'active wear' and stretching her neck told me at an informal coffee morning advertised in the parish magazine. Not in this room there weren't. 'In London there are oodles of men on career breaks or working in the finance and film industry who take days out. Mind you, I think they get through a few illicit substances if you know what I mean.'

'I do it full-time,' I said. 'My partner is expecting twins in three months.'

'Wow. How wonderful. I guess she'll be taking over then. When the numbers stack that high, you'll be running back to the office.'

'No, I'll have all three of them.'

I scanned the room, averting my eyes as they alighted on at least seven breast-feeding women. There was only one wall I felt able to look at. On it was a notice board advertising Tumble Tots at the Methodist hall, 'followed by songs and stories and activities'.

Still enjoying the unprecedented freedoms of looking after one child, I took Chloe to Tumble Tots in the Methodist hall where a man easily in his late seventies called Steve had constructed an assault course made from varnished wood with splinters big enough to spear a child's heart. This was the first hour; the second was to be for 'songs and stories'.

I put Chloe down on a mat where she sat and didn't move. I spotted Steve. He wore a paint-splattered tracksuit. He was the only other man in that vast place of worship where the children looked like ants and the adults chased them as they climbed on the contraption designed for catastrophe.

Steve gave me the once over. I was wearing a white shirt and chinos. I was trying to appear 'together'. It was a lie; a façade. I was a shattered vase held together with cheap glue.

'Ah,' Steve said.

'Ah,' I replied.

'I wasn't expecting you today.'

I scanned the room. There were familiar local faces, following toddlers who could actually walk. I saw Chloe sitting as still as a subject for an oil painting. I imagined someone might have told Steve that at some point a jaded bloke might turn up with his daughter in search of a kindred soul also living a lie and pretending he knew what he was doing.

'Well, I'm here,' I said.

Steve rummaged in his Tesco bag for life which, judging by his nicotine-stained fingers and the rattle in his chest like a box of ball bearings, wouldn't prove value for money. 'I've got my registration documents and the papers from my last inspection. I'm in the process of sanding and varnishing the kit. It's like the Forth Bridge.'

We both looked at 'the kit'; Steve with misplaced pride and I with a feeling of impending doom. It was nothing like the Forth Bridge. There were ladders roped to platforms where children wobbled like drunks and wooden cubes with jagged holes in which others sat steadfastly as mothers frantically tried to extricate them.

'How much does it cost for a session?'

Steve put his hand on my shoulder. 'A fiver for an hour. I haven't raised the price in over three years.'

'That's fine.' I handed him the five pounds.

He waved it away. 'You don't need to pay. Just do what you have to do and I'll keep out of the way.' Dave took a sheet of sandpaper out of his bag, walked over to one of his structures and started sanding the wood. I left him to it, took a trolley from a little girl adorned head to toe in Boden gear and stood Chloe up so she could hold on to the bar. The Boden child screamed. A woman wearing yet more 'active gear' peeled away from a group of chatting women, ran to the child whose blood was rapidly rising to the surface of her face, picked her up and glared at me.

'I thought she'd finished with the trolley,' I said, clearly having misjudged the situation. Chloe trundled away with

111

the trolley, actually using her legs. I could have cheered. I needed this child to walk before the birth of her twin sisters or I was done for. The woman turned away from me and hugged her child as if I meant to do it harm. I looked across at Steve who was industriously sanding his 'kit'. I realised then that he thought I was an inspector of some sort. If I had been, I would have closed his pile of whittled sticks down for good and marched him down to Social Services.

'What the hell do you think you're doing? We were using that!' the woman shouted. I could've taken issue here and said 'your child was using it while you nattered to your friends whilst jogging on the spot'.

'I'm sorry.'

Chloe trundled away, her nappy hanging like a payload ready to drop.

'Well, obviously she hadn't.'

'No. I'm sorry.' I could see that sorry wasn't enough. I held out my hand. I had seen this woman and her magazine-dressed child at other play groups. I introduced myself.

She looked me up and down. 'Caroline Waters. Sam Waters.'

'Sam?'

'My husband. Sam Waters, the gastroenterologist. I'm sure you know him.'

'No, I've never had a problem in that department.'

'Well, there you are. I'm sure you will.'

I wondered if she could see something I couldn't.

'We are sort of neighbours,' she added

'Sort of neighbours?'

'From a distance.'

'What's your daughter's name?'

Caroline Waters gave me a doubtful look as if telling a man the name of her daughter might be a risk. 'Sarah. You're married to Brigit Wheeler.'

'We're not married.'

Caroline wafted her hand as if ridding herself of a fly. 'Oh, well then. Bit precarious.' She actually tapped her ring.

'Insurance.' The diamond was like a huge egg perched on a tiny eggcup.

People began to disperse. Within a couple of minutes, tables were set up and covered with paper plates, pieces of wool, glitter and squeezy bottles of glue. Chloe was on the move. We had watched many an episode of Art Attack where scale models of the Eiffel Tower could be constructed with consummate ease from a hundred straws. A smiley face on a paper plate would be a walk in the park. While little Sarah, in her quickly commandeered apron, carefully selected her facial features from the various pots, Chloe got stuck straight in. The hands, which were mainly now her own, started grabbing things from other children. I tried to grab the glue. Chloe yelled at me and squeezed. The glue shot out of the nozzle and landed on the fair, immaculately combed hair of a perfect-looking boy.

'Oh, my God!' A woman with shoulder-length blonde hair pressed her hand to her mouth. She looked across at Caroline who rushed to her aid.

I left Chloe, went to apologise and introduce myself. 'I'm so sorry.' I should've worn a badge with 'I'm sorry' written on it in advance.

The mother of the little boy with the glob of glue now seeping into his thatch of straw-like hair smiled at me. 'It's okay. I'm sorry I reacted. It's just that Roddy has a little interview at the prep school this afternoon and I wanted him to look smart. 'I'm Diane Pargetter. Diane Quail is my married name. You must be…'

'Brigit Wheeler's partner. Shall I get a wet cloth?'

'I think Caroline's already gone for one.'

Caroline came bounding back with a cloth, so much like a pleased puppy, the thing wouldn't have looked amiss hanging from her mouth. She began dabbing little Roddy's hair.

Diane took the cloth. 'This must be rather alien to you,' she said to me as she dabbed away at Roddy's hair. Roddy was about three. He seemed too young to be going to school. 'We need to introduce you, so you don't feel left out.'

I was warming to Diane Pargetter/Quail who had in the midst of my doubt reached out and touched my arm.

Diane re-introduced Caroline Waters. 'That's Jilly Green,' Diane said, pointing at a short woman with bobbed obviously dyed blonde hair. Diane lowered her voice. I discovered over the years, despite Diane Pargetter/Quail giving perfect teeth to the famous and wealthy, she is a very decent woman. 'Olivia Rayner, Harriet Rickard, Angela Wallace are over there. They're a bit of a gaggle and hiss a lot, but harmless enough. That's Gaynor Tiller with little Brian. He's a handful, but lovely.' Seconds later, 'little Brian' smacked Jilly Green's precious son, Charles Julian, over the head with a Playmobil car. Jilly screamed, prompting Charles Julian to do the same after he'd come round from the shock. 'Little Brian' laughed.

Diane Pargetter/Quail nudged me and winked. I should've taken more notice of the wink. 'Oh yes, just on cue, we have another man.' Diane pointed at the door behind me. It felt like an episode of Blind Date where the wall was about to be drawn back to reveal the person with whom you have blindly chosen to spend an intimate weekend. I turned to look:

Trevor Mace was a stick of a man, a towering six feet five, like a very long straw that might buckle with the slightest touch. In the pushchair in front of him, in contrast to his father, was a boy about the same age as Chloe, and a doppelganger for the Michelin Man. Trevor spotted Diane and headed straight over.

'This is Trevor,' Diane said in a tone which sounded like she was setting us up as a couple who might have something in common. That thing in common and that thing alone was that Trevor and I were in the Methodist hall with children of about the same age. 'Chalk and cheese' and a multitude of other idioms fitted the situation like a perfectly crafted glove.

Trevor sat down on one of the child-sized stools, a daddy long legs perched on a tack. I held out my hand. He looked at it and handed me a wet halibut of a shake. Two middle-aged women, wearing A-line skirts and those round-neck polyester tops with longs sleeves and necklaces handed down from some long dead great aunt, entered the room and prompted an almost instantaneous hush. This duo possessed a power over the gathered assembly like something I have rarely seen before. Women scuttled, clearing the tables as if their lives depended on it. I realised that these two inoffensive-looking women were what people refer to as 'bible bashers'. I could imagine them cracking a disobedient member of the flock over the head with the spine of an unabridged version. I moved quickly, took Chloe's paper plate face from the pile of wool, furry felt and glitter and handed it to her. She looked thrilled with her handiwork as if the design was entirely intended. The likeness to Michael Myers out of the Halloween films was uncanny.

Diane left Trevor Mace and me together so that we could no doubt familiarise ourselves with one another. I know one should never take people at face value and I have learnt through the years to be kinder and more thoughtful than is instinctive to me. The moment was interrupted when Brian rammed a plastic truck into a little girl's mouth. The truth is, I could see from the off that 'little Brian' possessed an evil streak and that everyone within striking distance would always need to be on their guard; especially, it transpired, those queueing at bus stops.

Trevor stared at me with wide, grey, watery eyes.

I had that sinking feeling.

'I've not been well,' Trevor said. 'I suffer from depression.'

One look at Trevor and I was not surprised. His aura of melancholia was leaking out of every pore. 'I'm sorry to hear that.'

'My wife's a nurse at the hospital. Your wife is Brigit Wheeler.' He was listing facts.

I was searching for another man just like me; one who looked after the children; a man with whom I could form a bond for mutual support and maybe draw in others. Within a nanosecond of clocking him, I knew that this man was most definitely not Trevor Mace.

One of the women wearing an A-line skirt, her polyester top in duck egg blue and a perm so tight she looked like she'd had a face-lift, spoke. 'Gladys is going to lead the singing and Bea will be telling the story about the man who built his house on stone and the other who built his on sand.'

Gladys pressed a button. Piano music drifted from speakers above us. People started to sing. Children clapped. I looked at Trevor who had his hands clasped together as if in prayer and was rocking backwards and forwards like one of the possessed people in The Exorcist. Diane Quail gave a knowing wave. She was trying not to laugh. She nudged another woman next to her who also turned. I imagined they were taking the piss. I was on the back foot and on the back row with a depressive stick insect.

Bea, wearing the other A-line skirt and also a perm as tight as an Olympic swimmer's cap, started the story. In Bea's case, she was wearing the mauve polyester top rather than duck egg blue. She began the well-worn story about the two men and their houses built on two different types of foundation.

'The moral is, don't build your house without foundations. Don't use cheap materials. Build it strong and build it with the best you can find and the best people.' Bea made it sound like one of those documentaries about subsiding flats on the Costa del Sol.

'I suppose you do this because there are problems,' Trevor said over tea and biscuits.

'Problems?'

'You know…' Here he did a twitch. 'Issues.'

116

'No, I do it because my partner goes out to work. What I mean is, I do this and she does 'conventional' work. Mind you, I suppose this is conventional for women.'

Chloe was crawling about with Trevor's son who was called Linus.

'I had a breakdown. It's good to meet another man.'

Chloe and Linus seemed to be getting on well. They were 'bonding' as they say in 'The Complete Guide to Childcare'. Trevor and I most definitely weren't.

Diane Quail came over as we were leaving. 'We don't see Trevor very often.'

'What about the little boy?' I asked. 'It can't be good for him being around someone so sad and negative.'

'It's okay, they get help. His wife is wonderful, and she has a sister. At least he has time with his father. It really is great to see another guy.'

'Thanks.' I felt suddenly quite overwhelmed with emotion. Brigit and I were carrying a lot. She was carrying two children in her womb and I was carrying the guilt of not being a woman and being a fraud for pretending to even emulate one.

'You must come to the pre-school soon. I'll let you know when Marlon the Music Man is on the agenda. It'll be a great place to start! Cheer you up no end.'

I liked Diane Quail a lot even though they do now have a Ferrari, a slice of my son's admiration and skin like the French aristocracy.

12

NOW

Fact: Number of hours spent in public toilets, 3,210

The day has arrived for Em's driving test. People wish her luck, but secretly I know Ruby hopes she will fail. They will have to share the car.

'The Quails' kids have got a car each,' Ruby says as I take them to the bus. 'We shared a womb. We shouldn't have to share a car.'

Once again I am rendered speechless.

Ruby prods Emma. 'And she kicked me for nine months.'

'Actually it was eight. You were early,' I say. 'It was the only time.'

'Do you think you'll ever get a Ferrari, Dad?' Ollie asks hopefully.

'No. I don't think so. I don't suppose I'll ever be able to afford one.'

'You will when you write a best-seller.'

'Maybe.' I imagine that the chance of this is now as slim as a catwalk model.

I have to collect Emma and take her to the test centre for twelve minutes past eleven. No one can tell me the reason for this precision. I park outside the boys' school where Emma is in the sixth form and wait as the girls

118

filtering out give me the look, which makes me feel irritated and vaguely uncomfortable. I want to get out and tell them I am Emma's father, waiting to take her to her driving test for the second time and not some sleazy old git eyeing them up. They should be hurling those sorts of accusations at Geoff Tiller. Nevertheless, I am wearing an old coat and sitting in a Skoda in the car park of an old people's home facing the school gates, so I keep my head down and read the news summary on my phone. A man has swum the Atlantic holding a live chicken and the head of the Bank of England has maintained the same interest rate again. It hardly seems like an onerous job. He should try looking after kids. It would put the economy into perspective, that's for sure.

Emma loafs out of the school gates. She 'wanted a change', she got the grades, and we went along with it. She joined this school with the other thirty-nine girls with the best grades at the girls school, leaving her old school angry and significantly under par. Two boys follow her out, their eyes on Emma. Emma doesn't give a fig. She has come to accept that the boys aren't quite what she had expected, and pretty much how I described them to her before she took up her place.

'They just beat one another up in front of the girls,' she said when she first started. 'They're pathetic.' She had hoped for so much more than this.

'That's because they're seventeen. In the wild, they would have killed one another until only one remained as the leader and he would then have the pick of the women.'

'What if he was ugly?'

'Luck of the draw. With a skirt that short though, you'd be in with a good chance, even if he was ugly.'

Emma punched me really quite hard on the shoulder. They take no account of my ageing frame.

'You can get out. I'll drive,' she says, yanking my coat like someone might yank a child's to prevent it from walking out into the traffic.

119

We head off to the test centre. I am nervous. I am nervous not for Emma and the taking of the test, but nervous for the examiner if he or she has the courage to fail her again. Violence is not out of the question.

'He was an idiot,' Emma said when she failed the last time. 'I had to take the corner on the other side of the road. There was a woman about to cross. I had no choice.'

'You could have slowed down, even stopped.'

'She should've looked where she was going. Anyone filming the scene would have seen I was in the right.'

I don't pursue this. I have learnt at times it is best to remain silent and avoid culpability.

Emma has chosen to take the test in the yellow Peugeot. My mother is still talking about 'when I get back in the car'. This cannot happen, ever, while I am alive and my lungs rise and fall.

'I'm really nervous,' Emma says, stalling at the first set of traffic lights. The two boys walk past and laugh. Emma winds down the window and is about to give them the benefit of her wisdom. I grab her arm. I don't want to be seen condoning any sort of bad behaviour.

'Ignore them,' I suggest.

They look back.

Emma mouths a word from one of Ruby's rap songs.

The boys carry on walking. They obviously value their teeth.

'It's just a test, Em. Loads of people take it a few times. Your mother for example.'

'Yes, and she should still be bloody-well taking it.'

Brigit is a safe driver, just fast and erratic. The 'little knock' on the passenger door went unchecked for several days. 'There was a post,' she said. 'Just a scrape.' I took a look a few days later to see the door staved in. It required a new one at an unfathomable cost. The key is not to talk to Brigit when she's driving. This is because she presses and depresses the accelerator depending on the intensity of what she is talking about, bringing about a head-bobbing action, leading to feelings of nausea and ultimately vomit.

Emma does a couple of parallel parks and a bay reverse down a side road, cursing a woman on a Motability scooter for simply 'being there'.

'She's not disabled!' Emma complains as she tailgates the little vehicle. We pass the lady and I notice she only has one leg.

'Yep, she is,' I inform Emma. 'One leg.'

'She can hop. Frogs hop.' I can see Emma in one of the 'caring professions'. That lack of compassion could save the NHS a fortune.

We arrive at the test centre. I've been out with Emma constantly for a month and I am emotionally and physically wrung out. I do not have dual controls, just the handbrake and dashboard against which I can brace myself. We are on our second clutch, which will of course be the reason Emma fails this test, as it wasn't as good as the other one. It was so knackered; the plate had split in two!

'I've never seen one like that,' the man at the garage said, putting the bits of clutch on the bench. 'Don't know how it kept going.'

Emma parks well in the bay. It is a good start.

'They're watching from the window.' Emma points at a window in the test centre with the blinds closed.

'No, they're not. They're all out testing scary people like you.'

There is a waiting area and the tension is palpable. There are spotty youths and girls who look as if they've come out of primary school for the day. I am the only parent. All the others have their instructors with them. I'm wondering if this 'own car' is a good idea. These people know what they're doing. I don't, but I am an expert at doing things I don't know how to do. I've done it for nineteen years!

Emma hands over her licence at the window, signs a form. We wait. A man in a pink shirt appears from the back room where I assume the examiners must smoke like Romanian chemical factories.

'I'm Graham,' he says, shaking Emma's hand and ignoring me.

I imagine him thinking I might make a plea on her behalf. There's no chance of that.

Emma grins. She hasn't got the woman who now comes out and takes a terrified boy who looks about twelve outside to a Ford Fiesta with 'FIRST PASS' emblazoned on the side. I wonder if it makes any difference. Of course ours would read 'SECOND PASS'.

Graham and Emma pull away, and I watch until they turn right out of the test centre. Emma's statistical predictions of test route patterns and allocation of examiners has just gone down the toilet. It isn't a good start. I know what it's like being confined in a little car with an angry seventeen-year-old. It's frightening. They certainly don't cover it in the first or second 'Complete Guide to Childcare'.

'Do you think she'll pass?' It's one of the instructors frantically chewing gum. She must be dosed up to the eyeballs to do a job like this.

'She's a good driver. It's the stopping and the speed which might be her Waterloo.'

The instructor doesn't seem to appreciate this.

'How long have you been an instructor?' I ask.

'Seventeen years.'

I study her face.

'It must be very stressful.'

'It is. I've had seventeen years of anxiety.'

I think this is terrible and then remember that I have looked after our children for nineteen. I've got two years on her.

The forty minutes drag and there Emma is, coming up the road and parking. They sit for a while.

'She's passed,' the lady instructor tells me.

'How do you know?'

'She's handed the examiner her licence. He's writing out the certificate.'

Of course I am delighted. Emma has her long-desired independence. We live out in the country, which is fine for little children, but not so for big ones. She gets out grinning. I give her a hug and I know when I get home, I will be forking out big time for the privilege of putting another seventeen-year old on the road.

Ruby tries to congratulate Emma on her success, but the words, like a sharp chicken bone, get stuck in her throat. They will have to share the car. Emma has placed a whiteboard in the kitchen with a grid and filled in most of the squares for herself without conscience.

'Right then,' Emma says. 'I'm off.'

I realise she's going to drive this car on her own. For public safety reasons I make a knee-jerk response. 'Maybe I should come out with you the first few times?'

She looks at me as if I've just asked her to eat one of my fabulous slow-cooked stews nobody likes. (*It's a stew. Nobody likes stews,* I am told. The person who invented stews must feel utterly broken.)

'What and have you shout at me!' Emma shouts. She waves the pass paper. 'I passed. It's official. Big news!'

'No, to give you reassurance.'

'I don't need reassurance. I'm going to see my friends. They know I passed. It won't look that cool with my dad sitting in the back seat like the Queen.'

'I wouldn't be sitting in the back seat. I can't grab the handbrake from there.'

Emma scoffs, opens the car, and connects her phone to the radio. We are all informed, despite best efforts to the contrary, that we are still 'mother fuckers with semi-automatics' and Emma is gone.

13

BEFORE

Fact: Number of hours in front of the cooker 8,243

'My God, I look like a hippo,' Brigit kept saying, until I finally acquiesced.

'You do. Hippos are very beautiful though. Huge mouths.'

She would have hit me if she could have reached. I dodged her and she fell back onto the bed.

'No, they're not.'

'To other hippos, they are.' I hauled her up to the edge of the bed where she tried to fill her compressed lungs as Emma and Ruby continued to kick seven bells out of Brigit's internal organs.

We sat down for supper. I opened a bottle of wine. Brigit had a very small glass and I slugged half the bottle.

'You don't think they're going to come a month early, do you?' I asked.

Brigit rubbed her belly as if she were checking with the two occupants.

I was about as ready for these two as I was with Chloe, but twice as anxious. 'The Complete Guide to Twins' had done nothing but invoke panic.

Brigit's waters broke at midnight.

We called our friend to collect Chloe. We drove to the hospital along the rutted, frozen track, Brigit moaning with every jolt. As if I were a magnet, a police car came up behind us and flashed his lights. Of course there is never one when you need them, but always when you don't. The policeman did the thing with his hat, squaring it on his head and walked steadily to our car. I wound down the window.

'You seem to be driving a little erratically.'

Brigit made a contraction sound. The policeman glanced across at her.

'Twins,' I said. 'Any minute.'

The policeman's expression changed from curious to nervous. 'Follow me,' he said, pulling away and putting his foot on the gas.

We had a police escort to the maternity unit.

'You'll have your hands full,' he said before he left us at speed.

And some.

Brigit braced herself against the back of the lift. The porter looked on in concern.

'I've never delivered a baby,' he informed us.

The doors opened. 'Praise the lord!' I said.

We helped Brigit onto a bed in the delivery suite. The midwife examined her.

'Number one's ready to arrive.' She looked at me. 'Okay?'

'I wasn't expecting this.'

'What were you expecting then?'

I didn't get the chance to answer.

Brigit went into a serious contraction. We were all systems go. Once again I'd be reminded how utterly incidental men are post-conception.

Emma was born, smoothly and quickly. She was a medium-sized, very calm cantaloupe melon. They placed her under a lamp where she promptly went to sleep. Ruby refused to appear. The midwife produced an implement like a crochet hook and inserted it in a place crochet hooks

125

should most definitely not be inserted. Ruby came out shouting with indignation and has continued to do so ever since. I stared in awe at these two babies under the heat lamps who were, two minutes ago, still figments of my imagination. Here they were now, unaware that soon they'd be left in my care.

I was sent home at seven thirty in the morning. The carpet man arrived at nine. Our friend returned with Chloe. She couldn't stop because she had work. I watched as she bumped along the icy track to her structured day and turned to face an eighteen-month- old who was clearly putting all her energies into talking and not walking.

'I've discharged myself,' Brigit said when she called. 'The duty doctor's only twelve and knows nothing about babies. Can you come and get me?'

The carpet man banged the last tack into the floorboard. He looked at Chloe in my arms. 'Twins as well. God, you've got your hands full.'

And some.

Two weeks after the birth of Emma and Ruby, the Chief Executive left the hospital where Brigit was the deputy to 'spend more time with his family'. In fact, he was spending all his time with his family; just like me!

Brigit waved the advert. 'Do you think I should go for the job?'

'Well, is it what you want?' I didn't like to say that it was significantly more money and the cash would come in handy. I didn't say this because I felt silently ashamed for betraying my past where the man went out into the world of 'real work' and the women kept the home fires burning and did all the shitty stuff no one else in their right mind would choose to do.

'I'm not sure I can do it,' she said.

I could have said the same about my life. 'Of course you can. You've been doing it for the last three years. People think you run the place anyway.'

Brigit applied for the CEO job and was appointed. Everyone on the surface seemed pleased. I know, for a fact, there were male colleagues at the hospital who thought, because she was a woman, Brigit would be a pushover when it came to getting what they wanted. I know this because I heard them say it. They were wrong. Sam Waters, the gastroenterologist I was supposed to know, slapped me on the back when he saw me pushing Ruby and Emma in the city. I was searching for a public toilet to change a couple of nappies. He was gazing at the Rolex watches in the jewellers.

'Ah, you,' he said.

I knew he didn't know my name. 'Looking for a ring for Caroline?'

He looked sheepish. Perhaps not Caroline then.

'Brigit,' he said. 'Amazing. Must feel strange for you, not wearing the trousers.'

I looked at his mustard corduroys. Despite my attempts at being smart, my black jeans had a streak of raspberry Petit Filous down the left thigh. Perhaps it wouldn't have shown up on a pair of mustard corduroys. I'll never know. I don't possess that sort of blind confidence.

Brigit became a personal story in the local press but, before long, she also became the alleged cause of the problems at the hospital, which were never hers. The girls pointed at the television when Brigit came on to be interviewed. They went up and kissed the screen. I didn't tell Brigit. It would have broken her heart.

We decided to move. We found a bigger, grottier house we couldn't afford. If it had been a dog, someone would have put it down.

'It's got potential,' Brigit said.

I had a hangover the size of a much larger house and stood in the garden looking at the field that came with the place, thinking about Hugh Fearnley-Whittingstall and imagining right then that he was in better shape than me. Even today the field and the house still have this potential, but always a hundred litres of paint, ten tons of gravel and the will to do it are out of reach.

The move fanned a long-forgotten flame inside me. Its light had dimmed, but not quite extinguished. The house might have been a heap of 1960s prefabricated concrete with malignant decay but it did, however, have two acres of land covered in weeds with a grip like a great white.

We moved into our new (to us, but a pile of bricks to anyone else) home. Brigit's hours seeped beyond the beginning and the end of every day like oil leaking out of a pre-1970 British motorcycle engine. We had three children under the age of two. I interpreted sympathy and understanding from the women at the playgroups as pity. Feelings of inadequacy began to overwhelm me. I was also now the hostage to my unconditional love and responsibility for these three beautiful girls who needed me. To the outside world and as an article in the Sunday supplements about a family 'doing it differently', the whole thing might have looked like a dream and not a nightmare. Every now and then I closed my eyes in the hope I might wake up with a badge and a timetable driven by convention and not by full nappies and bottles of formula milk. Oh God, heaven forbid, I was living the life of a mother! I was beginning to rapidly understand that mothers were so much stronger than I was.

I surveyed the barren field that was our 'potential' garden and I suddenly realised how I would fill the hole my self-esteem once occupied: I would resurrect my dream of becoming a smallholder. I dusted down Hugh Fearnley-Whittingstall's books. I had only ever been a vegetable grower. Hugh was telling me this was only part of the equation. I'd done the two veg, but not the meat. Still not quite done with 'The Complete Guide to Childcare' or 'The Complete Guide to Twins' I bought 'The Complete Guide to Small-Holding'. I loved a glossy book showing the best something can possibly be by utilizing every prop and special effect available to emboss an utter lie on the cover

128

and the subsequent pages. There were children holding fluffy hens, chicks at their feet, a ewe and its lamb on a patch of straw, a basket of washed vegetables and a couple of handsome parents who'd just stepped out of a Burberry shop window. Not a smear of yoghurt or pureed carrot anywhere. What could possibly go wrong with my road back from half to complete man? I would be like them. I would become the glossy cover on the book of my life.

It was winter though and I could only watch as the rain hammered against the windows and the septic tank overflowed, sending a foul-smelling brown stream silently into our neighbour's garden. A man came to pump out the tank. It was humiliating having our waste products pumped out into a tanker standing in the driveway with **YOUR POO IS OUR BREAD AND BUTTER** written on the side. The smell lingered for several hours and no amount of Febreeze could shift it. I felt like putting a sign outside the house to inform the neighbours it was from the farm down the road.

'You're backing up,' the man said, a roll-up balanced on his worryingly swollen lip. 'Bloody baby wipes. You need to tell the wife to stop flushing them. I'll be out here every bloody week if she doesn't.'

'I'll make sure I tell her,' I said.

He went to his lorry and brought back a metal bucket. In it were three dead rabbits stinking to high heaven. He chucked them into the septic tank.

'That'll help,' he said.

'They're dead rabbits.'

'We don't use live ones, boy. They won't stay in the bucket. It gets the bacteria going. You need bacteria.'

I really didn't think I needed bacteria. He left me with the dead rabbits lying at the bottom of the septic tank and a sobbing Chloe who was convinced we'd just murdered Peter Rabbit, Flopsy and Mopsy and disposed of the bodies.

'It's not Peter Rabbit, love. I promise.'

Chloe continued to cry.

129

I didn't want to admit I was lonely. However, if you are the person you are admitting it to, then you most likely are. I felt like the last or first of my kind, searching for someone like me with whom I could share the trials and tribulations of nappy rash over a pint in the local pub.

'Oh, there are lots of guys looking after the children these days,' yet another woman fresh from the home counties with an Alice band and a string of genuine pearls informed me at a play group where women chatted while children clung to their breasts. 'Mind you,' the woman added, 'you've got to ask yourself why they'd give up their independence when women have done it for years. Good for you,' she added.

I took no consolation in this.

I went to toddler groups where I dipped in and out, searching for the elusive man who wasn't Trevor Mace from Tumble Tots. I was having nightmares about The Tweenies. Teletubbies and their bloody 'Tubby *tustard*' haunted the labyrinth of my unconscious. The hairs wore off my knees where I knelt to change nappies and I spent so much time in public toilets I looked like a loiterer waiting to get caught.

Brigit was barely in the door when I hit her with my idea.

'I can do this. I can run a smallholding. It will complete us.'

'Complete us?'

'Yes, join up the dots. Live the dream like we planned. It will fill the gap.'

I had become obsessed with this 'gap' that needed to be filled. I could see the gap, and I was going to fall into it along with my sanity if I didn't stuff it with something more stable. A smallholding was the answer.

'You look after three children. We look after three children under the age of two.'

'Well, actually I do the lion's share while you go out doing whatever it is you do.'

Brigit's rage was immediate and palpable. I had set fire to the powder keg. 'My God. Is that what you think?'

'Today, yes it is.'

'I thought we were in this together.'

'So did I. It's just that I've been left high and dry. I live off you, I rely on you for a roof over my head and I spend my time with three miniature people who respond like pissed people.'

Brigit burst into tears. 'You chose to do this. You said you could do it. I gave up time with my babies because you said you could take care of them. Now you want to become fucking Farmer Giles.'

'Hugh Fearnley-Whittingstall, actually.'

'Christ. You said you would do this.'

'Really? I chose to change nappy after nappy, make pureed meal after pureed meal, and wear the hairs off my knees? I even lied to the bloke who came to suck out the shit that it was the woman of the house who slung ten million baby wipes into the septic tank because I thought they dissolved. Now fucking Peter Rabbit and his mates are down there gobbling them all up.'

Chloe screamed. She was standing behind me. 'You said he wasn't Peter Rabbit.'

'No, no sweetie. It's a figure of speech. Peter Rabbit died a very long time ago. It was Mr McGregor, not me.'

Chloe screamed again and Brigit ran to her.

I emptied a few cans of Carlsberg and tried to read 'The Complete Guide to Smallholding' without feeling bitter. It was not possible. I was already loathing the buggers on the front cover. It didn't bode well.

We found middle ground. It needed ploughing.

'So, we get some essentials done to the house and we get the field fenced for some chickens?' Brigit finished studying my financial profile, the projections for egg production and the infinitesimal benefits of home-reared meat and every other conceivable thing I had in my rapidly expanding imagination.

I could see it all. It is a dangerous thing when you think you can 'see it all'.

131

Brigit was shuffling my extensive seed collection. 'What exactly is a 'walking stick cabbage'?'

'It doubles up.'

She went away shaking her head.

'You shake your head all you like. This is going to be the making of us.'

We decided to release the tiny amount of available equity we had in the house based on its never-to-this-day realised 'potential'. I rang the building society for an appointment.

'The mortgage is in another person's name,' the woman said rather curtly.

'Yes, my partner.'

'But your name isn't on the mortgage.'

'I live here.'

'That doesn't change the fact that your name isn't on the mortgage. You could be a tenant. I assume you don't pay it.'

'Not exactly.' I could've told her I looked after three children under the age of two. As if that wasn't enough, I was starting a mini farm as a bridge to access my former self when I wore a suit, had a badge on my door and people actually talked to me about the cost of pressure-relieving mattresses.

'Sorry,' she said. (You can say sorry in so many different ways. I took this to be both patronising and pitying.) 'You'll need to get permission in writing.'

Brigit wrote the letter. 'Sorry,' she said.

For my appointment at the building society I wore a pair of trousers without yoghurt down the thigh and an ironed shirt. I was shown to an office with a desk and two chairs. On the desk was a picture of a young couple taken at Disney World.

The young woman in the photograph with dark, long hair tied back, wearing a navy blue suit and looking very efficient, came into the room. I stood. I shook her hand. We both sat down and she read a file for quite some time before speaking.

'I'm Josephine Taylor, the mortgage adviser.' She turned the screen so I could see it. 'We need to fill in a few details so we can assess if the capital you would like can be made available.'

She started taking details. 'Dependants?'

'Three children under two. Do you have any children?'

'Not yet. I'm getting married next year and maybe then. It'll depend on my husband and his work.'

'Might he look after the children?' Maybe I saw the potential for a possible friend in my line of work.

'Not sure it would be his cup of tea.'

'Oh.'

'He works here in this branch.'

'What does he do?'

'Same as me at the moment, but he's destined for higher things.'

'And you?'

'Maybe.' She quickly moved on. 'So, income?' Josephine looked at me. I told her what Brigit earned. She tapped this into her computer. 'And you?'

'I look after the children. I write novels too.'

'So, what figure would you place on that?'

I had one in my mind, but it wouldn't have made any difference to the amount she had already entered on the screen. 'We're starting a smallholding. There will be costs, but the potential is…'

'I mean, your income now.' Josephine Taylor blew a stray strand of hair off her face.

I actually considered telling her about my cheque from the electricity board for having the now non-existent poles in the field. 'Well, I suppose you could leave my income off the form.' I couldn't bring myself to say 'zero'.

'So, Brigit Wheeler is the main earner?'

'Yes, I suppose she is. I paid the deposit for the house from the capital I had.'

'Okay.' She tapped her keyboard and turned to me. I accidentally looked at her knees. She pulled her skirt down

133

to cover them. 'So, what you're actually saying is Ms Wheeler carries you. You are in fact, a dependant.'

'I've never thought of myself as a 'dependant'. I thought dependants were children. I look after our children. They are dependant on me. We have three. They're all under two.'

'Yes, but Brigit Wheeler is the sole earner and therefore will carry the burden of the increased repayments. You are dependant on her. The children are dependant on her also.'

'Well, if you put it like that.'

'I can't see why we can't agree the funds. I'll just need to check it with my boss and then we can let Ms Wheeler know.'

'I can tell her,' I offered.

Josephine Taylor gave me a smarmy smile. 'No, we'll need to do that.'

I went straight home and cancelled my credit card with the building society, which was reckless, but not bold or sensible. Realising in my haste that I no longer had one, I applied for another. They turned me down on the grounds that the future eggs from our future fluffy chickens wouldn't be enough to guarantee the repayments. They also told me that the job I was doing for all my waking hours didn't qualify me for any credit.

14

NOW

Fact: Number of times we told you all 'we love you', 167,896 (and rising)

I am thinking about the things Brigit said to me because she is right. I wonder if there is 'The Complete Guide to Being Lost and Becoming Found Again' in glossy hardback with once lost and now found people on the front cover standing on a beach and gazing wistfully out to sea over which hangs a golden sunset.

I am emptying and repacking the dishwasher because the three mugs and four glasses won't wash if they sit with the rims facing upward. Even if the thing is on an intense three-hour cycle.

"I already did that," Emma says as she comes into the kitchen to make a cheese sandwich before I serve a sumptuous meal of chicken, capers and black olives.

'Supper will be ready in ten minutes,' I call out to people who are so intent on whatever they are doing I might as well put my mouth over the plug hole in the sink and shout down there.

Emma sniffs the air. 'Oh God, not bloody chicken, capers and black olives again.'

Once they loved this dish. I leapt upon this like an eagle on a spot of fresh road kill. I have hacked my way through

'Jamie Oliver's 15-Minute Meals', which take half a day and a serious shedload of machinery to prepare and, yes Jamie, you are right; 15 minutes to slam in a wok with a 'bish bash bosh'. I have pushed against the driving power of McDonalds for years. I find the wrappers dumped in the compost bin late at night as disturbing as someone leaving the severed head of a horse on my pillow. Perhaps I should have given in to the Golden Arches and allowed them to gorge and thus imbue a lifelong appreciation for my chicken, capers and black olives.

Ollie appears. 'This internet…'

'I know, it's crap.'

'You need to get everybody off the internet. It's the girls.'

'They're doing their homework.'

'Ruby's talking to her friends.'

'About homework?'

'No, about drinking and shots and stuff. That's not homework.' He sniffs the air. 'Not that chicken thing again. We always have that chicken thing.'

I get myself a beer and neck it to kill the pain. Six legless chickens have died in vain.

Chloe appears, holding two very large bottles of shampoo and conditioner.

'Do you think I should put these in my suitcase or just carry them separately?'

'Why are you taking two flagons of shampoo to university?'

Chloe looks at me as if I'm insane. 'Because people wash their hair when they're at uni, duh!' Chloe is going to train as a clinical psychologist. She says I am one of the reasons she has chosen this career.

Chloe sniffs the air. 'What are you cooking?'

'I'm cooking a meal you all used to love and now obviously hate. Your mother says I'm lost and I've got to find myself again by looking at things differently. Perhaps you could do the same with chicken, capers and olives.'

'Oh, that old chestnut. Thursdays.'

'Thursdays?'

'You've always cooked it on Thursdays.'

'Not every Thursday.'

'Every other Thursday. See, you don't even know you're doing it. You should have driven us to McDonalds. Emma's addicted to Mozzarella Dippers.'

'Are you serious?'

'Check her waste bin.'

Each revelation as the truth unfolds about our late teenage children hits me like a rubber bullet in the chest. I take a look at my lovely chicken, capers and olives and secretly confess to myself that I am pretty fed up with the dish.

The two bottles of shampoo and conditioner Chloe is still holding are large enough to keep a good-sized city salon supplied for a year.

'You're going to Bristol. There are places you can buy shampoo in Bristol, and food, and other vital supplies. I believe the main supply routes are still open. Although with Brexit you can't be sure.'

Chloe gives me the same sort of withering look as her mother. It roughly translates as 'ah, bless you, how sweet, you misguided little fool'. Bristol has obviously become, since I was last there, a hostile place where evil roams the streets, people scavenge in bins and the shops are empty shells where not the tiniest puddle of Australian Formula, shockingly expensive and quite unnecessary shampoo, can be found.

The day arrives for Chloe's departure. A pile of boxes, a couple of suitcases and two large bottles of hair products fill the hallway. There are bags of pasta, tins of beans and a variety of exotic foods I have never even heard of. No capers or olives. I conclude that Chloe won't be cooking my signature dish so she can meander down memory lane while she is away.

'Maybe you're right, Chloe. I suppose there could be a sudden shortage of hair products. An outbreak of intractable dandruff triggering panic buying and riots in the streets, leading to a broken nation with dull and lifeless hair. It is too horrific to think about. We should be stockpiling. I am reminded of my Auntie Mavis with a larder full of granulated sugar when someone announced there was a sugar shortage in the UK in the 70s. What they actually meant was that the Fine Fare on the London Road had run out because Laurence, the manager, had forgotten to tick the box for the re-order. On the heels of the granulated sugar was the tinned salmon, and again an oversight on the part of Lawrence at Fine Fare on London Road. When they moved Auntie Mavis into the nursing home, it took a transit van to shift the hundreds of yellow, solidified bags of granulated sugar and the five hundred and sixteen tins of John West salmon from her pantry.'

'You're so dramatic,' Chloe says.

'This is a dramatic time. You're leaving me.'

'I'm going to Bristol, Dad. It's an hour and a half drive.'

'Where they may or may not sell shampoo and toilet rolls and other vital items for survival.'

Ollie appears. He is coming with us. Chloe is his big sister and he takes this very seriously. None of our children have any difficulty expressing their emotions. I come from a place where men only cried when the factories closed or the pubs went dry or the football team got knocked out of the league cup. Crying was for girls. Not now though. The tears almost flow out of the television night after night. If it isn't '24 hours in A & E', it's idiots in some mocked-up jungle or someone who can't sing on 'The X Factor' who has a third cousin looking for a kidney, prompting the phone lines to jam with sobbing people offering their worn out organs from all over the world.

'I've got you a conker.' Ollie hands the shrivelled thing to his sister and she takes it with such genuine gratitude I want to cry. I haven't got her a conker. 'You can look at it and think of me.'

We are all welling up.

Ruby and Emma drift into the hallway. I am an only child, so sibling relationships are a mystery to me. I can't imagine what it must be like to have a sibling with whom it is possible to share some of the agonies of being a child. Yet another reason why I've never been eligible for the job of looking after four children.

'I'll be up to party,' Emma says.

Ruby starts to cry, along with Brigit, who is actually coming with us.

'I shall miss you so much,' Ruby says.

This starts Chloe off.

'Right,' I say putting the rest of the bags into the car.

We are fifty miles into the journey when the phone rings.

'Where are my hair straighteners?' Ruby demands.

I look at Chloe in the rear view mirror. She shrugs and grins at me. 'They're actually mine,' she says.

Ruby is shouting, 'I got them for Christmas! They were in the special stocking from Father Christmas.'

'Father Christmas isn't real,' Ollie chirps up. 'They lied to me.'

This comes up every now and then, and I can see the perpetuation of the lie through the generations does most definitely imbue a fracture of distrust in the bedrock of the relationship. His baby teeth have all fallen out now, so the tooth elf is no longer an issue. I have no reason to sprinkle glitter on the carpets as magic dust and leave tiny notes about tooth trees. I keep the teeth in little pots in my sock drawer.

We join a queue of parents taking bags out of cars and hauling them up to the halls of residence. The building is new and clean and well equipped. The walls are one single colour and fully painted, the windows fit properly in their frames and there are shades on the lights.

'It's nice,' I say. It's certainly in better decorative order than the place she's just left.

Chloe touches a wall. 'It is,' she says. 'It's lovely.'

The flat Chloe is sharing with five other people is perfect. Chloe's room has a view of parkland.

'Keep your windows closed,' Brigit says, closing the windows. 'There could be people lurking in the trees.'

Ollie presses his face against the window. 'That's so cool.'

'I'm nineteen, Mum.'

Brigit looks shocked as if this is a revelation and information which has been withheld from her. In the kitchen there are two young men. I say this politely as they are actually young boys who are pretending to be young men. I shake their hands.

'Yo,' the one with the dreads says.

I don't do 'yo'. 'Hi.'

'I'm Jet.'

The other young man shakes my hand. 'I'm Guy.'

I like Guy. He has a strong handshake and looks like he's come from army officer training rather than a CND protester from Greenham Common who hasn't had a wash for three months, lives on lentils and considers spray deodorant to be another notch in the demise of humanity.

'We can go back to my room and have a look at it,' Chloe suggests with a hint of panic in her voice. Parents roaming about a student house can only lead to embarrassment.

'We've already seen it,' I say. I'm happy to chat with Guy and Jet.

Brigit prods me really quite hard.

We go back to Chloe's room. I can see Brigit is struggling with the moment of separation. Ollie is more concerned about where his conker might reside during term time. Chloe places it inside an elephant-shaped candleholder. Ollie seems satisfied. He is ready to go. He's on a promise of McDonalds at the service station.

'We can FaceTime,' Chloe says, ready to push us out the door so she can go and apologise to Guy and Jet.

Chloe is pushing us away, back to the life we live and the one she is in the process, albeit temporarily (I like to convince myself), of leaving. I feel remarkably okay. I am not like most of the other fathers and it is my privilege to be this way. I am like the mothers who have spent thousands of hours with their children, carrying them and ultimately guiding them through each developmental stage. Brigit has played a huge role in this every step of the way. I couldn't have played my part without her when many women without their men easily can.

All of the parents here are infected though; with the emotions of loss and celebration, clinging to the cliché of birds and cages and open doors. Fathers are trying to hide their tears. Let them out, Clive, Harry, Brian or whoever you are.

I will miss Chloe, but she is ready to go. Chloe will FaceTime me on Monday to tell me she is okay, but more than likely to see if I am. I am as certain of this as the M5 being gridlocked on the way home.

Ollie is plugged into some sort of game on his phone. He has more collective gigabytes than anyone in the household because of a deal at the phone shop. Now he watches teenagers on YouTube who play games for vast sums of sponsorship and travel all over the world.

'How the hell can we be bloody well lost when we came this way? We have sat nav'. There are satellites in space telling us where to go and we can't even find the frigging M5!'

We are emotional.

'It's right!' Brigit shouts, pointing left. This is one of the things I love about her, and thank God it isn't really a necessary qualification for running one of the largest hospitals in the country.

We get home to a dark house because Emma and Ruby have gone to a party at some vague address where they will no doubt kip for the night and, I hope, steal someone else's maple-cured bacon.

15

BEFORE

Fact: Number of times we watched 'Beauty and the Beast', 182

The money came through into Brigit's account from the building society. As someone labelled as being 'carried' by my partner, I took no credit for helping to make this happen, refused to talk about it and turned it into a grudge.

'You have to stop looking at it this way,' Brigit said. 'It takes us nowhere other than down. It's 'our' money. I get to do my job because you do yours.'

I can't count the number of times Brigit has said this, but the feeling has never gone away.

We drew up plans to renovate our house. The quotes came in. The plans became less ambitious. The quotes came in. The plans became questionable as to whether they were worth implementing at all. We decided on a few fences and items of essential garden machinery.

'I need to get out there,' I said one weekend. I went 'out there' in the pouring rain, preparing the ground.

By twelve-thirty on Monday, the rain battering on the windows like skeletal fingers, the girls and I had done lunch in the shape of teddy bear cheesy toasts with Marmite and yoghurt. The girls were starting to throw food at one another. Chloe walked over to Emma and slapped her hard on the top of the head. Emma's face crumpled like a newspaper. Emma was inconsolable. She stopped breathing out, only in, until finally the outward breath came with such force, the sound almost punctured my eardrums. While I was tending to Emma's slapped head and irregular breathing, Chloe calmly walked over to Ruby and slapped her on the head. In response, Ruby sunk her two front teeth into Chloe's arm. Chloe screamed. I shouted. Seventy-five percent of the people in the room were making some sort of loud hysterical noise because they were inconsolably unhappy. Helping one unhappy person fix on a happy thought is one thing. A room-full of unhappy people is a room drained of happy thoughts, and I was struggling to find one.

I had to get out of the house. I had to do something. Brigit was cornered into making an unsuccessful hospital into a successful one or be removed. I was wringing my hands in despair when my charges were three beautiful little girls who asked nothing more of me than to be the best parent I could be. Maybe this was it; maybe I was the best parent I could be. Maybe I had reached my limits. It never mentioned 'limits' or failure in 'The Complete Guide to Childcare' and 'The Complete Guide to Twins'. I took the books and shoved them both under the bed.

While the children licked their wounds, I consulted Hugh Fearnley-Whittingstall and 'The Complete Guide to Smallholding'. I could do this. I had already heard Brigit's story about the people 'doing something' by dragging the dead bodies out of the sun. There were no bodies and no sun. I was going to do something to make the unhappy people happy again.

I found a number in the telephone book for a place where they sold chickens. I checked 'The Complete Guide to Smallholding'. It looked like a piece of cake. We would be those self-satisfied bastards on the front of the book with their fluffy chickens and their sterile vegetables. Chickens were the entrée into a smallholding, a mini farm, real work. Chickens were the solution to filling the gap between self-esteem and me. I would fill the void with chickens. If I was happy, everyone would be happy. Why hadn't I thought of it before?

'We're going to buy chickens,' I informed the girls.

'Quack, Quack,' Chloe said.

I could see we had a way to go.

Chloe rubbed her stomach. 'Mmm. I like chicken.'

'I'm not sure that's the sort of thing they want to hear, sweetheart. The eggs will be nice.'

The previous violence dished out by Chloe was now forgotten; Emma and Ruby clapped their hands together. I wiped them down from the catering pack of wipes, remembering to put them in the bin and not the pipe leading to the tomb of Peter Rabbit and his colleagues. There was no time to lose. I bundled the three of them into the Sierra as rainwater battered my back like a tirade of tiny hands. Ruby refused to sit and stretched herself out like a board. She started screaming.

'Please! Please!' I was well into begging the children to comply. I was a desperate man.

Ruby gave me the same look of contempt she sometimes gives me now when the roles are reversed and it is me acting like the truculent child. I pushed Ruby slowly into the seat and clipped the seat belt. We headed off in search of chickens.

The chicken place was called The Bird House. It looked like a hick town from a Western. There were cages and ponds and lots of other flappy things as well as chickens. I put Ruby and Emma into the buggy. I opened the door. An ugly goose with a large lump on its head came at us with its wings flapping and its beak open. I slammed the door and stood breathless with my hands pressed against it. I noticed a man watching us from behind a counter covered in bird shit. He was eating a sandwich very slowly and watching me with amusement as I worked the buggy through the door.

'The goose isn't very welcoming,' I said. The thing was still behind me, eyeing my backside.

'Great guard dogs. You need 'em.' He looked at the buggy. 'Nice bit of kit. Wife off for a pamper, is she?'

I was growing weary of these types of stereotypical comments from other men. I ignored it. The girls were frantically pointing at a parrot.

The man opened his paper, and ran his eyes over Pamela Anderson. I wondered if Pamela knew that fat men in chicken shacks drooled over her. She probably did.

The place was expansive. There were rabbits and other furry things and parrots. It should have been called Noah's Chaotic Arc. It was like a poultry supermarket. The parrot attracting the girls' attention was on a stand next to the counter doing that funny bobbing thing with its head. I held out my hand, for what reason I can't possibly now imagine, and the multi-coloured bastard sank his beak into the webby bit between my forefinger and thumb. Blood welled up like oil shooting from a well.

'He bites,' the man said with a grin, nodding at the sign hanging below the parrot's claws.

'Jesus!' I read the sign. MY NAME IS JACK. DO NOT TOUCH ME. I AM NOT FRIENDLY. 'That thing could've taken my eye out!'

The man laughed, revealing his half-digested sandwich. 'Only if you offer it to him. It's an African Blue, not a 'thing'. Sign not big enough?'

It was quite a big sign.

I left him and his deranged, bloodthirsty parrot and wandered around looking at birds. There were so many different chickens. I thought a chicken was a chicken; a bird with a tiny head and brain, confounded eternally about whether the egg came first.

Chloe stopped in front of some white fluffy chickens and pointed.

'Nice,' she said. 'Eggs.'

There were white eggs in the sawdust. I was gripped by a surge of excitement. I could buy these chickens and take them home right now. I didn't think becoming a smallholder could be that immediate. These would be my 'starter chickens'. It said so in 'The Complete Guide to Smallholding'.

Finally, finished with his sandwich and mentally undressing the already scantily clad Pamela, the man gave us his attention.

I pointed at the white fluffy chickens. 'I'll have four of those and a cockerel.'

'They're White Sussex,' the man said.

'Yep.' I could see they were white. I didn't know they came from Sussex.

'The hens come in threes. It's three plus one or six. Are you breeding?'

'Oh, I would think so.'

I saw the name Jim on a mug. 'Are you Jim?'

'That'll be me, boy.'

'I'll have six then. And a cockerel. I want eggs.'

Jim grinned to reveal so few teeth I was surprised he wasn't on pureed food. His chances with Pamela Anderson were, unlike him, looking slim.

'You don't need a cockerel for eggs. Only if you want chicks. You know, little chickens.'

'I definitely want a cockerel.'

Without another word, Jim went to the cage and, one by one, picked up the chickens by their feet and dropped them into two cardboard boxes. The cockerel took less kindly to the blood rushing to his head and made a peck at my arm as Jim carried him by.

'The birds aren't too keen on you today, boy,' Jim said. 'Or maybe they find you tasty.' He laughed at his little joke as the blood from my parrot peck continued to run down my arm.

I'd seen the ducks on the way in. I was on a roll. Chickens didn't somehow seem enough. 'I'll have three ducks as well.' I expected Jim to be impressed by this level of commitment to fowl. He remained impassive. I was coming to the conclusion that not even a dodo would impress Jim.

'You want Indian Runners?'

'As opposed to...?'

'Aylesbury, Muscovy, Mallard, domestic. You name them, we've got them. Or I can get them.'

I tried hard to think of a duck this bloody clever dick might not have, but I knew nothing about ducks. The only thing that came into my mind was…

'Donald?'

To his credit, he ignored this.

'Do the runners run?'

'They do.'

'Do they run fast?'

'Fast enough.' Jim wandered off and returned with a very tall duck hanging by its feet. It stared glassy-eyed at me as the person responsible for the world turning upside down.

'One Indian Runner. Good layer, easy to look after. Best put them in a separate house.'

I hadn't thought about houses. 'They live in houses? I thought ducks lived outside.'

'They live in houses if you want to hang onto the buggers. Mr Fox'll have 'em otherwise.'

'I'll have two Indian Runners. Are they actually from India?'

'Wolverhampton. They come in threes. You want a drake?'

'Do they lay eggs without one?'

'Oh yes, they can do that all on their own. If you want ducklings, you'll need a drake. It's the same principle as chickens, and people of course. You'll already know you need a bloke to make those.' He nodded at the girls who were palpably thrilled to be getting chickens and ducks.

'I'll have a drake then.'

Jim boxed them in one.

We went out into the yard to look at the houses I didn't think I needed. The houses were all flat-pack. I knew about

148

flat-pack. Flat-pack still makes me nervous. These were chicken houses. They weren't designer furniture. How hard could it be to put up a birdhouse?

'Are they easy to put up?'

Jim sized me up and blew a gust of acrid air through the large gap where his teeth used to reside. 'Even an idiot could put these together.' He grinned.

I was that idiot with just a hammer and a set of rusty tools my dad didn't want when he left to find a better life and another wife on the far side of town.

'Ok. I'll take one.'

'You'll be needing a duck house as well.'

'Really?'

'Oh, yes. Different design altogether.'

'What, more modernist?'

'If you say so, boy.'

I bought another flat-pack that looked just like the other one.

We loaded the flat houses into the back of the Sierra and the birds in the boxes on top. Jim tilled up the damage. He was tapping on the keyboard for ages.

'Four hundred and ninety-seven pounds. Call it four-ninety.'

Even with the generous discount, I was reeling. They were birds, some eastern European wood and a bit of mesh. I paid him on my credit card. Those birds were going to lay some pretty expensive eggs!

'When will they start laying?'

'Probably next year.'

'Next year?'

'They're not at 'point of lay' yet. Then you've got the shorter days. They don't like the shorter days. They don't lay on the shorter days.'

'What, like a protest?'

'Something like that. It's the light.'

'They don't lay in the dark?'

'Not regularly. They sleep in the dark. You don't shit when you sleep. Not unless the wife's put something in the cooking anyway!' This seemed to amuse Jim until he began to cough and put him on the verge of bringing up a lung.

I started to walk away.

Jim, being the vindictive country yokel I had surmised he was, waited until I reached the door and called after me. The girl's nappies were bulging to bursting point. It was all going to be a mess when we got home and I had just thrown a shed-load of poultry into the mix.

'What are you feeding them on?'

'Bread?'

'You got plenty then?'

'A lot of crusts. The girls don't like crusts.'

'Makes your hair curly,' Jim said. Probably the only line he possessed in an attempt to endear him to children.

'Well, that's not true is it? In the same way chewing gum doesn't wrap around your heart.'

'That not true either, boy?'

'No.'

Jim sold me a bag of mixed corn. I gave him back the generous seven pounds discount. We could have been Barry and Paul in the Chuckle Brothers doing the 'to you, to me, to you' thing again; the one Brigit doesn't find very funny.

I had just spent nearly five hundred quid on a flock of birds, which wouldn't be laying eggs until next year and then only when the sun was out.

I could still make it work. I was enthusiastic, just like Hugh Fearnley-Whittingstall was enthusiastic, except while he was making shed-loads of money writing books about his chickens laying eggs, mine weren't, even in the near future, going to do that. But this was the necessary investment. I was at the vanguard of making childcare a sideline and micro-farming my main role.

We drove home. I was excited and busy. The girls all fell asleep perched on their engorged nappies. I changed them while they slept in the car. Slowly, almost without noticing and realising the virtues, I was becoming quite an expert at looking after children.

I opened the boot of the car. One of the running ducks with the unfeasibly long necks poked its head out of the top of the box and had a good look around. It had a glint in its eye and a big beak. It quacked at me.

I unloaded the car, took the boxes of birds into the field. I only had a small lawnmower for a very large patch of grass. Here it was already a foot tall. The previous owners had cut it and made off with whatever machinery they used. I tipped the boxes onto their sides, opened the flaps and watched the birds gingerly step out into the light. Three of the chickens took off and flew many metres to the far side of the field. I didn't actually know until that moment that chickens could fly. I thought they were like penguins. Thankfully they stopped short of the fence and started pecking the grass. The Indian Runners did what they do best, and ran at pace into the other half of the field where predators on the hunt for a tasty duck no doubt lurked. Christmas had come early.

I planned to turn this piece of wild land into a blossom-filled orchard where I could while away the sunny afternoons thinking about the plot for the great novel I intended to knock out when I wasn't building birdhouses, or changing Weetabix-filled nappies. Within a few minutes the birds had mainly disappeared. I imagined twenty-pound notes flying out of my hands, and Jim counting them, eyed by his barbaric parrot.

I drove the car into the field where I could see the girls. They slept for two hours. The birdhouses were easy to put together with my dad's bequeathed and rusty tools. The light was fading. I lined the houses with straw. It started to rain. I began the task of rounding up the birds.

I realised within minutes I had made a mistake.

I found the cockerel and tried to grab him. He took a leaf out of the parrot's book and pecked me. I could see there were bridges to build between him and me. I grabbed a hen and the cockerel, who we decided to call Roy after my dad, and stuff them into the house. I searched in the bushes for the others but found nothing. I had lost four ducks and five chickens in two hours. I thought about consulting 'The Complete Guide to Smallholding', but I didn't want to look at how well the Burberry people herded their livestock without getting a spot of chicken shit on their Hunter wellies.

I fed the girls. Brigit came home at nine after being roasted at a public meeting about a building promised by her predecessor without having the money. I still only had two chickens in custody, which currently stood me at a hundred quid each.

'I'm not sure I can do this job,' she said.

This was not a good moment to announce her failings. If I could have a pound for every time Brigit Wheeler has said this through the years, I would have recouped my losses on the poultry. The truth is Brigit Wheeler can. She went straight through to hug her daughters and spread her love.

I followed her into the bedroom. 'I bought some chickens.' It sounded like a filthy confession.

'Chickens!' Chloe shouted. 'We've got chickens!'

Brigit looked genuinely pleased. 'Oh how lovely. How many?'

'A few. I bought a couple of houses too. They're not all in the houses though. Some of them are a bit free range.'

'And quack quacks,' Chloe added.

Brigit looked concerned. 'Ducks? Don't you need a pond for ducks?'

'No. 'The Complete Guide to Smallholding' says you only need a large receptacle of water so they can dunk their heads.'

'Ooh "receptacle".'

'It's a smallholding term. Bucket to you.'

'So, where are the ducks?'

'Wandering around.'

'What about the fox?'

'Probably wandering around looking at the ducks. I'll have to put them away soon. Dusk. The book says "dusk".'

'So they just come back?'

'Sure.'

'So, they're homing ducks?'

'They know where the house is.' I wasn't sure this was actually true. They did run off straight away, before I built the house.

'Mr Fox likes chickens,' Chloe added helpfully.

Brigit picked up the receipt for the birds. I took it from her. 'How much did this all cost?'

'We'll get it back with the eggs.'

'Not if you can't find the chickens.'

'A parrot bit my hand.' I held it up as evidence. 'It's still pretty sore.'

Brigit tried to grab the receipt.

'Lots of money,' Chloe said.

'Really. How much?'

Chloe didn't know how much. She was at that idyllic age where you simply plucked a twenty-pound note from the branch of the 'money tree'.

'Five hundred, with the houses and the feed and a cockerel called Roy. The hens are white from Sussex.'

'Five hundred pounds! You spent five hundred pounds on chickens! They're a fiver in Tesco.'

'They don't lay eggs.'

'The eggs are a couple of quid a dozen.'

'Not the same. Look, I'm trying to do something important here, for all of us, involve you and the children in a different way of living.'

'Five hundred pounds! I've just told you I don't think I can do this job any more.'

Normally, as another paid employee in the family, this would have been, to use the pun, 'water off a duck's back'. I took the accusation like a cricket ball in the nuts. You don't go around frittering away five hundred quid on a bunch of non-laying, absconding foul when you don't have a 'proper job'. Brigit didn't mean it, but I felt reduced, beholden, caged. This bloody well had to work. I was putting all my energies into a bunch of birds to make me feel whole again. Reckless and bold? Nope, just bloody stupid.

We went to bed in a poultry-induced silence. A noise woke me. It wasn't the girls. It was a screeching sound like something from a film about werewolves. I opened the curtains, which could have been replaced if I hadn't backed the wrong chicken. The moon was cinematically full, the light coating everything with silver. I saw something move on the far side of the field. I knew I needed to move fast. If I wasn't already, I was rapidly turning into one of those idiots Jim so eloquently described.

I ran down the stairs. I was naked. I grabbed the nearest coat by the door. It was a yellow see-through poncho from Alton Towers.

The field was wet. The grass twinkled in the moonlight. This moonlight was reflected back off the ground as if it were scattered with a lot of little jagged mirrors. I stood in awe. It was a beautiful night to be out. I went over to one of the little mirrors to see that it wasn't a mirror at all. They were not celestial shafts of light, glancing down on our little place either. The things I thought were mirrors were actually generous splashes of blood, wet sinew and the internal organs of birds. My increasingly expensive birds had been massacred. It looked like a scene from a Tarantino movie.

I sat on the wet grass. I put my hand down and lifted it immediately. There was a duck's head looking up accusingly at me. The head was tantalisingly close to its body. I imagined it dying, frustrated at this 'so close and yet so far' scenario. That duck would not be doing a whole lot of running in the future that was for sure. I saw a flipper, a chicken with its belly unzipped and its guts spilling out. I cast around desperately for any sign of life. I saw movement from one of the birds. I ran over to find a chicken on its side, throat open, eying me in an unforgiving sort of way. It was asking me 'why have you done this to me? I preferred

154

Jim and a cage.' I thought about wringing its neck. I thought about wringing Jim's neck! Even 'super vet', Noel Fitzpatrick, couldn't have got this one on its feet. I ran to the house and grabbed an empty beer bottle. The chicken with the gashed neck eyed me. It knew; it knew the bottle was empty and I hadn't got it for drinking beer.

'I'm sorry. I'm sorry for leaving you out and for this.' I was talking to a dying chicken. I slammed my bottle down into the grass a centimetre above the chicken's head. I missed. I did it again, this time hitting the target with a crack. The chicken stretched out its legs. It was still twitching. It was still alive. How could it be still alive with a flat head? I hit it again and again like some frenzied mad person; venting his rage for every vestige of harm anyone has ever done to him. The chicken stopped doing the thing with its legs and everything went quiet. I was breathing hard. I had murdered a chicken, with the blood of many others and ducks on my hands. Literally.

I stood up. The see-through poncho only reached the top of my thighs. The church bell struck midnight. I was standing in the centre of a field wearing an Alton Towers see-through poncho. It was so cold, my testicles had retreated so far into my body cavity, they were dangling somewhere near my epiglottis. From any angle this did not look good. A newspaper would have a field day with a story about ritual sacrifice. If someone had taken a picture right then, we'd have to leave.

It started to rain.

There was no easy way to break the news to the girls.

'Mr Fox and his little cubs are very happy,' I reassured them.

They weren't reassured. They howled. I should have lied. Brigit had her arms folded. There is nothing worse when you are up to your neck and scrabbling for an olive branch than someone with their arms folded.

Finally, Brigit gave me a hug. 'You don't need to do all this, you know.'

'Oh, trust me, I do, I really do.'

It was like a military burial after a battle. There were several modified shoe boxes filled with the jigsaw pieces of the birds they once were, but not necessarily all in the same box. Each box contained a note with a pictorial prayer, glitter and a crayon, should the bits of each bird miraculously reform themselves into one and have the urge to jot down its thoughts. Emma had drawn a horse for reasons best known to her.

Very early that morning, wearing more than an Alton Towers poncho, I dug the holes. We stood in front of them in a line. The girls were sobbing, not necessarily for the birds themselves, but for all the characters in the cartoons they represented. The potential PTSD was enormous.

'Hands together,' Chloe said. The girls, Brigit and I put our hands together. 'You need to say a prayer, Daddy.'

'Yes,' Brigit added. 'You need to say a prayer for the birds. One for the five hundred quid as well.'

She had no idea how much this hurt.

'To the God of chickens, please take these lovely birds into your heaven and look after them.'

The girls had their eyes squeezed tightly shut, praying as hard as it probably is to pray.

'There will be a few more stars in the sky tonight.'

Chloe looked at me hopefully. 'Really?'

'Oh, yes. A star for everybody. Everybody gets a star.'

'Which one is Mrs Barlow?'

Mrs Barlow was the old lady who lived down the road and shouted at all the children until her heart gave up. I was tempted to say she didn't get a star for being such a starchy old cow.

I pointed at the feeblest star I could see. 'That one.'

I didn't go back and see Jim for quite a while. I did go back though. I was determined. If it was good enough for Hugh, it was good enough for me. I bought four turkeys, three geese, five Indian Runners and six chickens. It sounded like that Christmas song without the partridge in the pear tree.

'You're a glutton for punishment,' Jim said as he took my cash without conscience. He was ogling a picture of Jennifer Lopez as if his feelings for her might one day be reciprocated. His optimism for landing a woman like J.Lo was as misplaced as mine was for becoming a successful smallholder. But I had no intention of seeing Jim again. I had plans to hatch my own birds in future and expand.

He was right though; I was a glutton for punishment.

16

NOW

Fact: Number of cakes made, 2,876

They are playing that Whitney Houston song on the radio, 'Where do Broken Hearts Go?' It makes me wonder about those parents who've given their years to ensuring their children are cared for – where do these parents go after the children stop being children and bugger off into the world and put every waking second onto social media? There must be a group. There are groups for everything. I can't find a group. Perhaps I should start one myself. It will probably be as successful as my search to find a collection of fathers doing what I do.

I look on Mumsnet and come across a bloke asking why it's so weird for a man to suggest to a woman that their children have a 'play date'. 'Maybe it's because their husbands don't like it,' one woman replied. 'Mine certainly wouldn't'.

I think about responding, but I don't want dialogue about something I already understand. I am fine being the last dodo if that's how it is. I really am fine. A little lost maybe, but ostensibly fine.

Ollie comes through wearing his school uniform, in a fashion. The fashion is, shoelaces tucked down the sides, shirt out and a hoody under his blazer.

'I'm ready,' he informs me. He looks about as ready as Marie Antoinette was for the guillotine.

I drop Ollie at the bus and drive into town to sit in a café where I can write some more of this. I have a booked call with Ollie's school. The head teacher won't talk to me because he 'works from the inside out'. It says so on his Twitter page. He works 'with the strategic interface', or at least that was how he described his role at the briefing we went to where he tried to sell us copies of his book on 'Managing the Strategic Interface Between Education and Society'. It must've taken him an hour just to write the bloody title.

I've been allocated one of Mr Atkin's sidekicks. Her name is Mrs Oliver and I can see she has tried to call me three times.

'I want to talk about mobile phones,' I tell her when we finally connect and she says 'hello' in a tone indicating that I am interfering with her important work. I actually thought the important work of the teachers was dealing with issues concerning the pupils. 'Carlton Community College has banned them. They take them off the kids when they arrive and they get them back at the end of the day. They canvassed the parents and eighty-two percent said yes.' I have my facts. Mrs Oliver listens in silence. I imagine her marking English homework and dunking a chocolate-coated Hob Nob as I speak.

'We will never do that,' Mrs Oliver informs me emphatically.

'But they're using them all day at school. They play games and watch God knows what.'

'We have a filtered internet, they can't even get Facebook.'

'They have 3G.'

'That's the parents' responsibility.'

'Not when they're at school. They use one another's hotspots. We can't manage that remotely.'

'We will not be banning mobile phones. It's a life skill.'

159

'I know it's a life skill, but I don't think it helps with learning. I know they game in the corridors. It's a battle with Xbox and PS4 all the time. Every day there's conflict at home. Schools need to play a part. You're always telling us it's a contract between home and school.' I can sense Mrs Oliver absorbing this well-documented fact.

'My son is sixteen and he has neither an Xbox or a PS4. He enjoys sport and would rather be outside.'

In one single cleave of her moralistic axe, this woman has reduced me. I am furious. I don't care or in fact give a flying fuck about her brilliant progeny and how everybody has sons who'd rather hunt for bugs than shoot the shit out of their friends on the screen. Despite being hands free (I need to say), I pull over into a layby before I slam my foot to the boards and drive into a wall.

'So, that's your final word on the matter?'

'Yes, it's the school policy.'

'Can I write to someone about it.'

'I suggest you talk to your son. Work it out between you. They need their phones for certain school tasks.' I can tell that Mrs Oliver will not be moved.

'Okay. My son has a detention. He received three behaviour marks.'

'That's right. We award a detention with three behaviour marks.' She makes it sound like an achievement. Go on, Mrs Oliver, tell me Perfect Fucking Peter has never had a detention in his bug-hunting life. 'We only award detentions to children who need to modify their behaviour. We get results here. You know that. We get results because we are clear with our pupils.'

Now I feel I have a delinquent child who cannot be controlled either at school or at home.

'We live fifteen miles out. Can he do it at lunchtime? He'll miss playing football with his mates. He loves football. It will be a punishment.'

'I'm afraid not. We only do detentions after school. The parents need to understand.'

'Understand what?'

'If the children are misbehaving then everyone loses out.'

'So we're all being punished?'

'I think it makes a point. School and home is a partnership.'

'So why not ban mobile phones?'

'It's a life skill.'

'You said.'

'I think you might benefit from coming to one of the Mind Map training sessions,' she said.

I've already been to one. I didn't really understand a word.

A man in a demob suit took the stage at the Mind Map seminar. 'I'm Farquhar,' he said with significant and undisguised pride. (The only Farquhar I could think of was the king with the short legs and the long armour in 'Shrek'.) 'The Mind Map is simply a way of mapping out the mind.' He paused, for what, I wasn't exactly sure. 'Setting out the clutter and ordering it on the page so we can make sense of what is going on in our heads. We have to teach young people to make sense of what is going on in their heads, where things are constantly swirling, in an age where this will only swirl more and more until…' Mr Farquhar didn't seem to know what happened after the 'swirling'.

I didn't stay for the custard creams and the beige tea. The second half promised to be even more thrilling: 'Having the cake and how to eat it.' I believe people get paid for this sort of stuff.

Now, I am late picking up Ollie, Emma and Ruby from the bus. I had to go to Tesco for cleaning products. I know my cleaning products like a pharmacist knows their drugs. I can take out a dirty bathroom with a Flash and Bleach in one hand and a Shower Shine in the other.

The trio are at my mother's house listening, no doubt, to stories when the world was a better place, before the Common Market and decimalisation. I get a text from Ollie.

161

WHERE ARE YOU? THIS IS AGONY. SHE'S TALKING ABOUT POWDERED EGG!

When I arrive, Ollie looks in genuine pain, gripping his stomach the way someone might if they'd eaten neat powdered egg. He mouths something rude which I ignore. My mother's going on about Emma's skirt and how she'll get arthritis in her hips.

'I'd say her armpits more likely.'

'It wasn't like this in my day,' my mother reminds us.

'Nothing is like it was in your day.'

I notice my mother doesn't have the button she's supposed to have around her neck.

'Where's the button you're supposed to have around your neck?'

'Upstairs.'

'And you're downstairs. If you fall down, you need the button to press.'

'I won't fall down,' she says with utmost certainty.

'How do you know?'

'I haven't fallen down yet.'

'It doesn't work retrospectively. It's about things which *might* happen. You don't build up points for good behaviour.'

'Oh, you can't worry about what's going to happen in the future. If you did that we'd all go mad.'

'So, you don't have the button with you at all times?'

'It doesn't work at the shops.'

'If you fall down at the shops, there'll be people to help you.'

'Not these days. They'll walk round you. They're too busy on their mobile phones to notice someone lying on the floor screaming for help.'

I'm inclined to agree with her on this one.

'I keep it by the bed, just in case I wake up in the night.'

Emma, Ruby and Ollie are all engrossed on their mobile phones.

'You press the button if you wake up?'

'They talk to you to make sure you're all right.'

'Are you serious?'

'They're very friendly.'

'You press the button when you wake up?'

'I don't always know where I am.'

We leave.

At home, they all go to their rooms.

I stand in the kitchen looking at my dog. 'We're alone, Claude.'

He wags his tail.

I open the fridge and look inside. I wonder if being dyslexic with words is like looking into the fridge and seeing the food, with no idea how to put any of it together to make a sensible meal.

There is a knock at the door. It is Dorothy and Ken from the cottage next door. They moved here from Manchester last year to be near their daughter and family who then moved to the Philippines a month after Dorothy and Ken arrived. I don't know if they took it personally or not. Dorothy has the look of someone who battles on, but slowly, inch-by-inch, she's becoming defeated by the sheer weight of life. Ken, a spindly retired accountant, stands next to Dorothy who is not spindly. She cleared the plate and left nothing for Ken, just like Jack Spratt and his wife. Ken is into 'pinhole photography', which is a mystery to me when you can take a perfectly good picture with your phone and never look at it again. Ken appears vacant, as if this visit has nothing to do with him. Dorothy is holding a piece of paper.

'Everybody hates us,' Dorothy says, then promptly bursts into tears, which I suppose is fair enough if this is actually true.

'I'm sure they don't.' I look at Ken who remains impassive should he be in some way incriminated in this ugly thing. 'Would you like to come in?'

I really hope they wouldn't like to, but they do. They follow me through to the kitchen as if expecting me to put this evident community-wide hatred to rest.

163

'Not finished the painting then?' Ken says, taking in the patchy walls. Ken's house is immaculate.

'It's a big job.' I put the kettle on and hope by the time it's boiled, Dorothy will have seen we don't hate her and leave.

Dorothy unrolls what look like plans. They are plans.

'Everyone has objected to our plans. There are some terrible letters on the council website. We're only going up two metres at the front. You haven't objected. Why haven't you objected?'

'Do you want me to?'

'Are you going to?'

'I hadn't planned on doing.'

Dorothy starts wailing. Ken puts his hand on her shoulder like he's supposed to and removes it as soon as she stops sniffing.

I make them a cup of tea.

'I didn't know you had plans,' I say.

Dorothy looks dumbfounded. 'You haven't seen them? Everybody knows we have plans.'

'I don't.'

'You don't check the council planning portal?'

'Sounds like some sort of time travel thing.'

Ken grins at this. I have amused a retired accountant. I must be really funny.

'Everybody checks the portal.'

'I don't.'

I take a bottle of beer from the fridge. I hold it up to Ken. He looks at Dorothy. She looks at her watch and shakes her head. Ken waves the bottle away. I slug it back. Dorothy lays the plans on the table. They want to change the shape of the roof of their little cottage to give them an attic room where they can actually stand up.

'Looks all right to me.'

'Really?'

'Yup.'

Dorothy is flabbergasted. 'You'll support it?'

164

'I won't oppose it. I'm all for home improvement as long as I don't have to do it.'

Ken shakes my hand so vigorously anyone would think I'd agreed to some sort of national treaty which could change the lives of thousands of people.

I see them out and I can tell I've made their night. I'm not sure my one vote of support will have much effect on the thirty-two letters of opposition, but it's done quite a bit for neighbourly relations. I think about re-gravelling the driveway. It is nothing more than a fleeting moment of madness.

I grab the hoover. It is as instinctive to me as the PlayStation controller is to Ollie. He has his headphones on and is lost to a world of carnage until I yell at him, several times, to come for his tea.

'Dad, can you please be quiet!' Emma shouts this from the top of the house.

I couldn't be further away, in a bedroom, hoovering. People simply shout from wherever they are and expect me to come running. I turn off the hoover.

Emma is revising. This will come back to me if she fails her exams.

Remember that day when you were hoovering and I was learning Young's Modulus of Elasticity?

No, I will say. (How can you single out one session of hoovering when there are nineteen years' worth to choose from?)

A question came up on that thing and I lost a grade and can't go to the university to do the course I want.

Oh my God, I'm so sorry, I cannot imagine myself saying.

I feed the dogs, cook macaroni cheese, and think about Dorothy and Ken poring over their plans with renewed vigour.

Brigit calls. 'The hospital is heaving. I've got to go down to the Emergency Department to talk to the staff. We've got ambulances stacking up outside.' It was the ambulance-stacking thing again.

165

'I'm cooking macaroni cheese. It's an emergency meal. Teenagers are stacking up outside the kitchen.'

Brigit says something, but it's while she's putting down the phone so I can't quite make it out. It was a short word.

Do I feel resentment? Yes, I do. I check my macaroni cheese while I wait for the peas and garlic bread. It is congealing. I look across the field where every species of British wildlife now lives in the undergrowth, probably alongside a couple of travelling families and a camera crew who used to work with David Attenborough but took a wrong turn and got lost. Hugh Fearnley-Whittingstall could forage in there for hours and probably squeeze a series of books out of it whilst straining some bramble jelly through his sock. The neighbours blame me for their nettles and all the spores the wind takes into their gardens.

Once I tried hiding behind a bush; Harriet Rickard caught me while she was walking her dog. 'Can't you do something?'

'I can't stop the spores and the bees.'

'You could cut it all down.'

'There's too much wildlife. I can't be responsible for killing all those little people. There's all the mice from Brambly Hedge, the snake from the Jungle Book and Peter Rabbit,' which was a lie because he was dead and eating up the crap in our septic tank. A rat scuttled out into the open. Harriet screamed. It was a piercing scream. 'And Samuel Whiskers,' I said. Harriet had already gone by then.

I look out over to the Rickards and imagine order and control, obedient youngsters and people with purpose and non-congealed macaroni cheese. As if it senses my late afternoon malaise, the barn owl appears and hovers over the Rickard's garden. There will be nothing there. Every rodent, snake and edible creature resides in our jungle until the weather gets cold and they begin to make their way to the house where they keep everyone awake and I have to call the pest control man who chucks a bag of rat poison into the loft where the rats then die and stink for six months. I bought a humane trap once, let the rat out into the field and I watched the bugger run straight back to the house. It was there before I was, and up the drainpipe just as rats are supposed to.

Emma and Ollie arrive to eat the macaroni cheese, the peas and the garlic bread. Ruby is with a friend and has taken the car.

'She always has the car,' Emma complains.

I point at her carefully crafted chart.

'No, it's her day.'

'It's always her day. Anyway, you owe me twenty-five quid.'

'It's pounds.'

'For petrol.' This must be the twentieth time Emma has reminded me about the money. I go and transfer it.

I have to leave. I'm going to Ollie's school for an evening on 'The Mental Well-Being of the Child: A Parent-School Partnership'. I can't find out if it's Mr Farquhar who's doing the gig or not. If it is, I'm heading home.

'You will check on Ollie every twenty minutes? He needs to be off his game thing by eight, bath, and reading for half an hour and not watching 'Bad Education' or 'Prison Break.''

Emma grunts.

I have said it. I should be covered. Em will deny it and Claude will have peed on the floor and Ollie will still be gaming when Brigit comes home from a congested hospital where the ambulances are piled five high. The dogs look at me as if to say 'why aren't you feeding us?'. I suppose if that's all you've got to think about, the space between each meal must seem like an eternity, especially when one of our years is equal to seven of theirs.

I don't possess a tie. I borrow one for funerals, but don't go to those if I can avoid them. I find them depressing. All this nonsense about 'a celebration of life' is lost on me. It's people clutching at straws. Our children have not been brought up with any religion.

167

'I'm a humanist,' Ollie declared after an obviously harrowing RS lesson.

'What did the teacher say?'

'That it's avoiding the question. I told her at least it's tangible.'

'What did she say then?'

'I got a behaviour mark for being cheeky.'

'You got a behaviour mark for that?'

Ollie looked sheepish. 'I might've said 'Duh!' at the end.'

'Fair enough. I would have given you two.'

I arrive at the school to find it is Mrs Oliver who is giving the seminar; her of the 'mobile phones are a life skill' and Perfect Fucking Peter for a son who is clearly happy knitting in the evenings and watching the sunset rather than killing a bunch of unarmed, harmless villagers on Minecraft.

'In the end, the mental well-being of our children is down to us.'

I wasn't sure if she was talking about the school, or the parents or this school/home partnership thing which works well when everything's hunky dory but becomes a shit-throwing contest when it's not.

I stick my hand up. It is a fit of pique. I don't know why I've put my hand up. The woman simply irritates me.

'Don't you think the issue of mobile phones should be addressed?' I say.

Parents are nodding vigorously like those dogs people used to have on the back shelf of their cars.

Mrs Oliver fixes me with an icy stare. 'It's a life skill.'

'Yes, but…'

She picks up her papers and like the press secretary for the White House, leaves the room. I do not like Mrs Oliver. I think about slashing her tyres, but I don't know which car she drives and I don't have a knife.

17

BEFORE

Fact: Number of zoos and parks visited (including repeats), 2,785

On the suggestion of Diane Quail, I enlisted in the local pre-school where they were holding the 'music hour'. I was as nervous as a man waiting for the electric chair. I was the ugly duckling frightened to come out of the reeds. I was Bambi staring down the barrel of a 12 bore. It was a pre-school for little children I kept telling myself. I had never been to a proper pre-school for little children before. Perhaps Trevor Mace was the standard of other full time dads. The thought of others like him roaming the darker recesses of these places imagining we might quickly bond and become besties filled me with the sort of impending dread I imagined was commensurate with someone waiting for a genito-urinary investigation by Dick Chaucer.

The previous night I had a nightmare where I was sucked down a huge pipe like a vacuum cleaner, clutching the girls to my chest. Skeletal arms reached through the walls of this tube, trying to snatch them from me. I crashed into a bright, yellow room with immaculately dressed women draped casually over furniture and perfect children doing perfect things. I sat in the middle of this room. Naked. My first instinct was to make sure the girls were unhurt and clothed. They were, but rather than the pink suits they wore when we left the house, they were wearing rags like Dickensian children. I grabbed a copy of The Tiger Who Came to Tea to cover my modesty. The women hugged their children to their chests and turned away in disgust. I awoke in the early hours covered in perspiration.

The car park in the village hall was full of vans and four by fours. I parked my Ford Sierra Estate with rotten sills and one hundred and sixty thousand miles on the clock in the far corner. I sat for several minutes getting control of my breathing. The village was quiet. The men had all disappeared into their world and I was about to invade the women's.

I took the girls out of the car and loaded Ruby and Emma into the double buggy, which was once called a pushchair. I could hear children shouting from within the hall. It sounded busy. I wanted to turn around and go home and watch the inane rabbit in the Hundred Acre Wood singing about 'trying a little something new?'

I took a deep breath.

A sea of buggies stood in the entrance hall. My heart was pounding. I hadn't been that anxious since asking Shirley Dawson to go to the cinema when I was sixteen. (She told me to 'fuck off'!)

I had two children who couldn't walk and one who could. I shunted the door open with the buggy and the thing got stuck. Women were staring at us. I almost threw in the towel which I could really have done with at that moment because I was sweating the sort of sweat people produce when they're in such a state of anxiety there's a chance they might never recover.

Then I saw Marlon the Music Man. He was another man. Perhaps this was it. Perhaps Marlon the Music Man would become my friend?

There were maybe twenty women sitting in a circle with children on their laps, sitting very nicely as they do in that utterly deceptive volume, 'The Complete Guide to Childcare' where there is a whole section on 'grounding the

170

child'. Marlon the Music Man was sitting in the centre of the circle with his legs crossed. I did a little coy wave. I wish I hadn't done a little coy wave because as soon as I did it I knew it didn't look good. Marlon waved back. (After Trevor Mace, I was wary of being too friendly.)

Marlon suddenly started singing, softly and sweetly like a choirboy at the altar. I could already see Marlon and I were as contrasting as the Ramones and Pavarotti.

Diane Quail appeared in front of me. 'Hey, it's so good you could come. With all three! That's brave.'

I hadn't thought of leaving a couple of them at home. It was illegal.

Diane helped me with the buggy. 'Marlon's only just started. Do join in.'

Join in? Join in? With the little soprano in the middle of the room? I really didn't fancy doing a duet with Aled Jones!

Marlon was singing about a drum which was being passed around the circle from mother to mother, and then from musically gifted child to even more musically gifted child. The mothers were passing two sticks and helping the children to tap the drum. I sat down with Ruby and Emma wriggling like maggots in my lap and Chloe hanging onto my hair should she drift away and be consumed by this centrifuge of madness.

'Oh, let's pass around the Gathering Drum,' Marlon sang in a voice so high I imagined someone squeezing one of his testicles with a pair of pliers. 'Pass it to one another, to my sister and my brother.'

I couldn't see any other 'brothers'. I was the 'brother'.

Emma grabbed the drumsticks from a little boy who started to cry. I felt no sympathy for him. Emma had only snaffled his drumsticks. In turn, Ruby snatched the sticks off Emma and stuck them in her mouth. People were looking at us as if we might do as a subject for 'Supernanny'. Chloe took the drumsticks from Ruby and threw them at a little girl wearing a miniature wedding dress on the other side of the circle. Both sticks caught the little girl in the centre of the forehead. The child began to shriek hysterically. I thought it was quite an impressive throw. The mother glared at me. People glared at me a lot in those days. In my defence, I wanted to say – just like Shaggy in his song – 'it wasn't me'.

Ghandi, disguised as Marlon in his smock, sitting cross-legged in the centre of the circle with his retrieved Gathering Drum, spoke slowly and calmly like those sort of people do. (Whatever he was on, I needed three times the dose.) 'A last song?'

People nodded enthusiastically. He didn't get a squeak out of me. I was happy for him to call it a day and bugger off. We wouldn't be forming one of Brigit's 'bonds'.

Marlon tortured us with one final song about the pitter-pattering rain and 'galoshes' – a word never used north of Watford or since the early 1900s by people in large country houses, as far as I knew. Marlon finished the song, dragging out every last crochet like a series of impacted molars, leaving us hypothetically soaking wet. Some of the mothers took this concept the full nine yards and actually pretended to dry themselves off. The madness was well and truly within them. Or maybe I was trapped in an Orwellian nightmare?

In a few well-practised moves, Marlon had his Gathering Drum and glockenspiels packed in his case and, with a little backwards wave, he was out of that place as quickly as Usain Bolt. I imagined the lucky bastard locking himself inside his Astra van with the funky rainbows lighting a roll-up with special leaves and swigging heartily from a hip flask before his next appearance at a village hall near you. Beware of The Gathering Drum!

The women remained in their circle chatting about the Gathering Drum as if there was a lot to say, and wasn't Marlon the Music Man 'the best thing'? The best thing since what? The last time someone brought some ancient and dubious pagan ritual to a children's playgroup?

I glanced around the circle of twenty women. What was the probability that seventeen of them were actually blonde? I should have checked my Gregor Mendel fact-sheet, I thought to myself, before moving on to consider how ironic it was that the Father of Genetics was a celibate monk.

A jaded-looking middle-aged woman with a face as furrowed as a ploughed field sat down next to me.

'You've not been here before. I'm Paula Butler, the pre-school leader. Been here for twenty years.' She said this like a woman who'd given up any prospect of parole. This was the damage twenty years of day-in-day-out childcare could do to a face that no amount of cement-like foundation could hide.

'No. It's my first time. Can't you tell?'

'Just make yourself at home. Everybody's really friendly. Your wife's Brigit Wheeler.'

'We're not married.'

'She's got her work cut out. I wouldn't do her job for all the tea in China.'

I got this a lot. Firstly they don't pay Brigit in tea, and secondly the people who tended to say this couldn't do the job if their lives depended on it.

Paula Butler wandered off to chat to the elderly woman behind the kitchen flap who was holding a teapot the size of a large watering can and, due to its weight, beginning to shake like Ozzy Osbourne.

A young woman with a big smile and lots of piercings came up to me. She was pretty, but stained around the edges by years of cheap roll-ups.

'It's great to see a man looking after the children,' she said. 'We always shared in the commune. Not something you normally see around here.'

The women were now bearing plates of exotic fruit you can only get from Waitrose or Asia. Ruby and Emma were crawling at speed. Chloe was already knuckle deep into a bowl of lychees and spitting the stones onto the floor.

'I'm April,' the young woman said. 'This is my daughter, October.' A little girl wearing a bright-red dress and bangles clung to April's leg.

I pointed at Chloe, Ruby and Emma who were diving into the fruit.

'We have a baby. He's at home with my life partner,' April went on . 'He's called Mick. He's a spiritual guru. We're only here for another week and then we're going back to the commune. It's in Spain. This isn't the life for us.' She leant into me conspiratorially and whispered: 'These women are all wearing disguises.'

'Disguises?'

'Oh yes,' she said with confidence. 'They're playing a part. They're frightened of being themselves, you see, so they have to be like one another. They're scared of revealing weakness, for fear of being torn apart by the others. You're not wearing a disguise,' she added.

I was wearing jeans, boots, a red shirt and a brown leather jacket.

'You might as well be naked.'

'Really.' I thought about my dream and my own fear of exposure. It was uncanny.

'We have to go,' April said. 'We only come for the music. Marlon's so wonderful. So connected with his centre. Sings like an angel.'

'He does.'

October held my hand.

'Is she called October because it was when she was born?'

April looked at me as if I were insane.

'It means 'precious jewel'. Time has no meaning in the commune. We live by the planets.'

I watched April leave, October in her arms. I saw them through the window, getting into a large green van, driven by a man with dreadlocks. It must have been Mick taking a break from being a spiritual guru.

174

One of the blonde women with two little boys in tow came up to me.

'I'm Claudia Bingham.' Claudia held out her hand. She was pale, thin and tall. 'You're with Brigit Wheeler.'

'I know.' I introduced myself. The girls were involved with the soft play.

'You look after your children some of the time, I believe?' Claudia said.

'All of the time actually. That and other things.'

'Oh. Other things. That sounds mysterious.'

'I write books.'

Claudia was suddenly interested.

'Really? Super. My husband's written a book. He's a builder, Robert. If you need a builder, he does all the work around here. It's going to be a movie.'

'Right.' A builder who had written a book being turned into a movie. I felt not an ounce of pleasure for him.

'I'll look you up,' Claudia promised.

I actually thought about giving the name of another author with books actually on the shelves. 'Nothing published yet, I'm afraid.'

'Oh.'

'In progress.'

'Robert's is out in October. A thriller. His agent thinks it'll make The Times best seller list. Very topical.'

'Is it about building?'

Claudia laughed at this and touched my arm. 'Oh, that's very good.'

The old lady had put down her gargantuan teapot and appeared at my side bearing a plate of custard creams.

'I used to bring my children here,' she said with a wistful look in her eyes. 'Everything's changed now. It's all so different.'

'This is Elsie. She helps out. Don't you, Elsie?' Claudia said.

I'm amazed she didn't pat the old girl on the head.

'I'm eighty-four,' Elsie said. She looked it. 'My daughter is sixty-one now. It was all a long time ago. It flies by so quickly. Make the most of it while you can.'

A woman with a very long nose came over. She peered at me from either side of her significant proboscis. 'I'm Angela Wallace. Roger Wallace, accountant, if you need one.'

'Right.' I didn't think I would have need of an accountant for quite some time.

'You're Brigit Wheeler's—'

'I know.'

A short fizzy woman, again with blonde hair, came bounding over with another woman, much taller and also with blonde hair. Anyone would have thought the Vikings had arrived, the men heading off for another rape and pillage fest while the women folk looked after the sprogs.

'Jilly Green,' the short woman said, shaking my hand firmly. 'Brigit Wheeler.'

This random throwing of names was quite disconcerting. I wondered if I should have responded. Perhaps with 'Elvis Presley' or 'Stig of the Dump'. The blondies were coming at me. The other woman was wearing leggings and a pair of muddy running shoes. She looked as if she'd romped over the fields.

'Quicky,' this woman said. I wondered what she meant. 'Olivia Rayner. We know you're with Brigit Wheeler. My husband is orthopaedic. Chris, Chris Rayner.'

An image of him sitting in a wheelchair flashed at me.

Olivia regarded me with a sad, sympathetic look. 'Chris says despite what Brigit does, we have to remember she is still a person.'

Someone put a hand on my shoulder. I turned to see Diane Quail.

'We're all sitting down now,' she said.

I rounded up the girls. I watched Olivia Rayner as she arranged her two boys on her lap, totally unaware of the impact her words had made. A woman sitting next to Olivia, a crying baby on her knee, sobbed quietly. Diane Quail sat down next to her and rubbed her back.

'Beatrice', Paula Butler who was sitting next to me whispered. 'Post natal. She's on the radar.'

'She looks very upset.'

'Husband works away. On the oilrigs. She only sees him a couple of times a year.'

We sang a few nursery rhymes I was to become so familiar with I could sing them backwards.

It was still raining when we left. The women came out of the car park. I could hear them organising play dates. I didn't like to ask. I saw Beatrice walking away on her own pushing her baby back to an empty house. I walked up the hill to our house, holding Chloe's hand, Ruby and Emma asleep in the buggy. The rain became heavy. I stood under a tree, the drops hitting the leaves. Chloe started singing 'Pitter patter raindrops, I'm wet through'.

Marlon the Music Man drove past and waved.

18

NOW

Fact: Number of times I wanted to chuck it all in, 840
Number of times I gave up, 0

I go swimming. I can do half an hour before the boredom becomes malignant and threatens to take over every cell in my body. I close my eyes as I crawl along, thinking of how I might restructure my life now that things are so changed and never to return to how they were. There is the house. There has always been the house, beseeching me to attend to its shortcomings. There are books to write in the spirit of Ernest Hemingway and maybe another stab at becoming Hugh Fearnley-Whittingstall.

There are four women in the pool, walking four abreast up and down. I stop and tune into their conversation.

'Her husband had an affair with her best friend,' the woman on the far right with the drinker's face says very loudly. The other three women look knowingly at one another. 'Never recovered. You wouldn't, would you. My Derek never strayed.'

I am the youngest person here because everyone else is retired. I am not retired. Instead, my hours have been reduced.

'I haven't seen you here for a while,' a man with white hair and a belly the size of a yoga ball says as I get changed.

'No. I've been busy.'

'I'm eighty-two. I've got ten grandchildren, and I swim fifty lengths every day.'

Bully for you.

He pats his belly as if it is a benefit of all this exercise.

I pull on my clothes, even though I am still wet, and leave. I don't want to talk to anyone about my life, especially an eighty-two-year old with ten grandchildren who looks as if he might be on the verge of giving birth to a couple more!

I drive to the library. The parking man is walking around the cars checking the tickets. He eyes me with relish.

'I'm just getting mine,' I tell him.

He gives me a threatening look.

I run to the machine.

He is still standing by the car when I get back. 'Nice car,' he says.

'It's a Skoda.'

'Yeah. Shame they don't change the badge. I don't think they'll ever shake off the image of it being the poor man's car.'

And here was me thinking it was the 'smart person's car'. I suddenly have a surge of deep resentment for Richard Quail and his Ferrari.

I go and get a latte. If he's there, I buy the young guy selling the Big Issue an Americano. I do this because I am lucky. I have a family and people who care about me. I have never lived on the street. I buy a copy of the Big Issue. Hugh Fearnley-Whittingstall beams out at me from the front cover. He is launching a campaign about reducing sugar and tackling the retail giants. What happened to the man who championed the blue carrot?

Libraries used to be quiet places for reflection and meditation. The librarians were always unmarried women who wanted absolute vacuum-like silence in which they could bury their own loneliness along with all the other lonely people as they tried to decode the unfathomable reference system in search of an elusive book on the

Guatemalan Red Spotted Beetle. Libraries aren't like that now. They are places of colour and light where people come to chat and drink tea. I wonder where all the old librarians went. Is there a place where old librarians go when they are done being dour and sad?

I find a table by the children's books. There is a small group of children in a circle with their mothers, cuddling characters from TV programmes I have never seen. I set up my computer, drink my coffee because you can eat and drink in libraries too. I have come to work on this book.

More children start to appear. I stop trying to write this 'great work' and watch them, aware that a man in his late fifties watching toddlers never looks good from the outside. I don't know any of the mothers, so I turn away and stare at a blank screen. Nothing comes. The 'great work' is destined to be a pamphlet at this rate. I think about Brigit and her packed day. I feel like someone who has worked for years in darkness and now, turned out into the light, I am blinded and rendered still. Brigit hasn't got time to reflect. I didn't used to have time to reflect. Looking after children for many years doesn't warrant reflection. It warrants getting on with it. Reflection, I'm beginning to think, should be left to mirrors and perfectly still ponds.

I examine the Bakewell slice I bought from the shop. It is gluten and wheat free and suitable for vegetarians and all the other dietary fanatics with the time to think about what's happening in the large intestine. Below the name it says 'filled with imagination'. 'Yes and fuck-all else,' I say loudly enough for an elderly woman nibbling a dry organic teacake opposite to give me a wrinkly scowl.

Someone starts banging a drum so expertly, I turn around to look. I am so shocked, I start to cough over my latte. It is Marlon the Music Man. It is definitely him, still wearing his Totnes smock. It's probably the same one from seventeen years ago when I took the girls to the playgroup for the first time. Marlon passes the drum to the first child who promptly puts the stick into its mouth. I think of our

180

girls and feel wistful. (Surely 'wistful' is for elderly people nearing the end of their time.) Marlon snatches it back. He was always very protective over his instruments. I spot a book on a shelf with the title 'Quick Reads'. The title is 'Breaking Free of OCD'. I think of taking it out and giving it to Marlon as a gesture for the weeks of torture he subjected me to.

Marlon is grey and thinning. Who wouldn't be, playing a bunch of homemade instruments in the age of iTunes, drum and bass and every conceivable childhood distraction? Who wants a wooden flute and a stick with a bell on the end in a time where encouraging children to Morris Dance is a form of abuse? Marlon is a testament to dogma and 'other world stuff', to a belief that the past can prevail. I think of April and October from the playgroup and wonder where they might be now, and whether October has changed her name to Tracey or Susan. Maybe April is working in the city with a penthouse apartment and the trappings of a capitalist fat cat. You can only chew wholegrain for so long before the stomach dissolves itself with hunger.

Marlon is engrossed with a glockenspiel in the way only someone like Marlon could be. Here's the thing though, the bludgeoning irony that hits me like a smack in the teeth: Marlon is still doing his thing. He is still making it work. He and I could be the same age, but he doesn't look lost. He looks at home, in the place he should be and not flailing around like a lanky tomato plant that has come away from its stick. Where I used to envy Marlon for being able to leave, I now envy him for being able to stay. My children are leaving me and I will be left like someone in a village hall after the dance when the music has stopped, the lights have come on and everyone, except the caretaker with a grudge against people having a good time, has gone.

Marlon packs away his Gathering Drum. I want it to be the same one Chloe and I held all those years ago when I was the only man in a sea of what seemed like hostile women, when they were just as anxious as I was. Marlon looks across at me. He can see I am staring. He comes over.

'Hi,' he says. 'How are you? Was it Chloe and then the twins?'

'Ruby and Emma.'

'That's it.'

'You remember?'

'Oh, yes. I always remember the little people. I'd be out of a job if it weren't for them. And I remember you. Not hard when you were the only man. Not easy. Even now.' He gestures to his group. 'Only women.'

'Do you ever meet any men looking after their children?' I sound faintly desperate; someone never quite able to give up the search for another of his kind.

'From time to time. Very few who do it day after day like you.'

'Chloe's just started at university.'

'No! I remember she had those beautiful big eyes.'

I want to hug this man, Marlon, in his smock and his van with the rainbows, which is probably a cube in some scrap yard. He remembers my girls. He remembers me. I have this ridiculous thought: maybe we could be friends? Maybe we were destined to meet, here in the library where once it was silent and now we can talk.

'Yes, she's still got those beautiful big eyes.'

He laughs at this. A truly genuine laugh.

'You're still going strong then?' I say.

'I can't stop. It's like being a parent, I guess. You never retire.' He waves his arm in the direction of the now chattering children. 'These are my children. We couldn't have any. It's such a privilege. I think they'll carry me out in a box from one of my lessons.'

'That would be quite a sight.'

We laugh together, Marlon and I. It will of course be a cardboard box surrounded by people wailing to some obscure Native American chant.

'I have to go,' Marlon says. 'Duty calls. Perhaps I'll see you here again. I'm always here on a Wednesday.'

I make a point of noting the day.

He notices the empty screen on my laptop. 'Waiting for the muse?' he asks.

'Something like that. Nothing coming.'

'Write what you know. Write about a man looking after his kids. The women seem to be doing very well on it.'

We shake hands. I watch him weave his way between the bookshelves with his bag of tricks like the Pied Piper with a job well done. It is eleven o'clock. I never thought I would look forward to seeing Marlon the Music Man. He is part of my history and I am part of his. We will be forever bound by the glockenspiel and the Gathering Drum. I try to write, but have to concede. Perhaps this hasn't been a wasted morning and might indeed be the first torn fragment of a much larger and detailed map I might use to find my way back to that person I once imagined I used to be.

I return to my car to see a note tucked under my windscreen wiper. It says...

Nice to see you. Perhaps we could have a cup of something next week. Marlon. Below he has written his mobile number. Did I ever imagine I would be drinking herbal tea with Marlon the Music Man? Probably not.

19

BEFORE

Fact: Number of picnics made containing animal-shaped sandwiches, 1,276

In 'The Complete Guide to Childcare' it didn't say how to fill a whole day. A day is a long time in the life of a child carer when the concentration span of an infant is about as long as it takes to eat a designer meal. This meant at least twenty individual activities every day to prevent a mutiny. On those glossy pages of 'The Complete Guide to Childcare' was a lot of dense text about emotional well-being and making sure children are stimulated in lots of different ways so their brains get 'three hundred and sixty degree exposure to the world'. Times three I calculated that to be one thousand and eighty degrees. The idea of a centrifuge passed briefly through my addled mind.

I had responsibility for not one, but three children to socialise and integrate into a world where their welfare outweighed my finer feelings by an infinite proportion. Where I come from there is a saying, 'if it doesn't kill you, it'll make you strong'. I wasn't dead; I was the sort of tired one feels with a protracted bout of glandular fever. I assumed I must have been strong. I stopped looking for a male childcare role model and someone I could aspire to be and realised he was in the mirror and looking like shit. I could whine all day long, or I could roll with it and whine at night to Brigit when I could no longer sing 'Tom Tom, the Bloody Piper's Son'. Quite frankly, I didn't care if Tom had stolen a litter of puppies, put them into a bin bag and slung them into the canal.

'Wine?' Brigit said when she came through the front door and immediately embraced each of our daughters with seamless delight.

I took it as a literal invitation and quaffed half a bottle straight from the fridge before handing her a small glass so I could neck the other half as I filled my glass.

'Good day?' she said.

I walked straight into it every time. Of course I'd had a good day. I'd spent it with our three beautiful children, helping to shape them with my tuneless singing. It was an impossible question, like someone asking if you're happy at knifepoint. If you refer to 'The Complete Guide to Childcare', I was living in frigging paradise 24/7!

'We watched a programme about a 'blue cow'. It got on a bus and went to places across the world. I'm writing to the TV people. It confuses the kids. We spent an hour looking for a blue cow getting on a bus. Then we had cow for tea. The girls made the connection. There was a lot of crying until I pointed out that particular cow wasn't blue. It cheered them up.'

'What fun,' Brigit said.

I imagined Brigit's day with meetings and coffee and difficult conversations about health funding and people who wouldn't do what they were bloody well told or paid to do. Brigit was good at this, has remained more than good at this for a lot of years until even her most ardent detractors have had to concede to this view.

'Yes, it was fun.'

The girls were sleepy. We put them to bed. I fell asleep on the sofa.

Brigit prodded me. 'You can't just fall asleep. I want to hear everything about them.'

I was no more capable of giving Brigit what she wanted than resurrecting myself from the dead.

Under the avalanche of nappies and regurgitated food, I couldn't see anything beyond treading water in a sea of domestic repetition. I was however becoming pretty good at what I did. I was staying afloat, and I was keeping the children safe, and I was beginning to believe there was a 'blue cow' who caught a bus every Tuesday from outside her field and went to places like the moon and the supermarket where the meat counter must have come as a bit of a shock. I was doing fine; until I met a man called Danny Ray and realised how much I needed Trevor Mace or someone truly on the back foot to help me shine.

'Danny Ray's coming down this morning with his triplets,' Angela Wallace told me. She was glowing like a woman in the midst of a hot menopausal flush. 'His wife, Cortina, buys some of her clothes from me when she's down from town.'

(I came to understand that 'down from town' meant coming from London to visit the country pile and make sure the locals were keeping it in order.)

'My first car was a Cortina,' I informed Angela. It was a heap of shit. I had to rebuild the sills with fibreglass.

We were singing a song about vegetables and holding up pictures of long carrots and voluminous cabbages, which did nothing to inspire my feelings of well-being when my vegetable patch resembled a piece of ground subjected to extensive nuclear testing. I felt a breeze of autumn air on my back. Everyone turned and there he was, an apparition in the doorway of the village hall. I hated Danny Ray on sight. Looking back, I now realise that surge of angry, vitriolic emotion was utterly justified.

Where I had streaks of yoghurt on my jeans and a shirt that looked like someone had taken it, screwed it into a ball and thrown it back at me, Danny Ray looked like someone fresh out of wardrobe and make-up in an advert for

186

Christian Dior. I would have been hard pressed to get a walk-on part behind Henry Cooper in an advert for Brut 33.

'Hi,' Danny said, scanning the women, their jaws resting on the soft heads of their children sitting in their laps. Danny had a voice smooth enough to make even a baby's bum feel like sandpaper. He gave a coy little wave.

I felt this surge of anguish. *Fuck off my manor* I wanted to hurl back at him. *With your wife who has the name of a 1970s car and your three little sprogs dressed like miniature surf dudes from 'Endless Summer'.* I was too gob-smacked to say anything. I knew it was time to throw in my hand without declaring my shitty cards and just watch this man take all the chips.

Paula Butler, the pre-school leader, almost fell over a plastic vacuum cleaner only the girls seemed to play with, in her desperation to get to Danny and make him feel utterly, undeniably, sick-makingly welcome.

'Oh, hi,' Paula said in a voice she'd probably been saving for Brad Pitt, but Danny Ray would do instead. I didn't recall this type of welcome when I arrived. I couldn't imagine why. 'It's so great you could come. Everyone's here.' It was true; the place was below the Plimsoll Line. Paula looked at me. I thought she was going to introduce me as the sole male, a majestic example of my kind. The sight of me clearly made her change her mind. I was missing Trevor Mace quite a lot. We should have exchanged numbers so we could bemoan people like Danny Ray and talk about our 'issues'.

Danny grinned a last-frame-before-the-credits-roll grin. He looked at Diane Quail and I was certain something almost invisible passed between them. It was obvious to me that Diane had, at some point in her cosmetic dentistry career, had her hands in Danny's mouth, which was big enough for both of them, and transformed his teeth into a set of polished piano keys with a spare octave. I hadn't even brushed my teeth where bits of burnt toast clung to them like the 'before' teeth in the adverts for plaque-busting toothpaste.

'Howdy, everyone,' Danny Ray said.

Who the hell, except the speccy-eyed Milky Bar kid, says 'howdy' and gets away with it? Danny Ray, that's who. The ripple of adulation almost ruffled my hair.

Danny ushered his three little boys into the hall. 'Orson, Clint and Bruce. They're all three years old.' (Of course they were, you dough head. They're triplets!)

We had a break. The well-oiled machine of book corner, free play, farm-based songs and exotic Waitrose fruit had gone to hell in a hand bag – all because a man tinged orange with Liberace teeth had walked into a village pre-school and turned the women into post-pubescent, pre-menopausal jelly.

Jilly Green finally brought Danny Ray over to meet me while the other women took over the entire physical and emotional welfare of Danny's three children with actors' names and neglected their own.

'Danny Ray,' Jilly said proudly as if Danny was something she'd crafted herself and was now making the point that this is what a 'proper man' should look like – not one who looked like he'd rolled in a ditch full of brackish slime.

Danny wasn't very tall, but what he lacked in height he made up with a shield of confidence strong enough to repel a nuclear warhead.

'Hi.' I didn't say howdy.

Danny shook my hand. It was firm and sincere. How I was hoping for Trevor Mace's halibut.

'You must be standing in,' Danny said quite genuinely. I almost lied. Danny's arrival had, it felt, changed the integrity of the atmosphere to the point where every electron in the room was seeking to bond with Danny's outer shell; except mine, of course. They were scrabbling to get away. I wanted nothing to do with this apparently perfect man.

'No, I do this full-time. I do other things, of course.' God, why did I keep saying this?

'Yes, he writes novels,' Jilly said in a perceptibly patronising tone. I honestly thought for a moment that Danny was about to show interest. 'Of course, Danny makes films.' Of course, he bloody well did. 'He's having a break between shooting. His wife, Cortina, is so beautiful.'

Danny tried to look modest, but it was like asking the winner of the Booker Prize not to look pleased. Any possible interest in the million words I'd tapped down to express my inner turmoil lay buried under the landslide of Danny's success. I could've slapped him.

He squeezed my shoulder. He was dicing with death. Then Danny gave me another firm handshake. 'It's really good to meet you,' he said.

I wanted to ask him if this was true. Chloe came over and hung onto my leg like a koala on a branch. 'This is my daughter…'

But Danny had turned back, without so much as a glance at Chloe. 'Catch you later,' he said.

I didn't take Danny at his word then, but he was right; I would see him later. Before Danny departed from the pre-school that morning, he played his hand and threw down at my feet what felt to me, but no one else in that room, like a gauntlet.

'Don't forget Danny's invited everyone to an afternoon of fun and games at his house at two until four. Everyone's welcome,' Caroline Waters announced with such undisguised excitement I thought she was about to collapse under its weight.

Danny waved at us like a retreating celebrity. Then he did the gun-pointing thing. Who the hell does the gun-pointing thing?

'See y'all.'

We went home for teddy-bear-shaped sandwiches and carrot sticks. The girls wanted to wear tiaras and princess dresses. Unbecoming for little princesses, they fought over the dressing-up box and slapped one another. I piled them into the royal carriage disguised as a clapped out Ford Sierra

Estate and followed the gilt-edged invitation to Danny's 'fun and games'. I couldn't wait.

Danny Ray's summer gaff was a vast renovated farm with a multitide of converted barns kitted out with oak and cast iron in a small-secluded valley with CCTV on every approach. Years ago, a cavalry of dairy workers had earned an honest wage before those with the time to dwell discovered it is possible to milk almonds and soya beans and compare the morality of eating cows, but not pets.

I pulled the trusted and still perfectly serviceable Ford Sierra up to the front of the house where a man in some sort of tunic sneered at it and asked me to park it round the back next to a rusted plough and a John Deere tractor on bricks.

Seeing the array of activities on the felt-like lawn, the girls rushed off. Outside the house with substantially more gravel than ours, the man with the tunic handed me some fruit punch.

'It's "sans alcohol",' he informed me with a wink.

The whole day was turning out to be a crushing disappointment.

I ventured onto the lawn clearly managed by the Wembley turf professionals. I found it difficult to take the whole thing in at first. It was like a miniature circus. There was a jester juggling and a woman eating fire. A man in a top hat came over to me and held out a deck of cards.

'Pick one. Don't show me, slip it back in the pack.'

I did as I was told.

'You see that tree?'

There was a card pinned to the trunk. I went over. It was my card, or at least one the same. The man tipped his hat.

'Impressive,' I said.

'Not really. It's a kid's trick.'

'Of course.' I had no idea how he did it, but I did find quite a few cards pinned to trees.

There were tables loaded with cakes and sandwiches, and I saw Caroline Waters and Olivia Rayner actually walking around with trays of canapés for grown ups I had never seen before. There were lollipops hanging from strings and people I vaguely recognised as locals pulling the strings to create a bit of sport. I had lost the girls and I stood on my own watching Danny Ray mingling in the way only someone perpetually used to a crowd can mingle.

Someone tapped me on the shoulder. I turned to see a beautiful woman wearing a white, body-hugging dress suited for a catwalk rather than a children's party. It was like one of those weird art-house films.

'So you are the one,' she said in an accent I recognised.

'The one?' I wondered if she might have been referring to Keanu Reeves in The Matrix.

'The only man among all these women who want to scratch each others eyes out because they want their children to be genius and their husbands to be the best.' She didn't think I was Keanu Reeves then.

I felt a little defensive towards my fellow child carers. After all, this woman standing in front of me looked as if she'd never been anywhere near a child. 'I wouldn't go as far as that.'

'I am Cortina Moldu,' she said. The Cortina I used to own didn't look anywhere near that good.

'Ah, Danny's wife.'

She laughed to reveal another set of perfect teeth. 'We are not married. He already has a wife, but she hates him. I am… how you say?...his bit on the side. But it is okay.'

'So the children aren't yours?'

Cortina put her hands on her hips and did a pout. 'Do I look like I had three precocious little brats kicking about in my belly?'

I looked at her flat, taught stomach. I had to concede that she didn't. She was nothing like the tired women dressed in 'active wear' or old denims, body warmers and hair scraped back in case it dipped in a dirty nappy or a pool of yoghurt. 'No, you don't.'

Even on this autumn day where it threatened rain, the sun came out and shone on Danny Ray and his carnival of fun.

'Where are you from?' I asked Cortina.

'Romania. A little place called Sigisoara. You will not know it.'

'Este un palet fourte frumos.'

Cortina looked at me with wide eyes.

'I used to live near Tirgu Mures.' I had forgotten most of the language, but remembered phrases, which never came in useful until then. We talked about Transylvania. I could sense people watching us, wondering why we so obviously had a connection.

'Life was very hard. Young people want to come to the West,' she said. 'This is better. It is not perfect, but better.'

'I believe Danny makes successful films,' I said.

'You have seen them?'

'No, I don't think I have. Can you tell me the name of one?'

Cortina laughed. 'Let me think.' She put her finger to her fabulous pout. 'Ah yes, Ingrid Does Innsbruck was very successful.' Cortina touched my arm. 'It has been very nice to talk to you.'

I watched her walk away, wondering, not unreasonably I thought, whether Cortina Moldu and Ingrid might be one and the same.

Despite Danny Ray's quick departure to his London life and dubious films, his presence left a tangible buzz among the mothers. I decided to kill it dead. This was my manor, and I was the only male child carer in the village. I was about to show everyone just how stupid I could be in my efforts to remind them, and myself, that I still had what it takes.

Three weeks later when the heavens threatened to drop their load, I decided to throw an 'open house' to counter the man with the teeth, the winning smile and the lottery winner's lifestyle. The girls and I made invitations and distributed them at the pre-school. I booked Marlon the Music Man for an hour. He took some persuading.

'So, what is it exactly you plan to do?' he asked not unreasonably.

'I'm having 'open house' with food and a water slide.' The water slide was a normal slide with a plastic sheet, a hosepipe and a gallon of washing up liquid. Danny had some purpose-built thing supplied by 'posh parties for posh kids' or something like that. There was also a bouncy castle. I had a pile of tractor inner tubes I had spent the morning washing.

Marlon seemed nervous. He was smoking in a way a crack addict without crack sucks on a cigarette to get more out of it. Marlon was an orderly man with an orderly box of instruments, which he packed away in an orderly fashion before buggering off to the sanctuary of his little van for a fag and a quick swig of Jack Daniels. 'Sounds a bit casual?'

'Not at all. All planned. Two until four, games, you, food and then out.' God, I sounded good. I was going for gold.

'Okay, I'll do it. It's my 'office afternoon'. The paperwork can wait. I can just do the health and safety stuff.'

I wondered how much paperwork a Gathering Drum and a box of glockenspiels could actually generate and what the health and safety issues might be concerning the said instruments.

'You don't have to do this,' Brigit said. 'It's something we can do at the weekend, together. They are my children too.'

I didn't tell her this was in direct response to Danny Ray. In a way, if the truth be known, I was using the children as an excuse to get one up. This was a 'me' thing.

'You don't have to be Super Dad.'

Yes, I bloody well did if was going to stop the constant buzzing about Danny Ray. I hadn't quite sunk low enough to tell everyone that Danny made porn movies. I imagined, with his teeth and his winning smile, this little thing might well be overlooked.

I was up at four, making pizzas and cakes. I decorated the field and the house with Christmas and birthday banners because it was nearly my birthday and I had seen a Christmas tree in the window of someone who celebrates Christmas 365 days a year and is sometimes on the local news for being eccentric and once for marrying his dog. I didn't have the sort of budget as Danny Ray. I had yet to make Enid Does Exeter, but I wasn't ruling it out. I was a desperate man, and desperate men do desperate things and all that.

Brigit hugged me as she left for work. 'I'm really proud of you for doing this. The girls will remember this day.' Brigit was right. They still talk about it.

Mothers and children began to arrive, the children bearing their invitations. Despite my resignation that I was the only one of my breed, I was still hopeful for another man to come through the gate who wasn't Danny bloody Ray. At this time, our house was simply partially built and not as it is now; an apocalyptic aftermath of artistic differences where people have spilt their decorative intentions on the walls, making it more like something a lunatic with twenty pots of paint might produce, rather than a bad bit of graffiti.

'I always thought this place had such potential,' Caroline Waters said, as she came through the warped front door. 'In the right hands, of course.' She obviously didn't mean ours. She had, on reflection, made a fair point.

I had laid the pizzas out on the table with cheese straws, carrot sticks from the garden and a bowl of oven chips not from the garden.

'This is amazing,' Jilly Green said, taking a chip and breaking it in half. Turning to Olivia she said, 'God, I have to be careful. I've had so much already today. I had a whole pack of Marks and Spencer's prawns. I'll be piling on the pounds.'

Olivia looked Jilly up and down. 'Yes,' Olivia said. 'It is a challenge.'

Jilly disappeared to the toilet where I assumed the aforementioned prawns were chucked up down the U-bend.

Children, in the same way as fluid, I have discovered, quickly occupy a space. They were already up the slide and the thing was rocking from side to side. I hadn't considered the potential for it to collapse. I had other things like nut allergies, dairy intolerance and Linda McCartney to worry about before the collapse of my structures. I ran to the slide, soaked the plastic sheet with the hosepipe, squirted enough Fairy Liquid to wash a thousand dishes and still keep your hands as soft as a baby's arse and shoved Charles Julian down the shute. He squealed with delight until he hit the end of the sheet and continued across the grass where he stopped abruptly in front of my compost heap. A lump of nicely rotting and warm vegetation landed on his head. He looked like Wurzel Gummidge with his screaming head on.

Jilly Green started running, her short muscular arms pumping like an express train, making the sort of noise frogs make when in the jaws of a cat. 'Oh my God! Oh my God!'

Other mothers started to run. It was a stampede of mothers! I guess the possible future Minister for Overseas Development should not have to harbour the memory of having shit on his head. Charles Julian continued to scream as if that alone might beam him out of the situation. Jilly picked Charles Julian up and then dropped him because he was slimy with Fairy Liquid and he was quite a chunky child.

Diane Quail, who was now by my side, started to laugh. 'Oh God, I shouldn't,' she said trying to cover her mirth with a hand sporting a diamond ring normally only seen on relatives of the Royal Family, 'but you couldn't make it up.'

'Oh, go on. Laugh at will,' I said. 'Did you do Danny Ray's teeth?'

This made Diane laugh all the more. 'Are you serious? I don't do second-rate work like that. Besides, the man's an arsehole. I wouldn't want his filthy mouth around my handiwork.'

I was beginning to feel the spring coming back into my step.

I had constructed an obstacle course from ladders and a dismantled climbing frame from the Early Learning Centre, for which I could never understand the instructions enough to put the thing together properly. If Dave at Tumble Tots could get away with it and charge a fiver, I felt justified in constructing my contraption for free. This was war, and I was bloody well going to win.

The sun came out. People gathered on a rug with the pizzas. Marlon arrived.

'This is lovely,' he said.

God, even Marlon the Music Man was impressed! I was on a roll. He got out his kit and the Gathering Drum sparkled in the rays of heavenly light streaming down on the grass despite looking like a head with patches of alopecia.

We sang about the seasons changing and lawns being jungles. The kids clapped. I clapped. Even Caroline Waters was smiling. This was my moment. I was back in the game.

I don't know if it was bitterness over his humiliation which prompted Charles Julian to open the large pen and let out the three turkeys, the ten chickens, the four geese and Roy the cockerel. Roy was at the vanguard. He had never forgiven me for bashing in the head of one of his wives with an empty Budweiser bottle on that moonlit night. I should have returned him, but I couldn't face the humiliation of telling Jim at the chicken place or the thought that Roy might be dispatched to the big hen house in the sky.

Roy stomped into the centre of what Marlon called his 'circle of joy'. Roy fluffed himself up. Some of the children delighted at the sight of Roy. He started running at the kids. Realising Roy meant business, mothers grabbed their offspring and ran. The dissipation of people prompted the chickens and the turkeys to hit the pizzas like an angry mob. Caroline Waters' children, Guy and Sarah, chased one of the turkeys. It dropped to the floor stone dead with, what I

196

discovered later, was a heart attack, and not uncommon in a 'distressed' turkey. I assume it must be a very common affliction during the Christmas period. Roy had children running for their lives with mothers in hot pursuit. I saw Charles Julian open the gate to the recently purchased pigs. I ran as fast as I could towards the little bastard. Roy was away and two pigs were gone before I managed to stop the third from breaking out. I watched the porkers head across the grass towards the sausage rolls where they bit into chunks of their distant relatives. Marlon was gathering up his instruments as fast as he could. This never happened to Hugh Fearnley-Whittingstall.

'Oh my God!' people shouted. But God was doing fuck all to intervene despite our house being only a few hundred metres from the church. I watched the pigs run out of the gate and onto the road. It was like dropping a box of bacon down a bottomless well.

'Stop them!' I shouted at Olivia Rayner who was holding James and Johnny and in no position to run after two Gloucester Old Spots.

'Don't be so bloody stupid!' she shouted.

Harriet Rickard was running in circles trying to catch her three children with Roy in hot pursuit of Harriet's backside. I lunged for Roy and caught him. I sustained a two-inch gash on my forearm and bear the scar today. I pinned him to the floor and wedged his neck with my bleeding arm.

'You bastard!' I said as I put my mouth as close as possible to where I suspected cockerels might have an ear. He eyed me with his beady eye and he knew; that big blue fucker knew what he'd done, and he was proud. He knew I was thinking of sending him off to the big chicken pen in the sky to become a burning star along with all the other chickens we'd been through over the years. He knew this, and he was having his day by ruining mine. My blood was dripping into his beautiful plumage. We were both breathing hard.

'I'm going to let go of you,' I said. I don't know why I imagined Roy could understand me. Perhaps I'd watched too many films where out of control animals become tame and communicate with their owners. I lifted my arm. Roy got up. We looked at one another. He went for my eye, took a chunk out of my eyebrow instead and went off in pursuit of a juicy child.

There was poultry everywhere, including my dead turkey. Chloe, Emma and Ruby were knelt around it, stroking its feathers and caressing its ugly testicular-looking head and sobbing. I thought about the vast hole I'd have to dig and whether I could chuck Roy in as well. Suddenly, I saw an old woman standing in the midst of the carnage of pizza slices, fairy cakes and sausage rolls strewn across the grass. I thought I was hallucinating. I thought maybe it was some old hag come to cast a forgetting spell so that this catastrophe would not exist as a horrific memory and spawn a thousand children's nightmares. I went over to her, blood seeping from my arm and my eyebrow like a victim of Mike Tyson.

The old woman was very small and wore a furry coat made from a number of animal skins. They must have been very cold without them. She looked at me with rheumy eyes and held out a hand so distorted with arthritis it looked like the twigs from Brigit's Easter tree.

'I'm Millicent,' she informed me. 'My daughter dropped me. You've been having a lovely time. Children and animals go very well together.'

'I'm afraid the party's over. Are you collecting someone.'

'No,' she said. 'I used to live here. Mind you, it didn't look like this.'

'No, I'm sure it didn't.' I have learnt over the years it is better not to go back to places you once knew because invariably someone has ruined it beyond human imagination.

'Still, everything changes. Except those.' Millicent was pointing at a row of pine trees at the far side of the field. 'They're seventy-five years old.'

'That's amazing. How can you tell? I thought you had to count the rings.'

'I planted them when I was ten. With my father. He died fifty years ago today.'

'Oh, I'm sorry to hear that.'

'Don't be sorry. It was a long time ago. Oh,' Millicent said, suddenly distracted. Roy was no more than a metre away and eyeing this frail woman with what I recognised as bad intent. She had so little meat on her, I wondered why he was bothering. 'You have a Blue Orpington.'

'Best keep away from him.'

'Oh no. They're very friendly.'

'This one isn't.'

Millicent held out her knotty hand.

'I think you'd be better…'

Roy edged towards her. Millicent bent down and stroked the bugger's back. 'He's lovely.' Finished with being petted, Roy wandered off to attack another child.

People were leaving. I saw Marlon drive away at some speed, fag on and smoke billowing through the open window.

'I wonder if I could sit down by the trees,' Millicent said. 'I'd like to sit and think about my father for a little while, say a prayer or two.'

I considered telling Millicent that if there was a God he most definitely was not in our garden that afternoon. He was probably being nice to people who weren't trying to upstage some porn filmmaker and do a variation on Hitchcock's 'The Birds'.

'Of course.' I carried a chair to the trees and left Millicent contemplating them and the seventy-five years which had passed since she dropped the seeds. I imagined she might need some time. I decided then to shelve my plans to cut the trees down for firewood, just in case Millicent was back to commemorate another milestone in her father's afterlife.

I have learnt that saying sorry is enough if it suits the occasion. 'Sorry' suited this occasion about as much as a bald man suits a parting. People were drifting away. Some of the children were holding back to shout at the free range-ness of the chickens, the turkeys, the geese and of course the pigs who could have been on their way to Minehead by then on a bus with Blue Cow.

Diane Quail came over with Jemima and Roddy.

'We had a great time,' Roddy said. 'A really great time.'

I looked into that earnest little boy's face and I could see he meant it.

Diane let go of Roddy's hand and took mine. 'You don't need to be Danny Ray, you know. Just be you.' Diane looked over my shoulder. 'Who's that woman talking to that tree?'

I turned to see Millicent who did seem to be in full conversation with the tree. 'That's Millicent. She planted those trees seventy-five years ago with her dad. He died fifty years ago today. She's come to have a little chat with him.' Just then it started to rain. 'Do you think Marlon will ever forgive me?'

'Oh yes,' Diane said. 'He needs the money.'

I watched the designer buggies leave and tried to herd the poultry and failed. I left them to the pizza slices. I would have to wait for nightfall and hope Millicent would coax God to come back and prevent any repeat carnage.

Chloe, Emma and Ruby sniffed their way through spaghetti letters, dippy eggs and soldiers. Millicent disappeared, leaving her chair and I have wondered since if she ever actually came.

'Has Turkey Lurkey gone to heaven?' Ruby asked.

'Definitely.'

'Where is she now?'

'In the resting place before we have a state funeral.' Turkey Lurkey's resting place was a bin liner in the shed.

I heard the rumble of some heavy machinery in the driveway. I really wasn't in the mood for another weird guest. I opened the front door to see a tractor with a box trailer. A tiny woman, wearing an oily boiler suit with the physique of Sylvester Stallone and the face of someone more suited to a teacher than a farmer, jumped down from the cab.

'I think I have your pigs. They were wandering. You can't have wandering animals. They can be vicious.' She clearly hadn't met Roy. 'Where do you want them?'

'God, I'm so grateful. I thought they were gone forever.' I held out my hand. We shook. She nearly broke my wrist. 'What's your name?'

'Sarah Harper.'

'You don't look like a Sarah,' I said.

'So what would she look like then?'

'Oh, you know what I mean.'

'Not sure I do.' Sarah Harper, I have learnt over the years, does not waste her words on idle chat.

Sarah drove the tractor to my pigpen where the third pig was waiting and disgruntled because it had missed out on the fun. We poured them through the gate.

'You look after your three children then?'

'Yes.'

'I see the wife driving off in the morning. You must feel like a duck out of water what with all them posh mothers round here.'

'Oh, you know.'

'I do. I've got four.'

'You run a farm and you have four children?'

'Yup. Three are older now, but there's Lucy. Do you want me to send her up?'

'Up?'

'To help out in the evenings. She loves little children.'

I was caught off guard. It hadn't occurred to me to get any help. 'Oh right, that would be lovely. I'll pay her of course.'

'No need. We'll have a bit of your bacon if you can keep hold of them pigs.' Sarah Harper laughed. I knew she was laughing at this townie trying to be something he wasn't at just about every level. There are no flies on Sarah Harper except in the summer when she has cow shit on her boiler suit.

I watched her spin her tractor round and roar off up the road, the pig-less trailer rattling behind her. Apart from Brigit, I have never met another woman quite as amazing as Sarah Harper. After all, Sarah had four children and, single-handedly, with the part-time help of her son, ran a beef farm. I should have felt intimidated. Instead, I have simply been in awe since the day I met her.

Brigit rang. 'My car's broken down! Keep the babies up, please. I need to see them. The AA are on their way.'

'They're falling asleep.'

'I need to see them. I miss them so much.'

If I could have done something about Brigit's 'missing' I would have done. I have often wondered if fathers out working feel the same magnetic pull to gather their children into their arms like a mother hen. I suppose the answer lies in the words 'mother' and 'hen'.

I kept Chloe, Ruby and Emma going. We sang songs, danced and by six I was knackered and losing the ground I never had in the first place. Someone knocked at the door. The girls ran to answer it. It was almost dark. A little blonde girl wearing a yellow dress, a duffel coat and green Dunlop wellies stood on the drive.

'I'm Lucy,' she said. 'My mum says I can come and play with your girls.'

The girls danced with delight. They pulled Lucy into the hallway and then into the front room where they began to show her everything from their books to their dolls. I felt the exhaustion drain from me to be replaced by weariness.

'Would you like a drink, Lucy?'

'Oh, yes please,' she said looking up briefly before turning all her attention back to the girls.

I handed her an orange juice. 'How old are you?'

'Seven.'

On a day when my livestock had tried to kill the local children, my pigs had made a bid for freedom, Marlon the Music Man was probably now looking for a safer job and consulting his solicitor, Millicent had come to talk to her fifty year deceased father, Lucy Harper thankfully walked into our lives.

20

BEFORE

Fact: Number of cheesy- Marmite squares made, 41,341

Lucy Harper came to us every day that summer. I used to pour out my woes and talk to her as if she were my therapist. I used to forget she was only seven. We visited zoos and donkey sanctuaries and the World of Marbles. Ruby took a marble out of a tray. A man wearing a rainbow waistcoat came running over. He wore a panicked expression. I assumed it was because someone had forced him to wear the waistcoat in front of the paying public and look like a right twat at the same time.

'Please put that back,' he said to Ruby.

She put the marble in her mouth.

'Oh, Jesus!' he shouted. 'The whole thing's going to come down.'

I leapt for Ruby and grabbed her.

'There's thousands of marbles on the line.'

Ruby was starting to choke.

'I need the marble!' the man in the waistcoat shouted.

'My daughter is choking!'

Lucy Harper pulled Chloe and Emma aside. They were both crying. 'It'll be fine,' Lucy reassured them. 'Your dad will sort it out. He sorts everything out.'

I turned Ruby upside down and held her by the feet and shook. The marble was heavy. It had to come out. I shunted my knee into the centre of her back. My internal organs were turning to mush. The man was still shouting about his marble.

'They're going to come down!'

'I don't fucking well care!' I yelled back at him. Ruby was turning blue. It was a parent's worst nightmare. 'Come on!' I would have given my life right then to save our daughter from choking. The marble fell from the back of Ruby's throat and dropped to the floor.

The man made a dive for it.

I kicked him really rather hard in the back and shouted, 'get out of the fucking way!'

He rolled over, his head striking the base of the structure holding all his stupid marbles. There was a rattle of things moving above us like thunder. Marbles began to rain from the sky. I grabbed Ruby. Lucy pulled Chloe and Emma out of the way. We stood and watched as the man lay on the ground, marbles raining down on him like large chunks of hail until the ground was covered with shiny, coloured glass.

'See what you've done!' The man pointed a shaky finger at us as he clambered to his feet looking pretty dazed.

'I saved my daughter's life while you were yelling about your fucking marbles!'

'It'll take hours to put this back together! If that little idiot hadn't removed the vital marble this wouldn't have happened.'

I wanted a fight. I wanted to batter him for caring more about his marbles than my beautiful daughter. What sort of a man cares more about marbles than the life of a child? The man at the World of Marbles wearing the twatty waistcoat, that's who!

'Do you have children?' I asked him.

'No, I don't.'

'Stick to marbles.'

Lucy pulled at my hand. 'I think we should go.'

We shuffled through the thousands of marbles scattered across the floor. I kicked a few into the car park.

We sat in the car and I calmed myself down.

'Are you all right?' Lucy asked.

'I'm fine. Thank you.' Once again I forgot that Lucy Harper was only seven years old.

One day, Lucy didn't come. She was helping her mother on the farm. Lucy was in great demand. I decided to take the girls to the beach. It was hot. It was crowded, deck chair to deckchair. I made sandwiches. I might as well have filled them with sand before we left. We crunched our way through them. We were having fun. I fell asleep in the sun and dreamt of a holiday I went on with a girlfriend to Tunisia. I got tonsillitis and took to my bed for a week. My girlfriend had a great time and met a local man called Brane. I remember the walls of the room and a painting with a child running into the sea. I think it was that image which woke me up. My charges were gone! I leapt to my feet. God knows how long I'd been asleep.

It is astonishing how, in times of such crisis, wall to wall nice people become blind to everything and unsympathetic to the fact that I had lost three children under the age of three on a beach.

'Nope,' a man with an Elvis tattoo on his belly said. 'I ain't seen nothing.'

'Surely, someone must have seen them! I mean there's three of them!' I shouted this at the people laid out like the aftermath from the battle of Marston Moor. I scanned the sea of oily bodies. People scream and shout on beaches because that's why they come from the cities and suburbia to let off steam and lose their kids in one fell swoop! I was in anguished agony. My guts were pouring into my feet and pooling on the sand.

'I've lost my kids!' I shouted. I wanted to cry. I actually wanted to let my jelly legs give way and collapse on the sand so someone more skilled, more in control of the situation could take over. The whole sorry saga reeled before my eyes.

I was a fraud. I was a man on a beach with the simple task of looking after three little children and keeping them safe. I had failed. While I was failing, no doubt Richard (I've got a waxy Ferrari and a family with unblemished skin) Quail had removed a couple of brain tumours and changed someone's personality for the better. In the same period of time, I had lost three children.

'I've lost three children!' I shouted again. It was hopeless. Shouting the same thing twice was akin to using the same key to open a lock which clearly didn't fit.

I changed tack. 'Oh Jesus, oh fucking Jesus!'

He wasn't there. Instead, a woman as brown and gnarled as a walnut and wearing many necklaces, came over to me and touched my arm. That was all I needed. I needed someone to touch my arm. In my view, if there was a whole lot more arm touching, the world would be a much better place. So, go touch arm today and make someone who has fallen asleep and lost three little children on a beach in the height of the tourist season feel better.

'It'll be fine,' she said.

I was immediately suspicious. I never trust people, especially grown up children who tell me 'it'll be fine'. I believe this was the root of my distrust along with all the other lies I've been told by 'The Complete Fucking Guide to Child Care' such as 'Your child is taking in your every word'. Yes, but in no particular order, so when they do speak they make no sense or respond when you yell that you've lost them.

I scanned the shoreline. There were hundreds of little children all with parents who hadn't lost them. I was brimming with panic. How was I meant to spot the Three Musketeers from that lot?

'Every child is an individual, who you will instinctively grow to recognise. This is what we call the mother's instinct'.

That was the other thing about 'The Complete fucking Guide…'; apart from pedalling shite, they only referred to

207

the mother when it came to the nitty gritty. The fathers were all too busy drinking wine and watching the telly. I was playing into their hands. I was a father trying to replace the mother when a mother wouldn't have fallen asleep dreaming of tonsillitis while her three little children went on a big adventure on a beach littered with possible paedophiles.

'What do they look like?' the nutty-looking women said.

What do they look like? What do three small children who make as much sense as a raving lunatic look like? The woman had this glazed appearance of someone who might have at some time had a marginal grip on reality, but this was now in the distant past.

'I've got three grandchildren.' She was very smug about this.

I didn't give a tinker's arse whether she had three million grandchildren. 'Yes, and you probably know where they are right now.'

'In America.'

I am not a mean person on the whole. At that moment though I did think a phone call to this woman with the news that her three grandchildren had gone missing in a car park on the outskirts of Washington DC might have levelled the playing field. She was of no use to me.

I left her and started running. I might have appeared as if I knew where I was going, I was running with such a sense of purpose. In fact I was just running. I was Forrest Gump and was going where my legs took me. My knees ached because I'd spent most of the previous three years down on them changing nappies and praying for sleep. I zigzagged between people, sending sand in the air. I apologised the first couple of times and then gave up. I didn't care. I didn't care if that sand permanently blinded them. Everything was reduced to the basic facts. Nothing mattered except my three little charges and the sword of Brigit's wrath and distress hanging over me like that sword of whoever it was. I was shouting. Ruby! Emma! Chloe! I was shouting for people who would not reply because children under the age of three do nothing at all to assist, or make any situation feel marginally better; other than breathe and smear stuff over their faces. They are sadists in the making!

I saw them. I stopped. I felt the vast pressure on my lungs and heart dissipate before the whole shooting match exploded like a zeppelin. They were holding hands by the water's edge, running in and then running out. They were wearing little floppy hats and Ruby was smeared in factor five million sun cream and looked just like the plate face Chloe made; like Michael Myers out of 'Halloween'. They were happy and safe. I was on the verge of hysteria with grief. Someone touched my arm. I turned to see Mrs Walnut standing next to me.

'My daughter is called Charlene,' she said. 'They were all caesareans, but healthy.'

'I've found my daughters,' I said.

She looked at me as if it was me who was casting random facts into the air like the wives of Brigit's colleagues. The woman walked away to speak of leftfield things to other people. I wondered if perhaps someone was frantically searching for her or had deliberately left her and driven off.

I took the girls back to our resting place where Chloe began to projectile vomit. I got a towel and held it to her. The other end exploded too. I grabbed another towel. I began to change her. She continued to vomit. There was sand everywhere. Sand is like water, but gritty. Ruby vomited over the pushchair and followed through. I grabbed the third and fourth towel. I looked at Emma and hoped beyond hope that she had a strong constitution. She didn't. It must have been the ham in the heat, or maybe a bug they all caught at the same time, exactly. Or it was a curse from hell to break me for taking a job that a woman can do so much better.

I ran out of towels, I was changing sand-filled nappies for Emma and Ruby. I resorted to using clothes. People watched in amusement. I am still traumatised by this. I have seen people do the most courageous things in desperate situations. I can only surmise that no one sitting around me saw this as anything other than 'par for the course' in the scheme of things. Children puke. It's what they all do so well. I wondered if they were laughing at me because they assumed I was another incompetent man. They were wrong. I was becoming an expert, and these three little people were my life.

I packed us all up as best I could with the exudate seeping out all over the place. Chloe held onto the double buggy as I hacked across the sand. I reached the car park beyond the dunes and started loading people in. Like a little genie, the old nutty woman appeared by the car. She was not, I concluded, of this earth.

'Have you lost your wife as well?' she said.

I got in the car as quickly as I could and drove away, leaving the stripy beach bag on the floor. I really missed Lucy Harper that day.

21

BEFORE

Fact: Number of baths run, 3,567

The health visitor was a stern-looking woman called Julia Madnam, an anagram waiting to be arranged.

She folded her arms and huffed. 'You've lost both their Child Health records?'

'I haven't lost them. We were late. They're at home. I know exactly where they are.'

'I really do need them for baby's weight and all the other vital things we have to record.'

'Well, if you write it all down or say it to me slowly, I'll write it down and I can put it in the book.'

'Oh no.' Julia Madnam waved her finger at me like a cross headmistress. 'It has to be me. Your job is to look after the book. My job is to provide the data.'

'Ok. I'll bring them in.'

Olivia Rayner looked at me sympathetically, James and Johnny both pretending to read books on the floor at her feet. I noticed Olivia had two folders with the boys names written on each. God, I was falling short at every turn. I needed folders.

Olivia saw me looking at the folders. 'Get a folder,' she said waving hers.

Julia Madnam was examining Emma's neck.

'You need to wipe the creases. There's biscuit in there. It can chafe.'

I went over to look. There were indeed lumps of biscuit in the folds of Emma's neck.

'I think you'll find the Dipro-Base cream will help with the chafing,' Caroline Waters who was sitting on the opposite side of the room pointed out. Olivia nodded her approval. She obviously knew what Dipro-Base cream was. Caroline only had little Sarah with her. The other two were with the nanny. Sarah was also at her mother's feet pretending to read a book intended for 12-16 year-olds because she was 'so advanced for her age'. The kid was one.

There were three other women I only knew by sight watching me now, tuning in to hear the horrors and the consequences of a man looking after his three daughters whilst the mother went out to earn the filthy lucre. I felt like the 'show-stopper', subject to hurtful scrutiny on 'The Great British Bake Off'.

'Do you see anything odd?' Julia Madnam asked me. She held Emma up to the light for everyone in the room to see. I felt like the subject with a rare and shameful disease in a lecture for medical students.

I examined Emma, pretending I knew what I was looking at. 'Odd?' It was like a Spot the Difference quiz. 'No, I can't see anything odd.'

Julia Madnam shook her head in dismay. She reminded me of Jeremy Paxman on 'University Challenge', making the students feel small for being thick. I was expecting her to throw the question over to the other side for a bonus point.

'With the colour of baby's skin?'

I looked at Emma's skin. 'No.'

'What are you feeding her?'

'The very best of everything. We have our own eggs and our own vegetables. I'm setting up as a smallholder. All organic. Peas, broccoli – which went to seed within a day – beetroot, beans, courgettes, pumpkins for Halloween and carrots. You name it, I'm growing it.'

'You said carrots.'

'Oh, God, yes. I've got carrots coming out of my ears. I haven't got the 'staging' right, so they all came at once. Lots of vitamin A. I mean, the kids could find their way out of the black hole of Calcutta, their eyesight's that good. Save a fortune on glasses if everyone did it. I should have brought everyone a bag.' I looked around the room. I didn't get the sense then that a bag of my delicious homegrown carrots would have been very welcome.

'How do you use the carrots?'

This was my chance to show these people who bought their pureed food in little expensive jars from the farm shops who in turn bought the stuff in bulk from Moldova and had it bottled in Basingstoke. 'I use the carrots and some other veg, a little seasoning, boil, butter and then mince it up. They love it. You can see how healthy they are.'

Chloe stopped playing with the little house in the corner and did a dance to show everyone how healthy she was. A point back for my team against Balliol, Oxford.

'The carotene,' Julia said.

'The carrots. They're organic.'

'It's coming out of their skin. If you look, you can see that baby's skin has an orange tinge to it. Look at the other baby.' She pointed at Ruby who was wobbling across the carpet with a nappy the size of a Jewson dumpy bag. Chloe had gone back into the little house and was kicking the cooker because she'd seen someone in our house do that before.

'What do you mean it's coming out of their skin?'

'You've turned the girls orange with too much carotene.'

'What do you mean *I've* turned them orange? You can't turn people orange. Even the Tango Man isn't actually orange, you know.'

'You can actually.'

Olivia Rayner was smirking, her two white and not orange boys at her feet.

'It's okay,' Julia said in a calm voice. 'It's reversible over time.'

I was struggling to see what was okay about an orange child.

'You've been giving them too many carrots.'

'I've got a lot of them. I thought carrots were good for you, help you see in the dark.'

'Nevertheless, you need to give them something else.'

I was thinking about the vast mountain of carrots. I had so many. Hugh Fearnley-Whittingstall would have written a bloody hardback, best-selling book on the 'million and one uses for the carrot' (without turning your children orange!).

I could only see the Tango Man in my mind. I had created two of them.

Chloe was playing in the toy corner and pretending to eat a plastic cream cake. I knew then what Julia was thinking. What she was thinking, was that I was some fanatical self-sufficient maniac who starved my children of yummy food, and that was why my eldest daughter was desperately trying to bite into a plastic cream cake with a still limited number of teeth. Chloe looked at us looking at her. I knew then what she was going to say… I was having what the spiritualists, with their crystals and joss sticks, might call a 'synchronistic' moment. In fact it was nothing more than the truth.

'I don't like carrots. I like broccoli,' Chloe said.

I couldn't look at Julia or any of the other women in the room. This was a thing of nightmares. This was worse than the dream I had about the pre-school. This was worse than turning up naked and sitting in a circle with my equally naked children and beating the shit out of the Gathering Drum.

'I have a glut of broccoli as well. I haven't quite cracked the 'staging' with that either.' I began to feel incredibly sad and, yes, fraudulent. I was in a room of mothers who quite arguably were better parents than I was; simply on the grounds of not turning their children orange.

214

Chloe came out of her little house. I wondered if she was about to do the dance of the orange children. No, it was even better.

'I have green poo,' she declared as she hurled the plastic cake back into the box in preference for a slice of rubber masquerading as a very convincing piece of meringue pie.

The rest of the measurements were conducted in silence. I left with the speed of a missile and the demeanour of a shamed man, two orange children, and the girl with the green poo. I drove home in the Sierra with the exhaust dragging on the ground. I was trying to be a smallholder and a novelist whilst looking after three children under the age of two. Driving home with Meatloaf banging out on full chat to cover the exhaust noise, I didn't feel like a smallholder or a novelist. I just felt small and unpublished.

The two orange children fell asleep. I watched them as they slept, their little orange eyelids flickering as they were probably having nightmares about carrots. I made a chocolate cake with Chloe and between us we ate half the mixture in my effort to give her a diet less influenced by vegetables. Hugh Fearnley-Whittingstall and I hadn't quite parted company at this stage. Flicking through his dessert section, I noticed a chocolate cake made with courgettes. I considered it briefly as I did have a mounting number of big ones, and consigned Hugh to the place where I'd stuffed 'The Complete Guide to Childcare' and its sequel. My children, I realised, were craving sugar and I had given them mainly carrots and broccoli.

The phone rang. It was Brigit. Brigit always rang at the times when my utter incompetence shone like the Kenyan sun.

I was about to tell her about our orange children. 'The children are…'

'Turn on the TV.'

I had started the ironing whilst Chloe also had a snooze.

'Just turn it on,' Brigit insisted.

There was some explosive action film on BBC1 with burning buildings. I flicked the channels, but for some reason the action film on BBC1 was also on the other channels too.

'What am I watching?'

'The World Trade Centre in New York.'

It didn't look real. Everyone remembers the images. Everyone was somewhere when it happened, and they will remember where that was until the day they can't remember anymore. I was doing the ironing. I remember where I was when John Lennon died, but nothing ever, I hope in my lifetime or beyond, will measure up to what happened the day the towers came down.

'Are you still there?' Brigit asked me.

'Oh, my God,' was pretty much all I said before Brigit left me to witness people being torn from their families as every second passed. It wrought human solidarity. What it did for me, as I stood with the iron in my hand watching people dying in colour on a screen while my children slept, was imagine life without them, and that imagined life was no life at all. They were orange, but they were alive and they wouldn't be orange forever. I kissed each one of them and I knew then that this was probably, despite the cliché, one of the most important jobs in the world. If not before, I realised then, this job required the best of me to produce the best of them.

22

BEFORE

Fact: Number of times checked for signs of breathing, 7,342

I bought, on what Brigit later described as 'another unfathomable impulse', six ewes from a man in Exmouth. I took the girls with me. We would be good enough to feature in a Sunday supplement. We were going to show those people existing on fast food in dense suburban areas what a bunch of clever-dicks we were for living off the land, shunning supermarkets and bringing Tesco to its knees, all with a truck-load of happy children less orange than they used to be.

Kevin lived in a caravan in two acres of ground, which looked like it had been strewn with the contents of a septic tank and the garbage cans from a block of flats. He had three pigs. These were very big pigs and would have given the wolf a rocket up the arse before he even had chance to think about blowing any houses down. I had read Hannibal, the sequel to Silence of the Lambs and I knew what pigs could do to people. One day there will be a headline: **PEPPA PIG EATS MUMMY PIG, DADDY PIG AND HER LITTLE BROTHER, GEORGE!!!!!!!** Don't say I didn't warn you.

'Don't mind them,' Kevin said, stepping into the mud in his socks and waving a wheel brace. In my experience, people don't wave wheel braces in the air for no reason unless they're limbering up to remove a very tight wheel. 'They won't hurt a fly.'

A rat, the size of Dick Whittington's cat, ran across the mud, got stuck, watched one of the three pigs charge towards him, and braced itself ready to become lunch. The pig bit the rat in half and that was that.

'They'll hurt rats though.' Kevin laughed at this.

The girls were screaming at the slaughter of Samuel Whiskers and I was sinking in the mud.

The lambs were sweet and fluffy.

'Will you be taking them for the wool?' Kevin asked.

I wasn't that self-sufficient. The thought of spinning had been discarded when I took the bicycle wheel to the tip.

'The meat.'

'Good eaters, these.'

This wasn't helpful in front of Chloe, who hugged one of the lambs. 'I won't let anyone eat you,' she promised.

'Do you deliver?' I asked Kevin. It didn't actually look as if Kevin ever left the swamp.

'They'll be fine in a box.'

'A box?'

'Oh, yeah.' Kevin produced a box and proceeded to stuff the lambs inside. 'You're not going far?'

'Thirty miles.'

'That'll be fine.'

I paid him. I can't remember how much. I do know though that one of my chops was as expensive as a side of lamb from the farm shop down the road.

On the bypass, Emma squealed. I didn't take any notice. We had three daughters. They did a lot of squealing.

'The lambs are out!'

Something brushed my arm. I looked down to see a lamb squeezing between the front seats with the ambition of driving the car. I pulled onto the hard shoulder. I was about to open the door. I stopped. Thank God I stopped. I had a vision of lambs running across the bypass. I could only think of shepherd's pie. I scrambled with the lamb to the back seat and one by one I tried to get them back into the box. I failed. The girls were all squealing with delight, the lambs were pissing and shitting everywhere, and I was hoping Kevin might have been scoffed by his pigs.

'Why?' Brigit asked me when she got home to see the little buggers springing about in the field like Zebedee from 'The Magic Roundabout'.

'I'm a smallholder.'

'Well, you're not, are you.'

'Yes, I bloody well am. I've got pigs, chickens and sheep. I grow veg. If that's not a smallholder I don't know what is. It verges on being a farm. If I had two of each and a boat, they'd called me bloody Noah!'

I was on a mission. I rented a ram from a farmer called Lenny Leatherhead to inseminate the six sheep we possessed, because that's what it said I had to do in 'The Complete Guide to Smallholding'. The ram was called Cliff.

'The wife likes Cliff Richard,' Lenny told me when he delivered Cliff.

'Right.' I could see that this Cliff and the other Cliff were like chalk and cheese, and this Cliff was most definitely not about to break into the chorus of Devil Woman.

Later, I peered out through the gloom to see Cliff mounting each one of my ewes until the blue chalk from the harness under his belly marked their back so darkly, there was no doubt he had done his job; several times. Cliff wasn't big on foreplay.

Lenny Leatherhead came to collect Cliff a week later.

'Looks like the boy's done his job good and proper.' Lenny said this with an undisguised tone of relish. I felt a sudden flood of sympathy for Lenny's wife. I imagined a nervous woman with watery eyes and Lenny's foreplay amounting to little more than 'brace yourself!'

'Looks like it.' I couldn't argue. Cliff had been busy and the ewes were gathered in the furthest corner of the field no doubt discussing what an unchivalrous shit he was.

Where Cliff eyed me with undisguised contempt, he bounded over to Lenny like a puppy and walked straight into the trailer. I handed over my hundred quid and Lenny left, no doubt to spread Cliff's seed at another idiot's smallholding and produce baby Cliffs and Cliffettes.

I went on a lambing course. It was sub-zero on Dartmoor. I pulled a dead lamb through a hole in a toilet cistern, twisting it and snaring it in the different positions the little devil might end up in the womb. I would never have equated a sheep's womb with a toilet cistern. That's self-sufficiency for you. We ate chocolate cake and people talked about crops, solar panels and a multitude of diseases affecting everything living. These people smelt of the earth and chicken shit and I knew I wasn't like them. I smelt of children's shampoo and Matey Foam. These people had chosen this life off the grid with their dreams of organic certification and I had blundered in by accident, as I had with childcare, like a man walking into a women's changing room.

'How's it working out?' A man in a camouflage jacket asked me. He was called Jack.

'Oh, okay.' My fingers were aching with what I was convinced was frostbite.

He squeezed my arm and stared into my eyes. I don't do the eye thing.

'How far are you off self-sufficient?' Jack pressed me.

I looked at his hands. They were rough and engrained with dirt.

'Oh, you know.' I was as far from self-sufficient as I was from writing that best-selling novel or my mother ever imagining I would amount to something she could share with her friends at the WI. 'It's a challenge.' It would have taken very little for me to confide, but I could see, just from the appearance of this man and the fusty smell of damp rising from his jacket, they would be wasted words. We were on different journeys. Jack's was to the nirvana of self-sufficiency and shitting onto sawdust in little sheds and

220

mine was 'the road to nowhere', as Talking Heads put it so succinctly.

I listened to these people talking confidently about the land and organic certification. I thought about my slaughtered chickens and the ones I replaced them with; and the hundreds of eggs I could never find. I thought of the pigs, big enough to rip a leg off and how I dropped the feed into the trough and ran for my life, hurling myself over the fence like an Olympian high-jumper. The pigs knew they were destined for bacon, and if they got the chance they'd have me first.

I joined the Smallholders Association and received a magazine where the members slagged one another off about propagation methods and tried to sell water buffalo to people with flooded fields.

'No!' Brigit said firmly. 'If you're thinking of buying one, you ring me. It's madness. This smallholding thing is getting out of hand.' She was observing the frolicking lambs and the cockerel trying to kill the chickens as she said this.

Between feeding the children, reading Biff and Chip books and being everything I thought a parent needed to be, I rang the woman whose name was Matilda about the water buffalo. I rang her because I thought a water buffalo might be big enough to fill the gap where my self-esteem used to reside. I never met a mother who felt the need to buy a water buffalo to pad out her child-caring days.

'We've sold her,' the woman informed me. 'We're moving to Milton Keynes with Tim's job. I want to die.'

'I'm sure Milton Keynes isn't that bad.'

She put the phone down. I have never been to Milton Keynes.

When the arrival of the lambs was imminent Brigit said, 'I need to talk to you.'

There is no way to say 'I need to talk to you' without it sounding ominous.

I followed her into the kitchen. Brigit stood by the window. Behind her, the sheep hobbled, their backsides begging to be cleaned. The birds pecked one another. I imagined the pigs reading Animal Farm and spreading the word.

'I'm pregnant.'

I noticed the sheep kept looking back over their lamb shoulders. I guessed they couldn't quite believe Cliff was gone. I wondered if they had any idea about Cliff's potential legacy, the mitotic cells dividing madly as they stood there in the damp with their multitude of parasites and disease constantly pushing them to extinction. I concluded in that moment, as I absorbed Brigit's news, that they had no idea about any of this, or they wouldn't be standing in a field waiting to become jigsaws of themselves in my freezer.

'Oh, my God. That's amazing.'

'Well, it's not is it. It was planned, if you remember. You make it sound as if it's a surprise.' Brigit was right. It was planned. Now Ollie was here, growing inside her, preparing to drop into my hands in however many months time. I have wondered over the years if 'the plan to have a child' means different things for men and women. For most men, I imagine, it must be like lighting the fuse of a rocket and retiring to a safe place. In my case it was like looking up and waiting for the thing to come down.

'No, I guess not. I just wasn't expecting it to happen so soon.'

'I really hope it's twins,' she said.

I pretended to share her hopefulness. It seemed so churlish not to. That would mean five children and only one me. I still had 'The Complete Guide to Twins'. I couldn't recall there being a section on twins times two plus one. I felt like the camel must have felt when whoever it was put the final straw on its back.

'Twins would be wonderful.' We were in for a penny, in for thousands of pounds. How can anyone have too many children?

'I can't go near the sheep,' Brigit announced when we were on our way for the first scan. 'There's a parasite that can affect the baby.' Sheep are not short on parasites.

Jackie, the scanographer started her scanning. 'There it is.'

I looked at the screen.

'A little singleton.'

Brigit promptly burst into tears.

'We hoped it might be twins. We already have twins,' I said.

Jackie eyed me as if I were insane. I think by that time, with my search for Blue Cow and the pot of gold stolen by Sly and Gobbo, the naughty goblins, I probably was.

'Are you sure?' Brigit asked.

Jackie stroked Brigit's arm. 'I'm sure, Ms Wheeler. But it looks very healthy.'

'I'm sorry it's not twins,' I said on the way home. 'It would've been nice.' I assumed it might be my fault until I checked and discovered only the mother can determine whether there are twins or not.

'I think the girls should go to ballet,' Brigit announced when we got home. 'We need to engage them in as many things as possible.'

I was hoping we might skip the ballet thing and move on to gymnastics or Thai Chi or football. The mothers I knew all took their perfect children to the 'master-class' where they pirouetted with an eye on the Royal Ballet. In the Midlands town where I grew up no one, and I mean 'no one', did ballet.

'Did you do ballet, Brigit?'

'No, I didn't. I'd like them to do it because of that. I want them to have the opportunities I didn't have.'

'I didn't do ballet either.'

'Not even the girls?'

'Not even the girls.'

'We should ask them.'

We asked them. They started to prance around the room with excitement. I was forced to read four books about Angelina Ballerina. Three times.

'Boys do it as well. You need to embrace everything. You set the example,' Brigit said.

'I set the example with everything. I set the example just by doing this stuff. It doesn't mean anybody follows it.' I was fearful of meeting Trevor Mace again. I could imagine Trevor Mace at ballet, talking about 'issues'. The man had lost any sense of dignity he might have once possessed.

'You're depriving them of growth. I can't take them every week. It breaks my heart. If they start though, I can come and watch.'

I took the girls to ballet. I couldn't be responsible for 'depriving them of growth'. Heaven forbid.

'It's not for everyone,' I kept saying to the girls in the car on the way. I said this several times, hammering the idea like a nail.

It didn't work. They were blind to my subtlety. They were excited. I was filled once again with dread.

We arrived in the Sierra which was, even by my standards, beginning to look a bit ropy. There were little darlings pirouetting in the car park.

Instead of a room of breastfeeding women where I felt it incumbent to turn away and read about 'dementia friendly parishes', I blundered into a room full of half-dressed five-year-olds and mothers with hairpins in their mouths. Two little girls screamed and froze on the spot, the two others ran into their mothers' arms and closed their eyes before screaming.

Claudia Bingham was there with her daughter. 'Oh, it's you,' she said. 'It's all right,' she said calmly to the screaming girls. 'It's only Chloe, Emma and Ruby's dad. I didn't think ballet would be your sort of thing.'

'I'm not doing it.'

'Oh, that's very funny.'

A boy wearing lycra shorts and black ballet shoes was limbering up. The girls started copying him.

I felt compelled to check one last time. 'Are you sure you want to do this?'

'Yes, yes, yes!'

The girls were issued with leotards, tights and shoes. I coughed up enough money to invoke a flashback to Jim and his bargain chickens and bugger all to show for it down the line. I followed the mothers through to the hall. The girls were skipping away. A woman who looked like an old headmistress held up her hand and came towards me.

'I'm sorry,' she said. 'Not you.'

I looked behind me. 'Not me?'

'We don't normally allow men to watch. For obvious reasons.'

'But my daughters are over there.'

'We have a special watching time at the end of term. I'm not sure the girls or the mothers will feel comfortable with a man. We've never had a man before you see.'

Someone touched my arm. I turned to see Jilly Green.

'It's okay,' Jilly said. 'He's one of us. Well, what I mean is, he does the 'mother thing'.'

I never thought Jilly Green would put one in for me, but she did. The headmistress reluctantly went back to her piano.

'Thank you.'

Jilly winked at me. 'You're welcome. I'm guessing you're new to ballet.'

'I am.'

Ruby got the idea of ballet quickly, hopping and skipping across the room. Chloe and Emma ran about with big smiles. The mothers were advising from the side-lines. I kept quiet, imagining my girls would never have the benefit of ballet wisdom. I was wrong. I learnt over the years that dance and the performing arts aren't about wisdom; they are about inspiration and expression. If I hadn't been 'the bloke who looked after his kids', I would never have known that, or that there really is a pot of gold at the end of the rainbow.

The pianist and ballet teacher all rolled into one was called Enid Flynn. She banged on the keys like Jerry Lee Lewis and called out her orders like a fishwife from Grimsby. I came to learn that Enid Flynn was a spinster, jilted once, apparently and literally at the altar. It wasn't going to happen twice.

'I let you off last week,' Enid said to me when we returned bright and early. 'Here are some pins and three nets. Their hair needs to be up. When I say up, I mean "up".'

I looked at the pins and the nets. 'Up?'

'In a bun. You know what a bun looks like?'

'Yes, round with currants in.'

Enid Flynn gave me the sort of withering look I imagined she gave whoever it was who jilted her at the altar, before she ripped off his head, cut out his heart and stuffed it in the neck hole.

'I expect discipline. It's important. I've had several students make it professionally. You never know with your girls. It's a uniform. A thing to be proud of.'

Chloe, Emma and Ruby were already stripped down to the basics and hoicking their tights up. I stood Ruby in front of me and pulled her masses of curls into a bunch on the top of her head. I scrunched it and began piercing it with pins. It fell apart. I developed an immediate respect for nest-building skills and could have done with a few. I did the same for Chloe and Emma, grabbing the chunks of hair and stuffing them into the nets. The girls looked like the people who worked behind the food counter in Sainsbury's.

'Go,' I said, pushing them through the curtain into the hall.

Enid was back in seconds. 'You need to do better than this. This isn't good enough.'

Jilly Green stepped into the breach. 'They look like they've been plugged into the mains.'

The following week, as if on cue, Nancy, the ewe, went into labour. It was ballet day. Nancy, even I could see, was in difficulty.

My experience with lambing was limited to pulling a dead lamb out of a hole in the side of a toilet cistern on a freezing cold day on Dartmoor. I was reliant on 'The Complete Guide to Smallholding'. Nancy couldn't get the lamb out. I knew what I had to do, but the gap between knowing and doing was as wide as the Grand Canyon. I inserted my hand. Nothing can prepare you for inserting your hand into the inner workings of a sheep.

'What are you doing, Daddy?' Chloe said from behind.

I turned to see the girls standing in a line wearing their leotards and full ballet gear.

'I'm trying to get the lamb out.'

I could feel the lamb. It was huge and facing the wrong way. I couldn't turn it because my hands were too big. There was blood and quite a lot of it. My hands and arms were covered. I was not only a man on the back foot in the ballet world. I was a man on the back foot in the ballet world with blood on my arms and a dying ewe called Nancy.

I crawled to Nancy's head end.

'It's okay,' I said.

Nancy wasn't okay. She was dying. I could see it in her eyes. The life was draining out of Nancy as fast as the cash slipped from my wallet when I went to see Jim at the Bird House. This was a mother fighting to stay alive for her child. I was a carer of children and not really a smallholder like the lunatics I had met on Dartmoor who made supper look like a crime scene.

'I need a vet.' Actually what I needed was a miracle and not to be doing what I was trying to do as well as look after three girls and prepare for a little lamb due to arrive.

Ruby started to cry. 'We'll be late for ballet.'

That was the least of my worries. If I didn't do something, Nancy and her impending child would simply be 'late'; as in dead as the dodo.

'Wait there.'

The girls stood in a line in their blue leotards with the little skirts, their tights and the pink cardigans in the field watching a mother fighting for her life. I ran to the house. I found the phone book. I flicked through it with my bloody fingers. I found a vet and covered the phone in blood also. There was a lot of blood.

'I need someone to get a lamb out of a ewe because it's too big and my hands don't fit. I need a woman. She's going to die. I mean, the sheep's going to die, not the woman. Can you get me a woman?'

I heard the receptionist take a deep breath. 'Can you repeat that?'

My emergency wasn't her emergency. I repeated it. 'I need a woman or a man with very small hands.'

She laughed. I suppose you would. 'The on call vet is a woman. I'll call her. She's petite. Will she do?'

'Yes, great. Tell her to put her foot down.'

'It's £50 for a call out and then whatever medication is required.'

'Yes, yes.' God, it was always about money. I was about to pay more for this visit than the cost of a professionally butchered whole lamb from Harrods food hall. They needn't have worried about any commercial competition from me.

The girls were twirling in the field, failing to entertain Nancy who was slipping silently beneath the veil. It looked like a macabre version of Angelina Ballerina.

The vet arrived within half an hour. 'Susan Leggett.' She took in my bloodied hands and decided not to shake one.

Without a word, Susan got down on the floor and stuck her hand inside Nancy. My only thought was 'thank God she wasn't a doctor!'.

'I need to snare the head.' She took a wire from her bag. We had done this on my course, but I now know that a toilet cistern bears no resemblance to a ewe's uterus.

228

Susan snared, turned and pulled. The head appeared. The girls were now into dancing in a circle of three. Like a pagan ritual. I had visions of someone taking a photo and sending it to the press along with the one of me staving in the head of a chicken with an empty Budweiser bottle. Susan pulled again. Nancy was white and so was Cliff and yet a huge black ram flopped onto the grass. I wondered if Nancy might have been seeing someone else during Cliff's visit.

Susan picked the ram up by its back legs and started swinging it like a Russian athlete preparing to throw the discus. I imagined her letting it go and sending the thing flying through the Rickard's kitchen window. I thought 'thank God you're not a midwife'. The thing bleated, probably to stop Susan swinging it around like a fairground ride.

Susan administered frighteningly expensive injections, which miraculously revived Nancy. I felt a surge of emotion and maybe the tiniest end of a wedge being driven between Hugh Fearnley-Whittingstall and me.

Enid was already banging the keys like Elton John playing Pinball Wizard when we arrived.

Claudia did the buns.

'We've got a big black man sheep,' Emma said.

Claudia looked surprised. 'You've got sheep?'

'We have.'

'Why? There's a perfectly good butcher down the road.'

'He's a small holder,' Chloe said.

23

BEFORE

Fact: Number of songs sung badly, 10,951

'Charles Julian is going to Abbots Bray,' Jilly Green announced at the pre-school.

Marlon had just released a new CD of excruciating songs, which we bought and played until I lost the thing between a copy of 'The Complete Guide to Childcare' and 'The Complete Guide to Twins' and almost the will to live.

'Gerald and his brother went there, so need I say more.'

No, she didn't.

'What about Chloe?'

'She's going to Charnwood Primary. I'm told it's very good.'

Brigit and I had attended the open evening. All the parents were there: Sam and Caroline Waters, Chris and Olivia Rayner, Harriet and Graham Rickard, Angela and Roger Wallace and Claudia Bingham without Roger. There was something going on, apparently.

'We could have ordered a coach and sung The Wheels on the Bus,' I said to Brigit who was trying not to look at people from the hospital. A man with a limp, who I assumed probably wasn't an orthopaedic surgeon or he'd have cured himself, collared her, leaving me to talk to myself.

Richard Quail appeared by my side. He smelt of expensive cologne; I was doused in Lynx.

'Hi,' he said. 'How are you? I'm after Brigit, wanted a quick word. Shop.'

'I'm—'

'Ah, there she is.' Richard Quail cupped my elbow. 'Laters.'

The lawyers were talking law of course and the finance people about the filthy lucre. It was more like a conference than an open evening for the local school.

Olivia Rayner was talking to a tall, elegant woman in a maroon suit. A little girl, who look like she'd stepped off the cover of a magazine for over-priced designer children's wear, offered up a plate of scattered digestives. I took two.

'You're only supposed to have one,' she said.

'Am I? Well, I've licked it.'

'That's disgusting.'

'I haven't really. It was a joke.'

'Well, you shouldn't say you did if you didn't. You're Chloe and the twins' dad.'

'I know.'

The little girl stood on tiptoe, actually took the biscuit off me and put it back on the plate. 'You're a giant.'

'No, I'm just tall. The BFG's a giant.'

'I don't like him. Mummy says he doesn't speak properly.'

'He has a lisp.'

'He should have gone to electrocution lessons like me.'

'Yes, you're probably right.'

Olivia Rayner waved away the digestives and rubbed her flat stomach. 'If I eat another thing today, I'll explode.' She pointed at me. 'Here he is,' she said to the elegantly dressed woman. 'Our token man; Brigit Wheeler's husband. She's part of the hospital.' Olivia made Brigit sound like a department. 'She deals with the office particulars, I believe. No one's really very sure. She's over there talking to my husband, the orthopaedic surgeon.'

'We're not married.'

'And I like to think you are. Okay?'

'I like to think Father Christmas is real, but it is unequivocally true that he isn't.'

Olivia was looking down. I looked down. The little girl with the biscuits was still standing next to me.

'Which he is, of course. Last year he left snow on our driveway.'

The little girl looked indignant. 'It didn't snow last year.'

'It came from the north pole. The snow is very durable at the north pole.'

'It would melt, silly.'

'Of course.' Olivia wandered off shaking her head.

'I'm Christine Taylor,' the elegant, tall woman said. I shook her hand. 'What's a token man?'

'Oh, I don't know. I'm just a man who looks after the kids. There's nothing tokenistic in my book. "Tokenistic" to me, roughly translates into 'you can leave whenever you like because you're not really making a difference. Leaving is not an option.'

'How many children?'

'Three.'

'God, that's brave. We've only got one and it's hard enough. Three! That's what you do?'

'I write novels and run a small-holding as well.'

'My God. Why?'

'Oh, you know. Child care is something I do part-time.'

'With three children?'

'I guess so.'

'That's amazing.'

'Is it?'

'Don't you think so?'

'Not really.'

Brigit kept looking back at me, apologising for the little crowd of hospital people closing in on her.

'Do you have a child going to the school?' I asked.

'I do. Just the one. Breda. I'm afraid I'm more of a career person than a natural mother. I've had help.'

'What do you do?'

'Less than you by the sound of it. I'm a journalist. Radio mainly.'

'Right.'

'The token man... I don't suppose you'd be willing to come onto the Saturday morning show and talk about men looking after children? You know, being the 'token male' in a nest of vipers! I mean it must feel like that.'

'Not all the time. Olivia's an acquired taste. Everyone has stuff going on.' I thought about Trevor Mace and his 'issues'.

'It'll be very straightforward, but it's an area of work I'm really interested in and we're doing a programme for local radio about the different care arrangements for children and the impact it has on them.'

'Okay.'

A man looking quite terrified came into the room and stood on a chair. He called for silence. No one took any notice. He banged a mug on the back of the chair and the handle came off. He held the handle up. Everyone laughed.

'I'm Geoffrey Brahms, the head teacher.' He had a lisp and the sort of thin, lank hair not even Vidal Sassoon using 'Australian Formula' could do anything with. He was shaking.

'It's a pleasure to meet you all.' He scanned the room like a terrified mouse facing a crowd of cats. He talked about the school, its achievements. I watched the men check their watches and the women make notes in little Moleskine books. Brigit was making notes too.

Mr Brahms disappeared as fast as Morrissey after one of his concerts to avoid meeting the fans he loathes so much.

Chloe started at the school in the September where our children would be measured, assessed and streamed and no longer subjected to my own brand and style of childcare.

233

'Of course, we expect Lottie to be fast-tracked to the Gifted and Talented group,' Caroline Waters announced in the playground on the first day. 'Sam's on the governors. He knows so much about education.'

'What, because he went to school?'

Caroline gave me the wasp-sucking look.

'I don't think they have a Gifted and Talented group here, Caroline,' I said.

'Sam's insisted they create one. You can't have those less able holding back the high flyers. Either that or they move Lottie up a couple of years.'

'She'll be at university when she's twelve.'

'She will have a gap year.'

'Thirteen then.'

'It's not unheard of.'

'True. They have documentaries about that sort of thing.'

'Sometimes, I wonder what planet you're on.'

'Me too.'

I could quickly see that Chloe would be the only one in the 'ordinary group', isolated by nothing more than the sheer brilliance of her fellow pupils.

I went to meetings at the school because Brigit worked long days trying to kick a hospital into a shape that looked like a hospital rather than some drifting, rudderless tanker.

'I can't carry on with this,' she said almost every Monday evening. But we were locked into the arrangement. She carried on. I carried on.

An avalanche of forms and paperwork came my way. Chloe would stagger out of school with plates for cakes and forms for allergies and issues with kiwi fruit. I didn't see the form about the kiwi fruit.

I gave Chloe a kiwi fruit to take to school. She liked kiwi fruit because she could eat them with a spoon like an egg.

'They put my kiwi fruit on the seat outside the school,' Chloe informed me when she came out of school at the end of the day.

Mothers were staring at me as if I'd done something offensive in the playground.

'Oh, my God!' Jilly Green said, her hand straight up to her mouth. 'You brought a kiwi fruit?'

'Yes, I did.'

'It's there!' Emma pointed at the egg-shaped thing wrapped in silver foil sitting in a dish on the wooden bench next to the pet cemetery where only Malcolm, an iguana once owned by the man who built this resting place, was buried in a Nike shoebox. To avoid confusion, the man was also called Malcolm.

I picked up the kiwi fruit and walked across to the reception. Mrs Davis, an acidic woman who made it quite clear that Brigit was a neglectful, career-centred bureaucrat and I was some low-life loser who had to look after the children because I wasn't fit for anything else, sneered at me. These were Mrs Dorothy Davis's words, not mine. (Olivia Rayner made a point of regurgitating them after informing the pre-school some months earlier that she had a photographic memory, yet couldn't remember which university she had been to when asked.)

To save her from the effort of smiling, Mrs Davis offered me her usual expression of disdain.

I held up the foil-clad kiwi.

'Chloe said someone put the kiwi outside the school. Thought I ought to check if someone was picking on her.'

'It was me.'

'You're picking on her?'

'We have a child who is allergic to kiwi fruit.'

'I thought they had to eat them, like nuts.'

'Not so. The guidance,' she looked to the heavens, 'says that such items should not be brought onto the premises. You had a letter.'

'Yes, I probably did. I get a lot of letters. You like your letters.'

'There's a lot to say.' Mrs Davis went to the back of her office and dropped two carrier bags full of egg boxes and toilet roll holders I had delivered at the beginning of the week onto the counter.

'I read the letter about bringing in egg boxes.'

'Have they been micro-waved?'

'Er, no. Didn't cross my mind.'

'You have to microwave them.'

'The egg boxes and the loo roll holders?'

'Yes. It was in the letter you supposedly read.'

'Well, I must have read the letter because I brought the stuff in.'

'Skim read.'

'Why do you microwave them?'

'Disease.'

'That's ridiculous.'

Mrs Davis held up her hands like someone threatened with a gun. 'I'm only passing the messages on. They come from on high.' Again, she looked upwards.

I took my egg boxes and bog rolls and chucked them in the bin on the way out. Edwina Curry still had a lot to answer for.

I went to a presentation on key stages. I realised then that some of the women worked in groups and moved around like a single organism. A woman, with the narrowest nose I have ever seen, spoke up from the centre of one of these groups where she was clearly the mouthpiece.

'I'm wondering,' she said, 'if some of the children will be starting at a higher level.' By some children, she obviously meant her child and those of the women in close proximity, the prodigies.

'Everyone starts at the same baseline,' Mrs Jones, the reception teacher, assured the woman.

The woman made a sort of disdainful snorting sound and folded her arms. 'Isn't there some sort of assessment? There's usually some sort of assessment.'

I imagined them testing embryos for IQ.

'We let them settle in first. There's more than enough assessment going on in the higher years. Children develop in different ways and at a different pace. We match progress and ability without making children feel less valued.'

The woman huffed again. She wasn't happy.

'What she means is…' it was Harriet Rickard who spoke, 'why isn't her little bloody Johnny already at the top of the class.'

People gasped. I gasped. Harriet was with the other group consisting of Caroline Waters, Olivia et al. The tension in the room was as taut as the 'active wear' many of them were wearing to limber up.

'His name is Bartholomew,' the woman with the nose said.

I knew the kid. He had her nose and I assume, later in life, he'd send her the bill for the plastic surgery.

'And no, I think I speak for our little group.'

The little group of women giggled. I stood in silence in my little group of one. I had nothing to add to this brick chucking. I thought you just brought your kids to school where they were taught to fear the nut and the kiwi, and take salbutamol whenever out of breath.

The meeting closed like one of those songs with no obvious ending and faded with whispered threats of taking the children out, or tackling the Education Authority, which, according to Mrs Davis, was obviously directly above her head on the right hand of God.

I was on my way out when Mrs Jones called me back. She handed me a piece of paper. 'I'd like you to sign this form.'

I looked at the form. This was a school which loved the form, but not the kiwi or the nut, or the non-microwaved egg box or toilet roll holder. 'What's it for?'

'It's a contract between the parents and the school. An agreement that you will play your part. Chloe is falling behind with her reading. We need to go back to the beginning with some basic books.'

People were still in the room, and silence fell like heavy snow. This was a conversation taking place in a room with twenty other people tuned in like they used to crowd around a wireless to get news during the Second World War.

'What do you want me to do?' I could literally feel people closing in until their scented breath brushed my skin.

'I will set you tasks at home to complete with her every day, then we review it.'

My blood was boiling. I wanted to rant. I wanted to spill out every drop of bile that had built up in me over the last few years and drown those supercilious little bastards in that room. I wanted to tell them how fucking hard it was being the last dodo with the big beak and no chance of finding a kindred spirit or another impossible bird with a big beak that probably never existed in the first place. I wanted to snatch my child away from that school and run. God knows where, but somewhere. This woman had exposed me and right then and there I hated every atom of her. I was failing my child. I was a man; a 'token man' trying to be a woman who hadn't got the energy or the time to help his eldest daughter decipher the fucking cat sat on the fucking shitty mat!

'Tasks?'

'Yes, tasks.'

'This is a school. I thought schools did the teaching. Why am I being given tasks?'

'It's a partnership. You have to understand that I already have my high flyers.'

'And Chloe isn't one of them?'

Mrs Jones smirked.

I wondered then why every child of a teacher isn't necessarily brilliant and why English teachers don't often write novels and why people who grow carrots don't turn their children orange. I looked at the other women in the room. Harriet Rickard touched my arm, smiling.

It was Caroline Waters who intervened. 'I'm sorry,' Caroline said, 'that we're all overhearing this.'

I thought, you're overhearing this because you're rubbernecking like a bunch of filleted giraffes.

238

'I don't think it's appropriate to be talking about this now. Chloe is a delightful girl. Ability is not just about academia.'

'Pretty but thick you mean?'

I watched them file out of the room. I like to think what Caroline said was in good faith, but I'd never felt so alone. I'd never felt so sad for my child, my little girl, who couldn't read a sentence on a page. I'd never felt so ashamed that I had a job which clearly, by anybody's standards, I couldn't do.

I saw the head teacher heading in my direction, like a man running through a war zone, fearful at any minute he could be the victim of enemy fire. He ducked over to me. 'I wondered if I could have a word.'

'Here?'

'Oh, yes, here is fine. It's about music.'

Ah, I thought. He's going to tell me that Chloe has a natural ear for music.

'Oh, right.'

'You play it very loudly when you drive down to the school. People are concerned.'

'People?'

'Yes, people.'

'You have names.'

'Quite a few people.'

Some of those who were leaving slowed to a shuffle, leaning back to catch the conversation, which was no doubt being conducted in public so Mr Brahms could demonstrate what a firm head teacher he was. The man needed every chance he could get.

'Oh, that's okay. I'll turn it down.'

'Right, good, that's great.' Mr Brahms was wringing his hands. I could smell his perspiration. This was killing him. He should have been an accountant and left the sweating to his clients. 'There's one other thing.'

'Okay.'

239

'It's not just the volume. There's a song you play and people…' here he looked at Caroline, Olivia and two women both called Sarah who not only looked alike, but wore identical shoes. 'People are a bit concerned.'

'People? Names?'

'Quite a few people.'

'What's the song?'

Mr Brahms took a piece of paper out of his jacket pocket. 'Yes, yes, I have it here.'

I read the song title. 'Where did you get that?'

He looked at Caroline. He got it from Caroline.

'It's the Ramones.'

Mr Brahms clearly didn't know who the Ramones were. He cleared his throat. I thought he was going to sing the song. 'It's called 'Beat up the Brat'.'

''Beat on the Brat' actually.'

'Not very appropriate for the school gates, wouldn't you agree?'

'Nope. I'm sorry. I didn't think. It comes straight after 'Rock Away Beach' and the kids were singing very loud and I couldn't hear.'

Mr Farnham put his paper away. 'I appreciate that.'

I left the 'high flyers' and the 'gifted and talented' with my little list of 'tasks' to complete at home because they obviously didn't do those at school anymore and went to sit in my car. The Sierra coughed into life. I wound all the windows down and gave them 'Pretty Vacant' at full chat by the Sex Pistols. It was a very cleansing experience.

24

BEFORE

Fact: Number of attempts at controlled crying, 1

Christine Taylor invited me to take part in a Saturday morning radio show.

The coffee at the radio station looked and tasted like sump oil. I sat next to a theatre director called Bill Lane. I'd never sat next to a theatre director before. I thought about telling him about my novel in the hope he might turn it into a play. I wasn't sure how many screenplays were based on novels yet to be written.

'We're just starting out in the provincial theatres before we take it to the West End,' Bill said with an air of confidence I could only imagine. Bill looked vaguely familiar. He caught me staring at him at this vague familiarity.

'If you're wondering, I did 'Cats' in the West End. And 'Oliver'.'

I realised I had no idea who he was.

We talked about wind turbines. There was a proposal to put them along the coast. Bill examined his nails, which were bitten to the quick. The phone lines were jammed with angry retired people who clearly hated wind turbines and had time to rant about them.

What do you think?' Adam, the presenter asked me.

'I like them. I think they're clean and beautiful and represent progress, capturing the natural resources at the same time.'

The phone crashed under the weight of 'Fucked off from Falmouth'.

Bill talked about his play. 'It's about the time when Exeter beat Brazil at football in 1904.' Bill wanted bums on seats.

Adam turned, pointed and introduced me to the invisible audience. 'So, house husband, home-maker, parent carer, stay at home dad.' He was chucking cliché's faster than I could catch them. 'How do you feel about those terms?' he said with a smug bastard's smile, one hundred and eighty on the dart board and goading his opponent to 'beat that'. 'After all, you do the job women have done for years.'

This was clearly not Bill's department. Suddenly, the thought of being a theatre director felt quite attractive.

'Does it matter what you call it?' I thought of raising the small-holding and the novels, but the sheep were gone, riddled with disease. Two turkeys had died of heart attacks and the chickens were still mourning the loss of Roy.

'Do you think they're derogatory terms?' Adam asked.

'Do you think they're derogatory, Adam?' I said

I was pissed off. I was tired. Ruby and Emma had colds and they were miserable. I had a cold. I was miserable.

Adam grinned. 'My wife looks after the children. I don't think she minds being called a housewife. Why do you mind being called a house husband?'

'I don't particularly. Would you?'

Adam shuffled his papers. 'It's different for women, I suppose. It's what they're used to. I guess they are the natural carers. Wouldn't you say that? It's hardly a career choice.'

'I made the choice.'

'A lot of people say it's not a proper job. I'm trying to be contentious here.' The bugger winked at me.

'It's not contentious. It's a very current and important issue that doesn't get talked about because a lot of women feel trapped.'

'So, 'house husband' is okay then? I mean, there seem to be a lot of men like you taking it on.'

'Like me?'

'You know what I mean.'

I just glared at him. I knew what he meant. Reaching over his mixing desk and slapping his face would have been wasted on the radio. 'Well, that's simply rhetoric. Two percent of men took paid paternity leave this year according to the BBC. Do I think it's a proper job? Do you?'

'That's not for me to say.'

'Why not?'

'Because I'm not a woman.'

'Doesn't matter. It's the way society views it. As a man you make up half the parents. Surely you have a view. Do you think it's a proper job?'

'I suppose the big question is: has it been worth it?'

'You didn't answer the previous question.'

'Bill, let's go back to the play.'

Bill was looking down at his hands. He clearly didn't want to engage in this debate. There was an uncomfortable silence. Adam put on the Carpenters. We've Only Just Begun. He faded it out not long after the Carpenters had only just begun. 'We've been talking about men looking after their children.'

Bill was still looking at his hands as if he was expecting something miraculously to appear.

'So,' Adam said. 'Is it worth it? After all, you don't get paid. People, and I'm not saying me, don't often view it as a proper job. Yet you've taken it on while your partner goes out to work. I think that's Brigit Wheeler, the CEO of our general hospital. You must feel a bit over-shadowed.'

'Has it been worth it? Well, I haven't earned any money for looking after the children as they don't have any to pay me. Unless you count the chocolate coins they get at

Christmas. I've watched my partner develop her career and save me at the end of the day when I could barely stay awake. People don't talk to me at parties because I don't have a badge, unless you count the ones with Noddy or Mr Tumble on them. I've spent hundreds of hours in public toilets where people have eyed me with suspicion. I bought a book called 'The Complete Guide to Childcare'. In this book it tells you what looking after children is like, making time for yourself, relaxing, nurturing, positive parenting, balanced diets (I don't mention the 'Tango girls'), controlled crying and cranial massage. I realised that in every picture it was the woman doing the task. There were men, but they were either bouncing a ball, reading a magazine or having dinner at a pristine table with a glass of Cotes du whatever.'

Adam was looking at the clock. If a man could have accelerated time, Adam was he. 'Thank you for that. We only have a few minutes. Maybe Bill could tell us a little bit more about his play.'

Bill suddenly gripped my arm. 'No,' he said. 'I want to hear what this man has to say. Was it worth it?'

Adam was waving his hand at the people behind the studio window.

'Every day. It's been a privilege for me and a huge sacrifice for my partner who has given every spare second she has to the kids. I got the lion's share though. I heard the first words, saw the first chicken pox spots and hosted a horde of kids whose mothers wanted them to catch it too. I should have charged. I'm watching the little people grow into big people. I've lived in a world most men never see. I've witnessed how amazing women can be, how resourceful and strong. I've seen them be hostage to their circumstances because they have no income and, despite the work, they are still dependants and, yes, unemployed. How can someone who works round the clock, seven days a week, be unemployed? My children have taught me patience when I had none, and kindness when I didn't know how to give it. They have shown me things most adults miss. We studied insects for hours and they are amazing, and some of them bite. 'So, yes. It has been worth it.'

I noticed that Bill had tears in his eyes. 'I have a daughter,' he said. 'I haven't seen her for eighteen years. I was always at work, following the next big production. I put my career before my family. I didn't watch her growing up. It's my greatest regret. It doesn't matter how many successes I've had, because I failed at the most important thing. My father left me, so I followed the pattern. I followed the path I thought fathers followed. I thought fathers were distant and austere.'

Adam looked frantic. He was pointing at the red light above the door. He mouthed 'we are still on air!'.

Bill dismissed Adam with a wave of his hand. 'I know we're still on air. That's why I'm talking. I wish I'd done more. I wish I'd given the hours to my daughter that I chose to give to my career; hours I can never get back. I envy you. I envy any father who has the chance to put right what so many fathers get wrong. I don't believe it's because they don't want to be involved. If they're like me, then they'll know it's too late. There are memories I will never have. I would say to any man out there with children, give them your hours and make those memories.'

The programme ended. Adam had beads of sweat on his forehead.

Outside the radio station, Bill and I stood in the rain. It was autumn, the familiar smell of decay; a prelude to pumpkins and rockets was in the air. Bill was racing back to the theatre. I was going back to runny noses and toffee apples.

'That was really brave,' I said to Bill.

'Nah, it wasn't. It was honest. I should have said it to my daughter.'

'Maybe she heard it.'

'She lives in Australia.'

'Oh, so probably not then. You should call her.'

'A lot of water under the bridge.' Bill shook my hand and walked away.

'It's never too late.'

'It's been a long time.'

'If you don't do it, it'll be even longer.'

Bill opened his car door and waved.

Brigit was waiting for me when I got back. She hugged me. 'That was amazing.'

'The presenter's just like the rest of them. He got my goat.'

'No, you were good. I mean the man who was with you, Bill. It was really moving.'

'Do you not think that's a bit ironic?'

'Why ironic?'

'That you were moved by the man who hadn't spent more time with his children rather than the one who has.'

'I didn't mean it like that.'

'He has a career.'

'And you don't?'

I didn't answer her.

25

NOW

Fact: Number of hugs, 317,874

'Oh my God! Oh my God! Oh my God!' Ruby runs out of the toilet.

There is vile-looking fluid pouring over the top of the bowl, running across the floor and soaking into the hallway carpet. 'We're backing up! You need to do something, Dad.'

Chloe is on FaceTime and laughing. She is a hundred miles away where the drains are connected to a labyrinth of other drains, flowing into an industrial sewerage treatment plant before they pump it out to sea where it drifts back on the tide to slop onto the shorelines of the cleanest beaches in the country.

'We're backing up! We're backing up! OMG, we're backing up!' Ruby sings to the tune of 'Footloose'.

No one moves. No one is going to move. No one is going to volunteer to unblock a drain overflowing with bodily fluids. There are people looking at me helplessly as if I am the one stuffing the U-bends until they can't take any more. I leave them huddled together in the kitchen fearing the blocked drain and head out to tackle the literally rising shit storm.

The drain is overflowing onto the gravel-less driveway. It is not a pretty sight. I lift the lid and survey the bubbling cauldron of loo roll and excrement. There is no subtle way to describe an overflowing drain any more than there is a full nappy.

Graham Rickard appears on the road. The Rickards have a habit of appearing from nowhere at a time of great inconvenience to engage in conversations about the comparative brilliance of their children. I don't want to talk to Graham right now about how Archie is going to be the Minister for Overseas Development or that Spence has rowed the Atlantic in a boat made from 'The Financial Times'.

Graham is carrying his copy of 'The Telegraph', which he collects from the box on the corner. Sometimes people steal his Telegraph. No one has ever stolen my Guardian.

'Oooh. Looks like a problem.'

Yes, the sum products of our family's digestive system are currently running out onto the road for the whole world to see. I would consider that a problem. I find it hard enough keeping our personal details private without having our intimate exudate flowing into the streets.

'I've got some drain rods,' Graham announces. Graham Rickard is the last man on the planet I would have imagined having drain rods. As likely as the Queen keeping a blowtorch in a lock-up in Hammersmith.

I hesitate.

I look at the drain.

Rods would be good. Of course, it doesn't mean he's ever used them. Graham wears shirts with cufflinks bearing golf-related things on them. People who wear cufflinks don't rod drains. People like me who wear Ramones T-shirts from 1982 rod drains.

Graham returns in the briefest of moments with a bag containing his drain rods and starts to assemble the first three. He is out of breath. He looks like a man desperate not to miss out on a spot of 'rodding'. I imagine Harriet seizing the opportunity for Graham, over a bubbling, shitty drain, to glean a few juicy facts about the shortcomings of our kids.

248

Perhaps I should tell him that some of this shit and piss has been emitted from the seventh most powerful woman in the city.

Graham starts screwing the other rods together. For someone who deals with ribbon-bound bundles of defence papers, I am impressed with his dexterity.

'We hardly see one another these days, and here we are unblocking drains,' Graham says.

I assume this is an entrée, but nothing else follows this. 'It's an odd sort of bonding experience.' I have a flash of an image of Trevor Mace from all those years ago. I don't need to bond with anybody now, especially over a burgeoning drain.

We feed the rod with the little plate on the end into the depths. Graham does a bit of shunting. Nothing happens. The water level continues to rise. I shout into the house.

'Are people using appliances?' I can hear a shower, the flushing of toilets and the washing machine. The house is veritably gushing with wastewater.

Graham is ramming away with such vigour, there is sweat on his brow. I refrain from mopping it with the J-cloth I've been using to catch the spillage.

'I'm wondering,' he says, 'if there might be a damaged pipe under the house.'

I consider the consequences of this and conjure the image of our multi-coloured, unfinished abode sinking into our own cesspit. What sort of clause would cover this on the house insurance I wonder?

Suddenly there is a gush. Stuff surges forth. It is very satisfying to watch. We are a couple of blokes admiring an emptying drain.

'A sample of that stuff,' Graham says, 'will tell you all you need to know about your lives.'

'What, that we're full of shit?'

He laughs at this. I have known, or at least been a neighbour of Graham and Harriet Rickard for nearly twenty years. We have probably exchanged no more than a few hundred words. Here we are laughing over a drain. Life never ceases to amaze.

'It's a key determinant in the criminal world these days,' Graham says.

'No shit.'

'Oh yes, I see. Very funny.'

'I know quite enough about our lives, thanks. You're welcome to delve around if you want, Graham, but if I were you I'd stick to defending the indefensible.'

I drop the drain lid back and we stow away the rods. I expect Graham to walk away, but he doesn't.

'Have you got a few minutes?' Graham Rickard has never asked me for a few minutes. I have always considered there to be a gulf between us. He is a high-flying criminal lawyer and I have looked after the children. Apart from the drain rodding, I am wondering where our common ground might lie.

'Sure. Come in.'

Graham follows me into the chaotic kitchen. There are pots and dishes piled up. I feel the need to apologise, but this is how we live. Out of this domestic mess emerge six people who I hope don't look so bad to the outside world; most of the time. Though inevitably surprised, Brigit greets Graham like an old friend. He and Harriet have stood in our kitchen maybe a handful of times when we've had a few neighbours around for drinks. They have never stayed. Graham kisses Brigit on both cheeks and then hugs her. He really hugs her. Brigit fractured a rib when she followed the bowling ball down the alley a few years ago. She still winces when someone squeezes her too tightly. She won't get it looked at. She encourages everyone else to use the services of her hospital. I imagine if the place caught fire, she would be the last one to leave.

Ruby and Emma are watching this unlikely display of neighbourly affection with expressions of bewilderment. Brigit signals for them to go as Graham continues to hug her. Uncharacteristically they do as Brigit asks.

'It's okay, Graham,' Brigit says.

I'm not aware that Graham has said anything to indicate it isn't, but Brigit has this ability to know things without the presence of words.

'Tea?' I offer.

Brigit starts rubbing Graham's back. He makes this guttural sound, which to me sounds like wind. I realise he is crying. This man who I imagined has never shown an ounce of emotion, is actually sobbing.

'God, I'm sorry,' Graham rubs his eyes, which look sore and bloodshot.

Brigit guides Graham into the lounge. I don't follow them. Brigit is the Queen of this sort of thing. I am better at consoling a hysterical child. I know about unicorns roaming the garden and the Easter Bunny and whether Father Christmas will come or not. I am still traumatised from the moment Ollie finally 'announced' that he knew the truth, and some little thoughtless bastard with not an ounce of imagination and irresponsible parents told him so.

'It's just a lie,' he said. 'You lied to all of us.'

I was reminded of the little girl at the school meeting with the digestive biscuits and the grudge against the BFG.

'I didn't lie. It's a beautiful thing to believe as a child.'

'I've known since I was eight.'

'Eight?'

'So, really it's you who's been lying, Ollie.' I know this didn't look good or responsible and could lead to issues in later life. Then let there be issues, I thought. Let there be issues where my son still believes in little people making toys in workshops at the North Pole. This was serious; I was fighting to keep Father Christmas alive! I was fighting to keep hold of a piece of 'us', but more importantly; a piece of 'me'. Ollie laughed. It was a laugh I will remember forever. It was the laugh of a boy entering into the real world where there are things that can harm him. Why would any parent want to expose their child to that?

'He never came. It was you who put the presents under the tree and the bag at the end of my bed. It's okay, Dad I'm fine about it.'

I wasn't. I came to believe again. I came to believe because there were enough children in the house to collectively collude with me that on Christmas Eve 'he' would come and there would be bells and a sleigh on the roof of the house; a roof so unstable it still struggles to support a large seagull. Belief is as strong as a steel girder.

Now I can hear Graham and Brigit talking in the lounge. I want to listen at the door. Sometimes I feel I should assert myself more in this world of adults, but it isn't my special skill. Standing outside the door, I feel slightly indignant. I got to Graham first. We did the drain thing together. We were bonding. Drain unblocking is not something you want to share with everyone.

I make the tea, slap a couple of Kit Kats on the tray and take them in. Brigit and Graham are sitting on the sofa together. He looks like a man on the verge of proposing, and I know his ring would be a fair bit larger than mine.

'Join us,' Brigit says.

I sit in the armchair with my hands pressed between my knees.

'It's okay, Graham. We're here to help,' Brigit assures him.

I can't imagine why Graham Rickard would need our help. He is wealthy, living in a house made of four other people's houses who now probably live in abject poverty. He has three aspiring and healthy children and a wife who paints pictures and is a pain in the arse. What more could a man want?

Graham gives me the sort of look I'd expect to see on the face of someone who's sustained a recent and resounding defeat. I feel conspicuous in his presence. Brigit gives me the look which says sensitivity is required and I might be best to keep my gob shut.

Graham is on the verge of making an ungodly confession. He is a murderer. He has five children by five different women. He is a pimp. He is Banksy.

'Harriet has dementia.' Graham immediately puts his head in his hands which, I imagine, is the only place right now where he can hide.

Brigit shuffles over to him and presses his head against her chest. My head is whirling. My immediate thought is that I must now think more kindly of Harriet Rickard and perhaps apologise for all the occasions when I have maligned her character. I decide against this. It would take too long.

'She's had it for ten years.'

Nope, I can't backtrack on all the derogatory things I've said about Harriet over ten years. It would be like shovelling up Ben Nevis and plonking it somewhere else.

'It's getting worse. We've talked about it and people need to know. She needs to be able to rely on friends. She says things she doesn't mean.'

'Oh, we all do,' Brigit says, glaring at me.

I glare back. I don't want to be in this room with my face pressed up against this fucking unassailable truth. It is a lesson I don't need to learn. *Always think kindly of people. You never know what goes on for them,* Brigit often says.

Graham pulls away from Brigit. 'I need to go. I can't leave her for too long. Her mother's there. It's like the blind leading the blind.'

Brigit rubs Graham's arm. Graham looks like he's had an idea. 'I don't know if this is true, but Harriet's mother, Sheila, hasn't been right in the head for years. She always says what she thinks regardless of the damage. I assumed Harriet was a chip off the old block. Now I'm beginning to wonder. I haven't been the best husband. I haven't always been there. You should be there for them, shouldn't you, Brigit?'

'It's not always easy. Relationships are very complicated. None of us know what goes on for other people. It's taken you a lot to share this with us, Graham. If there's anything we can do.'

Graham looks at me. Instead of the strident lawyer, bludgeoning weak defences with the blunt pencil of the law, he is small and frail. There is a hole in the elbow of his jumper and his jeans are frayed at the bottom. There are dark rings under his eyes and more grey hairs than brown. People look so different when they are on the back foot.

'There will come a time when we need to bring people in. I just wondered…' He is still looking at me, 'if someone could maybe pop round now and then, just to see if Harriet is okay. She gets lonely. I think she's been lonely for a long time. I have no idea what it must be like bringing three children up on your own. I spent most of my time at work, and I regret it. I really do. In fact, I used to stay at work or go to the gym until the kids were ready for bed. I left it all to Harriet, all of it.' Graham is still looking at me. He is doing the 'eye to eye thing'. I'm still very uncomfortable about the 'eye to eye' thing.

'It's okay,' Brigit says. She is still at the arm rubbing.

I am becoming fearful of friction burns for both of them.

'It's not,' Graham says. 'I had a couple of affairs. Meaningless tussles in cheap hotels.'

He points at me. I don't know why he's pointing at me. In my experience someone points at you when they're about to make an accusation.

'I don't know how you've done it. I don't know how you've taken the load with four kids. I know Brigit has played a huge part, unlike me, but you, I envy you. I've driven past your house every day and I've wondered how you've done this all these years, coped with the isolation, the drudgery of repetition and yet come out whole. I feel like half a man.'

I could right now tell Graham Rickard that over the years I haven't even felt like a fraction of a man, never mind a whole half. (Can you have a 'whole half'?) Graham might be shorter than me, but in terms of 'manliness' or whatever other people call it, he was always where I felt I should be and not knee deep in yoghurt and nappies. I don't know what to say. This is a revelation in its purest form. I don't know if I can take in all this honesty and 'sharing'. I was only unblocking a drain.

Brigit is nodding sagely at me.

'There you have it,' Graham says, finally standing and handing me his Kit Kat.

I don't really like Kit Kats. I'm more of an animal-shaped biscuit man myself. I particularly like the elephant. I always bite the trunk off first, then nibble the hide next.

Yes, there we have it. So much in such a short space of time. I feel exhausted. I need a drink, but it is only ten am. Perhaps a quick swill out of the bottle in the fridge door to take the edge off will suffice.

Brigit and I see Graham out. We both look down at the clean drain cover. It is a very satisfying sight watching the by-products of family sail by and back into the earth too close to the house for comfort because the builders didn't buy enough pipe. I know the building inspectors among you will be hunting for where I live, but I say to you: 'get a life!'.

'Good job,' Graham says. 'I'll leave the rods. You never know.'

I feel quite honoured to be the guardian of the rods.

Graham kisses Brigit and shakes my hand. It is a sincere shake. I can tell these things. There is nothing sincere about a wet halibut.

Brigit shuts the door and leans against it. 'Jesus! Poor guy.'

'He said he envied me. There was I envying him with his badge of honour and his perfect children.'

'And his dementing wife.'

'And that.'

'You should go and see Harriet. Check she's okay, like Graham asked.'

I shudder at the idea, but I will. In all the years of teaching the kids not to lie because the truth will set you free, I promise myself I will go and see Harriet Rickard.

'I will,' I say.

Brigit rubs my arm. With all the rubbing, she must be wearing the skin off her hands. 'I know you will. You're really good with people; small ones anyway.'

26

BEFORE

Fact: Number of nursery rhymes recited, 8,751

The day before Ollie was born, I took the girls to a park only a mile or so away. We often visited, traumatised the peacocks by chasing them and concussed the ducks with stale bread. Ollie was twelve days late and, unless he arrived by eight o'clock the following morning, Brigit would be induced in her own maternity department with at least two of our nursing and medical neighbours present.

'I might as well have it televised so they can watch it down the pub!' she said, quite understandably.

'You must be excited about having a new brother,' I said to the girls.

The six-year-old and the two five-year-olds looked at me as if I were insane.

'He's a boy,' Chloe said. 'We hate boys.'

They all nodded in unison. This sort of spontaneous and united hatred is always alarming. I didn't indulge them. They were a triangle and triangles are strong. I spotted a couple pushing a little girl on a swing to my right. The girls ran over and jumped onto the remaining three vacant swings.

I sat on a seat with my bag of half-eaten teddy-shaped sandwiches and watched these children swinging away. I'd never felt comfortable sitting in play areas full of little children as a lone male unless I knew some of the mothers and would make an animated show of talking to them. Short of holding a plaque bearing the words I'm one of the good guys!, I've always made a point of engaging with the girls so people would be quite clear that they knew who I was and not some stranger trying to lure them away.

I noticed the couple with the little girl watching our girls intently. I watched them intently so that eventually they could see I was staring at them. I had grown to be distrustful of adults in playgrounds. The woman smiled at me. I looked at the little girl and then behind the couple I spotted the motorised wheelchair. They lifted the girl out of the swing. She was probably Chloe's age, but profoundly disabled. They gently lowered the girl into the wheelchair, strapping her in. The man, who I assumed to be her father, kissed the girl on the forehead. I watched the two parents walking away behind the wheelchair. When they reached the gate, the woman looked back at me and smiled. Seeing them with their child, I felt guilty for having three healthy children when they had only one, disabled child who they clearly loved ferociously.

I heard a scream. Emma had fallen backwards off the swing and was howling like a wolf. I ran. She was lucid.

'What's your name?' I said.

'It's Emma, silly,' Ruby said. 'She's your daughter and my twin.'

'I know that. I need Em to tell me.' I held up my hand. 'How many fingers?'

Ruby counted. 'Four!'

I gave up after that.

Emma sat up. The ground was covered with soft tree bark. I rubbed the back of her head and a long line of clear snot rubbed off onto my jacket. I realised someone was standing behind me. I turned to see the mother of the little girl. She looked concerned.

'Is she okay?'

'I think she's fine.'

The woman peered at Emma. 'Do you want me to take a quick look? I'm a paediatrician. I'm Sarah.' She crouched down. 'What's your name?' Sarah asked Emma.

'Emma,' Ruby said.

Sarah laughed. 'Do you always answer for your twin?'

'She banged her head. She can't talk.'

'Yes, I can,' Emma said indignantly. 'She's just a blabber mouth.'

With clinical expertise, Sarah lifted Emma's eyelids and examined her eyes. 'Follow my finger.' Emma followed Sarah's finger. 'She seems fine. Keep an eye on her and just check her later on.'

'Thank you,' I said. I stood and shook Sarah's hand.

'You're welcome. You look after them?'

I looked at our three, back on the swings again. 'I do.' I didn't feel the need to tell her I was a small-holder and a best-selling novelist on the imaginary cusp of a breakthrough.

'My husband also.'

I looked across to see him giving their daughter a drink from a baby beaker. Our girls all used cups by then. They were making progress where their little one might not be. In that brief moment I almost suggested we got together, and I still wonder if I was right not to. In a way that father and I were two of a rare kind, but of course we weren't in many others. As I watched Sarah walk back to her partner and daughter, I wondered what it might be like to be a paediatrician, curing sick children and yet unable to do the same for your own. Sarah kissed her husband and said something to him. He smiled at me and waved. I watched them walk away.

I collected the girls and we drove home singing along to one of Marlon the Music Man's tapes, which at times I imagined using to garrotte him when he had sung about the planets revolving, the seasons changing and the icy winds that sting for the three-hundredth time. Yes, I remember them twenty years later and will only sing them for an unimaginably large fee. I also remember the couple and their daughter and I hope life has treated them as kindly as it has, in the main, treated us.

We arrived home from the park to find Brigit eating nut pralines and huffing about being induced in her own hospital the following day.

'He has to come in the next few hours. I can't go into my own hospital!'

I was having visions of delivering Ollie myself. I was pretty sure this wasn't covered in 'The Complete Guide to Childcare'. 'He might not,' I said, trying to prepare her for the imminent stream of people appearing at her bedside in the maternity unit. 'Sometimes things are just how they are.'

This was one of Brigit's stock phrases. She looked, if she could have got out of the chair, as if she wanted to hit me.

I put the children to bed. Brigit and I sat and watched television as we had for the previous twelve days to remind ourselves why we only ever watched the news. We stayed up. I rubbed Brigit's belly and spoke to Ollie about arriving. We watched a late- night documentary about a woman who suffered multiple orgasms throughout the day and how it was destroying her life.

'My husband gets jealous when I'm talking to other men and I start to moan with pleasure.' The woman started to cry. Brigit started to laugh. 'I can be in Tesco, in the vegetable section, and I can have one. I can be in a queue, the bingo. People stop and stare at me all the time.' Brigit was howling with laugher.

'It'll be the carrots!' Brigit said, doubling up and probably crushing Ollie. She sat up and groaned. She wasn't laughing. 'He's coming.' Ollie clearly wanted to watch the documentary.

'Are you sure?'

'Yes, I'm bloody sure! I've done this before!' Brigit doubled up again, enveloped by a surge of pain. 'Make the call!'

'There's no need to shout.'

'Yes, there bloody well is!'

I have often marvelled at the capacity and the contrast for women to become unnecessarily aggressive towards the father during the joyful process of childbirth. I have assumed, but never broached the subject, that during this time, women realise with stark clarity that, after conception, how utterly superfluous men really are. In my view it is not a good footing for the beginning of family life.

'Almost fully dilated,' the midwife informed me as if I needed to know. She was a practical, pragmatic woman called Claire. 'Right, onto the bed. Let's get this done.' A woman with a big smile came in carrying a box with all the necessary equipment. Her name was Dolly.

'How's Mummy doing?' Dolly asked Brigit who was now on all fours on the bed. Brigit gave Dolly a 'don't call me fucking 'Mummy', you flaky new-age hippy' look.

Ollie arrived an hour later with his hand over his head, relaxed and laid back; a style he has adopted to this day. It was the first time the girls had ever collectively slept through the night while their mother gave birth in the room below without gas and air and a midwife telling her to 'push' and the other calling her 'Mummy'.

'Can I do anything?' I offered.

The three women, including Brigit, looked at me as if I'd suggested we all sing a couple of verses of the 'Hokey Cokey'.

I cut the cord. I've done this four times now and every time it has felt like a concession to make me feel useful.

The girls appeared the next morning to find their brother lying in a cot at the end of the bed. They looked at him with disinterest and walked away.

Everybody was ready for school by eight. I was suddenly useful and gainfully employed. A childminder called Sybil came to collect the girls to take them to school. Sybil carried things in her bag to entertain the most truculent, obnoxious little brats. She thought Richard Quail was a God because he removed a tumour the size of a satsuma from her

261

husband's head. Richard Quail, I felt the need to point out, was of course not a God because God doesn't wear pinstripe suits or drive cars that scream 'success'. God has a white beard, a cream frock to equal one of those Doreen borrows from Demis Roussos and I believe is responsible for quite a lot of damage.

Sybil was a very emotional woman. The tears were literally welling up over her hands as she pressed over her mouth to stifle her screams of delight. This woman loved children like that little greedy bastard Winnie the Pooh likes honey.

'Oh, oh, oh! You look like the Waltons!'

Now, I do remember the Waltons and, if that memory serves me correctly, they were a bunch of hillbillies utterly bemused by life and dressed similarly to Dexy's Midnight Runners.

'You have a son,' Sybil said to me. She gave me a little shove on the shoulder. 'Well done.' It sounded like an achievement against the predicted odds.

Brigit gave me a shove. 'Yes, well done.'

Something happened after Ollie was born. It should have been Brigit and not me who went to the GP. Women get postnatal depression because they are exhausted and ground down by an avalanche of domestic duties, which slowly threaten to consume them. Whatever happened postnatal, I was the one who became depressed.

'I feel low,' I told the GP.

He took my blood pressure and looked at my eyes.

I still felt low.

He tore himself away from the screen, pushed his wheeled chair away from the desk and clasped his hands. 'What do you do?'

'Do?'

'With your time.'

'I look after our four children.'

'Ah.'

'Ah?'

He wrote something on his pad. 'What else do you do?'

I had stopped talking about the diminishing number of animals and the onions and the garlic I was growing because they required no effort. Perhaps I should have said something. 'I look after four children. I don't have time for anything else. They take up a lot of it.'

'My wife looks after ours.'

'Right. Then she'd know.'

'She does other things too.'

'Oh.'

'Parish council minutes, that sort of thing.'

'How many children do you have?'

'One. It's not an issue of numbers though, is it? One, three or five. They all need the same thing.'

'Oh, just the one.'

'It's a woman's job really. Don't you think?'

'Obviously not. I'm doing it.'

'Yes, but perhaps that may not be wise.' He wrote out a prescription and handed it to me.

'You've prescribed Prozac.'

'Yes. It'll help with the low mood. However that's really only one part of the problem.'

'Is it? What's the other part?'

He did the 'eye to eye' thing.

'I simply think you don't have enough to do.'

27

NOW

Fact: Cumulative number of odd socks, 368

Everyone is going to Brigit's PhD presentation. It is a three-line whip. People are also wearing the sort of expressions as if they have been actually whipped and are in excruciating pain.

Ollie continues to pull at his collar. 'It's a noose,' he bleats. 'Only condemned people wear nooses.'

'And it bloody well will be if you don't put a plug in it,' Emma adds sensitively.

She is wearing a dress which is, to anyone with half an eye, as excruciating for her as the tie is to Ollie. We are lined up for a photo and Graham Rickard, who has taken to popping round, takes a few snaps.

Brigit inspects them. 'Ollie, you have your tongue sticking out on every one. Retakes please Graham.'

'I'm not doing them again.' Ollie points at Ruby. 'She'll have it on Instagram before I can fart.'

'Ollie!'

'That's what Dad says.'

'That's a lie.'

Ollie shakes his fist at me. 'That's a lie!'

Someone knocks at the door and comes in. Lucy Harper appears and joins in the photo shoot.

'Yay!' she says in that 'Lucy' way. I have never really understood what 'yay!' means.

'God, you're so tall,' Brigit says every time she sees Lucy. This is because Brigit isn't very tall and everyone in our family is taller than she is. Over the years Brigit has become a minority group. 'I feel so small with you lot.'

'Perhaps you should move to the far east where people are generally smaller. Then it wouldn't feel so bad,' I say.

There is silence and rigid stares. I've clearly made one of my regular classic gaffs. I don't even bother trying to imagine what it might be. It will be too ridiculous to be believed.

'God, that's so racist, Dad.' Ruby is clearly stunned by my insensitivity towards people under five feet ten.

I glance at Graham Rickard who is still here. He looks as bewildered as I am. This height discrimination must be a new thing. I feel suddenly apologetic for being six foot three. I mean, it's absolutely obscene. There must be an operation I can have.

'But it's true. People in the far east are generally smaller.' I emphasise the word 'generally' in the hope of clemency. I appear to have dug either a second hole or made the first one deeper. People are looking at me not with sympathy but aggression and, yes, believe it or not, disbelief.

'There are some things you keep to yourself,' Brigit says. 'Remember the thing we discussed about 'the filter'?'

'Yes; the filter which imbues utter silence for anyone with an opinion. Oh right, so the next time you tuck your skirt into the top of your tights after you've been to the loo, I'll keep quiet. That's just in case I'm being prejudiced against people who like their dresses tucked into the top of their tights so their arses are exposed to the world.'

People groan.

Lucy gives me a hug. Lucy Harper and I don't need to say anything. She's always made me feel she's on my side when I've needed it most.

I see Graham out. He has enough problems without becoming embroiled in a convoluted debate about the need for height equality.

'How are things, you know, with Harriet?'

Graham looks down at his feet. I look down at them too. Looking at feet can sometimes be quite comforting. Unless of course, you have one leg. The absence of a foot could be quite disconcerting. Graham has smaller feet than me, but I don't say anything as I don't want to offend him or sound prejudiced in any way. Somewhere there is bound to be a group campaigning for equality for foot sizes. They would have my blessing if anyone could explain why children's shoes, a quarter the size of adult shoes, are four times as expensive.

'Harriet's having an assessment this week. There's a lot they can do with memory and how she can do things to make sure she can function at the highest level for as long as possible.'

I can see that Graham has already become embroiled by clinical jargon, 'a range of outcomes', 'the neural pathway' and 'projected prognosis'. I don't know why they can't simply say that Harriet Rickard is 'losing her mind'.

'It's hard though. The kids are being brilliant, but they've got their lives and they aren't around much.'

'I'll pop over.' I keep saying this, but I haven't done it yet. I don't think I've ever had a proper conversation with Harriet in all the time we have lived here. I'm not sure I'd know where to start. Brigit, of course, would say 'start somewhere'.

'That would be good. Thank you.'

I watch Graham go. He isn't the strident Graham Rickard I used to know. Or did I just imagine that? Did I see Graham as strident because I viewed myself as less so because I looked after the children, and progressively turned them orange? How the tables have turned. Or perhaps they haven't moved, and it is only perception that has shifted.

With that profound thought, I go back through the house to where the family are in the garden drinking champagne.

For some reason I turn when I reach the door. My foot hooks underneath it and I start to fall, my foot still trapped. I go down like a tree and hear something on the side of my foot click, or snap. I yell an expletive quite unfitting for the occasion.

'Holy fuck!' I don't have time to think about what that means. Even at six foot three it doesn't take long to hit the ground.

People look at me in the way they might look at a sideshow or a few fireworks intended to please but not intrude. They are laughing. I am down on the floor with my foot quite clearly hooked unnaturally under the door, moaning in justifiable pain. I gave up worrying about indignity years ago. People have seen me in flip-flops and socks bringing in the milk. After that there is not much further to go. My family are laughing. They are not moving. Even Lucy Harper is laughing. What the hell is there to laugh about? I imagine watching myself on You've Been Framed.

'I've bloody well hurt myself. I need to go to the emergency department.'

Brigit suddenly looks serious. Despite the father of her children lying prostrate on the patio, her concern is for her bloody emergency department and that I might occupy a seat or a stretcher or a space in a corridor reserved for a consumptive octogenarian. 'I hardly think so.' She is very protective of her emergency department. 'It's the weekend.'

I struggle to speak because the pain is suffocating me. 'So, if I'd done it yesterday, I could have gone? I need some help.' I unhook my foot from underneath the door. There is a bruise. It probably isn't broken, but there's definitely some damage to the tendon. 'I can't walk on it.'

'You'll be fine,' Chloe says. She is home especially for the occasion. She has a reading week where reading is an

267

infinitesimally small component. 'You'll be fine' is still her stock phrase.

'Do I look fine?'

'You can talk.'

'People who are terminally ill can talk.'

Ruby comes over and looks down at me. If she had been two, she would have almost definitely jumped on my head. 'That's such a dreadful thing to say.'

I am not in a good position to argue.

'How would you like it if you were terminally ill, Dad?'

Brigit looks at her watch. 'We need to go in twenty minutes.'

I am lying on the floor. People are behaving as if what is happening to me is occurring in a different time plane altogether. 'I can't walk.'

'You haven't tried.'

They go inside. Chloe returns with a cushion from the sofa and gently puts it under my head. I feel so grateful lying there in the cool autumn air on the patio with a cushion under my head. Some fathers aren't this lucky! I am on the verge of listing all the things I've done for them and wondering if my actions really do warrant being left lying on the patio to die of hypothermia. I imagine if I died, they would call someone to dig a hole.

'There,' Chloe says as if she has just done me the biggest favour.

I look up at her with such gratitude. 'You should do medicine, you'd save the NHS thousands. What would you do for someone having a heart attack? Give them a book to read?'

I manage after some time to get up. The side of my foot is swollen. I know though, the more I begin to move and try to function, the quicker any residual sympathy will slip away. I consider collapsing and feigning death. What's the point?

'I can't drive,' I tell the assembled group as we stand around the car.

Brigit drives because my clutch foot is buggered. We all feel nauseous because Brigit moves the accelerator with the changing intonation of her voice. This is not a criticism of women drivers. This is a criticism of Brigit's driving for which I have, on this rare occasion, full family support.

'It's Mum's day,' Chloe whispers quite threateningly in my ear. 'You need to be brave.'

I am being bloody brave. My foot is hanging onto my leg by a thread!

We arrive at a beautiful terraced house on the outskirts of the city overlooking the sea. It was the home of Nancy Astor, the first woman MP. They are now erecting a statue to commemorate and celebrate her. Brigit has quite rightly been tweeting madly about this because the word 'celebrated' needs to be repeated and celebrated as a word. No doubt she will go to the unveiling. It still staggers me how it's taken so long to get a statue of this remarkable woman when there is one for Kate Moss in Oslo.

I have this brief moment and imagine my statue being unveiled; a man doubled in pain and bearing a battered copy of 'The Complete Guide to Childcare' above his head. I am quickly pulled from this twisted fantasy and we are ushered up the stairs of this magnificent house to the top floor by a man wearing a long coat with the shiniest buttons I have ever seen. The image of Cinderella comes to mind, but I keep this quiet. I am hobbling, but the man with the buttons doesn't seem to give a shit either.

There is an array of canapés and drinks available. I spot a letter to Nancy Astor from the Queen. I take a photo. Brigit jabs me in the ribs. The man with the bright buttons waves his hand in a 'most definitely not' sort of way. I have been told.

I am introduced to the Chancellor of the University, the Vice Chancellor, the Dean and a few others wearing varying degrees of bling around their necks. I am introduced to the Mayor who looks woefully out of place because, like me, he is an ordinary person, except he has a chain which threatens to bring his forehead down to the shag pile and I have a tie borrowed off Graham Rickard now that we are besties. The girls look suitably mortified as people admire them and Ollie hits the canapés and the miniature cheesecakes in little jars, which are rather good even if they are only large enough to fill a cavity in a small tooth.

'So what do you do?' The Chancellor asks me.

I study his face to see if this might simply be standard patter. He has a nice round, kind face. I am standing in a room with some of the most qualified people within five miles. They have awards to show for their illustrious careers, and bank balances to reflect all the cumulative effort they have put in. I look at our children. I know they are the result in part of my efforts. I look at my foot. I wonder if the Chancellor would be so lucky to have his eldest daughter put a cushion under his head on the patio or whether Brigit might have found him a bed at the hospital.

'I've looked after the children for the last twenty years.'

He is incredulous. I assume this is because I have come straight out and admitted it without flinching. I don't mention the small-holding or the novels. I'm down to garlic and onions and a couple of geese that don't lay eggs.

'Wow. All four of them?'

'Yup.'

The Mayor appears at my side. 'He writes novels,' the Mayor says.

The Chancellor looks at me with renewed interest.

'I've read one. More the wife's cup of tea really. Nice cover though.'

'Really?' the Chancellor says. I imagine he's taking the piss.

'Well, a couple. Not best-sellers.'

'That's hardly the point.'

I'm liking this man more and more. I wonder if Brigit has had something to do with it.

'A novel is a hell of a thing to finish. I tried once. Took a pad on holiday. Wrote about six lines.'

270

I am suddenly distracted. 'I'm sorry,' I say to the Chancellor, 'is that…?'

'Yes, it is,' the Mayor says.

A man with grey, once blonde hair is talking to Brigit. 'Roger Taylor?'

'Roger Taylor,' the Mayor confirms. The Mayor doesn't strike me as someone who would recognise Roger Taylor if he was drumming in front of him. 'He's with 'The Queen'.' The Chancellor, the man I am thinking of adopting as my second bestie along with Graham Rickard, laughs.

'It's Queen, the group, Jerry, not *the* Queen. He's important, but not that important. Services to music or something. Not my department.'

The Mayor holds up his hand. 'No, Dougie,' which is obviously the Chancellor's name, 'he was on a stamp once. I bought one. You don't get on a stamp unless you have some weight.'

I look at the Mayor's belly and wonder why he hasn't featured on a stamp.

The Chancellor lowers his voice to a whisper. 'I was involved with Brigit's award and rightly deserved. Wonderful woman. You clearly played a big part. Brigit understands how things work, knows how to forge and maintain good relationships even with the biggest tossers you could ever meet. There are a few of those around I can tell you. But don't quote me. In fact I have to go and shake some of their hands.'

I meet the man who runs a zoo. His book has been turned into a film. He is being awarded a PhD for his work on animal conservation obviously. He looks relaxed. He has spent time with Matt Damon and Scarlett Johanssen who starred in the film adaptation of his book. I am a grown-up. I am not supposed to feel unchecked envy, but I do. He isn't even one of my friends and another little part of me still remaining is withering on the vine.

We are ushered again. There is a lot of ushering going on. The man doing a sterling impression of Buttons has his

271

eye on me. I assume he thinks I might lift something on the way out. Ollie takes a couple of canapés and stuffs them into his mouth and one of the cheesecake pots, which he slips into his pocket. We are led along with Roger Taylor, the zoo man, someone else who has done incredible work at the marine aquarium with things in tanks. We walk to a large marquee. There are more canapés and leather sofas. The girls, Ollie, Brigit and I stand with the other PhD recipients, their relatives and friends.

I check with the girls to see if they are all right.

'It's a bit much,' Chloe says.

Emma is staring at Roger Taylor. 'Is he famous?'

'He's the drummer from Queen.'

As if on cue, Roger comes over to us. He isn't as tall as I'd imagined and I realise it's unwise to touch on this subject as Ruby is likely to wade in and expose me for my prejudice against short people in front of one of the most famous drummers in the world. I think about telling Roger that I believe their album Sheer Heart Attack to be their best, but he may of course not agree with me, and he is in a better position technically than I am to give a view.

'This your family?' Roger asks, looking directly at me.

'Yes.' I introduce them with Ollie surreptitiously eating his cheesecake. He doesn't care about Queen. They don't call anyone a 'mother-fucker', so not cool at all.

'Amazing. Beautiful. You're a lucky man.'

He leaves us after giving this seal of approval and starts talking to Brigit again. I wonder if she knows who he is.

'You know that's Brian Taylor from Queen,' Brigit says when she finally comes over.

We all double up in pleats of laughter. Brigit has never been hot on names.

'Yeah, he was in a band with Eddie Mercury,' I say.

The tension of Emma being in a dress, Ollie wearing a noose and me feeling like a spare part lifts. Then I see him. This man wasn't at Nancy Astor's house. He is obviously also receiving an award; along with Brigit and Roger and

Andrew Lloyd-Webber's brother and the man from the zoo. There is no stopping the wave of people heading towards the doorway into a vast marquee where the presentation ceremony is taking place. I am caught in a current. This man and I are now only a metre apart. There is a surge and we are pushed against one another.

'Sorry,' I say.

He turns to me.

'That's okay. We're all in this together by the look of it.' He shakes my hand. He does the 'eye to eye' thing. I don't flinch.

'I suppose we are.'

We drift apart.

I have just shaken hands with Hugh Fearnley-Whittingstall.

28

CHRISTMAS PAST.

Fact: Number of regrets, 0

Now Ollie had finally arrived, and Brigit was popping into work to make sure the people covering hadn't taken over in a bloodless coup, I was a man with four children in his care. I reflect on the extraordinary chain of events taking an ostensibly fraudulent man, pretending he knew how to care for one child and ending up with four. I still don't know to this day why the authorities hadn't intervened and exposed the truth and got a documentary out of it or at least asked me to write an authentic column in a Sunday supplement.

On the last day before the Christmas holidays and Chloe's first term at school, Ruby, Emma, Ollie and I had spent the afternoon painting a Christmas scene for the wall on the village hall. Harriet Rickard, being the resident artist, had taken the lead. We had a vast piece of paper covering the floor. Ollie crawled across it, belched and regurgitated something orange onto the paper next to the baby Jesus in his crib. It did seem a bit disrespectful.

'It can be the moon,' Olivia Rayner said helpfully. 'Or a bauble.' Her sons, James and Johnny, were industriously colouring in the wise men and making a bloody hash of it. They looked like something drawn by a woodpecker.

'I notice Emma's drawn a horse.' Harriet Rickard pointed disparagingly at the five-legged beast Emma had produced. 'Not very Christmassy, would you say, Emma?'

'It's a donkey,' Emma said. 'There was a donkey 'cause fat Mary sat on it and went to Bethlehem with Joseph to have someone else's baby.'

'Well, I think you'll find she was carrying and about to give birth to the son of God, and that's why we call it Christmas; a celebration of Christ.'

My heart was pounding. I had a premonition of what was coming next and it wasn't a miracle. The crucifixion came to mind, brought forward from Easter, with me hanging on the cross.

Ruby put her hand up. She was drawing an angel beautifully, in the sky with a halo and wings. 'Excuse me,' she said.

I could see Harriet was getting irritated. 'What is it, Ruby?'

'I think Joseph was a very good man.' This seemed to lighten the atmosphere.

'Yes, he was, Ruby. Joseph was a very good man. That's a beautiful angel.'

'He was good because he looked after someone else's child and took Mary in because no one else wanted her.'

There were women glaring at me. Jilly Green was clutching Charles Julian as if he might be in imminent danger of becoming possessed by such blasphemy. Caroline Waters was gathering Guy and Sarah in her arms as if they might need to make a run for it. Olivia, Caroline, Jilly, Harriet and a bunch of other women who came and went through the year were all staring at me.

'Not sure where they got that from,' I said. 'There's all sorts of stuff about these days. No respect for tradition. Sorry.'

'Sometimes,' Harriet said, snatching the crayons off Ruby and Emma and one from Ollie's mouth, which was now blue, 'sorry simply isn't good enough.'

I was getting the impression she wanted a crucifixion. 'Well, maybe they picked it up from me.'

'I would think so,' Caroline Waters said with an affected air of resignation as if there was no hope for people like me. 'It's all about maintaining the magic. You'll be telling them Father Christmas doesn't exist next.'

There was silence. There were looks of bewilderment from the children as this ugly truth hung in the air, ready to be blasted into space. By me!

'Ha, ha, ha, what a ridiculous thing to say, Caroline. There's one thing to question the parentage of Jesus (this I think, went over the children's heads), but it's another to question the existence of someone we all know and love.' Here I got the attention of the children. They were all nodding furiously. It would seem that over the years I might have instilled some doubt as to the veracity of said fat man's existence and clawed myself back from the brink of becoming the modern day Scrooge. 'In fact, the children and I are all off to see him later.' This was a lie. 'We've already posted our lists to the North Pole.'

'No, we haven't,' Emma corrected me. 'You said it was a waste of a stamp and that we should put them up the chimbly. Then we said, they'll catch fire and anyway, Santa will only get them on his way down the chimbly and that will be too late because he'll already have our presents in his big fat sack.'

'Well, we will be posting them tonight. To the North Pole.'

We heard the bell at the school. It was the end of the day, the end of the term and the end of any magic about Mary and her virginity for a small group of probably permanently scarred children.

The Christmas scene produced by too many budding artists looked like a battlefield with dead one-dimensional animals. There were stars like nuclear explosions and houses clearly built by the man with foundations of sand. The wise men and the shepherds looked like men deposed. Only

276

Ruby's angel twinkled bright and beautiful in the sky not far from the orange moon made from Ollie's sputum.

It was still ten days to Christmas. Everything was closing until the New Year. I stood in the playground with the mothers eyeing me warily. I could only surmise that the truth about Mary had spread like an airborne virus.

Chloe came out of school laden with all the things they'd made to celebrate the season. There were paper chains, which looked like they'd been put together by a bunch of alcoholics with the shakes, candle holders designed for a pyromaniac and cards; a multitude of cards to every chicken, duck, goose, pig and sheep we still owned. There was even one for Roy who was now residing with Millicent and her daughter who still continued to insist what a friendly animal he really was. I couldn't help thinking of Ted Bundy and what a personable character he seemed until revealing his systematic slaughter of tens of young women. Roy, in my view, was just biding his time.

'Mrs Jones says we'll get everything we wish for,' Chloe said. 'That means I can go to the moon in my very own space rocket with glitter.'

I could see Mrs Jones on the other side of the playground dishing out her seasonal cheer and false hopes to anguished parents, reeling at the thought of letting their children down when they didn't unwrap a nuclear warhead on Christmas Day to nuke all the bad people.

'We can certainly do the glitter,' I said. I only had to hoover the carpet to fill a couple of buckets.

The girls' Christmas lists were long, in wonky writing, the words spilling off the page like a Dali painting. They looked like an order sheet for a Toys R Us warehouse. We put the lists in envelopes each with a letter, stuck on stamps and actually put them into the post box addressed to the North Pole, because I said that was what we were going to do. I was six years into childcare and a little part of me, probably my brain, actually believed they might get to the

North Pole. Despite the children having forgotten about her, I was still on the look out for Blue Cow.

'We need a tree,' Brigit said.

I bought a beautiful green artificial tree with colour-coded branches.

Brigit put her hand over her mouth when she saw it. I thought she was delighted. 'You can't be serious. It's artificial.'

'Yes. Just the job. It's even got the lights built in.' I plugged it in. The ends of every branch twinkled blue.

'It's got blue lights! My God, it's got blue lights.'

'I know. Told you.' I thought she was pleased.

'Blue lights on a green tree!'

'Look, we need to make things easy. We have four children, life is busy. We don't need a real Christmas tree with all the stuff. Anyway, Ruby told Harriet and the pre-school that Jesus was an illegitimate child. Well, he was an illegitimate child, but some other man's.'

'Yes, God.'

'Jesus!'

'Yes, God's son.'

'Have you gone mad?'

'It's Christmas. People lie and deceive at Christmas so everybody has a good time. And they buy real bloody Christmas trees that aren't like something from the set of Doctor Who!'

We went to buy a real tree from a real wood where a man I came to know simply as Terry for the next fourteen years took our photo and smiled a lot because he was taking money from people in a field who then had to cut down their own frigging tree and lug it home.

Terry handed me a saw. 'Take your pick.'

I looked at the saw. I wasn't expecting a saw. 'Isn't it already cut?'

'You need the fresh.'

'I'm happy with one already cut down.' I could see a row of trees leaning against his cabin. 'What about one of those?'

'Reserved.'

'Who by? Why should they get theirs cut down?'

'Because they're for the disabled people.' He grinned. Beyond his lips there was work enough to keep Diane Quail in full-time employment for quite a few weeks. 'You don't look disabled to me.'

Emma piped up. 'He said he was. He cut his finger. He cried. Mummy told him not to be such a big baby.'

I took the saw and went to cut down the tree and my finger at the same time. I tried very hard not to cry.

The girls wouldn't decorate the tree until Lucy Harper arrived. Lucy was getting taller and no longer seven.

They put on Last Christmas by Wham. I opened a bottle of fizz. I needed the anaesthetic.

I got out the old lights, rigged them up. They didn't work. I found a tear in the wire coating. I touched the wire. I don't know why I touched the wire. The current ran through my body like an eel. 'Jesus! Oh Jesus!' I shouted.

'It's his birthday,' Chloe shouted back. 'Happy birthday to Jesus, happy birthday to him,' they all sang.

I could have died, and my children were singing.

'I could have died!' I shouted above the music.

Only Ollie, sitting in his chair, was looking at me. Brigit was dancing with the girls to Last Christmas. They were all laughing.

'I'm still in shock.'

Brigit came and took my hand. 'You'll be fine,' she said.

29

CHRISTMAS PRESENT

Fact: Retirement age for this job, my last breath.

The blue icicle lights we drape around the house a couple of weeks before Christmas, to show we are in the Christmas spirit, are full of water. We have spent a fortune on lights over the years. Harriet Rickard is right; we are those people who spend money on Christmas decorations rather than something more permanent to make the house look good for longer than three weeks. We're like the people on one of those 'makeover' programmes where they use Velcro and PVA to cover the cracks and rising damp until the cameras leave, the presenters go on a 'detox' documentary and the house collapses into the basement.

        I hang the lights regardless. Ever hopeful.

        They don't work.

'They look awful,' Brigit says. 'We need some new ones.'

'We buy new ones every year.'

    I drive to B&Q because arguing the toss about Christmas lights is a waste of life. B&Q is full of industrious people covered in paint and brick dust who know what they're doing. When I'm here I feel compelled to buy brackets and screws or anything that might come in handy around the house. The shelves are almost devoid of Christmas lights apart from the drab-looking ones no one wants. I buy them and repair the rest. Masking tape has been good enough for the last nineteen years.

I am now hanging the lights in the rain on a Monday morning as I listen to people drive to work. Even after all these years, I am still affected by the sound of people going to work. Putting Christmas lights up feels like a legitimate activity for spare time, but not in the middle of the working day. Graham Rickard drives past and slows down. He waves. A man with the weight of the world, or at least a dementing wife, on his shoulders. I haven't been to see Harriet Rickard yet. I must do it.

The lights look much like they did last year. Emma comes back from walking the dog.

'A protest against Christmas?' she says.

'I love Christmas.'

'Then it should be reflected in the quality of the decorations. This is the kind of thing Scrooge would hang out.'

'They didn't have electricity when Charles Dickens was alive.'

'I thought it was J K Rowling.'

'Stick to empirical things, Em. Anyway, it's all they had. The two houses on the Fairway bought them all, prompting the government to introduce a programme of load-shedding.'

I turn them on. They start to flash. I can't stop them flashing.

Instead of assisting, Emma is laughing.

'They're supposed to be multi-functional.' I give up and turn them off. I am going to see Harriet Rickard. It is Christmas, and good things need to be done at Christmas.

The flowerbeds leading up to the Rickards' house are thick with weeds. Instead of bedding plants spilling over the edge in the spring like they used to, there are dock leaves and dandelions. The windowsills are peeling and the glass is filthy. Where our house isn't finished, the Rickards' is falling apart. Harriet was so fastidious. Now it looks as if she simply doesn't care.

Harriet's Renault is parked outside the house with L-plates on it. I knock on the door. It is Spence, their eighteen-year-old and youngest son, who comes to the door. He doesn't look surprised to see me. The teenagers never looked surprised. I guess so much comes at them, they don't have the time to be shocked.

'Hi,' Spence says in this deep gravelly voice, a shock after the squeaky little noises he used to make. He's almost as tall as me with wide muscular shoulders and sporting a goatee.

'I've come to see your mum. Is she in?'

'Yeah.'

I notice Spence has a black eye. 'What does the other guy look like?'

'I was drunk. I walked into a post.'

I admire his honesty.

'The post is fine.'

'Right.' We stand there, our lack of familiarity filling the silence. 'Shall I come in then?'

'Oh, yeah,' he says as if he's forgotten. 'Mum's in the lounge.'

The house, converted from four old cottages, is a dark labyrinth. I've only been in the place a handful of times and then only in the kitchen where I banged my head on the beams.

I find the lounge. Harriet has her back to me. She is sitting in a small conservatory overlooking the garden, which has also become unkempt and uncared for. I can see that where Harriet's hair was once blonde, it is now suffused with grey. I realise that Harriet is one of the genuine blondes and not one of the seventeen conjured from a bottle.

I don't want to make her jump, but she turns to me before I cough.

'My goodness, here's a surprise.' Harriet gets out of her chair.

'No, it's okay, don't get up.'

'Oh, don't be silly. I'm not disabled. I'm just losing my mind.'

I don't know whether to laugh at this. Harriet does it for me.

I sit down opposite her. Harriet is younger than me by maybe four years or so, but she looks a lot younger. Her skin is smooth, like someone without worry, as if every concern has been lifted from her and taken on by others. Like someone who has been excused responsibility; like a child.

'I thought I'd drop by and see how you are. I borrowed Graham's drain rods. He told us you weren't well.'

Harriet laughs. 'Graham always was the master of the understatement. I didn't know he had any drain rods. He's very secretive.'

Perhaps Harriet has an idea about the affairs.

She has lovely teeth. I've never noticed that before. I don't think I've ever looked, always too busy being irritated by her to see any virtues.

'Well, here I am. How's Brigit?'

'Oh, you know, busy, as always. The hospital's always full. Do you think we'll get snow?'

'Don't be ridiculous. Are we making small talk? I'm having a good day, let's not waste it on small talk. Save that for when I can't even recognise my own children.'

'Okay.' I feel a little nervous. I've only ever talked small with Harriet Rickard.

'I have early onset dementia, you know that? Of course you do. That's why you're here.'

I hand her the Christmas card.

'You normally send one of the children.'

'I thought I'd bring it myself this year.'

'That's very kind of you. Not one the children made then.'

'They're a bit past that and far too cool to send cards with Father Christmas on them. They send a picture on Snapchat wearing a couple of straps.'

'Do you remember that mural we did at the pre-school and Ollie dribbled on it and Emma drew a horse and Ruby told everyone that Mary was a slut more or less?'

'I do.'

'And that party you threw because you wanted to go one better than that arsehole Danny Ray?'

'You remember that? How did you know?'

'It was obvious. He comes along with his three little perfect sprogs and the funfair in his garden. You saw it as a threat. You didn't need to. I remember it all. You know he made porn films?'

'His girlfriend told me. 'Brenda Does Basingstoke'.'

'Ah, yes. I remember you talking to her. You know she was Ingrid in 'Ingrid Does Innsbruck'.'

'I did wonder.'

'What did you find to talk about?'

'I spoke a little Romanian. I used to live there. You can remember this?'

'Oh, yes. The past becomes clearer, I'm told, as the present slips away. A shitty trade off. I can walk to the top of the road and forget where I am, but I can tell you what I had for breakfast in 1999. It's very disconcerting. Not every day though.'

I didn't think Harriet had a sense of humour.

'Are you still painting?'

Harriet's paintings hang on many of the walls. They are impressionist, I believe. I don't particularly like them.

'The trouble is, I'm not doing anything really. Nothing sticks. I start a job, leave it and can't remember starting it in the first place, so I blame other people for the mess. Except there aren't so many people to blame these days. The children are all grown up. You must feel it too.'

'There's still Ollie. He's only twelve.'

'Yes, but the girls are adults, and twelve is when they start to get angry before they come back. Archie's doing law and Becca's in Australia living the life they live over there.'

Spence appears. 'Can I get you a coffee?'

'It's okay,' I say.

Harriet reaches over and takes my hand. 'Have one. Stay awhile. It's lovely to see you while I still know who you are.' She laughs at this. It is Harriet's prerogative. I laugh too, but it doesn't feel very funny.

Spence comes back with the coffee and some biscuits.

'What are you going to do, Spence?' I ask him.

'I'm taking a gap year.'

'Then what?'

Spence looks at his mother. 'I want to study art, like Mum.'

'Wow. That's wonderful.'

'Mum says you write novels.'

'I try to. Not very successfully. I've had four children to look after.'

'And all those bloody sheep, pigs and that cockerel. Do remember that cockerel, the one that escaped at the party?' Harriet says laughing.

'Roy.'

'That's him. I suppose he'll be dead by now.'

I haven't thought about Roy for years. I suppose he will be dead, along with all the other animals we had. The sky must be crammed with stars for each and every one of them.

'Graham's helping Spence to drive. His nerves are in tatters,' Harriet says after Spence has gone.

'I thought he'd passed.'

'Did I say that?'

'I think so.'

'I talk such rubbish. Did you know Geoff and Gaynor Tiller have spilt up?'

'I didn't.'

'No, you never did get the gossip. He was planning to go off with Phoebe from the Final Furlong. She had more sense and went back to the plumber. Geoff Tiller's such a tosser. I hope Gaynor takes him to the cleaners.'

I've never heard Harriet Rickard speak like this before. She turns to me. She has that faraway look in her eyes. Has she already forgotten who I am?

'Why did you do it?'

This sounds like the sort of question warranting a confession.

'Do what?'

'Look after all of those children for so long? You were the only man, apart from one or two weird ones who appeared now and again but never came back. It was such a tough call.'

I am taken aback by this. I'm not sure I can even answer. 'I wanted to do it. I thought it would be easy. It looked easy in the books.'

'Easy? God, there are so many easier things. Being a lawyer, telling other people their rights and getting paid for it is easy. Looking after children isn't easy. I was a crap mother. It's easy to be bad at it.'

'That's not true. You were a good mother.'

Harriet dismisses my comment with a wave of her hand. 'Oh, it's true. I pushed them when I should have let them do their own thing. Archie hates doing law. He thinks it's boring and Becca works for some fashion company. They're artistic, you see.'

'Like you.'

'No, I'm not artistic. I wanted to be, but I didn't have that little extra something it takes to be successful; that edge you need to stand out from the crowd. You know what I mean. It's the same with writing, I suppose. You have to give something a new spin or you get washed away on the tide of millions of others with the same dreams.' Harriet gazes out of the window at the mottled grey sky as if searching for something. Maybe she is. Maybe she is searching for the memories, which will one day elude her.

'I used to watch you with the girls. I used to wonder what it must feel like to be a man in a world of women, doing a job most men don't ever do. I used to suggest to Graham that he try it for a couple of weeks. He managed a day, like Tony Blair who said it was the "hardest thing" he ever did.'

I'm wondering why we're having such a conversation when, over the years, we have barely exchanged more than a few sentences and greetings. It feels as if someone has peeled the front away from Harriet to reveal what lies underneath and she is trying to catch up with all the things we should have said.

'I always felt a fraud. I didn't think it was a proper job. Did you think it was a proper job, Harriet?'

'Oh, my God, yes. Graham and I used to row all the time about how I was left to look after the kids and he went off to his chambers to consult and advise without culpability while I was changing nappies and pretending to be happy all the frigging time. My face used to ache with all that false smiling. I'm surprised my teeth haven't been worn away by the wind. Looking after the kids isn't even a job. It's something which has to be done. That's why women do it. They do it because it has to be done. If they waited around for the blokes, the kids would drown in their own pee and starve to death.'

I can't help but laugh at this and feel regret that we haven't had conversations like this many times before.

'Brigit ran the hospital. By the time we had three children under the age of two and her days were so long, we had to carry on.'

'It must have felt very lonely. I used to feel lonely.'

'But there were all the other women.'

'Oh yes, there were. But we were all in the same boat, assuming everyone else knew what they were doing and too scared to admit they didn't. At least you never made any bones about it. We met at playgroups and coffee mornings. You were there, but we were still alone. Most of the time we spent with the children there were no other adults.'

I am taken aback by Harriet's candour. 'I always thought you were as thick as thieves.'

'No, it's a lonely business being the main carer. You did well. Everybody admired you. I don't know any other men who could've done it. And Brigit, it must have cost her too, not to be with her babies during the day.'

'Yes, it did.'

Spence comes back into the room. He touches his mother's arm. 'Are you alright, Mum?'

Harriet looks up at him. There is a moment where I think she loses her thread. 'Yes, yes I'm fine. I'm tired.' Harriet smiles at me.

I guess this is how it will be for her – the periods of lucidity decreasing and those of bewilderment and confusion longer and longer until the final lock is turned and the door to the real Harriet Rickard is closed for good. I am left wondering if what she's said to me is real at all.

I get up and Harriet does too. I want to hold her in my arms, and I do and she hugs me. I feel her body shake and she is crying.

'I don't know if I should be happy or sad,' she says into my chest.

'Happy. I would go for happy.'

'Yes.' She sniffs, wiping her nose on the sleeve of her top. The old Harriet Rickard would never have wiped her nose on her sleeve.

I kiss her on the cheek and she kisses me back. I leave her sitting in the chair drifting back to the place where she will increasingly reside.

In the kitchen I shake Spence's hand. 'Good to see you, and delighted you're going to follow what's in here.' I thump my chest. 'When do the travels begin?' I realise I know the answer to this.

'Oh, you know, when I've got the cash together and made a plan.' The answer is that Spence has elected to be with his mother for as long as he can. 'Everyone's coming back for Christmas. A surprise for Mum.'

'That's wonderful.'

'Yeah. She's been a good mum, always there for us. We need to be there for her now.'

'Don't forget to tell her,' I say. 'Parents don't always know how they did.'

'Sure. Too right.'

Spence Rickard is growing up fast, as ours are too. I realise there comes a point when it is no longer possible to keep pace with this progression and the young people take the baton and run the next stage of the race while we concentrate increasingly on the memories and the route already run. I want to cry. All this child caring over the years has made me so emotional.

At home, in the drive, I try and get the lights working properly and succeed. I find the rest for the tree.

Everyone is home, we drive to cut the tree down. Terry still has his sales chart, peaking in the last two weeks before Christmas as always. This year he's selling venison burgers.

'Locally shot,' Terry informs the people queuing up. 'Her name was Bambi.' Few people appreciate Terry's sense of humour, but his trees are still very good value.

We argue over the tree.

'Blue spruce,' Ruby insists every year.

'Too expensive,' I say. 'Not Christmassy enough. You don't see blue spruce on Christmas cards.'

'You don't see Scrooge either,' Brigit adds, 'but he's alive and well.'

We buy a normal Christmas tree. I cut it down with Terry's blunt saw. Just like his yearly patter, he doesn't change the saws either.

Terry takes a few wobbly pictures and we leave for another year. I wonder how long it will be until Brigit and I come on our own?

'Until next Christmas then. It comes quicker every year,' Terry says as he always does.

'Well, that's just rubbish,' Emma says as she always does.

Everyone is home tonight, ready to decorate the tree. There are no interlopers. The doorbell goes and the girls scream when Lucy Harper comes into the house. Lucy is not an interloper. She is one of us and has been for a very long time.

'Still not agreed on the colour for the hallway then,' Lucy says.

I point out a couple of vaguely different yellow squares. 'I think you were responsible for those three.'

'So I was.' Lucy is twenty-five, but to me she will be forever seven when she was sensible and not such a bad influence on the girls. 'Anyway, what's everyone doing for Christmas? Party, party, party?'

'No, we're all here, and the Harpers over on Boxing Day like always.'

'I have plans for Boxing Day,' Emma says. 'A few of us are going to Bristol.'

'What!'

'Ruby and Chloe are coming too. We're here for Christmas Day.'

'Christmas Day! What about Christmas Eve?'

'There are parties, Dad,' Chloe says.

'Oh, my God, this is terrible. I don't know how many Christmases I've got left. Terry always says see you next year, but I know it's only to keep my spirits up. I might not be here.'

Ollie pipes up. 'Grandma's ninety-three. She's still here.'

'We're not related. I am the love child of the woman from the Post Office and the milkman who died when he was fifty-two. She left me on the doorstep and that woman who claims to be my mother picked me up because she thought I'd become Prime Minister, not some unemployed bum who looked after his kids.'

Chloe sits down next to me. 'It's okay, Dad. We'll get the balance.'

Emma gets up and grabs the white board they use for planning and then arguing over who uses the car. 'We can do a grid,' she says, 'so we know who's here and who isn't.' She starts making yet another grid.

'A grid! You're making a grid for Christmas! Christmas is a time for rest and relaxation, giving and family. It is not a time for grids!'

Emma points the marker at me. 'Exactly, Dad. For giving. It's exactly the time for grids.'

'You always used to be here at Christmas.'

'Dad, most fathers would welcome the peace and quiet.'

'I'm not most fathers.'

'You can say that again.' Emma has her pen poised over the chart. 'Christmas Eve? Let's have the schedules then we can fit the old fart in for a few minutes.'

'Party,' Ruby says.

Chloe puts up her hand. 'Party.'

'I'm doing taxi for money,' Emma says putting three ticks against Christmas Eve.

I feel choked. 'Christmas Eve! There's no one here on Christmas Eve when the house is silent and you can't hear a mouse.'

'Exactly,' Ruby says. 'We need to party while you can look after the mices.'

'Plural is mice. But we do stuff on Christmas Eve.'

Chloe rests her hand patronisingly on my shoulder. 'Dad. What exactly do we do on Christmas Eve? You like to watch Love Actually and reminisce. We're too young to reminisce. You've got to do stuff to be able to reminisce.'

This, I would agree, is a fair point.

'You have to make the memories. That's what you said.'

Also a fair point.

'What about Christmas Day then?'

Chloe rests her hand on my back now as if I might need the support. 'We're coming back after the party. We're here on Christmas Day, silly.'

'God, this is pathetic,' Brigit says, finally intervening.

'Look.' I point at Brigit.

'Don't point at me.'

'I'm pointing because there are seven people in this hallway, which should've been painted years ago. I need support here. Not some rational explanation that this is all part of the growing process and the caged bird thing about letting it fly free and all that tosh. These are the people I've cared for from embryos.'

'That's not strictly true, is it.'

'You know what I mean.'

'And now you should celebrate that they have friends, that they want to party.'

God I'm hating Brigit's facilitative thing right now. I want to lock the door and keep them all here. They are mine. I look at Lucy. She shrugs. She never used to shrug. She used to agree with everything I said and help with the implementation of various schemes. Now she has gone over to the other side. She is a bloody traitor.

'And you're no bloody use, Harper. I should have left you on the doorstep all those years ago.'

Lucy puts her arms around me. 'It's okay. You did good.'

'They're all leaving!'

'Yes, but they come back. We all come back. That's what I mean, you did good. I came back.'

'When did you get so bloody wise?'

'When I came to this house and saw a man who didn't know what he was doing, up to his neck in screaming children. One of us had to get wise.'

'We need to decorate the tree,' Brigit says, clapping her hands together like a teacher rounding up rowdy children at the end of playtime. 'Lucy, Champers in the fridge, Ollie you're on snacks.'

Ollie rubs his hands together. We won't see half of them.

'Chloe, you're on decoration sorting and Em's on music.'

Emma is busy finishing the chart of when people will be AWOL over Christmas. 'Ruby, you're on general management.'

People start on their jobs because Brigit is good at ordering people around and using the world 'we' meaning other people when she is allocating work because she still thinks she's at the hospital with teams of people they actually pay and not an army of reluctant volunteers.

I unravel the ravelled tree lights and plug them in. I stretch them out and test them. One set doesn't work. I check the masking tape where I've repaired the lights against official advice for many years. I've got to use these because the people on the Fairway sucking the National Grid have the rest, I assume, to illuminate their otherwise dull lives when they should, according to Harriet Rickard, be renovating their houses. Now, poor old Harriet won't be able to remember whether it matters or not. It doesn't.

I get the lights on the tree. Ruby hangs a bauble.

'There's a system, Rube. Lights first.'

'Jesus!'

'Yes, it's his birthday, so happy birthday to Jesus.'

'So you're religious now?'

'I am at Christmas. It's a time of sharing and being nice to people.'

Lucy comes in with the Champagne, which is actually Prosecco and you get four bottles for the price of Tesco Champagne. The lights go on. Wham start to play Last Christmas. Ollie sings 'I gave you my heart and the very next day you sold it on eBay'. I'm wondering if there's a 'we wish you a 'mother-fucking' Christmas' from some middle-class rapper pretending he's from Harlem rather than Hertford.

I turn the main lights out to see how the tree looks. It needs that final set. I cast them over the branches, plug them in. They don't light up. I wiggle the masking tape and touch the wire. The electric eel thing zaps up my arm and makes my jaw shake. I step back. I don't think I'm dead, but I could be in a parallel universe. If I am, everything is exactly the same as the previous one, where no one has batted an eyelid that I've come, once again, within an inch of losing my life.

'Jesus! I've just been electrocuted!'

People are drinking and dancing to Last Christmas.

'I said I've just been electrocuted!'

Brigit comes over and is about to touch me.

'Don't touch me! I'm live.'

'That's a good thing, then.'

'I could've been killed.'

The others are still drinking Prosecco and dancing. What do I have to do to engender sympathy?

Chloe brings me a glass of Prosecco. 'Happy Christmas, Dad.'

'Don't touch your dad,' Brigit says. 'He's live.'

The power goes, the lights are out and the music stops. We are seven people standing in the dark. The girls and Ollie start laughing. Brigit takes my hand. Evidently I am not live.

In the darkness, with people still laughing, I think of all the years during which I pretended to be this other person who was self-sufficient and wrote novels, when what I actually did was care for our children every single day. They are not a dream, or so far away that I need to go on a journey to find them. William, the man who played his recorder to my vegetables and converted me to cinnamon joss sticks, told me a story about the man who travelled the world looking for treasure, only to find it under a tree in his own back yard. While I am contemplating this, the electricity returns and all the lights, including the dodgy ones, come on. Everybody starts dancing again.

'I've been electrocuted!'

Lucy Harper comes over, making one of those mock sympathy faces. She pulls my arm.

'Come on. It's Christmas. You'll be fine.'

30

TODAY- LATE JANUARY.

Fact: Number of nights Brigit and I spent away from the children in 19 years, 5

I drop Emma, Ruby and Ollie at the bus stop and watch them trudge across the road like the condemned on the way to the gallows. Their heads are down, looking at the media feeds uploaded by people only metres away. Ollie turns to wave and steps out in front of a car. The car stops inches away and Ollie trudges on, the driver waving his fist at the back of Ollie's head. Ollie carries on oblivious, leaving me twitching in my seat.

On the way back home, I call on Harriet Rickard. She's having a bad day. The rate of her decline is alarming, though I know she and Graham have kept this secret for a long time. Barbara, the carer, is here, finally releasing Spence to enjoy the remainder of his gap year. Barbara is a local mother known to us all, one of those people who is simply good. Aspiring to her level of goodness and cleaning prowess is utterly futile. She even polishes the pipes on her radiators

'That woman's creeping around the house again,' Harriet says, pointing at Barbara as if she's a barefaced intruder wearing an apron searching for something valuable to steal.

'It's Barbara,' I remind Harriet.

'I don't know a Barbara.'

'Maybe not today, Harriet, but perhaps you will tomorrow.'

'I don't know a bloody Barbara. I've never known a bloody Barbara.'

We dip into the past briefly where Harriet feels at home. I touch on the subject of a younger Barbara. Maybe there is a flicker, but Harriet's eyes continue to follow Barbara around the room with undisguised suspicion.

'You remember Charles Julian, Jilly Green's boy?' I say.

Harriet suddenly looks bright-eyed and excited as if she's just thought of a great idea. She likes a bit of gossip, does Harriet, and I can be relatively sure she'll have forgotten it before she can pass it on.

'I do. He was such a precocious little brat. I remember your cockerel biting him on the arse.' Harriet has become a little looser with the vernacular these days.

'The gossip is that he's been done for selling drugs at Oxford. They've kicked him out.' I'm really not one for tittle-tattle, but I do have this on reliable authority from Diane Quail. Diane's gossip is selective and usually of some quality.

Harriet hoots with laughter. 'Ooh, that's a juicy one. Hey, Barbara!' This news has clearly found that loose wire and reconnected Harriet with the present. 'You know Jilly Green's little brat, Charles Julian?'

Barbara appears at Harriet's side with a duster.

Harriet looks at it in horror. 'Oh, you're a guest, you don't need to dust, leave that to the woman who comes round poking in my drawers like she bloody well lives here. Anyway, Charles Julian's been busted for possession.'

I am quite staggered how familiar Harriet is with the jargon.

'That's terrible.' Barbara struggles not to smirk.

'Nah, it isn't,' Harriet adds. 'Had it coming to him. He had his head so far up his arse he could see that dangly thing at the back of his throat.'

'Epiglottis,' I add.

'That's the one.'

I leave Harriet and Barbara to reacquaint themselves for the umpteenth time and return home. I don't know if I like Harriet more because her creeping dementia has loosened her up, or if I'd tried harder years ago and not been so precious, I might have liked her anyway. It's so easy to make assumptions and consign someone to being a person they simply aren't. I'm dreading the day when Harriet no longer knows who I am, cutting out the middle man in her visits to the toilet and becoming the recipient of bulk packs of incontinence pads. I will miss her. I like talking about the past and the children. It's a secret world where I can take her by the hand to familiar well-trodden territory where we both feel safe and sometimes a bit tearful.

Brigit and I have been talking lately and have probably made the decision, without actually saying it, to sell the house for practical and financial reasons. We both hate these pragmatic conversations in the same way as setting up a 'death file' feels like giving the thumbs up and opening the front door to the miserable bastard with the scythe.

'It's a tired house. Had a lot of wear. You'll lose out if you don't spruce it up,' the estate agent said, running through the vast list of things wrong with our home of many years. She was so dispassionate. This was our house, harbouring our memories. She gave us a 'now' value and a 'spruced up' value. The difference was significant enough to warrant some 'sprucing' with a shed-load of paint and some serious DIY SOS.

I haven't actually started this 'sprucing' because every time I choose a room and begin to clear it, I find things like photographs of the children on a beach or in a park that have slipped behind a cupboard. Despite it being just a building, we are in every nook and cranny of this place as if our molecules have blended with it to become one, which I know is ridiculous, but I do find the division between it and us hard to discern. The idea of selling it does feel like flogging an organ. These items and photographs pierce the now thick silence with their vibrancy. Most days I spot things I haven't seen before – a little drawing by Emma of one of her famous five-legged horses in pencil on a wall and a gold star Chloe has taken from a schoolbook and put on her headboard. These things stop me in my tracks and the minutes when I should be slapping paint on walls are lost to the memories these little artefacts invoke.

I decide to hit the hallway with some sort of green satin emulsion Brigit chose and no one liked because it is not reflective of who we are. It is bland and we most definitely are not. If we are a colour, I would choose a vibrant yellow with a few dark splodges here and there to account for my significant errors of judgement and dead poultry along the way.

I still can't bear to cover the test squares we made from the hundreds of paint pots, displaying our years of indecision and hopeless ideas of democracy. Instead, I start in a corner with a big brush really not intended for corners. I notice a Christmas decoration hanging underneath the stairs, hidden from ordinary view. It looks like it has been here for years. It is a little star, crayoned yellow with 'Chloe' written like an electrocuted spider on one of the points. I remember her making this and looking so proud, holding it out to me with little podgy fingers covered in glue for me to see. She was five. It could have been here for fifteen years. I see another; a little angel with cotton wool hair now thick with dust. It is one of Emma's, like something from a horror movie. I remember this too. I was there. This feels as precious to me as someone saying 'I was there' when England won the World Cup so long ago it feels more like a myth than something believable.

Where does anyone start on the job of eradicating twenty years of their own history and those dearest to them in the whole world? I am wrenched from this dilemma by the phone.

'Brigit's fine.' It is Sarah, Brigit's secretary. Sarah has called to tell me 'Brigit is fine'. Clearly she isn't. People don't randomly call to say 'someone is fine'. 'She had a fall.'

Brigit's hospital is twelve floors high. The image I have in my head is not good.

'What kind of fall?'

'In the car park. She says she tripped over herself. She's fine though. There was a lot of blood. She can't remember falling. I've just come back from the emergency department. They're looking after her really well.'

I'd hate to see someone who Sarah describes as 'not being fine'.

'I'll come now.'

'That will be good.'

I leave my paintbrush to dry to an unusable state and run out of the door.

When I tell the receptionist who I have come to see, she appears from behind her bulletproof window and takes me through the heart of the set of '24 Hours in A & E'.

Brigit is in a small windowless room at the back of the department, sitting up on a couch, her white blouse like a prop from a Tarantino movie. I am struck by how ashen and frail she looks.

'Oh my God, you look terrible,' I say, which is testament to why I am not in the health care profession. A neat line of stitches like a wavy ladder stretch from one side of the bridge of Brigit's nose to the other and beyond, holding together what looks like a far from neat gash. 'What happened?'

'I can't really remember.'

I can hardly hear her. This event has not only punched the stuffing out of Brigit, but taken her voice as well.

A bear of a man wearing maroon scrubs comes into the room, goes straight to Brigit and takes her hand and affectionately strokes the back. I stand and he comes to shake my hand.

'Pete, I'm the consultant on duty. Our leader has taken quite a crack on the head.'

'Brigit says she can't remember what happened.'

Pete takes Brigit's hand again. 'I know. A little worrying.'

'I tripped over myself,' Brigit says, still in a whisper. 'That's all.'

'The scan looks okay,' Pete says. 'No cracks or anything we can see to worry about. That doesn't mean you didn't take a hell of a bashing. That's a nasty cut. Something happened between you standing and then hitting the floor. Blood pressure's a bit low and I know those bloody 'regulators' are after us again because they've been down here with their clipboards and stop watches wanting to know why people aren't healing themselves more quickly.' Pete looks at me. 'I don't want to see this young lady in this hospital for at least a week.'

Brigit shakes her head and is about to challenge this.

Pete raises his finger. 'Ah, ah, ah. I've had people still feeling dizzy after six-months with bangs no worse than this. You need to slow down. Two weeks if possible. Can you do that?'

'She can,' I say. 'I'll look after her.'

'Ah yes, you looked after the kids, I believe. How many do you have?'

'Four.'

'Four? You looked after four kids?'

'I did.'

'While Brigit ran this place? God, we've only got one. She's two and a half. The thought of four is too much. My wife's a doctor too and keeps asking why she's the one who gets the short straw. I tell her it's because the women have the babies. They're programmed.'

'What does she say to that?'

'She throws things at me.'

'It's not the short straw.'

'Wasn't it Tony Blair who said he did one day with the kids and it was harder than being the Prime Minister? I take my hat off to you.'

Brigit nods at me affirmatively despite looking as if she's had ten tequila shots and five rounds with Tyson Fury.

I walk Brigit through the main entrance to the hospital and leave her on a seat while I fetch the car. I pass the League of Friend's stall where a man is pouring tea from a giant pot. I wonder if it is David Shaw from Brigit's carers' seminar. If it is him, he looks happy to be selling fairy cakes to the walking wounded and their nearest and dearest. I'm still not sure it's for me.

When we arrive home, I help Brigit into the shower and wait outside the door to make sure she's okay before making a cup of tea. When I come back, Brigit is in bed.

'You need to do as Pete says, Brig.'

She sips her tea without argument. Perhaps she will break the habit of a lifetime and become compliant. Or maybe this has really stopped her in her tracks.

I can't remember the last time Brigit and I were in the house on our own. This is of course what it will be like when all the children have gone. We look at one another in the silence when there is probably so much to say.

'I found this photograph of us on the beach.' I hand it to Brigit with several others I have been collecting on my bedside cabinet. 'I reckon it's twelve, thirteen years ago.'

'Oh, my God,' Brigit brushes her fingers through her hair where there are now flecks of grey. For me it is the other way round. Now there are only flecks of brown. I have been replaced by my father. 'We look so much younger,' she says.

'We were.' I take Brigit's hand. I can't remember the last time I actually looked at this woman who gave birth to our four children without any drugs and came through the other side as strong as she ever was, when I feel sure I'd be nothing but a husk of my former self. I notice little lines at the corner of Brigit's eyes and mouth where the years have etched themselves forever.

'You have to slow down,' I say.

Tears well in Brigit's eyes. 'I don't know how. I'm being pursued for things I can't change at the hospital. Everyone's working flat out.'

'They love you. Look at Pete. He cares about you. You matter to them. You matter to us.'

Brigit flicks through the photographs. There is one of me with the girls and Ollie at a park, taken by one of the mothers.

'I wasn't there.' She finds another with just the five of us. 'Or there. I missed those things. You didn't. You were there. Every time you were there.'

This feels like an accusation and my immediate reaction is to be defensive. I resist. I think of Harriet Rickard and why, after all these years, I like to spend time with her, to talk about the past she is slowly losing and I need to hang onto as much as she does. Without knowing it, Harriet gives as much to me as I try to give to her.

'You've been amazing, Brig. You're an inspiration to women everywhere and the kids love you. You've given more to our children than most men ever do with full-time jobs.'

'Do you think we made a mistake doing it how we did it?'

'Sometimes. Pete thinks women should do it by default. It's not true. Mind you, our lot got me.'

'Lucky them.'

'You think so?' I don't give her the chance to answer because I look at my watch and see the time. 'I have to get the kids.'

The bus is early for the first time ever. The three of them are sitting on a wall in silence. They throw their bags into the car and get in. Emma is about to ask one of her complicated inevitably consequential questions. I stop her and brief them by beginning with 'your mother's fine'.

'Oh, my God,' Ruby says, promptly bursting into tears.

'Does she have brain damage?' Ollie asks.

'No, they did a scan. Her brain is fine. Possibly even improved. We need to take care of her though.'

Once in the house, they run through to see Brigit. They are full of concern and Ollie is particularly keen to examine the damage to Brigit's nose.

'Bit of a mess,' he confirms. 'You'll definitely have a scar.'

Ruby calls Chloe on FaceTime. Chloe's shoulders and head beam into the bedroom from university, so everyone is here. The low winter sun sprinkles its late afternoon glow over us all as we sit on the bed where on many occasions we have all slept together because of the bear coming to get us after reading 'We're Going on a Bear Hunt'.

They pass round the photographs, laugh and remember all the bits not captured in that single moment and those extra times when Brigit was there as if she and I are indivisible as far as they are concerned. Brigit has no need to worry about how much she matters, but perhaps I need to tell her more often that, so many times, she was the glue that kept us from completely falling apart.

There are moments in life that stop you in your tracks. Brigit's recent moment is no doubt face planting in the hospital car park. Right now, this is one of mine. It takes me back to another when I was on that plane flying home from Toronto and watching Steve Martin in Father of the Bride 2. In that film, he sells the family home and, realising how much it meant, he buys it back at a greatly inflated price. I am certain without voicing it that we will not be selling our house just yet, or covering the sample squares, or taking down the handmade decorations from fifteen years ago. We will not be doing any of these things because this place is still full of us. It is brimming with the people we used to be and the ones we are still becoming. There is no room for anyone new.

My child-caring days are coming to an end and I'm finding it hard to let go of something that has taken up such a huge part of my life. Like it or not though, I became a carer and now I have a little time to give to Harriet and at last to Brigit who deserves it more than most.

We did it our way and there is no turning back.

'Lucky them,' Brigit says.

'What?'

'Before you went to pick them up, you asked me if I thought they were lucky having you as the full-time parent. There's your answer.' She waves at the mob sitting on the bed.

The photographs have prompted a cascade of great and ridiculous memories of sheep, pigs and vicious parrots, a cockerel called Roy who bit the now shamed Charles Julian on the arse, gluts of carrots, orange children and a multi-coloured house where Brigit and I will no doubt live until they wheel us out because we are hostage to the treasure trove of memories it harbours and willing captives within our own story.

A line in a Steve Martin film prompted me to change my life and set out on a journey most men may never know because it is the thinnest premise you could ever find to commit such a crazy act. I never really imagined that line would apply to me, but it does and I can say it now.

This is about as good as life gets.

ACKNOWLEDGEMENTS

I couldn't of course, have written this novel without having some experience of the subject. Nevertheless, there are many people who helped me to survive and write the thing- our children, Grace, Evie, Hana and Otto to name four. Without you, I would not have enjoyed such richness in my life, or felt so utterly exhausted. I will be forever in your debt, which sounds ridiculous when you come to think about it. I love you from the bottom of my ragged heart.

I would like to say a special thank you to our extended family-the Nicholls; Marc, Sadie, Tanya, Romilly, the recently arrived Penelope Celia and of course to the late Shelagh, (to whom this book is dedicated) the matriarch, the oracle who often made the most insurmountable problems look smaller and the light at the end of the tunnel appear a little closer than it actually was. Here's to you 'sweetie pie'.

I would like to say a huge thank you to my friend Professor Alan Borthwick OBE for simply being sensible when I have often been without the capacity to be so. To David Roberts for the dedication on the Jonny Walker show and for being a loyal and wonderful friend for most of our lives. 'Rock on' my friend. To Sophie Duffy, the bravest of people, who believed in me and reminded me I could write, even when I didn't believe it myself. To Margaret James who once again told me to get this stuff on paper and to all the wonderful Exeter Writers who tolerate my ramblings and still renew my membership. I would also like to thank Phil and Judith Ward for keeping me on the straight and narrow when it comes to thinking straight and for taking me just as I am. I am very grateful to have such good friends.

There are always so many people to thank through life's journey, and I know if I make the list any longer, people might feel left out when you all matter so much. Finally I would like to thank my partner Ann James, the fabulous mother of our four equally fabulous children. If my life were a show rather than a pantomime, you would be the star.

Simon Kettlewell 2021

ABOUT THE AUTHOR

Like the narrator of this story, Simon Kettlewell has also looked after four children for a very long time. For the purpose of authenticity this book is inevitably shaped to some extent by this experience. Some bits have been extracted from the author's twisted imagination, but he is still too exhausted to remember which ones. Simon lives in Devon with a variety of animals in a multi-coloured house where people come and go like passengers at Crewe station.

You can find him at…

Website- simonkettlewell.co.uk
Twitter- @SIMONKETTLEWELL

Also by Simon Kettlewell

Bread for the Bourgeoisie

Dead Dog Floating

The Truth About Us

The Truth about Her

Printed in Great Britain
by Amazon